MYS   532253

Andrews, Sarah

MOTHER
NATURE

MOTHER NATURE

◇
◇
◇

Sarah Andrews

ST. MARTIN'S PRESS ⚉ NEW YORK

Design by Maureen Troy

Library of Congress Cataloging-in-Publication Data

Andrews, Sarah.
    Mother nature   /   Sarah Andrews.—1st ed.
        p.   cm.
    ISBN 0-312-15591-3 (hardcover)
    I. Title.
PS3551.N4526M6   1997
813'.54—dc21   96-52649
                                                    CIP

First Edition: May 1997

10   9   8   7   6   5   4   3   2   1

For my parents,
Mary Fisher Andrews
and Richard Lloyd Andrews,
with great love and respect

ACKNOWLEDGMENTS

I WISH TO THANK:

Deborah Schneider, Elisabeth Story, and Kelley Ragland for championing this book during a tough market.

Mary Hallock, Clint Smith, and Robert J. Bowman for their constructive criticisms of the manuscript.

Christine Scheib and Damon Brown of EBA Wastechnologies, Santa Rosa, who reviewed the manuscript for technical accuracy, and who shouldn't be held responsible for any errors that might have crept back in during final revisions. Deputy Sheriff Will Conner of the Sonoma County Sheriff's Office, who provided coaching and advice regarding scenes involving the Sheriff's Office, and who likewise shouldn't be held responsible for the questions I neglected to ask him. Kim Cordell, hydrologist, for explaining the effects of stream channelization on flood dynamics in the Laguna de Santa Rosa.

Anne McGinley of Action Mortgage, Santa Rosa, for sharing her knowledge of patterns of development and population growth in Sonoma County. Judy Hubbert of Hubbert's Training Stables, Sebastopol, and horse lover Rhonda Azevedo, for sharing the trials and tribulations of horse ranching in the wet season. Suzi Kaido and Dick Norton of Manzanas Products Co., Inc., for the tour of their plant.

Certain parties who shall remain nameless, for being such horse's patoots that they irked me into writing this story. And last but not least, I thank certain other parties who choose to remain nameless, for telling me where a few political bodies are buried.

MOTHER
NATURE

I DROVE FIRST TO THE ROADSIDE DITCH WHERE JANET PIN-chon's body had been found lying in a shroud of dry oak leaves. From the airport, the map guided me northward through a fog-bound city made of sherbet-colored boxes crowding hilly streets, across the Golden Gate Bridge through wisps of cloud and thin December sunlight, and up a congested freeway past the far fingers of San Francisco Bay. I was surprised to find California so dim and dank: television had led me to expect a sunshine-and-orange-groves California with tanned gods and goddesses driving convertibles down wide suburban boulevards lined with palm trees.

From the north end of the Bay, the hand-drawn map the Senator's assistant had given me led inland over a hilly divide covered with buckskin-colored grass. The odd round rhythm of the hills was broken by tall windbreaks made of eucalyptus trees, and the sky hung low and gray overhead. I drove in silence, my shoulders hunched close to my ears against the chill, wishing the heater in the truck worked better, and ruing the ignorance that had led me to leave my down parka at home.

Dank. Dim. Gray. It was fitting weather to visit a scene of death.

The pint-sized Japanese pickup truck I was driving puttered along in the heavy stream of traffic as I descended now into a broad plain. The gray overcast bent down to swallow the ground, blurring the summits of the hills beyond. How different from the crisp winter openness of my native Wyoming.

I held the sketch map across the top of the steering wheel and watched for my next turn, U.S. Highway 12, uncertain from the crudeness of the map how far away it might be. Ten miles later, in the middle of a city called Santa Rosa, I spotted it and swung westward through a grove of pink and white oleanders, leaving the city for its surrounding malaise of suburban sprawl. After a few miles, tract housing in turn gave way to a jumble of chain-link fences, disused land, and building supply centers.

In an effort to avoid being hit by a kid in a jacked-up truck on monster tires who was making a wild lane change, I missed the turn that came after that. I pulled off to the right and waited for a chance to turn around. Almost two minutes passed before I saw an opening in the rush of oncoming cars. I stomped the gas pedal to the floor and bolted forward, inserting the little truck none too deftly between an Izusu Trooper and a BMW, whose driver retaliated by riding my back bumper like a lamprey, giving me the finger. I had been warned about Californians and their love affair with the automobile, but no one had told me that their love was a jealous one, where too many drivers compete for too little road. As I made the turn onto Occidental Road, I saluted him back.

Occidental Road carried me into softly undulating pasture land studded with spreading oaks, a landscape that held a sad, winter-dead beauty. In places, the gnarled arms of the oaks almost touched over the middle of the road. The dry stalks of last summer's grass and wildflowers stood like stiff sentries, lining the sodden roadside ditches with a forlorn trash of brown, unlike the fresh contours of snow I'd seen along the Rockies early that morning.

The ditches worried me. Most roads in Wyoming have broad crowns leading off to wide shoulders banked to guide the runoff away from the pavement. Here there was no shoulder, and the drainage ditches were as deep and steep-sided as Wyoming's irrigation ditches. They were way too close to the edge of the pavement for comfort. I found myself veering toward the center line of the roadway. I've had a phobia about ditches like that ever since my older brother drowned in one of the irrigation ditches when I was a child.

Beyond the ditches, horses stared glassy-eyed over board fences. Some abstract part of my brain marveled at this luxurious use of wood, where barbed-wire would have edged Wyoming's pastures. *This is Em Hansen distracting herself as best she can from a growing sense of panic,* I mused bitterly, *and it's not just the ditches that have her tensing, it's the job. Her arms and jaws are uncomfortably tight and she is barely breathing. Will she survive this latest flight from reason? Stay tuned for further reports.*

I asked myself once more why I'd let myself in for this task. *I'm a geologist,* I told myself firmly, *not a detective. What am I doing here?*

What's the difference? a hyperrational part of my brain countered. *Geologists solve puzzles, too, so what makes better sense than a geologist being hired to investigate the death of a geologist?*

Yeah, but I used to do the geology first. The damned murder investigations were a sideline. Happenstance. Now everything's ass-backward.

Tut, tut. Changes, changes.

Too much had changed in my life of late.

The sky seemed to press against my head. The landscape looked closed in, the farmsteads stunted and crammed together, and the narrow, shoulderless blacktop seemed to scrape between those ditches. Each bump in the pavement jarred me, reminding me that I should have used the rest room at the airport while I had the chance.

I cursed the worn suspension on the tinny little truck and glared out the windshield, reviewing the arguments against hiring me that I had laid out to Janet Pinchon's father: "I don't know California geology," I had said, "and besides, if I drove in there in a truck with out-of-state tags, I'd stand out like a sore thumb. Undercover investigators are supposed to blend in, not rent billboard space announcing that they're in town."

"Rent a car at the airport, with California plates."

"No, I don't think you get it. Rental cars look like rental cars. They have little stickers on the back bumper that say Hertz and National.

They have velvet seats and weird dashboards, nothing like what a geologist would drive. They stink of interloper. There's no way it would work."

"Then a private vehicle will be available," he had soothed. For some reason, this had brought an unkind smile to his lips, as if he were enjoying a joke at my expense.

"And I cost five hundred dollars a day," I had asserted, certain this would be a suitably indigestible sum.

"Fine." He hadn't even blinked.

My mouth had gone dry. I needed that money. It had been six months since Blackfeet Oil Company had disappeared into the dark night of corporate raiding, and I'd become nothing but a shiftless mooch on my friend Elyria, unable to find another job in the oil patch, uncertain where else to go or what else to do to make my living. Senator Pinchon had caught me with my last few petro-dollars huddling for cover at the bottom of my bank account. It must have showed on my face, because his smile had grown much wider. He knew he had me.

It had taken me fewer than twenty-four hours to pack and make plane reservations, and now here I was in California pretending to be a private investigator. At least I'd had the sense to wear wool socks.

As Occidental Road began a slow descent into a sleepy drainage, I saw my last turn, Sanborn Road, and took it. I drove more slowly now, watching, staring into the ditch on the right. The spot where Janet Pinchon's body had been found was marked by an X on the sketch map, but the map had been drawn without scale; the seventy miles I'd traveled between the airport and Highway 12 was three inches long on the map, and the six or seven miles I'd driven since covered four. How far along this road was the site?

I pulled the truck to a stop and fumbled a stack of eight-by-ten-inch glossy photographs out of my attaché, some ghoul's overzealous imitation of police photography. Amazing, the people who show up at crash sites, but the Senator's assistant said he had been able to purchase both the prints and the negatives for a surprisingly reasonable sum.

The area shot was the third picture down, sandwiched between a grim portrait of the sprawled remains and a close-up of the dead woman's left hand. Holding the area shot up, I let off the brake and rolled slowly along, scanning the roadside, trying to match the fence posts with those in the photograph.

A truck thundered past me and I swerved, almost sinking a wheel into the ditch. Papers began to spill out of the attaché and onto the floor, slithering sickeningly, underscoring my growing nausea over what I was doing.

Stopping again, I set the brake and bent to pick up the fallen papers. As I stuffed them back into the attaché, a crisp piece of blue watermarked stationery broke loose from the rest and slid toward my thigh as if attacking me.

I pushed it away like it was on fire and covered it with a photograph. What I couldn't cloak was its presence, or the challenge spoken by the familiarity of that slanting handwriting.

Snatching it back out of the stack, I folded it twice in places where it hadn't yet been folded, cast about for its envelope, and stuffed it resolutely inside.

The damned handwriting covered the envelope, too.

Ms. Emily Bradstreet Hansen, it read, *c/o Elyria Kretzmer, 3236 West 30th Street, Denver, Colorado.* The return address was even worse, like a fist squeezing my heart: *Mrs. C. H. Hansen, Iron Mtn. Road, Chugwater, Wyoming.*

My mother. She had written to apologize.

Apologize! As if that could bring my father back, or erase all those years of pain . . .

I cast my eyes nervously around at the dim landscape, trying to kid myself that I was now far enough from Chugwater and Denver to escape any more letters. Why did Elyria have to go and press this one into my hands as she drove me to the airport? And why hadn't I just dropped it in the trash as I hurried down the concourse? Elyria was right, I'd have to deal with this someday, but she didn't understand: too much had changed too fast, and just when I could deal with it the least.

Hands trembling, I grabbed for the photographs again, put the truck back into gear, and inched along, trying again to spot that place where the body had been found.

A Cadillac hauling a horse trailer roared around me, oblivious to the axle-eating ditches.

Was I looking on the correct side of the road? Was there truly anything new I could discover by coming here, two weeks after Janet's death, when a whole sheriff's department had already combed the landscape? Santa Rosa had seemed a big and prosperous city, and not so far from the urban wonders of San Francisco that its sheriff's department would be backward and ignorant. It seemed an increasingly good idea to just give up, maybe take a swing through the nearest town for a bite of the fabled California Cuisine, and head home to Denver.

If Denver is my home . . .

Think positively, I told myself. *At five hundred dollars a day, you can hang out for a week and make enough to run away to Mexico. Just go through the motions, bill the old fart, and get gone. He won't miss the cash.* But even as I dreamed this dream, I knew my damned Puritan conscience would never let me do it.

The message on the blue stationery crowded in on top of this bit of self-defeating virtue, reaching into my brain with long, guilt-provoking tendrils. Puritans. Why hadn't Mother stayed in her native Boston, and left me to be whelped by someone with a heart? I willed the ditch to command my attention, rolled down the window and glared into it.

Then I saw the place. A fence post more crooked than the others, right next to a skinny oak. Stopping the truck with its right wheels teetering on the scant three inches of gravel between the pavement and the ditch, I set the emergency flashers and the brake and stepped out, taking the photographs with me.

The ditch was nearly three feet deep here, the sides extremely steep. Fragments of yellow plastic police cordon tape still fluttered from the fence above it, but nothing lay within it now but wet grass and a scattering of leaves. Why were these ditches so large, and so deep? I looked up at the clouds. Did the rain come in torrents here, drowning the roadways and fields around them? I held my breath, stiff with fear at the thought of this ditch brim-full of dark, roiling waters coursing past my feet.

The sound of the idling truck engine consumed the silence.

Chill air reached inside my jacket, probing with damp fingers down from my collar and up from my waist. I shivered and hunched my shoulders, looked around. I was standing downhill from a ranch that was bigger than its neighbors. Even though there was no livestock in sight, the fields had the awful barren aspect of overgrazing, and stood naked of the oak trees that graced the nearby spreads.

Well back from the road on a shallow rise stood a large two-story wood-frame house. It jutted bleakly from the dark earth like a ship-wreck on a deserted beach, its only companion one forlorn palm tree. The house was older than its neighbors, its boxy shape and ornate trim suggesting the local rendition of Victoriana, but the dry clapboards that shielded its sides were gray with age and lack of paint, and its tall win-dows stared blankly across the empty landscape. I thought at first it must be abandoned. But then I saw that I was being watched.

A big bruiser of a fellow. He stood at the head of the lane that led up to the house, kind of lurking behind one of a pair of stone gateposts like it could conceal his mass. There was nothing inconspicuous about his stare, either, even from a hundred yards away.

Figuring turnabout was fair play, I reached behind the cab of the truck and fished a compact pair of binoculars out of my gear bag. Lay-ing them on the roof of the truck, I focused them in and stared back at him. Even from that distance, I didn't like what I saw: head drawn down between his shoulders defensively; mean, distrustful eyes, the kind that belong to the sort of overpowered coward folks call a bully; cruel mouth set in a childish pout; filthy work clothes slung over an overweight, sloppy frame. His hair was thinning and I could make out a heavy jaw darkly in need of a shave.

Seeing that I'd spotted him, he drew himself back, awkwardly try-ing to stuff more of himself behind the gatepost.

Revulsion filled my stomach. Was I looking at the creature that had killed Janet? *You look crazy enough. No, that's too easy. The sheriff's de-tectives would have spotted you long ago.*

An engine coughed into life up by the house. Lifting my gaze from the binoculars, I spied a second man, this one sitting behind the wheel of a battered yellow truck. He had it rolling, soon hurtling, down the long driveway toward the gateposts, where he pulled up by the big galoot and leaned his head out the window to say something to him.

I switched back to the binoculars. I'd managed to bump them, so I missed a moment of their interchange while I realigned them. The big man was frowning—no, pouting—his eyes trained defiantly on the ground. The man in the truck gestured forcibly, bullying the bully. He was a much smaller man, but the derisive look that contorted his dark face told me he was fully accustomed to ordering the big oaf around. The oaf pointed my way. The smaller man waved him summarily into the truck, glaring from under thick black eyebrows that met in the middle. The oaf cast one more distrustful look my way and then conceded, shambling over to the truck and climbing in, his head hanging in grudging defeat.

My heart sank. It had been a tawdry little scene. Here I was prying into people's lives again, and already I had found at least one life I'd rather leave unpried. With mounting distaste, I realized that as they lived right by the place where the body had been found, I'd eventually have to talk to them.

I shrugged my shoulders violently, refocusing my attention on the ditch. For all I knew, I was hundreds of miles from the place where Janet Pinchon had been killed and from the person who had killed her. This was just a ditch in rural farmland, right? Just the sort of place you'd dump a body if you didn't want to be seen doing it. The big guy was probably just some disadvantaged human chaff who had grown leery of the stream of cops, reporters, and rubberneckers who must have been harassing his family for the past two weeks.

To hell with the ditch, I told myself. *The photographs probably tell more about Janet Pinchon's death than the setting.* I put down the binoculars and stared once again at the lurid pictures. The second showed the unnatural angles her hips, knees, and elbows had assumed in death, as if she'd been reaching for something to grab hold of as she exited this life; perhaps her bicycle, which lay farther down the ditch, its forks bent and front wheel hideously twisted. I had wondered, when I first looked at this photograph, if she had simply been hit by a car while riding. But no, Janet's body lay prone, and a close-up photograph showed that the ugly blotching of postmortem lividity had formed while she lay supine; at minimum, she had been rolled over, and more likely killed elsewhere and moved to this spot. The next picture added further grisly evidence to the story: a close-up, showing bruises where thick, angry fingers had gouged into her neck, grasping her from behind. Not the work of a hit-and-run driver.

I glanced reflexively up toward the ranch house where the ungainly man had gone, hoping for another look at the size of his hands, but he was nowhere in sight.

Taking a quick breath, I held the photograph of Janet Pinchon's sprawled body at arm's length, superimposing black-and-white death on the dew-drenched weeds. The act disgusted me. It was unreal and vilely titillating, like watching cheap television. I hadn't even known this woman; how in hell was I supposed to do this job?

Placing the photographs of Janet and the bicycle on the hood of the truck, I reexamined the next, and the next. The victim's neck, showing the prints of those large, cruel fingers. The victim's waist, revealing a sloppy effort at tucking the snug jersey back into skintight spandex bicycling shorts that had been yanked to one side. I swallowed hard to steady my stomach.

Something stopped me at a close-up of her left hand, a detail I presume had been photographed to illustrate an odd welt on her wrist, but that wasn't what caught my attention. I glanced at it again, trying to figure out what had. A hand's a hand, right?

Closing my eyes a moment, I tried to breathe down deeply into my abdomen, but found that the muscles were so tense that I couldn't draw air past my rib cage. I concentrated, forcing my stomach to relax.

Hands. Wrists. Left.

I reopened my eyes and examined my own left hand. It was softer than it used to be, the calluses and torn cuticles healed since the days when I worked in the oil fields, or the days long before that when I worked with my dad.

A vagrant memory wisped through my brain, of riding horseback with Dad when I was four years old, checking the fences. *For once, he has taken me instead of my brother. His strong arms hold me snugly on the saddle in front of him so I can see the world from where he sits. The wide Wyoming sky is awash with evening color. I am supremely happy. . . .*

I squeezed my eyes shut, trying to blank out the memory, but my mother's blue letter paper was not to be ignored, not since that August evening four months past when the first letter had come, saying, "Your father's dead. His heart. He went quickly. Couldn't reach you by phone. Call for date and time of memorial service."

At the time, I'd been so numbed all I'd been able to think was, *Why did I have to hear it from you, Mother?*

Em! my brain prompted. *Do your job!*

My eyes popped open. I stared at my hands. The minute hand on the watch on my left hand ticked hypnotically around the dial. Suddenly the watch came into sharp focus, and I looked again at the photograph. No watch. I took mine off and compared my hand to the one in the picture.

They could have been twins, right down to the pale line left where the watch band had been, the sign of a woman who worked in the sun.

At that moment Janet Pinchon came alive to me, a young woman trying to make it in a difficult world. Perhaps, as her father seemed to suspect, her death had something to do with her profession, or more specifically, her job. Perhaps she had learned something fatal, or made a mistake, a miscalculation, too green at life to handle it any better.

I held the photograph to my heart. No matter what her story, Janet Pinchon deserved better than to end up alone in a ditch, the final page of her life left unwritten.

I resolved to find her killer.

2

I SHOULD TELL YOU A BIT MORE ABOUT HOW I CAME TO BE SEN-ator Pinchon's private investigator. It began with a phone call from a person who rather officiously identified himself as the Senator's confidential assistant.

"Would you please repeat your name?" I said. Perhaps my tone was a bit snarky, but he had awakened me from a nap, and nothing he was saying seemed to make sense.

"This is Curt Murbles," he reiterated, taking such pains to make his name sound dignified that I began to believe he was telling me the truth. Nobody would joke about being named Murbles; it sounded too much like a fart in a bathtub.

"Excuse me, Mr. Murbles; my ears are somewhat bad. Too many years working on drilling rigs." My standard excuse for inattention. "What can I do for you?"

"As I said, I am George Harwood Pinchon's confidential assistant."

"Who?"

An exasperated sigh. "George Harwood Pinchon, United States Senator for the State of California," he intoned, clearly appalled at my ignorance.

"Sure," I answered, in one of those *I knew that* tones.

"This *is* Emily Hansen?"

"Yeah . . ."

Murbles must have thought I was making fun of him, because his tone soured from officious to snappish. "The Senator has an important business proposition for you. Be at Denver International Airport tomorrow, ten-fifteen. The United Airlines Red Carpet Lounge. Don't be late; he has less than an hour between flights."

After he'd hung up, I had decided that the whole conversation had been either a bad dream or a hallucination. But an hour later, when Elyria came home from work, she confirmed that Pinchon, at least, was real. "Ambitious, high-handed. But then, that describes most of them," she said, as she dug absentmindedly through her mail, her smooth hair shining against the lapel of the winter coat she had yet to remove. I was amazed that she could make even as mundane a job as sorting her mail an act of grace.

So I'm going to jump into a small swimming pool with a big shark, I mused, as I studied my roommate-landlady. Today she was dressed entirely in a warm gray save for a deep ruby scarf. A fine spray of water droplets glinted across the crown of her head and her shoulders. Droplets? I looked outside, and saw that it had begun to snow while I was asleep. Winter had come to Colorado.

"So what do I wear to a meeting with a senator?" I asked, staring at the place where my right knee was coming through my blue jeans. Dressing Em was a pleasant, homey game Elyria and I liked to play. There is only so much you can do to make a plain, garden-variety, medium-everything person like me look (to use my mother's term) "intentional," but if Elyria sold sow's ears, you'd think they were all silk purses.

"Your indigo flannel suit with the narrow skirt, crisp white silk blouse, black pumps with the heels. Those red Venetian glass beads. Serious yet subtly extravagant, the color scheme patriotic. It says if he wants to do business with you, he must prepare himself to pay well for your time." She slid a letter opener into the first envelope and slit it as neatly as a butcher filleting a salmon.

"Sounds nice, but I don't think I'll bother," I mumbled. I wasn't feeling that formidable. I squirmed farther down into the damask cushions of the couch, watching for her reaction.

Elyria dropped the first envelope efficiently into the wastebasket she kept by the door for this purpose, and ripped into a second. "Oh? Why not find out what he wants? Have you something to lose?"

"Just my status amongst the unemployed," I muttered.

"Do you good," she continued, as she ejected envelope number two and read quickly through a begging letter from some foundation or another. "Morons! I sent them *one* check for *fifteen* dollars over a year ago. Since then, they have spent at least *twenty* dollars sending letters asking me for more. They expect me to support such poor planning?" Elyria is an economist, specializing in minerals. She notices things.

"Then why are you reading it?"

"Touché. No, really, Emily, find out what the man wants. You've hardly left the house since you came back from your father's funeral. It's been, what, four months? Hmm?"

I know I'm in deep shit when she calls me Emily. Yes, here she was, bringing up The Topic. I tried in vain to avoid it, my voice rising nervously: "Don't you think it sounds funny, though? Total stranger calls me up and says his boss has a business proposition for me? Hell, Elyria, I might get whisked into a private jet and taken to Saudi Arabia, never to be heard from again."

Elyria gave me a wilting look over the top of the page. "Firstly, my dear, the Saudis are a more civilized people than you might imagine. Secondly . . ."

"Secondly, I need the money? I don't need no stinking money. There's always the Dumpster behind Safeway."

"Secondly, you're not the white slavery type," she continued, perfectly stone-faced. "Slave masters prefer willowy hothouse blondes with cushiony bosoms, not earthy cowgirls like yourself. They don't make harem pants in denim."

"I'll pack my own, then. I don't have one of them nice coin brazeres, but that don't matter, I'll jus' rustle up sumpin' outta Scotch tape and a couple dimes, little girl like me."

Elyria affected deep interest in another piece of mail. She knew she'd won, and being at depth a compassionate person, she was leaving me a residue of my pride.

◈

DENVER INTERNATIONAL AIRPORT looks like a giant Martian meringue landed in the windy prairie twenty miles east of Denver. It is a lonely place, at one and the same time too large and too exposed for human scale. It's so sprawled out that the parking lots seem halfway to Kansas, and an underground train playing goofy tunes is required to move the glazed-looking travelers from one concourse to the next.

I was in fact late, having misgauged traffic, and when I reached the B concourse, I was confronted with another problem: there was not one, but two Red Carpet Lounges. I flipped a coin and tried the east one first, and was informed by the creature at its entrance that my coin had misled me, there were no senators there. I dashed across the Disneyland-style concourse to Red Carpet Lounge West, argued my way past the snippy raisin at that desk (who could apparently *smell* that I was not a member), and ascended the long escalator to the lounge's sun-drenched, rarified heights, wondering why I detected the scent of brimstone if I was going *up*.

My stomach was doing flips by the time I walked into the lounge, only to find myself faced with the task of trying to figure out which of the overstuffed, graying men seated there was the junior United States Senator for California. When I gave up and asked the demurely tailored odalisque at the upper desk, she pointed to a man seated not twenty feet away.

He was the obvious choice, in retrospect: the photogenic one with the commanding stage presence and the extra half inch of sumptuous wave to his hair, betraying more than a touch of vanity. As I presented myself, the Senator narrowed his eyes for a moment, then inflated his chest, spread his thick arms along the back of his chair, and slung one leg onto the opposite knee, sizing me up with a contemptuous, self-satisfied glare.

Confidential Assistant Curt Murbles managed to look down his nose at me from a sitting position. He had a rangy build with large hands and feet, and limp, thinning hair the same color as his oily skin, and as he watched me, he ran his long, bony fingers up and down the shaft of his fountain pen.

"Senator Pinchon," I murmured, offering a hand to be shaken, "I'm Emily Hansen. Pleased to meet you."

"Miss Hansen." He did not shake my hand. Definitely a put-down, coming from a politician.

Murbles took over the preliminaries. "Sit down, Miss Hansen. The acoustics are in our favor here, but you *will* keep your voice low."

I settled myself tentatively on the front edge of a thickly upholstered leather chair and smoothed my skirt, feeling like a schoolgirl in the principal's office. *Okay, I'm here; now tell me what I did wrong.*

The conversation was short and to the point. The Senator's daughter had been murdered and the Sheriff's Department wasn't getting to the bottom of it fast enough. The Senator, apparently satisfied with what he saw in me, topped his summation off with, "I hear you're good with this sort of thing," as if that was all there was to that.

"Excuse me, sir, but who gave you my name?"

"An associate," said Murbles.

I didn't like the sound of this. Besides, I hate being told no. It always presses me to behave rashly, or as in this case, lends an assertiveness to my tone that is born more of irritation than self-confidence. "I'm sorry, but I'll have to know more."

The Senator seemed to like that. His face assumed a more self-satisfied arrangement of curled lip and lowered eyelids. "His name is Jacobson. His daughter knew you at school."

Marcie Jacobson. Yes, that fits; her father's in the House. How the old school tie doth bind. But there was still something very wrong with the picture. I fell into arguing my lack of qualifications. Which, as I've already described, concluded in my agreeing to take the job.

So I began to ask what questions I could think to ask, making an attempt at a confident, professional effect, but Murbles soon interrupted me, emphasizing the confidential nature of my "errand": "You may present yourself as a friend of the deceased, but you know nothing of the family, not even their names."

"All right."

"You have never met either the Senator or myself."

I nodded.

Then the Senator spoke. He leaned forward and fixed me with what he must have fancied was his most charismatic, arresting stare: "You will report to me and me only. Is that clear?"

"Yes, sir."

"And if you find anything in her activities that connects to mine, you will call me immediately and do nothing more until we have spoken. Is *that* clear?"

"Yes, sir, but—"

"No buts. You will report to me daily."

As they rose to go, I turned to the Senator and asked, "How may I reach you, sir?"

"Curt, give her the number."

Murbles extended a card with a phone number on it. "This is the private line into the office in Washington," he said, releasing it without touching me, as if I had a disease of the skin. "Give it out to no one."

I shot venom at him in a look and turned back to the Senator. Something was still bothering me. The whole proposition was misshapen. "Sir, why me? There are private investigators available right there in California."

"Because you're a geologist, and a good one. I want someone who can get inside."

Vanity is a potent drug. When administered during a season of pain and loneliness, it can be addictive.

3

So here I was in California, pretending I was a professional private investigator. What a laugh.

I hung around the ditch site for another few minutes, looking westward. The open pastureland on which I stood dropped off gradually toward a bottomland that supported a line of trees that I presumed marked the course of a narrow stream. A quarter mile beyond, the ground rose sharply to the encircling hills, here richly textured with neatly planted vineyards, there covered with an opaque wall of trees. It was a landscape of soft winter grays, each receding screen of trees a fainter tint, appearing flattened like the fading layers of a Japanese print. Overhead, the sky was rich with moisture, a paler, shiny gray tinged with opalescent pink, like the nacre that lines a shell.

I wondered if the heavy clouds were children of the cold current that swept the shore.

I had never seen the Pacific Ocean. When I was a child in land-locked Wyoming, my Uncle Skinny had told me about it. He said you could stand on the shore and look westward and not see another bit of land anywhere, no matter how clear the day. The idea of all that water had horrified me. I had dreamt of it almost nightly for a month, a frightening dream, for always the water was cold and quiet as death. For a moment the embrace of that long-forgotten dream once again enfolded me, throwing my thoughts into disarray.

I closed my eyes and literally shook myself, intent on staying focused on the job at hand, and picked up the information I had scribbled when I met Senator Pinchon.

I stared at the one scant page of notes. It wasn't much to go on. Janet Pinchon, aged twenty-four, dead two weeks. Home address: 3006 Via Robles, Santa Rosa. Education: bachelor's degree from somewhere in the California State University system, the Senator could not recall which campus. Friends: unknown. Boyfriends: unknown. Employment: geologist with a small environmental services firm somewhere in Santa Rosa; the Senator didn't know the name, but he understood that she had left the job immediately prior to her death. The Senator couldn't say why. He discouraged further questioning along this line by informing me peremptorily that "the family" had not heard from Janet for some time before her death. This was the part of delving into murder that made me queasy: the way the problem seemed to spread, rather than contract. I wasn't just investigating the riddle of who killed Janet Pinchon, I was also delving into why her daddy didn't know more about her; and if he was not interested in her life before she was dead, why he was now; and why he thought a geologist from out of state could succeed where a perfectly good sheriff's department had so far failed.

IF I WAS going to find out who killed Janet Pinchon and why, I was going to have to devise a plan. Twice before I had been involved in murder investigations, but only because I found myself in the middle of things and had to fight my way out. But this time I was an outsider. This time I first had to fight my way in.

On the principle that it was easier to fight on a full stomach than an empty one, I reached for the Senator's assistant's map to figure out which way to drive to find a little lunch. For this, the map was useless. No detail. No scale. Understand, I am truly a geologist. Geologists live and breathe maps. We can read maps symbols better than words in a book. We suffer sensory deprivation and consider committing manslaughter when some idiot hands us a bad one.

So I tuned my dead-reckoning sense to *B* for burrito, which took me back toward Santa Rosa, forsaking the farmlands for suburbia. Twenty town-house-modern developments and five bland concrete strip malls later, I got lucky: huddled in a far corner of a shopping center, I found a storefront taco joint with unadorned Formica tables. A row of customers, including petite mamas with smiling *niños* and short, swarthy laborers, stood at a tall counter ordering *burritos grandes* "to go" in Spanish from a stone-faced *señora* with shining coal-black eyes. By some divinely guided luck I had found the place: cheap and *auténtico*. I smacked my lips in anticipation of my first taste of Cal Mex, wondering just what variant combination of tortillas, beans, and cheese might await me.

The woman behind the counter eyed me expectantly, stubby pencil poised impatiently over the order chit, her dark eyes aimed in my direction but not troubling to see me. I examined the menu plaque over the cook's window and opened my mouth, ready to place my order in Spanish, but after a second, sheepish glance into the opaque dignity of her gaze, I chickened out and spoke English. "Hi. Super chicken burrito with guacamole and lots of hot sauce. Please."

The woman scribbled my order. "Drink?"

"Just water."

The woman tallied my tab and tax, then pointed to the sum with her pencil. I paid. She tore the order off her pad and slipped it into a metal clip over the cook's window, handed me a plastic fork and knife wrapped up in a thin paper napkin, and turned to the next customer, a gawky blond guy decked out in neon-colored bicycling spandex. I supposed my water would arrive with the burrito.

I headed for the table closest to the window, and was even more pleased when a teenaged female with waist-length black ringlets hustled up to the table to deliver a basket of corn tortilla chips and two little crocks of salsa. Wasting no time, I shoveled one of the chips into the salsa, popped it into my mouth, and closed my eyes, the better to concentrate. Chip: thin, salty, trace of lime, perfect crunch. Salsa: spicy, about a seven on a scale of ten, but not too hot to dull the tongue and keep the flavor from blooming through. I meditated for a moment on the herb I couldn't identify, munched down three or four more chips, then spread out my papers and got to work.

I had my one scant page of notes and those nasty eight-by-ten black-and-white photographs. Not much to go on, but every investigation has to start somewhere.

The bicyclist sauntered over and sat down facing me at the next table. The overhead lighting gave his white-blond hair a luminous green sheen, rather like it was made of plastic. He locked eyes with me and hoisted a bottle of Gatorade to his peach-fuzz-fringed lips, guzzled noisily, clunked the bottle down on his table, and sighed contentedly as he wiggled his narrow ass into a more preferred arrangement in the stiff plastic chair. Either I was hallucinating, or he gave me a little wink.

I peered back at him. What was he, nineteen? Hell, he hadn't even filled out yet, if indeed he'd finished growing. Did he really presume to catch the eye of a woman more than ten years his senior? And had he truly picked as the subject of this campaign Forgettable Em the Wyoming Wallflower? But yes, there it was again, the old one-eye. What a prince.

"Hi," he said.

I sort of smiled. I couldn't help it: his performance struck me as funny.

"You new in these parts?" he asked, mistaking my smirk for a welcome.

Just passin' through, pard, I wanted to say, with a little extra zinger like, *and passin' for sure,* but he'd caught me. If it was that obvious I was from somewhere else, I wanted to know what I was doing wrong in the camouflage department. "Why do you ask?"

The skinny little snake grinned. I didn't like his narrow teeth any better than that insolent look in his eyes. "It's your belt buckle. Babes 'n this hood buy shit that looks like that down at the mall, but like I say, it's shit, and yours is real." Smug, smug, smug.

I wanted to smack him. But as Em Hansen, undercover investigator, I forced myself to give impulse a backseat to information gathering. Janet had been found wearing bicycling clothes, ergo she was a bicyclist. Here was another bicyclist. "I can see by *your* outfit that *you* are a *bicyclist*," I quipped.

The kid rolled his head back suavely and lowered his eyelids to a level I suppose was meant to be sexy, but served mostly to make him look like an intoxicated gecko. "Check."

"Know a bit about bicycles, then?"

He let out a snort.

"Okay, bicycle man," I said, turning over my file to obscure the label and pulling out the last black-and-white photograph in the lot, "what you think of this number?" It was a picture of Janet Pinchon's bicycle. Ever so casually, I laid a napkin across the twisted front fork and wheel, so that it would look like a normal bicycle just lying in the grass.

The boy swagged himself over to my table. "Duke's the name," he drawled, gazing into my eyes.

"Em Hansen. The photo, Duke."

Duke gave me yet another wink and applied himself to the photograph. "Nice ride. Merlin frame, a custom job. Oh, and looky here at these shifters. State of the art, don't come cheap. The whole setup, oooh, I'd say three and a half, four K. Where'd a nice babe like you get all that dough?" Then, quick as a bat catching an insect, he snatched the napkin away and saw the nasty twist in the front wheel and forks. His face fell. "Hey, what'd you do to it? This is sacrilege!"

"Just a little altercation. Nothing another K or two can't fix. Calm down."

"Yours?" he asked, looking at me askance.

"Sure," I replied.

Duke's scowl deepened. He spirited an inconspicuous pair of reading glasses out of one of his jersey pockets and narrowed his view to one section of the photograph. "Okay, hot stuff, then what color is this thing?" he demanded, disappearing the glasses again and jabbing a stained and callused finger at the frame.

"Huh?"

Duke peered at me sharply. "Right. You don't know. Not your

bike, is it?" He flipped the photograph over and read the label on the back, which idiotically declared, "Bicycle in ditch."

I was beginning to get plenty annoyed, which is to say I didn't like being caught lying. *I* was supposed to be the detective asking the questions, not *he*. I returned his stare with one I hoped was equally virulent.

Our staring match was interrupted by the arrival of my lunch. *"Burrito grande de pollo?"* asked a girl with sloe eyes and a black braid long enough to sit on. I pointed to my place. The girl landed an enormous tortilla-enshrouded mound in front of me, cantilevered a similar one down in front of Duke *Bicicletas,* then through some sleight of hand made additional little dishes of green and red salsa appear on the table.

I plucked the photograph out of Duke's hands and began to stab into my food, eyes pointedly anywhere but on him.

Duke let out a nasty snort. "That's a police photograph, isn't it? You some kind of detective, or are you just playing at it?"

I swallowed hard, but that mouthful of burrito halted its descent halfway from my mouth to my stomach and hovered. The fact was, I didn't really know where the photographs had come from. Curt Murbles had *told* me they had been taken by a "little Mexican meddler" who had been cruising with his police scanner going when Janet's body was found. He had given them to me with a sneer, humoring me, and only because I'd insisted on at least seeing a picture of Janet. "Wrong-o, Duke, these are not police photographs," I growled, perplexed at how quickly this skinny little dweeb was getting under my skin.

"Aw, c'mon, babe, you can tell the Duke." He arranged his lips into a pout.

I'd had enough, and said so: "Duke, honey, I'm not sure I altogether care for your attitude."

Duke grabbed for the photograph. I stabbed his hand with my flimsy fork. He jumped back, a hostile grin blooming across his bony face. "Duke likes a filly with spirit!"

I planted my elbows on the photograph and leaned my face into my hands. "Listen, Duke, do me and my burrito a favor and leave us in peace, okay?"

Duke got up, pulled a plastic bag out of his jersey, and deftly maneuvered his burrito into it. "Okay, have it your way. The Duke can take a joke." He made a kissy little pucker, swiveled his hips, and headed for the plate-glass door. As he shouldered it open, he paused a moment and said, "By the way, darlin', Merlin frames are a nice silver; color film would be wasted on it. You pay that much for a titanium frame, you don't paint it."

I stared at him, not even bothering to fake an *I knew that* look.

Then Duke delivered his *coup de grâce:* "And that was Janet Pinchon's bicycle. I ought to know, I helped build it. I don't know what you're doing with those pictures, but I can find out." Then he whipped a pair of orange wraparound reflective sunglasses out of yet another pocket in his miraculous jersey, mounted them on his bony nose, flashed his Hollywood smile from hell, and said, "Enjoy your lunch."

The door slammed shut behind him.

My first impulse was to run out the door after him. I wanted to catch him so he couldn't tell anyone about our conversation, but I wasn't sure what I'd do with him once I had him. Fold him up like a card table and stick him in my suitcase?

Instead, I just sat there and prayed. I realized that my hands were shaking. *Relax, Em,* I told myself. *Santa Rosa looks like a big town. You'll never see or hear from the little turd again.*

I cut a second bite of the burrito but couldn't eat it. I wasn't sure what scared me worse: that I'd come within a millimeter of blowing my cover, or that I clearly didn't know what I was doing. Because if I didn't know how to do this job, I ought to go home.

I got a doggie bag for the rest of my burrito, carted it and my papers and photographs back out to the truck. I put the burrito on the floor, overrevved the engine, and missed my shift, but finally managed to find reverse and maneuver out of the parking lot without hitting any of the gleaming Camaros that were parked all around me.

Eleven-thirty. The blinding milk-white sky of half an hour earlier had given way to a hazy blue, but the vault of the heavens still seemed to loom only a few hundred feet overhead. I drove down the street to the first gas station I saw and pulled in, parked next to the public phone, and dialed the special number the Senator had given me to use to report in. It rang once. Twice. Three times. I waited, tapping on the glass of the phone booth. When a voice finally came on the line, it was not Senator Pinchon's. "Murbles," it said.

"This is Em Hansen. I'm in Santa Rosa. Were you able to make me an appointment with Janet's roommate?"

I heard an unpleasant sound, something like muffled laughter. "Why, yes, she'll meet you at noon at her apartment. Don't be late."

Noon? Shit! I hoped it wasn't more than twenty minutes away. "What's her name?"

"Suzanne Cousins."

"What have you told her about me?"

"That you were a friend of Janet's," he said dryly, as if only a cretin would need this repeated. "She asked if you were coming to pick up Janet's personal effects." Another smirking snort. "I told her you had been deputized by Janet's mother to do so."

This was good. This meant I didn't have to fabricate a reason to be pawing through Janet's things. But why did Murbles seem to think this was funny? "Won't she wonder why a family member isn't picking up her stuff?"

"Don't ask impertinent questions, Miss Hansen."

The day was past when I could trouble myself to be impressed by some jumped-up politician's personal assistant, and I fantasized squishing this one like a cockroach. "It's my job to ask questions, Curt. And I'll decide which ones are impertinent." *Fellah.*

Silence.

"Come on, *Mister* Murbles."

"The Senator is a busy man," he said, as if I was implying that he should be more interested in his daughter's belongings, which I was.

"How about his wife?"

"She is indisposed."

"She's got maybe siblings?"

"Two brothers."

"And?"

"They are busy also."

Nice family. Everyone's too busy for little Janet. "Cousins? Aunts? Chauffeurs? Garbagemen?"

Murbles' voice flowed like ice water over the line. "Miss Hansen, *you* have been delegated. I rather thought this would be useful to you in your investigation. Would you prefer I inform Ms. Cousins we are canceling the—"

"No. No, this is fine." I counted to ten.

Around eight, the line went dead. I stared at the hand that held the telephone receiver. It was shaking with anger.

I leaned against the cold glass of the booth, trying to become calm. Why was all this being so difficult for me? I had never been one to suffer fools gladly, but neither had I let them get me so riled so fast. I tried to remember what Elyria had told me about dealing with things when you're down. When Elyria's husband had died, she had grieved robustly and with style, greeting each new challenge openly and with grace. Why was I drawing into myself, lolling on the couch for months, and then running away somewhere I'd never been to find out who killed someone I'd never met?

Get a grip on yourself, Em.

Well, sure, Elyria lost her husband, but she wasn't out of work at the time. And now that my life's falling apart, Elyria's is on the rise: she's fallen in love, and three's beginning to be a crowd. And I'd always thought that Mother's drinking would put her in an early grave, and that I'd go home to the ranch and help Dad run it, and live on there in peace and happiness, running the ranch myself until I was old and gray.

I closed my eyes and took a very deep breath. When in doubt, I've found that spite can take me a long way. I decided that squishing the Senator's personal confidential assistant like a cockroach would be too hasty and merciful a death. Perhaps, if I ever got to Washington, I would instead leave roach bait out on his desk. I imagined him salivating at the sight of this tidbit, sweeter than a doughnut, more succulent than foie gras. . . .

I focused my mind on the Senator. Why did he suspect that his daughter's profession had a bearing on her murder? Was it instinct, or did he know something he hadn't told me?

I decided to dial that number again, get assertive, demand to speak with my client. While the phone rang, I perused a rather vulgar bit of misspelled graffiti inscribed on the coin box. When I heard Murbles' voice again, I announced, "This is Em Hansen. I'd like to speak with the Senator."

"Miss Hansen, the Senator is not *available.* What do you *need?"*

"I need to report, as instructed."

"I shall tell him you called."

"And I have a question for him," I added hurriedly, lest he cut me off.

"What is your question, Miss Hansen? I will ask him and call you back, or more likely, I can answer it myself."

I braced my feet and puffed out my chest as if this guy could see me through all that phone wire, and addressed him like he was some irritating, balky horse I was trying to break to saddle. "No. I will wait until the Senator is available." *"You will report to me and to me only,"* hah! Senator, *do you know what your help's up to?*

"Suit yourself."

"And tell me, Mr., ah, Murbles"—I couldn't help pronouncing the name as if I were speaking through a length of sewer pipe—"what *is* the best time to reach him? I'm on the road, and so he can't call me." This technique had always cut through a lot of stalling when I worked in the oil business.

"There *is* no *best* time. But I will tell him you *called."*

The line disconnected, leaving me staring at that line of graffiti. I decided its author was my kind of guy.

4

I PRESSED THE BUZZER AT 3006 VIA ROBLES, WHICH TURNED
out to be half of a duplex on a dusty street at the southwest edge of
town, where a seedier, more tumbledown variant on civilization met
the farmlands. No one answered. I checked my watch again. Had I really set the thing right? *Maybe the clock in the truck is on Pacific standard
time, which would mean, uh, let's see, I traveled west and the earth rotates
counterclockwise when viewed from over the north pole. . . . Where is Suzanne
Cousins?*

I mentally rehearsed my story. *I am a friend of Janet's family, and I
called her folks and asked if I could do anything for them and here I am.* From
there I figured to guide Suzanne into a few questions, like, *Tell me,
where was Janet working just before she died?* This had to be handled with
sensitivity, of course, but if I was going to infiltrate Janet's professional
sphere, I had first to find out where that sphere had been.

The door opened.

At first all I could see were her eyes. Gray, like smoke. They searched
deep inside me.

I blinked, looked again. Suzanne's eyes were still looking at mine,
but no longer into them. With their intensity diminished, I could notice that they were surrounded by lavish dark lashes and framed by a
straight, level brow and slanting cheekbones. Her lips were full and she
was blessed with a tumult of sandy blond hair that fell in waves past
her shoulders. Which were broad and muscular, yet soft. Her body was

swathed in a soft tunic and stretchy leggings the color of ripe fruit. Her feet were bare.

I remember thinking, *This woman would have been burned as a witch in Salem.* Tallying the sheen of gray in the hair and the spray of crow's-feet that curved around cheeks no longer softened by the kiss of youth, I gauged her to be forty or at most forty-five.

She spoke in a deep lioness purr: "You're Emily Hansen?" The tone was cordial, but lacked the inviting challenge of that first glance.

"In person."

She turned—a fluid, integrated motion that swept through her body—and led me into her abode.

Which enfolded me in the softness of exotic fabrics and spiced air, the richness of space occupied by treasured objects. Prisms hanging on satin ribbons in the windows sprayed sunlight in its elemental wavelengths around the room. Inviting cushions decked the sofa and spilled across the floor in decadent splendor. Photographs in homemade frames drew my eyes about the walls, and on a low table, the bleached vertebra of what must have been a whale was lovingly displayed among bowls of smooth pebbles, flower petals, orange skins, and sage.

I was fascinated, and yet disappointed. This decor had to be Suzanne's effort, not the practical surroundings of a geologist who rode an unpainted bicycle.

"Janet's room is through there," Suzanne was saying, pointing down a short hallway. "Everything's in there, except the things the police took."

I wasn't fully listening to her words. I was too distracted by the matter-of-factness of her manner. I had expected the heaviness of sadness, maybe. A woman swept up in the tragedy of her roommate's death. Or a stoic, perhaps, austere and tough, but certainly not this. I hadn't needed an appointment: I could have knocked on the door and said, "Hi, I'm from the Salvation Army, I'm here for Janet's stuff," and Suzanne would probably have said, "Fine, it's down the hall and to the left." I marched down that hall thinking, *Okay, so the rest of the apartment is Suzanne,* this *room is going to tell me something about Janet.*

But hope sank like a failed soufflé. Janet Pinchon's bedroom was tidy and faceless, as if someone had moved systematically through the room, cleaning away any suggestion of personality. Her bedding was folded on top of her bed, her floor swept, her few toiletries grouped on the top of her dresser, where Suzanne must have placed them after removing them from the bathroom. The walls were devoid of decoration, the few posters and photographs laid neatly on top of the stack of blankets. I unrolled one poster. SAVE THE WETLANDS, it proclaimed.

I heard breathing right behind me and spun around. Suzanne was leaning against the doorframe, arms folded across her stomach, watching me. "Lock the door behind you when you leave, and don't let the cat out," she said, turned, and left.

"You're going out?"

"That's correct," she called from the middle of the living room. I heard car keys jingling, and the rustle of jacket greeting shoulders.

"But I need to pack Janet's stuff," I shouted after her.

"Take your time." I heard the front door open.

I hurried back into the living room, catching Suzanne halfway out the door. "But I need to talk to you!"

Those gray eyes narrowed in a different kind of challenge. "About what?"

"About Janet."

"Janet's dead."

I opened my mouth. "Yes, and—"

"That was sad."

Was sad? *Was* sad? My mouth sagged open. It must be that some of the things I'd heard about California were true, and I was staring eye to eye with a grand practitioner of the religion of This Minute and Now.

"She's your roommate, and you—"

"I hardly knew her."

"But you lived with her. Can we get together later on?"

"Sure. I'll call you." As in *don't call me.*

"But you don't have my number."

"Write it on a piece of paper and put it by the phone."

"No, that won't work," I said. "I don't have a place yet."

"So you call me, then." With that, Suzanne Cousins strode out the door, climbed into an ancient Jeep Cherokee, cranked the engine, and bolted away from the curb.

IT TOOK ME until early evening to scout enough cardboard boxes from liquor stores to pack Janet's things. I dawdled, hoping Suzanne would return.

And I took time (as I carefully placed each item into whiskey boxes printed with poinsettia and holly and big red bows for the Yuletide season) to look for anything that would suggest why someone would want to kill Janet. Nothing popped out at me. I even leafed through a few of her books (as I stacked them in vodka boxes printed with joyous reindeer), but no startling slips of paper fell out of them. I felt like I was Christmas-wrapping a funeral.

I began to justify the empty feeling of the room, speculating that Janet had been a woman who lived within the undoubtedly vast and special universe of her mind. Or maybe she had had an allergic reaction to her roommate's sensuality. The books in particular helped me feel better about her. They were a rich little cache, the carefully chosen favorites of an educated mind: classics like *Anna Karenina;* texts and field guides on geology, ecology, astronomy, botany, and ornithology; a few choice science fiction paperbacks that had been lovingly read and reread until the covers flopped open as if on tiny hinges; an eclectic survey of nonfiction trade paperbacks delving into ecopolitics, emerging nations, philosophy, spiritual experience, and religion. Clearly this was a library born of many years' devoted browsing through obscure bookstores, a treasury of favorites winnowed from whatever broader sources a well-educated woman might encounter. No casual fiction, no frivolous cookbooks, no *People* magazine–type effluvia. I packed Janet's books with care.

By the time I'd carried all the boxes to the truck, my back was aching. The bed called me. The quiet simplicity of the room had begun to grow on me. I began to long for it like a hermit crab must long for a more comfortable shell. I wondered briefly if Suzanne would let me stay for a while. It wasn't yet the end of the month; might not Janet's rent still be good? I could win Suzanne's confidence, interview her at leisure, get tidbits of insight that would, of course, prove earth-shattering. But as the minutes and hours ticked by, it became clear that Suzanne Cousins would not be returning until I was safely gone.

There were, altogether, ten boxes of books, one box of toiletries and things like pens and pencils and miscellaneous geologist's gear, and one box of shoes. The clothing I folded politely and stowed in three boxes and a couple of suitcases I found underneath the bed. There was not a single piece fancy enough to require more tender handling. I stuffed the bedding into a big paper-towel box scrounged from a nearby supermarket, and was able to fit all remaining bits of stuff into one twelve-bottle whiskey carton. I left the furniture, figuring that as it matched the dresser and bookcase in Suzanne's room (Suzanne had a queen-sized futon on the floor—no single-bed monasticism for her), it probably went with the apartment.

I took one last look around the room, glancing into the closet and under the bed to make sure I'd gotten everything. Underneath the bed, up against the baseboard, I saw a slip of paper that turned out to be a business card. HRC ENVIRONMENTAL CONSULTANTS, it read, and gave a local address and telephone number. Janet's name was below and to the right, with "Staff Geologist" printed just beneath it.

This card I slipped into the back pocket of my jeans. I smiled, at last sure of at least one essential bit of information.

Thus, with the residue of Janet's worldly goods stowed in the back of the truck, I set out in search of a motel, certain I had missed some-thing obvious.

5

THERE ARE A FEW INANIMATE OBJECTS IN THIS LIFE THAT TRULY give me the creeps. Among them are motel rooms. A person of taste would say that this is because motel rooms, like Janet Pinchon's apartment bedroom, are so terribly, awfully bland. A paranoiac who watches too much TV would say it's because motel rooms are lonely places where people get killed. A Californian with New Age leanings would tell you it's because people with bad energy have slept there before you.

Room 132 at the Wagon Trail Motel was no exception. It languished beside Santa Rosa Avenue south of the city limits in a neighborhood of trailer courts, discount emporiums, and auto repair shops. The Wagon Trail was no longer in its salad days, but the rates fit within the limit of my already stressed credit card.

A Mexican woman of about my age made an impression of that poor overused piece of plastic, pointed to number 132 on a map of the complex, and said, "Nice room. Very private. It's on the corner around back." She smelled of garlic and cumin. She had a short, rounded body grown rounder from childbearing and a head of shining black hair that was to die for. She observed me with the gaze of the ancients, that sober, dignified watchfulness of the *indígena* that quietly maps your bones.

I drove the little truck around to the back, parked it outside of my room, and stepped inside, wondering just how awful my new home was going to be.

On an awfulness scale of one to ten, it was about seven. Cinder-block modern architecture, circa 1960. Velvet painting of lateen-rigged ship at dock done in ten tired brushstrokes. Drapes that wouldn't quite close. Worn peacock-blue shag carpeting. Stained bedspread. And the steady rumble of trucks and whooshing of passenger cars ripping past on Highway 101, which bordered the back of the motel, was mind-numbing.

I fiddled with the curtains for a while, trying to close the four-inch gap. Despairing, I opened them wide, which gave me a panoramic view of a chain-link fence and the highway beyond, the back of a liquor store, its inelegant Dumpster, and its weak security light, which only made the evening gloom beyond more eerie. I settled for leaving the curtains not quite closed.

Now that I'd officially made my nest, my first order of business was to bring Janet's boxes in from the truck so they wouldn't be stolen. I smiled wryly at the self-image I was cultivating: Em Hansen, itinerant monk, now transporting the bones of a little-known martyr to a distant shrine.

My second order of business was to make some instant coffee in the little plug-in pot supplied by the motel. The result tasted enough like mud that I poured it into the toilet.

Which in turn made me feel so sorry for myself that I indulged in my third order of business, which was to phone Elyria, just to let her know I was okay.

She wasn't home.

Loneliness engulfed me so suddenly and deeply that I left an un-characteristically long and detailed message on her machine. I gave the name of the motel, the city, the area code, the number, the room ex-tension, and a stiff-upper-beak version of how I actually felt. I was sure I sounded on the edge of hysteria, the timbre of my voice rising throughout. I hung up in disgust.

And slid into a funk, about how Elyria was probably going to marry this guy Joe Finney, with whom she was no doubt right at this mo-ment having a nice, companionable dinner, and how that meant that when I got back to Denver, I was going to have to look for another place to live. Gak. And with what money?

Right, money. I had something over two hundred dollars left in my checking account. My credit card had been very nearly redlined before I left Denver, and now it was further burdened by a plane ticket, which, being a last-minute affair, had cost a bunch. Meals on the road would not be cheap, and this room was going to throw another brick on the load every day I stayed. It occurred to me also that I'd need gas for the truck, and there would be phone calls and maps and photographs and who knew what else. I checked my wallet. I had that one Visa card, a Chevron card, an automatic teller card to my checking account in Denver, and twenty-four dollars in cash. Berating myself for not thinking to ask for a retainer before starting the job, I made a note to bring it up when I phoned the Senator in the morning, got back into the truck, and wandered off in search of dinner.

What South Santa Rosa Avenue offered by way of cuisine looked questionable, so I drove all the way into downtown Santa Rosa, where I found a nice brew pub called the Third Street Aleworks. After dining heartily on barbecue beer shrimp and wheat beer, I handed the waiter my credit card to conserve my cash, but a minute later he returned and ever so discreetly handed it back to me. "Excuse me, ma'am, but this card is beyond its limit," he whispered sweetly, as if the cute little slip of plastic had had one too many. My face averted against embarrassment, I promptly paid cash.

That left me with only fifteen dollars and change, which would hardly get me through the next day. I set out in search of a bank with an automatic teller machine, figuring about a hundred dollars would tide me over until I got my advance.

I found a Bank of America at the first corner. The automatic teller machine looked across Third Street onto a central square featuring a big evergreen decked out in colored lights for the holidays. Littler trees all around it were ablaze with miniature white lights, and the light staffs were rigged with Christmas gewgaws. Ho, ho, ho.

I checked to make sure the B of A would accept my card, stuffed it in, and stood poised to type in my Personal Identification Number. When the screen lights came on, I began to type, but no, it seemed the machine didn't want my PIN first, like any self-respecting ATM in the Rockies, it wanted to know whether I intended to do my transaction in English or Spanish. I punched *English* and then my PIN. Or thought I had. The machine asked me to enter it again.

Beginning to feel pretty exposed on the late evening sidewalk downtown, I glanced around. There was very little traffic moving along the street, and no one abroad on the sidewalk. Except one man. A big, tough-looking man. Who was moving straight toward me. His face harsh and haggard under the streetlights. He stopped five feet behind me. There was a second machine, damn it; why didn't he use it?

I typed faster, managing to punch my PIN in wrong a second time. I typed again. Wrong again. The man moved up closer behind me. I tried a fourth time, and a fifth, now forgetting my correct PIN entirely. The machine spat my card back at me.

I pressed my card back into the slot of the other machine. It promptly came back out. Only then did I notice that the screen display read, *Out of Service.*

Now stuffing his own card into the first machine, the man said, "I hate these things. It did that to me last week. You type in the wrong number a couple times and the machine thinks you're a crook or something, freezes your card access to your account. Now you've got to come during business hours to get your account cleared again." He shook his head. "Pain in the butt."

I drove back to the motel in a daze, wondering just when I had begun to get so paranoid.

◈

BACK IN MY room, there was a light flashing on my phone. Knowing that Elyria was the only person who had my number, I dialed her back without even tagging the motel desk for the message. "Hi," I said, when she answered.

"Em? Hello, I was about to return your call."

"You hadn't called yet?" *Huh?*

"No. I just came in a few minutes ago," she said, her diction growing more formal, which meant she was nervous about something. "Er, your mother called just now. When I mentioned that you were in California, she said you must look up your aunt Frida. She gave her number."

"You told her where I *am?*"

"No. But such a coincidence: the number she gave for your aunt is your same area code. Have I met Frida?"

"Damn it, Elyria, you didn't give her my number, did you?"

"Do you have a pen and paper?"

"Elyria!" I was shrieking.

There was silence from the other end of the line. For a moment, I thought she'd hung up. When she did speak, it was softly, and with a note of resignation: "No, I didn't give her your number or tell her where you are, just that you are in California. That's a very large place, as I recall. I'm not so insensitive that I'd presume to push a reconciliation on you. I think she gave your aunt's number out of social reflex. Heaven help me I should suggest the woman was concerned about you—I don't know her, don't know her limitations, don't know half of what she's done or not done for you. All I know is how you feel about her."

As Elyria's voice flowed through my ear, my mind slipped. I am five years old, hiding in the closet in my room. At home. In Wyoming. My mother is calling me, her voice soft and concerned. She says it's okay for me to come out now. *No,* I think, *that can't be her voice!*

Elyria's voice said, "Em, when *are* you going to answer her calls?"

The memory vanishes, locked back in my head, replaced by a vast emptiness. Into the telephone I whispered, "I've got to go now. Sorry. Call you another time," and put it back on its cradle.

6

IN THE MIDDLE OF THE NIGHT, I WOKE UP FREEZING COLD AND dug through Janet's boxes until I found her blankets. Cocooning myself in their warmth, I stared at the light that seeped in through the gap in the curtains, weirdly illuminating the unfamiliar shapes and masses in the room. When the first gray of daylight finally mingled with the harsh yellow of the security lights, I showered and put on a good tweed suit that dated from my petro-baroness days and left early for breakfast and my first assault on Janet Pinchon's former employer.

Outside, I found the sky a thick gunmetal gray. No bright sunrise horizon to the east, no early morning birdsong over the oil-stained asphalt. I climbed into the little truck and set out in search of bright lights, coffee, and a newspaper to set my world back in a more bearable register.

I found a deli across the street from HRC Environmental Consultants, Inc., the place where Janet Pinchon had worked. The avenue was a long run of sleek new pavement bordered by new "tip-up" prefabricated buildings styled in air-raid-bunker modern. There were no cars yet in the parking spaces; in fact, the whole office park was so damned plain-Jane sparkling clean and devoid of wear that I wondered if the builders hadn't yet gotten around to installing the people. I parked the truck behind the deli and wandered by on the sidewalk, making a quick reconnaissance of the area. HRC Environmental Consultants crouched along forty or fifty feet of a building landscaped with withered rhododendrons cruelly misplanted in hard clay soil.

I looked at my watch. It was early, not yet seven, long before anyone might be arriving to work. The deli had big windows and a great view of HRC; just the place to lie in wait and plan my assault.

An astonishingly cheerful woman took my order. She wore a crisp chef's apron (apple green to match the Formica tabletops) that exaggerated her ample bosom. Her name, Reena, was machine-embroidered in tomato-red thread across the leading acreage of her left breast, and she leaned toward me with so much enthusiasm that I wondered if I were her first customer ever. "May I take your order?" she inquired in a rich, deep voice accented from somewhere east of Athens.

"Ah, yeah," I mumbled, my own voice still clabbered from a night's disuse. "Ah, two eggs, toast, and hash browns. And coffee."

"And can I interest you in some fresh-squeezed oranch juice?"

"What the hell." Damn the torpedoes: I'd have the ATM card cleared up in time to pay for lunch.

"Excuse me a minute," she caroled, pressing the electronic keypad on the front of her cash register. When the machine *ding*ed to indicate that it had arrived at a sum, her face broke into a smile of beatific triumph. "That will be nine dollars and three cents."

"Nine—*what?*" I clasped the pocket that had my wallet in it.

Reena's eyes popped in alarm. Her hands fidgeted. "Four-fifty for the aiks, toas, and home fries, one-fifty for the coffee—unlimited refills!—and two-fifty for the oranch juice. Fifty-three cents tax."

"Hold the OJ," I muttered, embarrassed. I pulled out my wallet and bowed my head over the ten and five ones that cowered in its murky depths between a disintegrating credit card receipt and a fortune cookie fortune that read, "You have a curious nature."

Reena was silent. I looked up to see her hand wavering over the keyboard of the cash register. "It's new," she whispered. "I don't know how to subtract—"

"It's okay," I said, a little too loudly, slapping the ten on the counter. "I shall savor every sip. Keep the change, please. I'll be over there." I spun around and headed to the counter under the window, humiliated at leaving only a ninety-seven-cent tip.

As I sat down, I saw that someone had parked a car in front of HRC Consultants. Had they gone inside? No, no lights on yet, and a big man was ambling from the car toward the deli door. He wasn't quite looking where he was going, more absorbed in counting change out of his pocket than watching his footing. His large, soft frame lurched as he came up over the curb.

He shoved open the deli door with one shoulder, still concentrating on his pocket change, but his lips parted into the sort of smile one sometimes sees on the face of a sleeping child. He planted his large feet wide to stop a slight swaying in his body. I had thought at first that he was drunk, but now that he was close I could smell no booze. His head drooped forward at the neck. He was probably six foot three, had dark freckles on milky skin and a rich thatch of graying red-brown hair. He was fastidiously groomed, his hair freshly cut, his fingernails trimmed and clean, and his penny loafers polished to a high shine. He wore neatly pressed charcoal-gray flannel slacks and a muted red tie. The commercially starched collar of his pin-striped shirt and his narrow belt formed cofferdams against the descent of softening jowls and abdominal muscles that were taking the big middle-aged slide, but he was not so far gone as to seem sloppy.

He called out a greeting to Reena in a vibrant baritone: "My, mymymymy! Reena, you are the apple of my heart. Good morning."

Reena surged to the counter, a smile exploding across her wide face. "Good *morning,* Mr. Ryan. How *are* you?" she sang.

The tall man looked up from the task of counting out change with fumbling fingers and renewed his own full-lipped smile. "Reena, Reena; it *is* a lovely morning, isn't it?"

I looked outside. Gray murk.

"Why, Mr. Ryan . . ." Reena warbled.

"If only because you are in it, sweet Reena. The usual, what ho." He pursed his lips into a pixilated air-kiss that pulled his cheeks forward like taffy. "And *when* will you call me Pat?"

Reena disappeared into the tiny kitchen behind the counter, leaving a deep-throated giggle hanging in the air behind her. Pat Ryan cast a pile of crumpled bills and a handful of change across the counter and stuffed two singles into the tip jar by the register. Then he waved to someone in the kitchen. "Morning, Ahmed. How's tricks?"

"Is good, Pat," a voice replied.

Then Pat Ryan swung toward me, catching me staring. His brushy brown eyebrows rose skyward, hoisting open some of the sweetest, sleepiest, most intensely blue eyes I've ever seen. Even as grouchy as I was feeling, this yanked a smile clean out of me. He bowed courteously. "Good morning, ma'amselle," he purred, starting to move my way. "I thought no one was a worse insomniac than I."

My smile became a grin, and when he gestured inquiringly at the stool next to me, I nodded happily. "Em Hansen," I said, reaching out my hand to shake his.

"And what brings you into our midst, Ms. Hansen?" he asked, enclosing my hand in the warmth of his own.

"I'm a geologist," I said. "Out here looking for work," I added, laying in my cover story. "Are you with HRC?" Ryan? Maybe he was even R!

Ryan nodded, a flicker of irritation muddying his eyes.

"Is HRC hiring?" I asked. Subtle old Em.

Reena bustled up to our counter with two big mugs of steaming coffee and a handful of little tubs full of half-and-half. Ryan emptied three into his mug and stirred, his fingers limp and fumbling. When he looked up, his smile was no longer a happy one, and he pursed his lips several times, as if exercising them before a difficult athletic feat. "You want to work for H, R, and C? Brave woman."

"Why d'you say that?" I revised my prior speculation: Ryan was employee, not employer.

"Aw, don't take me too seriously, I'm just kind of like that."

Like what? I wondered, but asked, "Isn't it a good place to work?"

He poured on the charm again, though it had lost its cheer: "Aw, well, my dear . . . HRC is a nice enough place to work, I suppose, if you're looking for some experience, but you're a few years older than your standard entry-level kid, or do I miss my guess?"

"The crumbs of my thirtieth birthday cake are long since stale, Mr. Ryan," I intoned.

He elaborately pursed his lips. "Just so. And by the cut of your jib"—he gestured toward my tweed suit—"I would guess your prior experience is in something that pays rather better than environmental consulting. Such as petroleum . . ." He let this last word roll out like an oil slick on the Persian Gulf.

I made a mental note: *This man may seem half-asleep, but he isn't stupid. A geologist, no doubt; deductive logic, intuitive leaps* . . . "Is oil-patch experience a problem?"

Ryan pursed his lips and mouthed several words before choosing one he would voice. "Oh . . . Mr. H and Mr. R and Mr. C have a thing about oily types. H and C are civil engineers, which means they don't much understand what geologists do, and R is a hydrogeologist, which is by no means to be confused with a geologist."

"How so?"

Ryan's eyes roamed the room. "Let's just say hydros don't play nicely with the other kids. Don't share the toys, always want to be team captain but never just a player. Abstractionists amok in a concrete universe. My own self," he said, laying his long fingers across the fine pinpoint cotton of his pressed shirt, "they suffer to employ because I emphasized certain other accomplishments than geology on my resume. I had to hide my oily years, may they rest in peace. I hid them between the service and my tenure with the Water Board."

My mental gears shifted to fast forward, filing and assessing information. *The army. Muscle tone lost and hair graying, face on close inspection sprayed with the first fine wrinkles. Mid-forties plus, makes that service Vietnam—marines? He likes lots of starch around his neck—which fits with a stint in the oil patch during the late-seventies, early-eighties boom.* "The Water Board?"

"You're not a Californian, I see. So you're not registered, either?"

"Slow up, please; you're losing me."

"The California State Water Quality Control Board. I was lucky, in a way, to be one of the first laid off from the oil biz, but it sure was fun while it lasted."

Pat Ryan clearly knew a lot and had a lot to say, but he was leaving out so many essential cars in the train of his thoughts that I felt like a caboose that had come unhitched and rolled onto a siding. I wondered again if he was a drunk who hadn't been to bed yet, but no, there definitely wasn't any eau de booze on his breath. "Water Board?" I repeated.

He turned his thousand-yard glaze out across the street, which was waking up to the first few sorties of commuter traffic. "Aw, I suppose it's not so bad as all that."

The conversation was beginning to make me feel a little hazy myself. I wasn't a caboose on a siding, I was a spaceship that had gotten sucked into the slipstream of an existentialist fugue. Doggedly I said, "The Water Board is a state government regulatory agency?"

Pat's focus swam back toward me. "Yes."

"So I want a job at HRC. So how do I package my qualifications?"

"Qualifications? Just tell them you want to learn about tanks," he said. Suddenly he sat up straight, a happy twinkle in his eyes. "Yes, perfect! In fact, just today they're interviewing to replace a geologist we lost. I bet if you walked in there this morning, they'd have you interviewed and out before they figured out you weren't on the schedule!" The thought tickled him so much that he threw back his head and began to laugh at the building across the street as if it were a bully he'd managed to blindside.

"Who do I ask to see?" I asked, as Reena slid our breakfasts in front of us.

"Rauch. He's the hydro guy. Hollingsworth is gone as usual doing expert-witness testimony, and Carter was last seen exiting stage left to

Hawaii with wife number three. Ask to see Rauch, say you're expected. And here's what you do: you don't have your forty, either, do you." It was a statement.

"What's a forty?"

"Right. So you say, 'Mr. Rauch, I've heard you run the best shop in town, and I'm looking for the best experience." Play to his ego. You can't miss it, it's a rather large feature. You say, 'I'm not registered, but I have X years' experience field-mapping'—something vague like that—'and I plan to sit the registration exam next time it's offered. And here's what I'll do about my forty, Mr. Rauch. I'll work the first week for free, that way it costs you nothing to give me a trial, you even pocket whatever chargeable time I accrue. Then, if you like me—' " He slapped the counter, warming to his blarney. " '*When* you see how *much* you like me, you send me for my forty.' "

"Please translate."

He looked up at me politely, as if I were a conductor on that little mental railroad of his and I'd just asked to see his ticket. "California registers geologists under the Division of Consumer Affairs. RG, Registered Geologist. You can't call yourself a geologist for hire without it. Regulator talk for here's the hoops you have to jump through. And the fed OSHA—"

I grimaced.

He rolled his eyes. "—Occupational Safety and Health Administration—says you can't work on a contaminated site without a forty-hour health and safety training course."

"So why would Rauch hire me on trial if he couldn't send me on a site?"

He steepled his fingers. "My dear, he does it all the time."

"Breaks the law."

"Precisely."

"And what happens if I get hurt on his site?"

"He *could* get his greedy little buttocks jailed. Or sued. Or both. But of course, as long as we are ignorant of the regulations . . ."

Red flags flew up in my head. Maybe Janet had quit to stay healthy.

And maybe she threatened to blow the whistle on Rauch, and he didn't like that, and— Excited, I swilled my two-dollar-and-fifty-cent orange juice without tasting it. "So I tell Rauch I want to learn about tanks," I prompted.

"Yeah."

"So *you* tell *me* about tanks, so I can act like tanks are the only thing that keep my heart beating."

"Tanks."

"Yeah." Hel-*looo!*

"Right. LUST." His cheeks bunched in an elaborately prim smile.

"LUST?"

"As in Leaking Underground Storage Tanks."

"Tanks."

"No really, the County Health Department calls it the LUST program. You'll catch on soon enough," he said. He popped the last of his English muffin into his mouth and chewed. When he'd swallowed, he rose and dusted the crumbs off his necktie and slacks. "Gotta go. Gotta be at my desk when the man gets in, look earnest, keep my job another day." He turned to go but briefly glanced back at me, his smile completely absent. "You'll probably want to dress a little more humbly, my dear, so your oiliness doesn't show. Oh, and don't tell them you know me. It wouldn't help your cause."

I REMAINED THROUGH two refills of my coffee mug, maximizing caffeine gained for cash spent, and watched the inmates of HRC Environmental arrive for their day at the salt mines. They were a morose lot, shuffling in with hunched shoulders and drooping necks, except for the only female in the bunch, a young boopsie who fairly bounced up the sidewalk. And a middle-aged guy who drove up in a shining BMW. He stormed into the building like there were heads in there that needed knocking together. I figured him for Mr. Rauch, my quarry.

I fiddled absently with my watch, the image of Janet's watchless wrist floating back up into consciousness. So the work she did for HRC dealt with leaking underground fuel storage tanks: what about them? I supposed that a leaking tank meant that whatever petroleum product had been in the tank was now outside the tank, which spelled contamination. I found that rather hard to get excited about, having worked for so many years in and around the petroleum *finding* business, where crude oil got spilled as a regular thing. And how much could leak out of a tank before somebody noticed? Wouldn't they catch the problem after, say, ten or fifteen gallons?

I did heed Ryan's warning about my attire, a problem easy to remedy. Before setting out to storm the Bastille of job interviews, I made a run back to the motel and changed. The suit I had on amounted to the only clothing fancier than blue jeans I had brought with me, but Janet had worn the same sizes I did, and by gum, I had all her clothes. You might think it a little gutsy to wear a dead woman's clothes to interview for her job, but her tastes had been remarkably unobtrusive, running to common, off-the-rack styles in don't-notice-me blues. Perfect camouflage, and it was kind of comforting to put them on, like I had a friend in town who'd support me as I went through the agony of interviewing for a job.

While I was at the motel, I tried to phone the Senator but got Murbles again, who again claimed the Senator was unavailable. As what I needed most just now more than anything was the money, I avoided another pissing match and kept to basics, trying to sound productive first before I hit him for the cash: "I've boxed Janet's belongings. Shall I take them to the Senator's California residence?" Yeah, that was a good idea; he'd give me the address, and Mrs. Pinchon would be there, and I could chat with her, and . . .

"No." For just a moment, he sounded flustered, almost human: "Just hold on to them for now." But then he recovered himself, demanding brusquely, "Is that all you have to report?"

"No, there's one more item of business."

"Which is?" he drawled, sarcasm oozing out of the telephone and into my ear.

I took a deep breath. "At our first meeting we failed to arrange for my retainer," I announced, managing to sound a little indignant. "I'll need a week in advance. Thirty-five hundred dollars. A cashier's check will do."

He chuckled. It wasn't a pleasant sound. "Working through the weekend, are we?"

"You'd rather I dawdled?"

"Out of funds, dear?"

I was sitting on the end of the bed, clutching the phone, and could see myself in the mirror over the writing desk. A vein was beginning to bulge in my forehead. *Yes, out of funds. Broke. Indigent. On the skids. Are we done with the humiliation now? Might we proceed with the business at hand?*

Silence seemed to work on Murbles. With boredom dripping from his voice, he finally said, "Okay, where shall I send it?"

I hadn't planned on letting him know where to reach me; that would mean giving up what slim control over our communications I had. But I had no alternative mail drop set up, and was already so humiliated that I didn't want to get caught sounding like I hadn't thought this through, so I gave him the name and address of the motel. "Cashier's check, FedEx, tomorrow morning," I concluded, and rang off in a huff. After the check arrived, I told myself, I would move anyway, and to a better motel.

◈

LIKE MYSELF, JANET favored one hundred percent cotton clothing, so it was fortunate that the woman at the front desk had an ironing board to lend. She emerged from her residence, bringing a tiny baby to the desk in the cradle of one arm. The baby lay utterly relaxed, eyes closed in slumber. The woman maneuvered expertly, bringing me first the iron and then the ironing board with her free arm.

"Beautiful baby," I said.

"Thank you. You have children?"

I hesitated, embarrassed by the question, then shook my head. Motherhood was an alien thought to me. I felt like a child next to her obvious womanhood, a noninitiate, a girl until I became a mother myself, if that ever happened.

"Sisters and brothers?" she asked sympathetically.

I opened my mouth and closed it again.

"None?" She was amazed.

"I had a brother once," I said. "He died when I was very young."

She shook her head sympathetically.

"I hardly remember him," I said hurriedly, and started out the door.

"Wait," she called after me. "Don't you want your message?"

Message? Oh, the flashing red light on my phone. Surely she had misdirected the call. "Wasn't that call for someone else?" I suggested politely.

"It wasn't a call."

That stopped me. I waited, half in and half out the front door, iron and ironing board growing heavy in my arms. "Someone came *by?*"

"Yes. The message is, 'Say hello to the *girl* in Room 132.' It's from a *man."* She laughed duskily, rolled her dark eyes. "Or should I say *boy."*

Who in the hell? "He leave a name?"

The woman raised one shoulder coyly and gave me bedroom eyes. "Duke," she replied, pitching her voice low and sticking out her chest, baby and all. Then she threw back her head and indulged in a full belly laugh. *"Qué macho!"* The baby's eyes fluttered open; he smiled and fell back to sleep.

Another day, in another life, I would have shared her laughter. I should have been complimented that she presumed I wouldn't be interested in anyone as ridiculous as Bicycle Boy Duke, fresh-plucked road chicken and self-styled boulevardier. But in my gathering paranoia, it didn't seem funny at all that I'd been that easy to spot. My mind raced. It must have been a fortuitous sighting; he'd been out driving around—had to be driving, because he couldn't have kept up with me on his bicycle, and who would ride a bike down this part of town?— and had seen me, had followed me. Why? Surely not to continue his flirtation. No, he had known Janet, had been more than a small bit hostile toward me, once he thought I was messing in her affairs. Hadn't he? Then what was this, harassment? Or was he crazy? I forced a smile. "He leave a number?"

The motel manager shook her head. "No, 'Say hello' was all."

BY THE TIME I was steering the little truck back toward HRC Environmental, I had Duke stuck back into his proper pigeonhole, safe and unthreatening. He had probably just happened by on Highway 101 as I was unpacking the truck and decided to play an I-know-where-you-are prank. That would amuse his pea brain. That had to be it. *I can handle this,* I told myself.

But as I marched up the cement walkway to the reflective glass front door of HRC, I knew I was not, in fact, handling it. I was disconcerted by my own reflection. The harsh daylight that bounced off the pale walkway caught every line in my face, exaggerating the weight of fatigue and pain that had accumulated in the months since the layoffs and my father's death. I looked old and haggard. My mouse-brown hair was in need of cutting, and just as I reached the door, a puff of wind blew it all askew, and I noticed a bad suitcase crease I hadn't gotten ironed out of Janet's blue skirt. Smoothing the crease, I put my shoulder to the door and walked through it.

The door opened into a small outer office. Just inside, I encountered a girl with a haircut worse than mine who was seated behind a small Formica-topped desk with a computer screen and keyboard on it. I recognized her as the young thing who had bounced up the sidewalk earlier in the morning. She took two bovine chews at her gum and scratched an eyebrow with one long, pink fingernail before asking if she could help me.

"Um, yes," I replied. "I'm Em Hansen. I'm here about the geologist position."

Chewy stopped cold and squinted at me, her gears taking a moment to mesh. "You got an appointment?"

"Sure." I pulled my head back in staged indignation.

Chewy scrunched her shoulders up in a pose that might have aroused some sympathy in me if I'd been a male yak. "Sorry. I'm new here. Still learning."

I smiled magnanimously. "No problem."

"I'll let Mr. Rauch know you're here. Your name again?"

"Hansen. Emily Hansen."

She pulled open a drawer in her desk and riffled through a file. "I don't see your resume here. You got another copy?"

I stiffened.

Chewy grinned conspiratorially, one of those pig-face numbers where you get to see the inside of the grinner's nose. "No problem, I bet he's got it right on his desk." She struck a few keys on her computer to stabilize some task and started for the inside door.

Before she was even out of the room, the street door opened again and a sunburnt fellow five years or more my junior lurched in, mouth agape and eyes bugging with fear. He wore black lace-up shoes with brown socks, corduroy slacks, and a suit jacket that clearly belonged to someone else. He moved as if he had a rod duct-taped to his spine.

Chewy stopped short of the door and stared gape-mouthed at him, uncertain whether to continue her task or tend to this second intruder. "Yeah?" she blurted.

His voice was a bit high and squealy: "Hi, I'm George Benson. I'm here for an interview about the geologist position."

Chewy stood frozen like a fawn in the headlights of life, her mouth sagging open, her little gears clearly jammed.

I shrugged my shoulders to catch Chewy's attention and looked sideways at George Benson, as if to say, "Who's he?" then tipped my head encouragingly toward the inner door.

Chewy's jaws started working her gum again. Finally fate, or perhaps a minor earthquake, tipped her toward the inner door, and she hurried away into the bowels of the building. I followed close on her heels. When she saw that I was behind her, her chubby little hands whizzed around in confused gestures, one of which sort of pointed me into a room with a big table and some cheaply upholstered chairs on casters. "Can I getcha some coffee or something?" she gasped. "Mr. Rauch is kinda, ah—running late today."

"Sure. Black." I let myself into the conference room quickly, before George Benson could catch on and outrun me. Suddenly it was of deep importance to get this job, a real job, a geologist job, and I wasn't going to let any young punk in a borrowed suit jacket swipe it out from under me.

I could hear Chewy's voice somewhere down the hallway, a sibilant whisper, cajoling this Mr. Rauch to come out of his office. A harsh baritone growl issued an unintelligible answer. The ensuing debate went on for a while, giving me time to size up the framed credentials that were arrayed around the conference room walls. Rauch, Frederick William, was a Certified Hydrogeologist who had been educated at one of California's state universities, one I didn't know. He headlined the display between Theodore R. Hollingsworth (B.S., civil engineering, same school), and J. Thomas Carter (B.S., engineering, same again). My attention was next drawn to a company brochure that was ostentatiously displayed on the table. It included a statement-of-qualifications section that listed resumes of each member of the professional staff. Janet's had not yet been removed. I filed away the information that HRC had been Janet's first job after graduating from Sonoma State University, where she'd taken a double major in geology and environmental studies, which meant that Janet had been an environmentalist as much as she had been a geologist.

At this point Chewy reappeared with the cup of coffee. A thin-lipped man followed close on her heels, the hot-tempered Beemer-driver I'd scoped out from my breakfast perch. Chewy gave me a worried smile and chirped, "Mr. Rauch, this is, ah—"

"Em Hansen," I said, presenting my hand to be shaken. "I'm pleased to meet you."

Rauch did not shake my hand (reminding me a little too much of Senator Pinchon), but instead eased himself into a chair, making a point of leaving me standing.

From close range he was strongly athletic, in a tight-assed sort of way, and I was struck by the way he had moved. His joints all swung smoothly with each stride and shift of posture, greasing the air with arrogance and a kind of self-satisfied glory in his physical self. "Hansen? I don't have her resume, Cynthia," he barked, nailing the receptionist with a look of contempt so acidic it could burn through steel. "That's because you haven't *given* it to me yet, *isn't* it?"

Chewy struck her soon-to-be-dead deer pose again.

"Find it, Cynthia. *Now!*"

Chewy vanished.

Rauch turned his gaze on me. His complexion had become florid and splotchy, and his jaws bunched around lips now bent in a travesty of a smile.

Recalling some of the power moves I'd learned in the oil business, I grasped the back of another chair, moved it three inches to the right—thereby establishing it as my territory—and sat in it, spreading my elbows out on the arms so that I'd look as large as possible. The chair lurched off kilter as a caster let go.

Rauch's unfriendly smile widened.

Before he could speak again, I said, "Mr. Rauch, I'll just run down the high points of my resume." I stretched my right foot out casually to counterbalance the leaning chair, trying to make it look like I preferred, even enjoyed, teetering two inches to the left. And found that in fact I was enjoying myself. I was forming a new persona on the spot, getting to know it at the same time Rauch did. "I'm a geologist with six years' experience . . ." I began. What had Jack Ryan said? Hide the oil-patch experience?

Rauch continued to stare, his self-satisfied smile souring into a disgruntled pout.

Don't like losing, huh? I held up a hand with its back to him, cheerfully imagining that each finger meant what the middle one did, and began to enumerate my professional prowess, drawling it out. ". . . in field mapping . . ." (I stiffened my thumb)" . . . and project work . . ." *Yeah, that's vague enough!* (I stiffened my index finger) ". . . which means I'm no stranger to hard work." *I salute you, you sheep tick on the livestock of life* (I stiffened my middle finger). "My education——"

Here Rauch cut me off, his smile spreading wide enough to crease his cheeks for the first time. "The position doesn't call for an *oil* geologist."

My mouth fell open. "How——"

"I can spot you people a mile off." Rauch stood up, his smile spreading into a predatory grin. "Nice meeting you," he hissed, and headed out of the room.

"No, hear me out," I informed his back.

He turned halfway back, clearly enjoying himself.

"Mr. Rauch, you're going to hire me, because it will save you money." I suddenly had his full attention. It was something in his eyes. They got duller, like he was looking inward at that sensuous little place in his narcissistic soul that felt really, really good. I continued, gaining momentum. "I'm going to work for you for a week free of charge. That way you get to check me out at no risk and see what I can do. Then, when you've realized you can't get on without me, we'll discuss my salary."

Rauch looked like a snake that had just had autoerotic sex, all slithery and sloe-eyed. As his mouth opened, I wondered if a narrow forked tongue might whip out. "All right, Jensen, leave your phone number with Cynthia."

"That's Hansen."

"If she calls you, report in the morning," he said, already turning again and heading into the hallway. "Seven A.M. Wear field clothes. You'll assist Adam Horowitz; maybe it'll speed that bastard up. Cynthia!" he shouted. "Get a phone number from this person. Then send in the next Christian."

As his muscular frame receded down the hallway, I measured him with my eyes, computing how much concrete it would take to hold him underwater long enough to effect drowning. And as I made a mental note of the time he'd said to report, I was already composing my letter of resignation, which was going to be written entirely in words four letters long.

7

By the time I got back to my motel, there was a message for me to phone Cynthia. I was in.

That meant that the next thing I had to do was get a set of field clothes together so I could go out on the job. If geologists have a uniform, it's a pair of blue jeans, a khaki shirt, boots, some kind of sturdy jacket if there's weather, and a mapping vest.

I had brought my own boots and jeans, a good pair of ropers, low-heeled and well broken in. Unfortunately they were red, and they lacked the steel toe that I supposed OSHA required. I considered hitting a Sears for a khaki work shirt, but I wasn't sure the Senator would agree it was a business expense. Instead, I raided Janet's wardrobe again and found everything I needed: shirt, down jacket, steel-toed boots, and mapping vest. A Filson vest is a specialty item made of canvas. It's all pockets, sort of like a fishing vest, except the pockets are larger and specially shaped for the kind of gear and notebooks a geologist carries. The back is one great big pocket designed to hold a mapping clipboard. Thus garbed, a geologist can move about any kind of landscape or work site in durable comfort, ready to carry specimens home for documentation, paperweights, or general office decor.

The Filson vest slid on comfortably. Going through its pockets, I found the usual handful of trinkets geologists carry, including a hand lens strung on a braided nylon ribbon and a credit-card-sized plastic card called a grain-size chart, both used in describing rock and soil samples so that the descriptions are more uniform from geologist to geologist.

A geologist's hand lens is very special, a shaman's eye into the microscopic mysteries of the profession. I peered through Janet's lens at the chart, admiring the shapes of the printed grains of sand. The lens was a ten-power Hastings Triplet, and well used. It flipped open easily, and the black paint on the outside of the cover was worn through to the brass where Janet's fingers had habitually grasped it. My fingertips warmed the brass just as Janet's had. With reverence, I slipped its ribbon around my neck and let go. It fell to just the right level on my chest, resting against my heart, low enough to stay inside the shirt when I leaned forward, but easily grasped and drawn out when I needed it.

I tried the boots on last. They fit perfectly, almost down to the way my toes and arches rested inside the hills and shallows her feet had worn into the soles. I was beginning to know Janet, to feel her presence. I knew her taste, how big she was, her habits with her hand lens, even how she stood within the soles of her boots, and as I walked up and down the worn carpeting, I felt for just a moment that I was both myself and Janet. Coming to a stop in front of the full-length mirror on the closet door, I found myself looking into the glass to see if I could see her.

I found that I truly liked this person-who-was-no-longer-here. It was a gentle, tender feeling that eased my loneliness. As I looked into the glass in search of her fleeting visage, I thought, *One more time into the field, friend, one more time.*

◆

NEXT STOP, THE bank. The teller politely informed me that she couldn't help me with my problem, citing security requirements. I begrudgingly thanked her for saving me from stealing from myself and dialed my bank in Colorado. A woman at the Colorado bank crisply informed me that she'd truly love to help me, but wasn't I aware that my account was overdrawn?

No, I was not aware of that. Would she please read back my last ten debits?

She did. I'd forgotten to write down a check. Three hundred dollars worth of overdue health insurance payments. "Don't I have overdraft protection?" I whined.

"Yes, with your credit card, but that's currently at its maximum. We're so sorry we can't help you."

Figuring I'd better save those last few dollars for lunch the next day on the job, I dug that half-eaten burrito out from under the seat of the little blue truck and tried to believe the night's rest had improved it. It did at least serve the function of temporarily killing my appetite.

I SPENT THE rest of the day digging through public records of Janet's murder, which means I went to the Sonoma County Library and read the local newspapers.

The reference librarian seemed almost joyous to be able to help me in any way. I made a mental note of her, in case I ever needed anything else from the wilds of the public library: slender in a middle-aged sort of way, shoulder-length brown hair with a squiggly permanent wave, an ingratiating smile, and sparkling, yet slightly sleepy blue eyes that alluded to a much less sedate youth.

The librarian was pleased to inform me that the daily newspaper published in Santa Rosa was called the *Press Democrat* (or more affectionately, the *PD*), and pointed out where to find recent issues within the wide sweep of the modernish building. The *PD* was several sections long, with Sunday supplements and lots of four-color advertising inserts.

I sat down and searched through the issues immediately following Janet's murder. Her passing was apparently not sufficiently noteworthy to warrant much mention, just a short recitation in Section B, identity withheld pending notification of family. The next day's paper followed up with a minimal presentation of facts: name, occupation, lack of leads, and brief statement of loss from roommate Suzanne

Cousins. I was beginning to get incensed on Janet's behalf for this over-whelming lack of interest when my friendly reference librarian showed me a map atlas called the *Thomas Brothers Guide to Sonoma County*. It showed that the ditch site was much closer to a town called Sebastopol than it was to Santa Rosa. She suggested the event might therefore have drawn more notice in the Sebastopol paper.

I made a copy of the map page, which showed the ditch site.

Luck was with me. Sebastopol published a weekly called the *Se-bastopol Times & News*. I pulled out the first issue published after the murder. I found a short bit buried in a summary entitled "County Sher-iff's Log" for the date of the murder:

Sanborn Rd.: The body of Janet Pinchon, 24, of Santa Rosa was found with her bicycle in the 7300 block. The Sheriff's Department is investigating.

As the Sebastopol *Times & News* was abundant in such small-town charm, I got to perusing it. The whole paper was only twelve pages long, plus the obligatory advertising inserts. Aside from the County Sheriff's Log, there was a City Crime Log, a Fire Log, City Govern-ment Briefs, Editorial page, several regular columns, a sports and school page, and notices of births, marriages, deaths, obituaries, legals. I learned that there was mounting concern over pedestrian safety in city cross-walks, that local no-growth interests were arguing the fate of a pro-posed low-income housing development project in the vicinity, that the Analy High School Tigers were doing okay football- and basketball-wise, that three joyous local couples had announced the births of chil-dren in recent weeks (two girls, one boy), and that the local Safeway supermarket had chuck roast, lightbulbs, and Huggies on sale. Not ex-actly a large haul on information, but somehow very soothing.

Then I noticed a sidebar column entitled "In Brief." Along with summaries on a quarry accident, a particularly glorious fender bender, and minor outrage over a defaced sign, was one paragraph on Janet:

'ACCIDENT' BAFFLES SHERIFF'S DEPARTMENT

SEBASTOPOL—The sheriff this week is working to determine the cause of death of a Santa Rosa woman who was last seen leaving her home for an evening ride on her bicycle. The body of Janet Pinchon, 24, was found in the ditch bordering Sanborn Road early in the morning of Nov. 30. An investigation into what at first appeared to have been hit-and-run manslaughter is now being conducted as first-degree murder. Investigators have not yet determined whether Pinchon's death was caused by heavy blows to the head and body, or by asphyxiation due to strangulation, according to Det. Sgt. Joe Harding of the Sonoma County Coroner's Office.

Leave it to a small-town rag to savor the details.

This account told me several things. It let me know that Janet's odd roommate, Suzanne Cousins, was the last person who admitted to seeing Janet alive. It gave me a bit more information about the timing of events, and it gave me the name of a person in the Coroner's Office to approach for further information. That an attempt had been made to make her death appear to be vehicular manslaughter, I already knew.

I glanced at random through the other logs for the date Janet's body was found. There was a notation under the Fire Log. Under Miwok Mills Fire District, I found:

> Propane leak, 8056 Miwok Station Rd.; motorcycle accident (moderate injuries), 11287 Trimbe Rd.; medical aid, 7342 Sanborn Rd.; Mutual Aid to Graton Fire Dept.

This suggested that an ambulance had been called when Janet's body was found, which meant there was a medic at the Miwok Mills Fire District I could contact. This was good; I began to have a few people I could chase down for further information. In fact, I liked the idea of seeking out the medic much better than making a cold call on the Sheriff's Department or the Coroner's Office.

About then I noted an unease in my stomach, a sensation not un-like the onset of gas. Something was wrong. What? Was it worry over my impending performance in the geology job I had hustled myself into? Was it the fly-on-the-wall sense of dislocation I had arrived in California with, now growing into full-blown anomie? No, those were both there, but there was something else, something about the news-papers.

It was fifteen minutes later, as I was leaving the library, that I finally sorted out what was wrong. It was so glaringly obvious that I couldn't believe I'd missed it: nowhere in the spare reporting was there a men-tion that the dead woman was the daughter of the United States Sen-ator from California.

8

THE MIWOK MILLS FIRE HOUSE WAS LITTLE MORE THAN A COF-
fee urn with a garage full of fire engines and rescue vehicles attached.
It lay at a crossroads a mile west of the ditch site, tight in by a small
cluster of weather-beaten shops and houses.

At first I thought no one was home at the firehouse. I stood on tip-
toes to see over a big sign that read SPAGHETTI FEED SUNDAY NIGHT
ALL YOU CAN EAT $10 and peered in through a window, but could see
nothing but gloom and hulking fire engines. The sense of vacancy
matched the mood of the rest of Miwok Mills, which was comprised
of two bars, a convenience store, several large industrial buildings, a
few abandoned shops, and a much-vandalized bus stop surrounded by
very modest cottage-style houses with picket fences. One of the old
storefronts sported new paint and a sign reading, COMING SOON: MIWOK
BAKERY AND CAFÉ. Three unsettled-looking Latinos watched me
closely from the bald face of one of the saloons, which looked like it
had been teleported intact from a Mexican border town: chipped
stucco walls in a fading robin's-egg blue, one tiny window, a dark doorway, and no sign.

It was getting on for dark and cooling down rapidly. I knocked on
the firehouse door again, ready for an excuse to leave, but now a light
came on deep inside, throwing an interior doorframe into stark silhouette. A man filled the doorframe and paused, his face engulfed in
shadows, his backlit blond curls a corona of light. As he crossed to the

door by which I stood, he moved with a lanky grace. He opened the door, looked me up and down, smiled shyly, and blushed. "May I help you?" he asked, shoving his hands into the pockets of his snug blue jeans. He was a tall man. A tall, muscular, rosy-cheeked, blue-eyed, damned good-looking man with an unassuming manner.

It took me a moment to reply, so distracted was I by the wild disorganization of those flaxen curls and the sandy eyelashes that went with them. It had been a long while since I'd noticed a man. I'd been too busy grieving and hiding at home, but here I was out in the world asserting myself again, working on a job. I felt exhilarated and frightened. I wanted to visit with him and I wanted to run for it. I said, "I hope so. I'm looking for whoever went out on a medical call on Sanborn Road a couple of weeks back. I'm . . . I knew the woman who was killed, and, um, I'm trying to learn all I can about how she died."

The man averted his eyes in sympathy. His blush deepened. "I'm sorry—"

"For the family, sort of," I prattled on, feeling increasingly embarrassed at my line of falsehoods. "I hate to ask, but it would help everyone get through it. The loss, I mean."

The man extended a thick, callused hand. "Jim Erikson. I went on that call. Come in." He led me back to the tiny office and indicated with a wave of his hand that coffee was mine for the asking. I nodded yes. He searched around awkwardly for a mug that was reasonably clean, filled it, and brought it to me. That left him standing very close to me, but then, it really was a very small room.

He towered over my five foot five, hunching slightly as tall people sometimes do to try to make themselves appear smaller. The effect was endearing, the more so because he was clearly a very trim, fit individual brimming with physical vitality. I'm trying to say that I liked having him close to me. As soon as I realized this, I stepped back and stared at the floor.

Erikson twisted uncomfortably and stuck his hands in the pockets of his jeans.

"So you're both a fireman and an EMT?" I asked, trying to stick to business.

"Yes. Most of us are."

"So you were the fireman on duty when the call came in for Janet?"

"On call. It's an all-volunteer department. I'm an electrician. I work for myself, so I take a lot of early morning and rush-hour duty." He was staring at my hands now. Unconsciously imitating his posture, I had stuck my hands in my jeans pockets, too. I pulled out my left hand and made a display of scratching an itch on my face, right where the light would prove that I wore no ring on that third finger. "Did someone phone the firehouse here with the report about Janet?"

Jim's cheeks once again grew pinker. "No, it was a typical call, it came through 911—dispatch. Except that it was what's called a 'coroner's call.' Your friend was already, ah—"

"Dead. Um, yeah, I suppose she died the night before sometime." I tried to catch his eye again, but he was staring resolutely at the floor.

"I think so. I secured the scene until the sheriff and coroner could get there, because we're a lot closer. When the coroner got there he said she'd been gone awhile."

His euphemisms were getting a bit thick. "Listen, I'm not squeamish about this. In fact, I've seen the photographs that guy took."

"Oh. Yeah, he arrived just as I was leaving." He frowned, then chanced a quick look into my eyes. "Well, there's not much more I can tell you."

I weighed the wisdom of smiling too coquettishly in the middle of a conversation like this and decided it would fly in the face of the cover story I had fed him. "Was it obvious to you that her death was no accident?"

"Oh, I see what you mean. No, I wouldn't have thought for a minute it was accidental. The scene was all wrong. The way the bicycle was farther down the ditch than she was, and the way her clothes were all crooked." He fell silent and shook his head, the pale curls shifting slightly with the motion. Blushing deeply now with the abject embarrassment of one who is telling another something painful and intimate, he said, "And of course, the lividity—that's a sort of bruising effect that develops after death—"

"Yes, I've seen it before." I tried to give him a look of reassurance, but his eyes were once again glued to the dirty concrete of the floor.

"Well, it was fully developed, and on the upper side of her body, not pooled at the bottom like it would have been if she'd died in that position."

"I see. One thing I wonder, if she was so clearly dead, then who phoned for an EMT?"

"Standard procedure. Our district, we roll. Fires, automobile accidents, downed phone wires . . ." He shrugged his shoulders, pulled his left hand out of his pocket to rub the back of his neck. No wedding ring!

Smiling foolishly, I sipped my coffee and swallowed, trying to cover my smile with the cup. "Do you know who made the 911 call?" I asked.

"That would have been Mrs. Karsh."

Clearly someone he knew. "Who's Mrs. Karsh?"

"She lives right there by where your friend was found."

"Did she find her?" I persisted, falling into his use of euphemisms in spite of myself. It was not Janet that had been found, but her body.

The medic curved his spine in a new kind of embarrassment. "I really don't know."

"She lives in that two-story Victorian with the palm trees, and the stone gateposts out front?"

"Yeah."

I tensed at the thought of that barren expanse of land, the unpainted, derelict house, and the hulking man trying to hide himself behind the gatepost. "I saw a big man there."

"That would be Matthew, her son."

"Is he as dangerous as he looks?"

Jim Erikson considered this for a moment. "No, I don't think so. Everybody says he's just an overgrown kid." He chanced a quick smile, now that we were back on what he felt were more neutral topics.

"Oh. And the sheriff's deputy," I added quickly. "What's his name?"

He thought a moment. "Dexter relieved me."

"Great. And do you know the name of the guy who took those photographs?" I smiled encouragement, and not just to stimulate his memory.

A thin beeping sound interrupted our conversation. Abruptly Jim Erikson straightened up, all self-consciousness vanishing from his posture. He grabbed at a slim black gadget mounted on his belt, pushed a button to silence the beeps, and pulled it up into the light to read it. To me he said, "Excuse me. This is a call. Um, why don't you come back another time?"

"Oh, sure. No problem. I'll ask Mrs. Karsh."

At this, Jim Erikson shot me a perplexed look, then shrugged his shoulders, turned to his dispatch radio, and listened. "Miwok Mills respond," a squelchy voice barked over the wire. "Truck in ditch, 12775 Oakwood. Man down."

Erikson said, "I have to go," and quite firmly herded me out toward the front door.

"Thank you for your help," I said, smiling winningly, but my words were drowned in tooth-rattling thunder as the fire siren roared into life overhead. Jim Erikson wasn't listening, anyway. He had already jumped into his turnouts and was behind the wheel of the rescue vehicle, firing up its massive diesel engine.

FROM MIWOK MILLS, I followed Occidental Road back eastward, winding down off the line of hills that lay west of the ditch site and the Karsh ranch. The road dipped down into the bottomlands, passing over the sleepy stream—Laguna de Santa Rosa, the Thomas Brothers' map informed me—that ran between the hills and the turnoff to the Karshes'. I wondered idly why this sleepy, narrow little stream had been named "lake" in Spanish.

The road was elevated along a causeway to either side of the bridge, which was much wider than the Laguna and passed at least ten feet over it, suggesting that engineers had built the road to stay high and dry during periodic flooding. I slowed, looking around. The design of the causeway and bridge tallied with the architecture of the system of ditches. In my high school geography lessons, California had been held up as North America's example of a Mediterranean climate, which meant the seasons could be divided into a wet and a dry. The region would receive all of its rainfall in a few short months, saturating the soil. If the area was then visited by a heavy storm, it would flood. The farmers had dug those deep ditches to make certain that their fields drained quickly, keeping their crops from spoiling and their livestock from getting mired. With my geologist's eye, I scanned the darkening landscape, measuring the breadth of the floodplain of the Laguna de Santa Rosa. A lake it might indeed become.

It was ink dusk when I drove between the stone gateposts toward Mrs. Karsh's stark Victorian farmhouse. Ink dusk is a quality of atmosphere that my father would point out to me of an evening, as we'd ride in from tending the herd. He'd smooth his hand across the sky as if painting it with his palm, the better to admire this moment when the sky turned a dark blue that was not yet black. It's a time when the last bounced light still picks out the larger masses in the landscape such as trees and shrubs clearly, but smaller details are swallowed by the night.

In ink dusk, the lines of the Karsh farmhouse seemed softer, almost welcoming. I say almost. In fact, it would have taken a much sweeter camouflage to take the eeriness out of that setting, not to mention the memory of that strange man who'd tried to hide his ungraceful body behind the stone gatepost. If I hadn't known there was a woman inside that farmhouse, I would have delayed the visit to a daylight time or I would have brought someone with me for protection.

I did drive slowly and cautiously up the driveway, watching for the big man, and for the little one with the battered yellow truck who had fetched him home from the gatepost. I saw no sign of either of them.

There was only one light on in the farmhouse. I was just deciding to come back by daylight after all when a dim porch light came on at the rear of the house. The front doorway remained darkened. I took a deep breath and continued up the drive, musing that people who put twenty-watt bulbs on their back stoops are either not expecting much company or they're trying desperately to save funds.

As I pulled up beside the house, the mass of a square tower came into view just behind it. The light from the back porch threw a ghostly illumination across it. It was more than two stories tall, and no more than twelve or fifteen feet on a side.

I stepped out of the little blue truck, procrastinating over approaching the door, telling myself that if Mrs. Karsh wanted company at this hour, she'd come outside and meet me. She met me halfway, appearing inside the screened door to the kitchen, hand against the wire mesh as if touching the gathering night. "Can I help you?" she asked, echoing the words I had heard not a half hour earlier at the firehouse. Her tone was distant yet reasonably hospitable.

"Yes. I'm Emily Hansen," I called out, unconsciously getting formal with my name to match her reserve. "I'm a friend of Janet Pinchon's. I hate to trouble you, but I'm trying to learn about Janet. The man at the firehouse said you were the one who called the ambulance." When she didn't respond, I added, "Can I ask you a few questions, please?"

She didn't move from the doorway. "You'll excuse me. For a moment I thought you *were* Janet. But of course, you can't be."

That stopped me for a moment. *Why, because I'm the same size? Because I'm wearing her jacket?* "You knew her?"

A pause. "We were—acquainted." The tone was civil, urgently polite, yet shy and doubtful.

I moved a few steps closer, oddly drawn to her. I decided to make small talk for a moment, to ease into an acquaintance. "Is that a water tower?" I asked, gesturing toward the square tower.

Her gaze jerked toward the tower. "Ah, yes . . ." One of her hands floated up toward her breast in uncertainty. "A tank house. Yes."

Wrong question, for some reason. Why? "Would it be better if I came back another time? I realize it's pretty strange, just dropping in like this."

"Well . . ."

"I'd have someone introduce us, but I'm not from around here. I'm sorry."

Mrs. Karsh at last relented, pushing open the door and stepping to one side. "You'd better come in, Emily," she said. "You'll catch your death out there."

❖

I GET NERVOUS even thinking about that house. I don't like to remember it, and it's hard for me still to put my finger on what upsets me so in the memory of that first meeting. Perhaps it's just that I don't like to remember how happy I felt at her first faint welcome.

I was only ever in her kitchen, but a kitchen can tell you a lot about a woman, if you're paying attention. Mrs. Karsh's kitchen was what you'd call homey, if you were stretching things. More accurately, it lacked in the niceties of modernization. But here, too, I was thrown off, because it reminded me of my grandmother Hansen's kitchen up in Casper, and I loved my grandmother dearly.

And like my grandmother's, Mrs. Karsh's kitchen smelled wonderful. There was a stew simmering on the stove. I began to salivate.

In the fuller light of the kitchen, I got a better look at her. She was perhaps sixty-five, gray-haired and already a bit hunched, but the remnants of an aristocratic prettiness still played around her face; something in the bones that curved just so under smooth but sagging skin. Behind a pair of bifocals, her gray eyes had a dreaming, unaffected quality that was rather lovely, and spoke of an intelligence given to private contemplation. The effect was appealing, almost alluring, in a way I hadn't expected in a woman of her years. She was dressed in practical clothing and wore no makeup, again traits I had always found comforting in my father's mother.

"Please sit down," she said, gesturing toward an oak chair with the kind of pressed-wood design that Sears Roebuck sold from their catalog in the early part of the century.

I settled on the chair, nestling into its faded red gingham cushion, and looked around. The room had a forlorn, yellowed look to it. The stove from which that seductive aroma wafted was a stocky gas model with bullnosed corners and heavy cast-iron grates over the burners. The refrigerator was a small thing that probably dated back to the fifties, and the cabinets were plain painted wood, no frills of molding or hardware. There was no dishwasher. Everything was tinged with the dirt that accumulates over decades of use without repainting. The place might have been altogether depressing, except for a fiery splash of bright red geraniums that grew beneath the window, and that wonderful smell of stew.

My first thought was that Mrs. Karsh had no money, but the large size of the house and the extensive pasturelands argued wealth. So why the frugality? Were this woman's assets all invested in the land, or was she just accustomed to her surroundings, and disinclined to change them? I wondered what the rest of the house was like. Peering through the doorway into the dining room, I saw old furniture and dust. Only one narrow pathway across the hardwood flooring showed signs of foot traffic, this leading to a staircase beyond.

She lives in this kitchen, I decided, and glancing through another doorway, spied a narrow bed with a yellow chenille spread. Mrs. Karsh's hand went up to her breast. I glanced away, embarrassed that she had seen me staring. My eyes came to rest finally on a plate of store-bought oatmeal cookies on the table next to a crumpled paper napkin and a partially filled mug.

"Would you like some tea?" Mrs. Karsh asked awkwardly, gesturing toward a teapot that sat snugged up on a trivet over the pilot light on the stove.

"Please," I said, immediately wishing I had turned her offer down. Mrs. Karsh got up and reached the teapot down in front of me and moved slowly toward the cupboard, where she meditated over the small array of crockery. She selected a yellow cup and saucer, studied each at length, lining them up carefully with the correct slice of her trifocal lenses and running a thumb around the edges, then exchanged the saucer for another with no chips, the unconscious motions of a woman most usually alone. She placed the cup and saucer on the table in front of me, never looking directly at me, as if she were setting a place for someone who had not yet arrived.

I poured the tea. It was hot enough to set up a wisp of steam, and when I picked up a pitcher of cream that was near my place, I found that it was still cool and sweating, as if it had been taken from the refrigerator shortly before my arrival. I took a sip. The warm liquid radiated comfort through my body, intensifying my appetite.

Mrs. Karsh eased herself into a chair across the table from me, shifting around a bit as if to take the pressure off an uncomfortable joint. Then she pushed the plate of store-bought cookies my way and settled back, interlacing dry fingers over a plastic place mat. Her face came to rest in a polite smile.

How I longed to take one of those cookies. They looked hard and sweet, the kind that are stamped from a mold, each exactly like all the others. My mind played little greedy tricks on me, rationalizing that, broke as I was, every crumb could be important to my continued survival. I forced myself to concentrate on business, averting my eyes to the mug and crumpled paper napkin that had been left by the third place mat on the table. I noted that the mug had an inch of tea in the bottom, and the cookie crumbs that lay scattered around the napkin, and wondered who had been sitting there before I came. Mrs. Karsh? No, there was another teacup by her place, beyond a clutter of condiments and miscellaneous kitchen table incunabula. A fine new leather-bound notebook rested by the uninhabited place, conspicuous in its expensiveness. It lay open to a page of notes, a couple of diagrams with arrows and circles, the first showing how a $40,000 gross monthly income would be divided to address circles labeled "Bank," "Trust," and "RConst." From this last there was another arrow leading to "DK." The second diagram was the same, except that "Bank" had been replaced by "W-A," and "DK" got a bigger piece of the pie and "W-A" got a smaller one. I took all this in at a glance and looked away, as Mrs. Karsh clearly stiffened as my eyes rested on it. A moment later, she slid a hand across the table and quietly closed the notebook.

Clearly I was not the first person to pay a call on her that evening.

Stringing together the few clues present on the table, I surmised that her earlier caller had been a man (she had chosen a mug rather than a teacup), and that he had left not long before I had arrived (the tea was hot and the cream still cold). Had it been the big man I saw by the gatepost the day before, or perhaps the little one who had fetched him back to the house? No, I couldn't see either of them owning such a fine notebook, or for that matter sitting to tea and cookies.

I looked up. Mrs. Karsh was watching me, her gaze retreating the moment she saw me looking. I cleared my throat. "Thank you for seeing me, Mrs. Karsh," I began.

Her fingers tightened their grip on each other, and she tilted her head at a patrician angle.

I said, "I'm trying to find out what I can about Janet's death. It will help the family in their grief," I added piously. "The man at the firehouse said you phoned in the report, so I thought you might have been the one who found her."

One hand rose to her breast, and she shook her head slowly from side to side, a ruminative, habitual gesture. Mrs. Karsh lowered her gaze to her place mat. "Oh dear, yes . . . a terrible thing to lose a daughter."

"I can see that this was difficult for you," I suggested.

"What?" She looked up.

"We were talking about the morning you found—"

Mrs. Karsh's voice suddenly grew firmer and more businesslike. "Excuse me. Yes, I telephoned to the firehouse. My handyman found the—your friend on his way to work that morning, and I phoned and then went down to see if there was anything I could do. Of course, there wasn't," she concluded apologetically.

"Your handyman?"

"Yes, Jaime. Jaime Martinez. Won't you have some more tea? Or a cookie?"

I caved in and took a cookie, chewing ravenously. "What time was it when the—ah, she was found?" I asked, wondering why no one had noticed Janet's body earlier.

"You're hungry," she said, suddenly agitated. "I, ah, have stew on the stove."

"Oh, no, I'm fine! Really. Thanks anyway," I replied, clutching my hands together under the edge of the table to keep them off that plate. "Ah, what kind of a morning was it?"

Mrs. Karsh's gaze wandered again, perhaps following a mote of dust floating in the air of the quiet room. "Jaime comes at six-thirty, so I suppose it was about then, perhaps a little after. That morning the fog was particularly thick."

Morning fog. A standard occurrence. So visibility had been limited. Motorists would have been concentrating on the road, not its edges; and at that hour, it would have barely been getting light.

"What time does the fog settle in along this valley?"

She looked studiously at her hands and spoke quickly, as if trying to hurry toward the end of our interview. "Usually by nine or ten. Always by midnight. Unless it's not coming. Occasionally it's clear, you see."

"Ah. And the man who took the photographs. When did he arrive?"

Mrs. Karsh looked straight at me, her eyes politely blank. "Man?"

"Yes. Taking photographs."

Mrs. Karsh smiled the bright smile of a child who has just remembered a right answer under pressure of embarrassment by Teacher. "You mean the police photographer."

"No, someone else. Someone who took pictures before the area was cordoned off. He must have had a police scanner, to arrive so early."

"Oh, ah—yes, that man."

"Did you know him?"

A pause. "No." Her hand returned to her breast.

Had I asked a wrong question again? "Ah. But you did know Janet?"

Mrs. Karsh's gray eyes turned opaque. "Yes."

I began to feel irritated at the way she seemed to be avoiding my questions, but at the same time I felt badly, like I was goading the poor woman. Plunging forward, I asked, "Socially?"

"Well . . . she rode her bike out this way, you see."

"I see," I said ironically, because I didn't. I waited, willing her to elaborate.

She didn't. Her inward stare began to intensify, drawing her entire body inward, like a bug curling up against attack. Her eyes going dark, she said, "I'm sorry, but you see, I have a slight headache."

"Perhaps I should go," I offered, wondering why I was being so compliant. Either this woman was totally unaccustomed to company, or she knew something she did not want to report.

"Yes, I suppose that would be best."

As she said this, I was surprised to find how disappointed I felt. I didn't want to leave, I wanted to stay and eat cookies and sip tea. Not only was the kitchen a comfortable place for someone with my memories, but there was something intriguing about Mrs. Karsh, perhaps a hidden spark of passion as suggested by those red geraniums and the rich cooking. It gave her a fey quality that appealed strongly even through her reticence, like the faint light of a fairy floating out of reach over the heath that draws an Irishman toward a cliff. "Could I come back another day? I'm working tomorrow. I've been hired by Janet's old company," I said, clinging to the conversation. "But perhaps the next day?"

"Janet's company?"

"Yes, HRC Environmental." I waited. When she said nothing more, I prompted, "Saturday?"

"Saturday? No, I won't be here Saturday."

"How about Sunday?"

"Oh, Sunday I'll be helping the boys at the firehouse. . . ." Her voice trailed off like that fairy light dissolving into the mists.

"I'd like to come back sometime when Jaime is here, too."

She closed her eyes, like that headache was starting to really clamp down on her.

"When's Jaime here?" I asked.

"Oh, only very early mornings. Then he goes to work in the vineyards."

"Really? I thought I saw him down by the road yesterday around eleven A.M."

She rose to see me to the door. "Jaime checks back some days when there isn't much work," she said, pushing the door open.

Something nearby outside caught her notice. Her spine straightened. Her eyes came suddenly alive and her dry lips spread into a strange smile.

I stepped past her into the dim pall of the porch light, squinting to get my eyes used to the darkness as quickly as possible, but it wasn't difficult to see what had caught her attention. The big, hulking man who had watched me from the gatepost was lurking in the shadowy doorway of the tank house.

I gripped the porch handrail.

Even in this dim light he stood out harsh and menacing, and at this close range, frightening. He was big, well over six feet tall, around two hundred fifty pounds of soft yet powerful flesh. His hair was thinning on top but long and stringy at the nape, where it was pulled back with a knotted string. The whiskers on his face grew in a rough, unkempt pattern around swelling cheeks. Enormous grubby hands clenched malevolently, pawing the air in slow, hypnotic circles. His eyes were sunken pools in a face contorted with a toxic mixture of fear and hatred, and right now they were aimed straight at me.

Mrs. Karsh broke the silence. The entire quality of her voice had changed, transformed from fading reticence to a rich, melodious, almost theatrical tone. It wrapped unctuously around me, drawing me into an unexpected, unnerving intimacy. She said: "This is my son, Matthew. Matthew's just been in his playroom, haven't you, Matthew? Matthew dear, this is Emily. Emily is a friend of Janet's." She smiled, "You remember *Janet,* don't you?"

Matthew's enormous fingers flared hungrily. Was he remembering her, or thinking of me? I in turn was gripped with feeling, a toxic mixture of fear and guilt. Something about Matthew was terribly familiar, and not just because I had seen him before.

He didn't speak.

I didn't speak, either. I couldn't. Something had frozen my vocal cords, something old as death. Something that unhinged my mind, hurling it into a dark and primitive place. In this space of darkness, I began to worry. I worried that I couldn't move, wouldn't speak or cry out if I needed to. My ears began to ring. Watching those ugly, clenching hands maul the air between us, I could see them closing around Janet's throat, hear her gasp for air, twist, shudder, and die, her neck now limp and broken, her tender skin mottled with enormous, hideous bruises.

Suddenly light bathed the scene, bright and dancing. Matthew drew back into the doorway like a spider retracting his fat body from sight. The light bounced, swung wildly. The sound of a large engine broke into my awareness and groaned closer. Someone was driving up beside the house, pulling up alongside the little blue truck. I could see the vehicle now out of the corner of my eye, a big, high-clearance truck, making mine seem small as a toy. A man stepped down out of the cab and walked over to my little blue truck, leaned down and stared into the cab, cupping his hands around his face to cut the glare on the glass cast by his headlights. After some moments, he turned and joined us.

He was a man of advancing years, yet still startlingly handsome, almost beautiful. He stood tall and straight and magnificent, like a proud adolescent posing in front of a mirror. He enjoyed a full head of perfectly white, lushly wavy hair that glowed regally in the truck's headlights. He wore khaki slacks, heavy work shoes, and a twill shirt in a brilliant turquoise blue, as bright as his eyes. As he joined us at the stoop, he bestowed on us a self-satisfied smile, examined me with interest, and said, "Hello again, Dierdre. Evening, Matt. Who's this?"

I looked at Mrs. Karsh. In the moment of his arrival, her shoulders had slumped forward and her smile had collapsed to a small crimp. Gone also was the vibrancy of her tone as she said: "Val Reeves, Emily Hansen."

Val stepped forward and gripped my hand in both of his, like the

Pope bestowing a blessing. His hands were warm, and I was surprised to discover that they had the dry feel of my father's, though not as rough with calluses. I looked more sharply at him. Was this a man who worked with his hands? He widened his smile into a showy grin, displaying a row of even, perfectly white teeth, and stared deeply into my eyes as if he'd mislaid something of a personal nature inside my head. "Emily," he pronounced, and then, apparently satisfied with his performance, he turned back to Mrs. Karsh. "Dierdre, I left my notebook on your kitchen table."

"Oh, certainly, Val. I saw it there after you left. Go right on in."

After Val Reeves passed into the house, I glanced back over to the door of the tank house. Matthew Karsh was gone.

Gone, and yet I felt his presence; an almost tactile reverberation of his mass. It hung in the doorway like an anomaly of gravity, heavy and frightening. And the enchantment that had played between mother and son stretched across the dooryard to me like the thick, unlovely web a black widow spins.

I heard the screen door close behind me. Mrs. Karsh's voice came to my ear, once again rich and low, for my hearing only: "Be careful going out. People drive fast on that road at night. You could get hurt."

9

SLEEP ELUDED ME UNTIL THE SMALL HOURS. I LAY AWAKE IN THE darkness in that unfamiliar bed, unable to shake the thought that this distorted son of a fading woman might be Janet's murderer. My suspicion made no sense: one so billowing with malice and so proximal to the crime would not have escaped the Sheriff's notice. A creature like that would have drawn detectives like flies to dung, and if he were guilty, I couldn't see anyone so rudely constructed staying together through even the mildest interrogation. Interrogation is a hideous pressure; I know, having been questioned as a witness. I felt like confessing to a crime I hadn't committed just to get out of the chair they'd sat me in. The Sheriff's detectives would have turned the screws and squeezed a confession out of a Matthew Karsh like toothpaste out of a tube. Within minutes. But they hadn't.

On the rare occasions that I managed to clear Matthew Karsh and his mother from my brain, I found that fickle organ veering off into more personal problems, fussing over the job I had to do in the morning, or where to go for Christmas. Concern over filling Janet's shoes was just stage fright, but why anxiety over Christmas should badger me on this particular night, I could not fathom until I recalled how fully Mrs. Karsh's kitchen had pricked a nostalgia for my grandmother Hansen's, where we had always gathered for Christmas when I was a child.

Christmas. Grandmother Hansen was long dead, and now so was

my father. I imagined that Elyria would be preoccupied with Joe Finney this year, and I couldn't go home; spending the holidays on the ranch alone with my mother was out of the question.

Well, there was Aunt Frida's. Hadn't Elyria said she was somewhere in California? How had I lost track of her, after Uncle Bert died? I wasted further mental energy trying to imagine why Frida had left Wyoming, giving up a perfectly good horse ranch. And even more odd, come to think of it, was the fact that she hadn't come to my father's funeral. Between abortive attempts at counting sheep, I thought of phoning Frida, even searched the local phone book for her number, but didn't find one. I cursed myself for having been so quick in my fear and outrage with Elyria that I hadn't taken down the number when I'd had the chance.

❖

THE NEXT MORNING I struggled to find my way to HRC Environmental through a thick, ground-hugging fog. It flowed like milk through the beams of my headlights. Distances were hard to gauge. Large objects like buildings and other cars appeared suddenly and too close, or stayed frustratingly hidden.

The weather suited my frame of mind. I had awakened from a dream about Dierdre Karsh, and much as I struggled to tap back into the illogic of sleep, I couldn't remember what had happened in the dream, just that she had been in it, but it left me with the sensation of something exquisitely sweet right next to something frightening. Awake, I felt lonelier and more exposed than ever.

I had climbed out of bed and dressed quickly, hoping I could don Janet's undoubtedly saner mental state with her field clothing. No luck. All the way through the fog to HRC, the dream had continued to dog me, as if Mrs. Karsh were still with me, sitting just behind me in the truck.

It was six-thirty. Half an hour to go until I started this new "job," and my stomach was grinding. At the deli, Reena was smiling her thousand-megawatt smile, enough to drive the ghosts far enough away that I could jolt myself the rest of the way awake with two fine cups of coffee. I ordered a side of two eggs sunny-side up. That left me with three dollars and seventy-five cents cash to my name.

As the coffee hoisted my eyelids to full wakefulness, I felt a growing excitement: I was about to learn what Janet had been doing with her working hours, that work that had seemed important enough to her father that he would hire a private operative to bring it to light. Ah yes, the inscrutable Senator Pinchon. I chewed my eggs meditatively, wondering once again what he already knew that he wasn't telling me.

At seven sharp I was waiting at the front door of HRC Environmental, wondering where this guy Adam Horowitz was. The door was locked and the lights were still off, so I just huddled against the front wall of the building, trying to shrug off the chill of the fog. The minutes inched by. At last someone appeared in the front office, pulled up a blind, and greeted me with a thoroughly bitter scowl. He was slender and sunken-chested and still young enough to be fighting a severe case of acne that covered his weaselly face and what I could see of his scrawny neck. He shoved open the door and narrowed his eyes. "You're Hansen," he insinuated. "Where the hell have you been?"

"I've been right here, waiting for you," I replied, sucked into his adversarial attitude like a cow into quicksand.

"Damn it to hell," he muttered, already turning his back on me to stomp through the office. I barely caught the door before it slammed shut, had to break into a trot to catch up with him.

The drive to the work site was forty-five minutes of seething noncommunication against a background of AM news and yak turned up piercingly loud. I gathered that we were inching northwestward along Highway 101, but I still couldn't see much except for short patches where the fog mysteriously disappeared. The whole time Adam cussed under his breath and gripped the wheel so hard his knuckles blanched. I began to wonder if he was sitting on a pile of tacks.

At length we turned off the highway and onto a winding two-lane road that led gradually uphill past more vineyard and orchard land. As the ground rose, the mist began to clear, and finally we broke out into a gray overcast. The trees took on a flat gray-green paper-cutout effect against a background of pearl-gray mist. Then we popped into a little town, pulled up by a mom-and-pop grocery store, and Adam spoke directly to me for the first time since he'd opened the front door of HRC Environmental: "You stay here with the backhoe. I'm working the rig down the street. Don't tell him nothing, just take notes."

"What's the backhoe doing?"

Adam rolled his eyes in exasperation. "Pulling a tank, what else?"

"I *see,*" I mocked, wondering what had happened to my self-esteem that I was sparring with a juvenile. "And all I'm supposed to do is *watch?*"

"*Observe,*" Adam parried witheringly. "Earl knows what to do. But having a *geologist*"—he named my profession with abundant sarcasm—"on site makes him more *legitimate.* Don't worry, he'll add ten percent to your hourly rate and pass it on to the client." He looked suspiciously at my Filson vest. "You don't got a clipboard, *do* you? Goddamn it, I suppose you'll have to use one of *mine.*" He reached behind the seat and spirited up a portable plastic file box and pulled out one of two aluminum clipboards. He gunned the motor of the truck. I got out. Gravel spun around my ankles as he left.

I looked around. I was in the parking lot next to the store. The pavement had been cleared and marked with yellow paint over an area maybe fifteen feet by twenty, right next to a concrete pad that looked like it had once held a set of gasoline pumps. Truncated pipelines projected up from the earth like hungry eels. Twenty feet away to my right stood a large backhoe, and parked next to it was another pickup truck with camper shell and a flatbed trailer that must have hauled the backhoe. The logo on its door said EARL'S EARTH MOVING, INC.

Earl was an immense, ovoid man with a narrow, balding skull and jowly, sagging chin a quarter inch thick with whiskers, like his hair and flesh were melting from the top of his head and settling to the bottom.

As I approached his truck, he was sitting behind the wheel slurping coffee out of a twelve-ounce polystyrene cup. He turned to watch me. I smiled. Coffee addiction is something to which I can relate.

Earl paused in his ritual and pursed his rubbery lips in midslurp, eyes half-closed in the rapture of gathering steam off the hot liquid. "Who you?" he grunted.

"Geologist from HRC," I replied, imitating his telegraphic speech.

"Huh?"

"New."

"Uh. You insteadda Adam?"

"Yuh. He's down the street, we need him. He was in a hurry, I guess."

Earl pursed his lips again, this time in amusement, and shook his head side to side very slowly. "That kid always got his BVDs in a bunch. Well, les' gedda work." He knocked the last third of his cup back in a gulp audible half the way down to his middle and unwedged himself from behind the wheel. It was a tall truck, but as he stepped down, his eye level didn't drop. "Go on getchersef a cuppa coffee. I'll have this asphalt off fore you know it."

Inside the store, I found a large coffee urn next to a dusty display of fishing lures. As I stepped across the threshold, I'd set off a bell somewhere, and presently I saw an elderly man working his way through the displays from the back of the shop. He was a pleasant old codger with a narrow neck and just a few pet hairs combed fondly across the top of an otherwise shiny skull, and he had dark eyes that seemed enormous behind beer-bottle-bottom glasses. "Can I help you?" he sang.

"I'm with the backhoe out here. I just wanted some coffee."

He grinned ear to ear. "Take all you want, little missy, it's on the house!"

My heart sank as I thought of Adam's words about how Earl would charge my time with a ten percent markup. At that, I didn't even know how much I was costing Earl. "No, I insist on paying." I pulled my wallet out of my back pocket and pulled out one of my last pathetic wrinkly dollar bills.

The man held up a hand, cheerfully refusing to take my money. I would have dropped it and run for it, if I'd had it to spare, but just then the front door *dinged* open again and another old coot shambled in, sucking his teeth. "Hey, Phil! What's the story? Your gas pumps is gone. You want me to drive all the way into Cloverdale to fill up?"

"Sorry, Stan," Phil soothed, "County Health Department says my tanks is leaking, and I have to pull 'em or fix 'em, so I'm having 'em replaced. We'll be without for a little while. This little lady here is helping out, aren't ya now?"

I smiled primly.

Stan bared his false teeth at me. "Hah! I heard about you bloodsuckers! Damn gummint says we got to bury the tanks so we don't burn the place down, so we bury them. Then you come along and say we're pollutin' the ground, so they gotta come out. Then you put your snoopy wells all over the place and who's gotta pay? We do! We pay and pay and pay!" He had raised his cane and was shaking it at me, knocking packets of corn chips off a display as the thing wobbled out of control.

"Now, Stan, it won't be like that. Will it, missy?" Phil said, smiling hopefully.

I began to think I was in a bad movie, or at least a bad dream. Backing away brandishing the steaming coffee and clutching the clipboard across my front for protection, I mumbled something articulate like, "Gosh, I don't know, I'm new here."

"Some excuse!" the old man shrilled. "A man works hard his whole life, and for what? You young punks come in here like you own the place, say we're messin' up your environment. You whine like pigs! You try working with your hands!" His cane clattered to the floor and he shook his gnarled, spotted hands at me in fury, his ancient head locked forward with anger.

Suddenly something in me rose up, and words flew out of my mouth: "I'm not a punk! I've worked hard myself. *These* hands have mended fences in a high wind at ten below, dammit, and I won't be spoken to this way!" I was shaking so hard I dropped the clipboard, and the coffee sloshed onto my bare skin, scalding it.

With shaking hands, I switched the cup to my undamaged paw. I'd never lost my cool like this before, ever. Or had I? A weird sense of déjà vu slipped through my body like a wave of nausea.

Both old men stood frozen in place, watching me like I was a rabid mountain lion. Muttering an apology, I picked up my clipboard, turned, and hurried back outside.

◈

EARL PHIPPS WAS already at work ripping up the asphalt concrete that covered the gasoline tanks. He worked steadily, ripping and pushing the broken pieces aside with the bucket of the backhoe, working the levers and brakes from his bouncing throne in the middle of the craft. After the paved surface was up, he started scooping up the earth, great bucketfuls of the gray and tawny layers of pebbly soil. I pulled out the clipboard and took notes, things like, "Commenced work at 8:04 A.M. Removed asphalt concrete." It looked suspiciously like a daily drilling wire report from an oil rig, but what did they expect of a lowly ex-oil rookie?

Six feet down, Earl struck the top of a tank, a dull *thunk* reverberating over the *grrrs* and *whumps* of the backhoe. He got out and took a look, peering into the hole from a respectful distance away from the edge. "There's the unleaded. A one-K," he commented sagely.

"A thousand gallons?"

"Yup. Put it in in seventy. The old leaded ought to be here to the right. It's been there longer. A five-fifty."

"Five hundred fifty gallons."

"Yup. Hauler oughtta be here soon. Yo, Vince!" he hollered at a man who was just then wandering up. "Speaka da devil!"

Vince was a rangy guy dressed in a navy-blue coverall with his name embroidered on the chest. He snubbed out a cigarette he'd been smoking, rubbing it on the sole of his steel-toed boot and slipping the butt into a pocket. "The county on its way?" he asked.

Earl nodded. "Wonder who's coming," he said.

"Hoping for Lucy, eh? Always chasing skirts, ain't ya, Earl. Real ladies' man."

"Lucy's good at what she does," Earl said demurely.

"Uh-huh." Vince batted his eyelashes at Earl. Then he turned to me. "And who's this bit of lovely?"

I was just sticking out my scalded hand to introduce myself when a small sedan with a government license plate pulled up next to the backhoe. Out bounced a very appealing young woman carrying a clipboard and a hard hat. Everything about her was buoyant—her smile, her musculature, her bosom, her stride. "Hi, Earl!" she sang, waving an arm high over her head. "Oh, and Vince! Well, the gang's all here then. Let's hustle a bustle, why don't we?"

After a few minutes of this low-key horsing around, they got back down to work. Lucy had not yet noticed me, which was fine, because it gave me license to watch the proceedings like the fly on the wall the Senator had hired me to be.

Phil, the old man who owned the store and this hole in the ground, had wandered out to watch, too. He stood shyly by the corner of the building, his gnarly old hands jammed into his back jeans pockets, his eyes bright with interest and a feverish variety of hope. Stan, the old coot with the cane, stood next to him, his expression as dark as rain.

Earl lumbered back into the backhoe and swung the bucket back into the hole, removing the remaining soil and the pea-gravel backfill from the tops of the tanks. When they were clear, Vince jumped down into the hole and peered into the tanks through what was left of the pipes, checking to make sure they were empty. Then he dropped a load of dry ice into each to settle the fumes. Earl got the backhoe bucket under one end of the leaded gasoline tank and tipped it up, making room for Vince to pass a sling under it. They repeated this at the other end of the tank. When they had the thing adequately trussed, Earl passed a chain through the slings and prepared to hoist the tank out with the bucket of his backhoe.

"This is the big moment," Lucy chortled, speaking to me for the

first time. She was hugging her clipboard with all the gooey enthusiasm of an ingenue at a bridal shower waiting for the first touching little present to be unwrapped.

"What are you looking for?" I asked.

"Contamination."

Earl shoved a lever and the tank lurched into the air, swung, settled, and turned slowly on the chain. A heavy reek of rotted gasoline
roiled up from the pit, washing past my nostrils in a nearly palpable
wave.

"Bingo!" Lucy shouted. I turned to look at her. She was smiling
cheerfully. She scribbled something on the form on her clipboard. "It's
a stinker, all right!"

Phil shuffled toward me, still smiling. "How's it look?"

I cringed. What could I say? Forget about your retirement funds?
"Ah, I'm not sure. I think Lucy just said she thought maybe there was
some contamination."

Phil's eyes still held mine brightly. He did not comprehend what
I'd said. "Well, I hope it's nothing bad."

"Why don't you wait inside? I'm sure Lucy will be in shortly."

Lucy was hollering to be heard over the engine of the backhoe. "I
win again, Earl!"

Earl waved magnanimously.

Fixing a manic grin on my face, I again urged Phil to go inside. Smiling his confusion, he did.

I turned to Lucy, my hands itching to slap her. "You're happy it
leaked?" I demanded.

Lucy cocked her head to one side. "Oh, it's just a game Earl and I
have. He's kind of cute: statistically, ninety percent of them are leakers, so I almost always win. Get it?"

"But—"

"Oh, come on, you can't let life get serious. This is just a job. *Someone's* got to do it."

"But isn't this going to cost that old man over there his life savings
to clean it up?"

"Oh, maybe not. If he plays his cards right, the SB2004 Fund will pick up the cost of cleanup, or the bulk of it anyway." To Earl she shouted, "Just set it over there, Earl, and pull the other one, too. Vince, see if you can knock some of the crud off the bottom of that tank, check it for holes."

I said, "What's the SB2—"

Lucy cocked her head at me again. "You're new, huh." With a peremptory lifting of her golden eyebrows, Lucy shifted her clipboard to the other side of her chest and prepared to lecture me. "It's a state law set up to cover this kind of problem, promulgated in 1992," she intoned, relishing the legalese. "The tank owners pay into the Fund each time they have the tanks filled. Monitoring is done on a regular schedule. They have to show that the tank is pressure-tight, and that the gas-in-gas-out inventory tallies properly, or they can't get their tank-operating license renewed. If it's a leaker, the tank removal and the first ten thousand dollars of the cleanup is their problem. If there were no water-supply wells within range of the plume of contamination, we could just maybe monitor it for a while, but this is right near all these houses." She pointed to a place where a downspout from the roof of the store was quietly funneling the morning's dampness into the excavation. "See how fast that water's moving through that soil? If that well next door doesn't test positive for benzene, I'll eat my hard hat, honey." She turned away for a moment and hollered at Earl. "Hey, Earl! Dump some bentonite in there, will you? You're turning this hole into a percolation pond!" Back to me, she said, "So this one'll go for cleanup, that's all but certain. But if they keep moving forward with the job in good faith, they can apply for reimbursement from the Fund."

"Apply? Doesn't the Fund always pay?"

Lucy shrugged. "It all depends on where they are on the priority list. The Fund is not bottomless, after all. Private residential tanks get paid back first, then small businesses, then large, then agricultural tanks."

"And if the Fund won't cover this job?"

I must have let the hostility I was feeling seep into my voice, be-cause Lucy lowered her eyelids halfway, oddly echoing the venemous gaze of the old man with the cane. "He has to take responsibility for his property. You know how it is: mess up, clean up."

My neck had gone rigid. "What a solution. Now we can all pay higher taxes to care for him in his waning years." I pulled a pen out of the pocket of Janet's Filson vest. Wondering just how Janet had felt when she faced jobs like this, I wrote: *10:45: Representative of County Health Department has mastered the art of officious bullshit-chucking.*

BY NOON, BOTH tanks had been hoisted, examined for holes (none were visible, but there was a lot of rust), and lashed to Vince's flat-bed truck for removal to the tank graveyard. The store owner had dutifully signed a form from Lucy that documented a release of toxic materials into the soil, obligating himself to the next level of investi-gation. Earl had scraped out the remaining pea gravel with his bucket and grunted his way down into the hole to take soil samples for analysis, to document the degree of contamination.

It was my opinion that this was a waste of the old man's money. What did it matter how much contamination there was? I could not only smell but see the leakage: the soil underneath the tanks had turned an unnatural bluish gray, the fumes arising from the hole were quickly giving me a headache, and a rainbow sheen of hydrocarbons was blos-soming on the water that was draining into the hole. But Earl labeled the samples, recorded them on a chain-of-custody log, and busied himself packing them in a cooler, probably smacking his rubbery lips over the analytical fee markup to come.

I at least made headway with my real investigation. Being naturally garrulous, Lucy had no compunction against talking about Janet Pin-chon. "She was okay," Lucy was saying, "kind of hard to talk to. Sort of a fanatic, really."

"What do you mean?"

Lucy tipped her head in thought. "She hung out with those lunatic fringe types a lot."

"Who exactly?"

She shrugged. "I do my best not to get involved. You know, the herbs, drumming, and moon ritual gang. Goddess junkies."

The sensuous image of the uncaring Suzanne Cousins filled my mind's eye. "You think Janet was really into all that?"

Lucy's attention began to wander. Other women were clearly not central to her interest. "Who knows."

I tried to make my questions include the wonders of Lucy. "Did you do government oversight like this on many of Janet's jobs?"

"Not many. HRC's kind of an old boys' club. No, that's an understatement. Anyway, Janet didn't get out on much Phase Two work. Well, she sampled wells some. I watched her do that a few times."

"Wells?"

Lucy looked at me out of the corner of her eye, one of those how-can-you-be-so-dumb looks. "Groundwater-monitoring wells. Like your pal Adam is installing down the street."

Through my teeth, I asked, "What else did she do?"

"Mostly Phase Ones."

Doggedly I asked, "What's a Phase One?"

Lucy didn't bother to answer this question. Not only was my ignorance beginning to bore her, but Earl was moseying toward her. "Lunchtime," he rumbled. His face went kind of squishy. Unless I miss my guess, he was trying to look cute.

Lucy glanced at her watch. "Why not?"

Earl jerked his head my way. "That's it, toots."

"Right." I handed him his hard hat and scribbled the quitting time down in the little box on my job sheet so I wouldn't have to make eye contact with him. It drives me nuts being shucked off for the Lucys of the world, even by the Earls.

The two of them wandered off toward a second cooler that Earl had packed with drinks and sandwiches. Scrounging the last few dollars out of the bottoms of my pockets, I bought the cheapest sandwich Phil had to offer (egg salad) and headed down the street to find out what I was supposed to do for the afternoon.

◆

ADAM WAS HARD at it spitting vitriol at two subcontractors who were drilling shallow monitoring wells with a little truck-mounted rig. Watching Adam at work didn't do much to improve the flavor of the egg salad, but I told myself that working with him could be no worse than mucking out a horse barn with a kicking stallion in the stall. Mind you, I've mucked some pretty sour manure in my day. I cleared my throat so he'd know I was there and took another bite of my sandwich.

Adam spun around on one heel, looked me up and down with an expression that made me wonder if I was crawling with eels, and barked, "Don't you know better than to eat in the exclusion zone?"

I froze, my mouth crammed with egg salad, and mumphed, "Huh?"

"You stepped right over my yellow caution tape!"

I looked back at the route I'd taken in. He was right, there *was* a yellow tape fluttering around most of the site, sort of tied to a truck bumper here and wrapped around an old tire there, but I'd come onto the site through a wide gap in the tape where the driller's helper had apparently taken it down so he could push wheelbarrows full of augered soil toward a stockpile behind the building. So much for site security.

Adam marched past me and rerigged the tape, cussing viciously— something about snot-nosed bimbos from hell who eat sandwiches and don't even wear hard hats in an exclusion zone. When he was done, he stomped over to the tailgate of his truck, picked up an indelible pen, and began to make notes on his clipboard.

I indulged myself in glowering at him while scratching my nose with the middle finger of one hand, and then sauntered over and draped an arm tenderly around his bony shoulders. "Adam, dew drop," I cooed, "the tanks are all pulled. I help you now, right?"

Adam went all stiff, his shoulders jamming smack up under his ears. When he realized I wasn't going to volunteer to take my arm away, he writhed out of range, signaled to the driller, croaked, "Half hour," climbed into the cab of the truck, and tried to look totally engrossed in a paper sack full of sandwiches. His face had gone kind of white. I wondered if I'd overdone it.

The driller shut off his rig and wandered over to say hello. Graying hair pulled back into a thick braid extended from under his hard hat halfway down his back. A diamond stud winked from one nostril. "Having fun with old Adam?" he inquired.

"Barrel of laughs." Appealing to the driller's gray hairs, I inquired, "How old is that kid, anyway? I mean, he can't have more than a year or two on the job."

"Just over a year. He's on the HRC plan: hire kids straight out of school, hang them out to dry for a year or two, then fire them when they start to agitate for more money."

"No backup?"

"Aw, some of the companies we drill for give their kids a cell phone so they can call the office when they have a question. HRC's so cheap they make him run down the street here to the pay phone. But then, Adam never phones; he's too proud to admit he's in a jam, if in fact he knows when he's in one."

"Does he do an okay job?"

The driller shrugged. "He could be worse. We can generally keep him out of trouble."

"How do you do that?"

"Aw, hell, we drill five days a week, fifty weeks a year. We could do these jobs in our sleep. The budgets don't allow for any real science anyway. It's just wham–bam, punch your holes in the ground, get in, get out, thank you ma'am. So take it easy on the kid; he's way over his head out here."

I felt like a prize shit. Beating up on a scared kid used to be beneath me. Maybe Elyria was right, I was losing my grip. "So far over his head he could get hurt?"

The driller squinted at me. "What's on your mind?"

"I hear the woman I'm replacing is dead."

"You talking about Janet Pinchon?"

"Yeah."

The driller looked at his shadow on the ground. "Nice girl—or woman, excuse me, but they're so young."

"Is there anything I ought to know about her and any safety violations?"

The driller shook his head in frustration. "There's not a company we've worked for that's done it by the book. You a mole for OSHA or something? Listen, Adam's a pain-in-the-butt kid, but he's trying."

"No, I'm just trying to watch my own back."

"Good idea, 'cause like I say, these companies like to hang their people out to dry, wring every last drop of earning power they can out of them. We can't get away with that. A man gets tired, we insist they take time off until they're safe to go on the site again, because we're handling heavy equipment all day long, all week, all year. But these engineers and geologists, they'd run them around the clock if they could, put 'em on salary so they can charge overtime and not pay it."

"So what did she work on?"

The driller swept a hand across the scene. "This sort of stuff, sometimes, but she didn't just do tank yanks and well installations. She did those Phase Ones."

"What's that?"

"I don't know much about them, except it's everything *before* you bring us in."

"So she'd be working alone?"

"Yeah. With no one to watch her back." Shaking his head sadly, the driller walked away.

10

I TOOK WHAT WAS LEFT OF MY SANDWICH BACK OUT BEYOND the exclusion-zone tape and settled on a bus bench across the road, nibbling on the sandwich like it was my last meal, poor though my appetite had suddenly become. I dug into my pocket. I had two quarters left. *Hell,* I thought, *this might be my last meal if Murbles doesn't have that check waiting for me at the motel.*

At the thought of being paid for what I was doing, sharp little fingers of guilt scratched at my heart. Maybe that was my problem, I was having an uncertainty attack. I wasn't sure I was on the right track. I'd spent the morning learning what Janet seldom did for HRC; how was I going to learn what she did most of the time, and how was I going to figure out what, if anything, it had to do with her death?

I stared across the street at the drilling site, trying to understand what Adam and the drillers were doing. Certainly this kind of mess caused a lot of financial pain to the property owner, and money was an age-old motivation to kill. But Janet didn't cause the mess, so why kill her?

As my appetite became slaked, my mind bogged down in the details, the big picture still too fragmental to be grasped.

I stretched and admired the view. The fog had long since burned off, revealing the shapely shoulders of surrounding hills. The little crossroads community sat in a narrow, steep-sided valley carpeted with vineyards. A red-tailed hawk cruised for dinner overhead. I felt sleepy.

Mother Nature was looking awfully pretty today. How nice it

would have been to visit this town, this whole county for that matter, for any other reason than to dig into the nasty side of human nature. I would have preferred to hike up one of these hills into the chaparral, relax, and enjoy life. I told myself that I would have preferred to have a friend to walk with, to talk out what was on my mind. I would have preferred a great many things to the monastic life I was living.

I closed my eyes and chewed slowly on the remnants of the sourdough roll that had surrounded the smashed egg in my sandwich, thinking that I'd phone Elyria come evening, see if I could get our friendship back on an even keel. She was right, I'd been letting my problems get in the way of things. It wasn't her fault that she had gone forward with her career and her love life while mine slipped away. It was hard times for all geologists. And my love life was a thing of distant memory. For the thousandth time, I wondered, *I made the right decision about Frank Barnes, didn't I?*

Frank. I hoped his wife was good to him, and could make allowances for his dark moods. I hoped she liked to fish for trout with dry flies up by Yellowstone, and camp out with him under the stars, and— *No, don't think about that.*

I looked back up at the sky, but couldn't distract myself. Thoughts of Frank kept coming. Word on the grapevine was that he would be a father soon. A good one, I imagined.

My own father had been the best in the world.

I threw my sandwich wrapper in the trash barrel by the bench and lurched to my feet, grudgingly thankful to have Adam to pit myself against. With luck, he would behave badly enough to keep me distracted from my wounds until quitting time.

11

WE WORKED, OR SHOULD I SAY I WATCHED, THE DRILLERS
built wells, and Adam fussed over his scratchy little notes until just about
two, at which time Adam put highway cones on all the well heads,
scowled at the site, the driller, and the drill rig, and indicated with nearly
inaudible grunts that the site was tidied up enough that we could leave.
I walked up to Adam and said, "What's next?"

"Sampling," he hissed. "And you're going to help, Goddamn it."

Me? What was the implication, that I had been goldbricking? I
thought of pointing out that I wasn't even getting paid for this. *Except
if you figure the five hundred a day Senator Pinchon's paying me, but that—*

My mental gears jammed, completely confused about who I was and
what I was supposed to be doing there. Was I Em the geologist, Em
the investigator, Em the nearly worthless rookie tank yanker, or was I
someone else entirely? After all, I was wearing Janet's clothes, I was
having her argument with Adam, I was doing her job. . . .

I hurled myself into the truck, ready to dive into any task just to get
it straight who I was, what I was doing there, and why.

AS WE DROVE to the next site, I reminded myself that I was here to
investigate a crime, not to get into personal fights with pencil-necked
geeks. I vowed not to react to Adam's vitriol, to instead treat him with
the kind of consideration I'd show any other mangy coyote that had a

foot caught in a trap. "So, Adam," I murmured, "you looked like an old pro, like you've got a lot of experience. You been doing this a while, eh?"

No answer.

"You must be quite valuable to HRC; they give you an awful lot of responsibility."

Still no reply. I wondered if he saw through my bromide, and was just trying to control his disgust.

I decided to lay the butter on a little thicker. "Have you had a management course or something? I saw how you handled the drillers. They're a tough lot. You got to really keep them in line, give them lots of direction."

Adam's posture softened. He put an elbow up on his windowsill, even cocked his head to one side, really suave. "Nah. I just know what to tell them."

"Well, I'm hoping I can learn a lot from you. I mean, I'm hoping you'll teach me. I mean, otherwise I'm kind of at sea here."

"Yeah, I know," he preened.

I glanced his way again. He was fighting to repress a satisfied smile. "A deal, then?" I offered, trying to repress a wave of nausea.

"Well, now I realize it'll take you quite a while to learn all this. You got to be willing to do hard work. Outside, any weather. Got to be tough. I'm not so sure a female is going to like that."

I had to take a deep breath to restrain myself. "I'm willing to try, really I am." And then, in an ever-so-natural segue, I asked, "It sounds like you've had to work with some difficult women. Has a woman worked for HRC? You know, like someone who put women in a bad light for you?"

Adam's face clouded. "Well, yeah. There was this bitch who was here until just a while ago—you're replacing her, I guess. Prissy little thing, real bad attitude. I told Rauch, I said, shit, you get a female in here, and she won't quit whining until she gets the softest work."

"You came to work here first?"

Adam lowered his head in a slightly more marked sulk.

"What was her name?"

"Janet," he muttered.

"Oh, I heard about her. Didn't she die or something?"

Adam scowled. "Yeah, but that had nothing to do with this. Shit, she croaks and Rauch starts talking about her like she was a saint or something, did the best work in the company, walked on water in her free time. Shit."

Ah, jealousy. Adam had hated Janet while she was alive because she was his competition in grade, and now that she was dead, she continued to haunt him by becoming an object of sympathy. A very toxic mixture. Or was there a message to be read between the lines? *Had* Janet been a goof-off? A prima donna? Or was Rauch putting on a show of sorrow to deflect suspicion from himself?

Adam turned from southbound Highway 101 onto a wide, high-speed secondary road that carried us westward across the north end of the Santa Rosa plain through bottomlands planted with grapes, and several miles later turned south onto a road that snaked up into the line of hills I had seen rising west of the ditch site. My interest sharpened. I tried to get Adam to tell me a little more specifically why he held Janet in such contempt, but something about the job we were approaching had him upset, above and beyond his usual state of emotional uproar. As we turned south on Highway 116, a two-laner with wide shoulders, Adam's knuckles grew white on the steering wheel and he fell into monosyllabic muttering.

"Highway 116," I said sharply, trying to snap him out of his internal pissing match. "Doesn't this cross Occidental Road near Miwok Mills?"

Adam twisted up his face and whined, "The Gravenstein Highway," in the same kind of tone grade-school kids address kindergartners. "Goddamn pet names for roads. Can't they just call it 116?"

I got to reading the hand-painted signs posted on trees and telephone poles as we bounced along the curving blacktop. Little ones advertised

Hi-Weed Mowing, Rototilling, and missing cats, while bigger sandwich-board signs advertised local events like concerts, Christmas bazaars, and of course, the Miwok Mills Fire Department's Christmas Spaghetti Feed. It was like driving down a two-lane community bulletin board. "Gravenstein like the apple?" I asked, admiring the groves of apple trees we were passing.

"And it's graven*stine*, not graven*steen!* Can't they even pronounce the language right?"

Adam was right, the apple farmers were mispronouncing their German, but was this a reason to run one's blood pressure through the roof? "You don't like this part of the county?" I inquired.

Adam shot me a look of combined rage and panic. "We're back in the hills now, sister. Bunch of redneck farmers and Volvo-driving trust-fund hippies sitting in hot tubs."

"Um—"

"And they all own *dogs*. You gotta watch 'em like a hawk. No respect for a working man. *Shit!*" Adam screamed, swerving to miss a bicyclist who had veered too close to the inside edge of the shoulder for Adam's taste.

I glanced in the rearview mirror on my side just in time to see a skinny kid raise one arm of his neon green bicycling spandex in the international salute of forced copulation. It was the Duke, in all his plucked-chicken glory. "Hey, pull over!" I yelled. "I need to talk to that kid."

"Bull-*shit* I will! He's probably writing down my license number right now, or worse yet, the name of our company, and he's going to sue me! Sue *me,* and *I* was the one minding my own business and staying in my lane! Goddamn shithead bicyclists think they *own the road!*"

I sighed and slumped back in the seat, resigned to my fate. This guy Duke was just going to make me nuts, that was all. Too bad he hadn't seen me; then he'd follow us to wherever we were going for sure, and I could grab him by his slippery spandex and demand a few answers.

Adam was still displaying the reeking underside of his paranoia as we turned and dropped down off the ridge of hills toward the east. I watched for glimpses of the Laguna, figuring we were within a mile or two of Occidental Road now. At the bottom of the hill, Adam stopped to open a gate of welded stainless steel that hung between tall fieldstone posts like the ones at Mrs. Karsh's house, and we passed into a yard full of long, steel-roofed industrial buildings and parked in front of what was clearly the office. A crisply lettered sign set tastefully low to the ground declared that we were at the corporate headquarters of Misty Creek Winery.

The cement parking bumper nearest the main door read "Karsh." I turned quickly to Adam. "Is this Karsh any relation to the woman who lives on the other side of the Laguna, down on Sanborn Road?"

"How the fuck would I know?"

"But we're sampling monitoring wells here?"

"Yeah. Four wells. There was a diesel and a gasoline tank over by the shipping barn. We pulled them six months ago. Bad leakers; six inches of product floating on top of the groundwater. We have a skimmer going in the center well to get what we can."

"And the other three wells?"

"The regulators have us sample them quarterly for a year, to document the level of contamination on the site."

"You drilled these wells, too?"

Adam's expression darkened from low clouds to thunderheads. "No. Janet."

Aha! Janet's father was right; she worked right here, doing geology. Karshes here, Karshes there. There must be a connection! I went on the alert, head on a swivel.

Adam's head was swiveling, too. He was grumbling, "Stay here. I got to check in. And keep the doors closed!" Cracking his door slowly, he peered this way and that, then jumped out and ran toward the office door.

Before Adam's skinny legs reached the doorway, a Doberman pinscher darted out from behind the neatly planted shrubberies, blocking

Adam's path. It went into a crouch. A low, full-throated growl resonated from its throat.

"Git!" Adam shouted, his voice rising frantically to a squeal. "Hey, the dog's loose! Hey, someone come get this goddamn thing!"

The office door swung open and a tall woman in her middle years with flame-red hair, a long nose, and plump cheeks stuck her head out. "Tina!" she called. The dog wheeled, braced, looked confused, cowered, and came to her. "Bad girl. How'd you get loose?" she cooed, rattling a cluster of costume jewelry as she stroked the animal's narrow skull. "Aww, that man yelling at you? Come in here." To Adam she said, "Sorry," and tossed him a large, condescending wink.

Adam lowered his head. "We're here to do the wells. You'll keep her in?"

"Of course. How long will you be?"

"Out of here by five, trust me."

The woman retreated into the office, the dog held loosely by the collar.

Adam hurried back to the truck and backed it quickly away, turning past the office block toward a cluster of storage barns at the back of the main factory building. "You got to watch out for that dog," he was saying, gesticulating fiercely with his free hand. "She's trouble. There's two of them; sisters. They let them out together at night when the gate's locked and everyone's gone, to patrol the grounds. They usually keep at least one in the kennels during the day. You see only one of them, you're maybe okay, but you ever see them both at once, you jump for the highest spot you can find; they're attack dogs, and don't you try to pet them!"

Sure enough, as we pulled up to the end of the buildings, we were greeted by a second skinny Doberman, this one a brown to the other one's black. Like her sister, she at first cowered, but this one broke and ran away the instant Adam opened the door. "This one's okay, but don't get close," he cautioned.

"I've never heard of timid guard dogs," I offered.

"Dangerous. Worst kind. Hard to predict a piss-head dog with the heart of a fucking chicken. They're psychotic. It's like either one of them's only half a dog, but you get them together, they'll try anything. Just watch your back."

◆

THE AIR HAD a slicing dampness to it, threatening rain. Between the buildings I could glimpse the bottomlands of the Laguna, that broad dish of land out there just waiting to flood. I imagined all those steep-sided ditches filling, the water rushing, now brimming over the top and setting the roads awash. . . . My mind even fed me the image of Janet's sodden body, swept along by the deluge.

Give me high ground in a rainstorm. I do not like to argue with water. Most easterners don't understand water, or know its power. They've never seen a landscape hit by the passion of a western storm, seen it shed the waters into steep-sided gullies that are one moment dry and the next shoulder-high in roiling, churning water. Crops are washed out, or rot, when the rains come too hard and too sudden. No one had to explain the image of the biblical flood to me, where farmers saw their lowland universe consumed by waters, and prayed for the salvation of just a spot of dry land.

Surveying the flat ground around the winery, I told myself that I had just been around Adam too long, and was catching his paranoia. But I did say a prayer that I be allowed to just stay warm and dry until this job was done, and promised the Great Whatever out there that I would buy a good rain slicker over the coming weekend.

The three wells we had to sample were spaced in a large triangle scattered in between the buildings, such that I could not see from one to the next. Adam did a lot of cussing as he set me up with a whiny little pump and the truck battery that powered it, and with tubing and bailers and leaking drums of expelled contaminated water. My job, he explained, was to watch as the well water was purged into the drums and to monitor a bunch of gadgets that measured the temperature, pH, and conductivity of said water. He handed me another one of his forms. "See, what you do is, every five minutes you take a reading,

and mark it down here. See, the water's really muddy right now. It'll
take a while. When the water's running clear and the temp and so forth
have been stable for three readings, it means we're getting a true sample from the soil, not just the degassed water that's been sitting in the
well casing. Then you come get me, and I'll show you how to collect
the sample." Having said this, he got back into the truck and disappeared around the corner, leaving me sitting on an overturned plastic
milk crate for a chair, holding the clipboard on my knees as a desk.

The pump whined away.

I thought longingly of the nice, warm office, wanting nothing better than to march over there and strike up a woman-to-woman conversation with that redheaded secretary and find out just what had
transpired on this site between Janet Pinchon and anyone named Karsh.
But no, the readings I was supposed to take were timed too close together, and if there's one thing I believe in, it's not screwing up the
collection of scientific data.

It had clouded over again, was beginning to spit rain, and starting
to get pretty brisk. I zipped Janet's jacket up snugly around my throat
(wondering how long it would take before its nylon shell wet through
and the down fill began to compact), stuffed my hands in my pockets,
and began to hum, waiting for the five-minute timer on my watch to
go off. After taking the first reading, I got up and began to do *demi-
pliés,* kind of bouncing up and down to keep warm. When the fresh-
ening breeze began to whip my hair into my eyes, I checked my watch
and moved over into the lee of a row of huge wooden brewing barrels that smelled of vinegar, each about a story tall.

I had three and a half minutes to go before my next reading, and
the water running into the barrel was still turbid. With the growing
chill beginning to ram my shoulders up underneath my ears, I drew
farther in among the barrels. The reek of vinegar grew stronger. Beyond them, a door to the adjacent building stood open. I glanced at
my watch. Three minutes to go. I went in.

It was no warmer inside, but at least it was out of the wind and wet.
I looked around. The concrete floor had a large hole in it, from which

emanated an enormous Archimedes' screw about four feet in diameter. I followed the screw with my eyes up to the second story of the building, trying to reason out its function. It appeared that the screw would carry materials up to a conveyor that fed a hopper that in turn fed a heavy press. The press stood six feet tall, and was served by plate-steel beds that wheeled back and forth on tracks and a huge hydraulic ram.

"What you think, young lady?" came a voice behind me.

I jumped and turned. A short, aging man with a still proud chest but sagging jowls stood between me and the doorway. As I faced him, his eyes popped, and he took an involuntary step backward.

"Are you okay?" I asked, stepping toward him.

The man put a hand to his chest. "It's okay. I—you just look like someone." He spread his mouth in a wide show of teeth that gleamed here and there with eighteen-karat dentistry. The eyes were feverishly bright, yet sad and pensive.

"I'm sorry," I said, making small talk to put him at his ease. I had a strong suspicion who I must have looked like, but I knew better than to jump right in with the obvious questions. "I guess I'm not supposed to be in here, but you see, I'm sampling that well out there, and I just wanted to get out of the wind, and . . ."

The man shrugged his shoulders and began to rock back and forth on his well-shod feet. "Oh, it's okay, dear. There's nothing going on in here anymore anyway. We don't press apple juice these days. Only grapes. We're a winery now." He looked around slowly, longingly, taking in the pattern of girders in the roof, the stacks of disused pressing blankets on the steel carts, waiting for apple mash that wasn't coming. "No, just grapes these days." The man was expensively dressed, his steel-gray hair was neatly combed in tight waves back from his forehead, and his hands looked neatly manicured.

"Are you Mr. Karsh?"

"Yes," he said vaguely, continuing his walk down memory lane.

"I'm Em Hansen. I met someone named Karsh just last evening. Any relation? She lives down on Sanborn Road."

The broad sort-of-smile on the man's face grew heavy. "Yes," he whispered. He turned away, starting to leave.

"So this was an apple-processing plant," I said brightly, willing him to turn back and talk to me some more. "I suppose a truck dumped the apples into the sump in the floor here, and the screw would grind them and carry them up to the second floor."

Mr. Karsh turned back, passed a hand lovingly through his hair, then pointed up toward the press. "Yes. The hopper up there mixed the apple mash with rice hulls to hold the mash up for pressing, then we'd open the chute and fill the pressing blankets there. We'd get a stack of them, see, all held in place by those wooden frames, and then that ram presses the whole stack up from the floor against that head plate, and out goes the juice. There's a cistern down below that catches it." His face fell further as he came back to the present moment. "Best juice in the county, we made. Next building, we made apple sauce and canned them both." He sighed. "Nowadays it's all grapes."

"You talk like you've worked the line."

The man's eyes shone longingly. "Yes. Came here fresh out of the army, right after Korea. Worked the line for ten years: machinist, trucking, whatever needed done. It was a young man's world back then."

While we'd been talking, the brown Doberman had wandered quietly in and tucked its head up under his left hand. Mr. Karsh ran his index finger gently along her muzzle and up between her eyes, soothing her.

My watch beeped at me, time to take a reading at the well head. Torn over whether to stay and keep investigating or go and do a good job on the simple task Adam had set me, I said, "Excuse me, I have to run outside a moment, check my equipment. I'll be right back. I want to hear more."

I was half a minute late taking the reading, but scribbled it down quickly anyway, figuring that it would just have to do. Then I reset the timer on my watch and hurried back toward the doorway.

Mr. Karsh wasn't there. I cocked an ear, trying to figure out where he had gone, but heard no one, only the rumble of a distant forklift and the odd groan of a door somewhere moving on rusty hinges in the wind.

So this was an apple plant that had been retooled as a winery. And this Mr. Karsh, was he a self-made man? The plant had been here since before the 1950s, when he had come to work as a skilled laborer. Had he earned his way in and bought out the owners? Or was he only a manager, perhaps a man so wedded to his job that the history of the plant felt like a litany of his own successes and failures? And just what relation was he to the Mrs. Karsh I had met? Brother-in-law? Cousin? Husband?

I heard a sound behind me and turned. The woman with the red hair came bustling in through the doorway, her still curvy figure bouncing with bone-deep cheer and enthusiasm for her task. She was carrying a cordless telephone. "Have you seen Wilbur? Mr. Karsh? Man about that tall, with a barrel chest?" She gestured to Mr. Karsh's height, a few inches less than the altitude she commanded on her spindly high-heeled shoes. "There's a phone call for him."

"He was here a few minutes ago."

She sighed in cheery exasperation. "He's out looking for that boy of his," she gossiped. "Mama Karsh dropped him off an hour ago, and things always go to hell around here when we have him. You'd think he was five years old, the way he gets into trouble. Will just worries himself sick about him." She turned to leave, then looked back over her shoulder. "You see him—the boy, not the father—don't worry, he's harmless. He looks kind of scary, real big and hulking." She pantomimed a looming thug, arching her arms away from her sides. "Just ignore him. Well, I better find Will; this call's important. See ya." She hurried away, her heels clicking rhythmically across the concrete and crunching as they hit the gravel driveway. I watched her go, a flurry of brightly colored fabric jostling over a supple body that joyously defied the call of gravity and middle age.

I had a sinking feeling that I knew just the oaf she was talking about. It had to be Matthew Karsh. So Mrs. Karsh had "dropped him off"?

What did that mean? And things always went to hell around the winery when he was about? Exactly what kind of trouble was he likely to get into? And where did this "secretary" get off talking about "Will" and herself so proprietarily as "we"?

I went back outside and stayed close to the instruments until it was time to take the next reading, musing on the relative pleasures Mr. Karsh might find between a bouncing redhead and a graying woman distracted by a damaged son.

A couple of trucks went past. Somewhere in the depths of a nearby building, I could hear a heavy forklift operating. A moment later, I saw Mr. Karsh in the distance, passing out of one building and hurrying into the one that echoed with the groan of the forklift. The groan stopped. Mr. Karsh came back out of the building, leading his ungainly son. As I had guessed, it was Matthew Karsh.

The two were downwind of me and quite a distance away, so I couldn't hear what the older man was saying to the younger, but by his gestures, I gathered that he was cajoling him to settle down and behave in whatever way he hadn't just been behaving. Matthew was scowling. Mr. Karsh touched his arm one more time, tenderly, even piteously, and hurried back toward the office. Matthew watched him go. He stood with his shoulders slumped, his head hanging, and his lower lip stuck out, just like a little boy who's had his toys taken away. *How interesting it must be to do business with a distraction like Matthew,* I thought dryly. And as I thought that thought, he looked up and saw me.

Whatever was wrong with Matthew Karsh, his eyes were as sharp as an eagle's. His body stiffened from flaccid disappointment to alert, thirsting menace. He kept watching me. And I watched him, nervously, afraid to turn my back to do my job. Several minutes passed. My watch sounded, calling me to take another reading. What to do? I gauged the distance between us, reckoned the time it would take him to reach me, dragged a foot across the gravel to calibrate my ear for the sound he would make on approach, then turned and scribbled the numbers down as fast as I could.

When I looked up again, he was gone.

Suddenly I felt silly. Hadn't the redhead just told me he was harmless? What was wrong with me? Relax, I told myself. It's broad daylight. Just finish your work, stay right out here where the passing trucks can see you, and do your Goddamn job.

I turned back to the well, rechecked my work, and noted my observations. The water was clear now, and the last two readings had been nearly identical, so it wouldn't be long before I could search up Adam, collect the water sample, and get the hell out of there.

I closed up the clipboard. As it clicked shut, I heard a low growl. I turned. Saw both Doberman pinschers, charging at full speed, shoulder to shoulder, straight at me.

I turned and ran, dashing for the nearest high place, right through that doorway and towards the Archimedes' screw.

The dogs rushed after me, sluicing between the barrels and through the door and scrambling up the steps like they were as flat as the driveway.

At the top of the stairs above the screw, I grabbed the rungs of a ladder beside the hopper, swung up, and shot into the attic space, ripping one knee of my jeans on a girder as I clambered frantically into the dust and squeaking steel. When I had stabilized my grip on an upright of the roof truss, I turned and looked down.

The dogs stood at the foot of the ladder, growling from deep in their chests.

"Git!" I yelled. "Go on! Go on home with you!"

The black one leapt at the ladder. The brown one whipped around in a tight circle, snapping at the third rung.

Furious to find myself treed by livestock, I made smoochy noises at the lousy mutts, lest they think I was truly scared. Which I was. My whole body was beginning to tremble with the let down from the adrenaline that had just hammered through me.

Half a minute later, I was still sitting there cussing at the dogs, getting cut in half by the edge of that girder, hanging on with one hand

and beginning to probe at a trickle of blood on my knee with the other, when I became aware that I had more company than just two canines.

Matthew Karsh stood just inside the door, feet planted and chest heaved up under his sloppy chin in a burlesque of pridefulness. His face was cruel with triumph, his lips retracted from his mossy teeth in a grimace of horrific glee. It was a child's pose distorted onto the body of a man, that defiant "gotcha" posture so popular among preschoolers who need to get even. He shifted excitedly from foot to foot, showing himself to me, but keeping his bulk carefully inside the doorway, his victory display for me and me only.

I tried to look casual, unimpressed, even though the girder was beginning to cut like a knife. "Hi, Matt," I said. "What's the haps?"

"I've *got* you," he replied, in a deep, nasal voice.

I shrugged. "Nah, let's not play that game." I shifted on the girder, dangling one foot toward the top of the ladder.

"I wouldn't *do* that. They could *eat* you."

On cue, the brown dog raised her growl to a sharp bark and leapt at the ladder again.

Matthew rocked far enough that his face loomed for a moment out of the shadow. His eyes were agleam, the whites visible all the way around the irises. It was not a pretty sight.

Okay, I counseled myself, *you're in a bit of a bind here. You've been treed by a pair of neurotic dogs who answer to a psychotic master. So what are you going to do about this?*

I was surprised to find that I felt charged up, stimulated by the challenge. Now that the tension of possibility was broken by action, life had become suddenly simpler, more defined. I let this insight sink in while I tried to craft my next move.

Move, that was it: I was playing chess, getting a perverse thrill out of this experience. I wasn't proud of that.

I was just thinking that the best maneuver might be to climb down the ladder far enough to incite the dogs into a fit of barking, in the hope that someone else might hear them and come find us, when Matthew threw a switch mounted in a big metal box by the wall.

The floor shook and moaned as the Archimedes' screw began to turn, its four-foot gullet and polished metal edges slithering like a hungry snake. The screw made a grinding noise as the great spiral blade pulsed toward me. As if the suggestion of sexual violence was not obvious enough, Matthew began to rub the front of his pants with one giant paw. Then his head whipped around, ears alerted to a sound I could not hear. Then he was gone.

A moment later, Will Karsh reentered the room. Seeing what was making the floor shake, he slapped the switch off, bringing the screw to a halt, but the dogs still paced wildly, patrolling the base of the ladder.

"Could you get the dogs down from there, please?" I yelled.

Will Karsh jerked his head back in search of the source of my voice, eyes squinting into the darkness. When at last he saw me, he did something I found almost as disconcerting as what his son had done: he just stood there. Eyes blank. As if watching TV.

"Okay, I'll just start down, then," I called, and swung myself onto the top rung. "You can just call these dogs off any time you want."

The brown dog leapt at my bootheel and sank her teeth into it, dangling for a split second before she dropped. "Now, Mr. Karsh!" I hollered, my voice rising into a scream.

He just stood there.

A high, bright whistling came from the doorway. The dogs dropped back to all fours and turned toward the sound, then scrambled back down the stairs. The redhead had entered the building, all smiles and jangling jewelry. Sizing up the scene at a glance, she awarded me a cheery smile. "I see you've met our girls!" she called. "Coco, Tina, you come. Come!" she commanded, snapping her fingers and pointing at the floor to either side of her spike heels.

The dogs fell all over each other in their hurry to do her bidding. She petted them, giving them lovies and talking to them like they were a couple of slightly unruly two-year-olds: "Now, girls, you been chasing the nice sample person? That's not nice. You're only supposed to scare thieves, and they come at nighttime, now don't they?" She trailed off into some choice ookum-snookums stuff and then, glancing up toward me, she added, "It's okay to come down now."

By the time I'd gotten down the ladder and descended the stairs, Mr. Karsh had wandered out the door, eyes blank, as if nothing unusual had happened. I turned to the redhead, who was now holding each dog firmly by its collar. "What was that all about?" I demanded. "He just stood there, didn't even try to call them off."

"They don't mind him much."

"Oh, no? Then why does he keep them? Doesn't he worry about the liability of keeping attack dogs around that he can't control?"

"Well, it's usually not a problem."

"And why's it a problem today? Some little detail about that psychotic son of his?" I spat.

"Oh, Matthew? Like I said, he's harmless."

"He set those dogs on me!"

"You think so? Huh. Well, you didn't get hurt, did you?"

I gasped for words, trying to figure out how to explain to this woman that her words weren't making sense. But then I looked more deeply into her eyes, and realized that what I had mistaken for frivolity was an illusion generated by the featurelessness of those soft brown lakes. "No, I didn't get hurt."

"Well then, you'd better get back to work, hadn't you?" She massaged one dog's neck sensuously with her thumb, her grip growing threateningly slack on its collar. The dog began to growl.

"Sure. Why not," I replied, letting my face reflect her hostility. "But you lead; I don't want your little pals getting any ideas."

With a withering smile, she turned and left, the dogs trotting beside her like outboard motors.

I waited a moment, brushing myself off and straightening my clothes, and checked my knee gingerly to make sure the bleeding had stopped. Then I realized that Matthew must have left the room via an inside door, which probably meant he was still in there. Still inside and watching from a safe distance. Watching and smiling as he saw that his father and the redhead were sweeping away his tracks. Yes, I could complain about this, but they would gloss it over, say it was really my fault; that much was clear.

I hastened back outside, uncertain which way to turn my back to protect myself. Suddenly the wet and windswept driveway seemed the warmest place in the compound.

In my absence, the drum had filled to the brim. Contaminated water was now sluicing down the sides in quantity, puddling in the gravel, and sinking into the ground. I glanced at my watch. I'd missed two readings.

And Adam was just coming around the building.

12

WHEN ADAM SAW THE OVERFLOWING BARREL, HE JAMMED HIS fists onto his bony hips and snarled, "Say the three words, Hansen!"

"Which are?"

"You fucked up."

So much for my career as an environmental geologist.

"And what the fuck happened to your knee?" he spat, as if my injury were another personal insult to him.

"Adam, honeycup," I sighed, "what can you expect from a fuckup like me?"

My head was heavy with anxiety and exhaustion as we drove back to Santa Rosa. Adam gave me the silent treatment the whole way. I had disappointed him. Woe betide me. I was too upset by what had happened in the apple shed to care.

Back at HRC, Adam drove around to the back of the building and hoisted one of the roll-up doors and barked, "You! Help me unload."

Fine, I thought doggedly, *I'll help you get your gear out of this truck. And then you leave. I have work to do. Records to search. I'm going to stay here all night if I have to, and find out what, if anything, Janet Pinchon did to piss off the Karshes.* I jerked open the back of the camper shell and hauled cargo boxes off over the tailgate of the truck. Adam stacked them on the shelves where they belonged, cussing under his breath the while. When we were done, he turned to me and said, "You just head on out the back way here."

"You go ahead, I'll just walk back through the office," I asserted. "My truck's out front. See you Monday."

Adam pointed one skinny finger. "The back way. I have orders."

Suggesting that someone above him did not trust me was downright insulting. Never mind that what I was planning warranted that distrust. "Someone gave you *orders?* Who?"

Adam pinched his face up like he smelled something putrid. "Rauch. He said don't let the new girl alone in the building. You don't *really* work here. No W-4 form, no nothing. You live in a *motel,*" he sneered. "I know; I had to phone this morning to find out where in hell you *were* and I get a Mex broad says, Wagon Trail Motel, what *room* do I want! Rauch probably thinks you'll fall down in here and *sue* us."

I laughed mirthlessly. Rauch had been content to send me out on a job site with no OSHA training and no clear insurance status; surely my personal well-being didn't worry the son of a bitch. So that meant there was something inside the building he didn't want the new person to see. But whatever it was, it was going to have to wait. I wasn't willing to mug Adam Horowitz for the right to stay; I might get rabies.

After being ushered out the back way, I walked around front toward my little blue truck in the dark, trying to figure out a plan B. I was just in time to see Pat Ryan fumbling with his keys by the front door. "Evening, Pat!" I called.

Pat stopped, wobbling like a bear dancing on its hind legs. "Well, why, Em Hansen, isn't it? How is every little thing?"

"Fine. I got the job, thanks to your coaching."

"So I hear. When do you start?"

"I already did. I just came back from pulling my first tank."

Our paths had now converged at the front door, and a gentle breeze carried the light perfume of an early evening beer to my nostrils from Pat's lips. "Yanking tanks," he said. "Oh, that you should sink to such humble labors from the greater glories of the oil patch."

"I'm a big girl, my ego can take it."

"Saint preserve!" Pat caroled, as he spied my ripped and blood-caked knee in the glow of the security light by the door, "Mymymymymy, whatever happened to your knee?"

I set my jaw, uncertain what to tell him. "Just had a little bad luck," I finally answered.

"Let Uncle Pat take a look."

"No, really, I'm fine. Say, are you heading inside? I don't have a key yet."

"Em, my dear, as it happens, I left my attaché by my desk. Did you leave something inside? May I get it for you?"

I thought quickly, fashioning a likely story. "Well, actually I just wanted to get into the library, maybe borrow some books, get a leg up on contamination and groundwater, that sort of stuff. If you can just let me in, I could lock the door behind me when I leave."

"Library? No such a beast," Pat said mournfully. "Consulting firms aren't very interested in educating their employees. You're used to the oil patch, where employers understand that a well-educated, up-to-date employee finds more of the commodity in question. Here in environmental services, you *are* the commodity. They wouldn't want to lose time educating you: that time they can't charge for."

"Well, I—"

"But I'll tell you what, you're in luck after all; Pat Ryan will look after you. You just wait a moment while I retrieve my attaché, and I'll take you home to Mother."

"Excuse me?"

"I have such books at my place, dear lady. You wouldn't turn down a steak grilled expressly for you by none other than Patrick John Ryan, would you? I just happen to be at liberty for the evening, you see, and—"

Steak? Food? "I'll just get my truck and bring it around by yours," I said, preempting an offer to give me a ride, certain his blood alcohol was already pushing the legal limit. "I'll follow you home."

❖

PAT RYAN WASN'T kidding. The man could fry a mean steak. As I leaned onto the railing of the tiny balcony of his apartment nursing a beer, he delicately seared two fine chunks of T-bone over a tiny hibachi. I looked on lovingly, mapping out just which bite I would present to my molars first, and which one second. I love the tender bit on the north side of the bone. To hell with my arteries, I was raised on a cattle ranch.

As the meat sizzled, Pat hunkered down and took a warm wet washcloth to my knee. It stung a little, but the cuts proved shallow, and after daubing a bit of antibiotic ointment on them, Pat declared me fit for service.

When the steaks were done, he shoveled them onto paper plates and whisked them onto the little Formica-topped table in the dining nook off the kitchen. Russet potatoes emerged from the oven and turned thick pats of butter to golden liquid, and somewhere in the proceedings he had rustled up a couple of crisp green salads and had heated some sourdough bread in the oven.

My knife sank through the steak with almost no resistance. I poised a morsel between my lips. I bit. I chewed. I moaned. I was in heaven.

Pat smiled happily at my appreciation and spirited a bottle of wine out of a cupboard. From a drawer under the kitchen counter he retrieved a cork puller. The only other thing in the drawer was an inexpensive bread knife. In fact, there was very little in the entire apartment, at least in the parts I'd seen; just a plain-Jane couch and cheap coffee table in the tiny living room, a small TV, the table, and two plastic-upholstered chairs with tubular metal legs. "You live alone?" I asked rhetorically, taking a seat at the table.

Pat worried the tines of the cork puller into the neck of the bottle and eased out the cork. "Here in Santa Rosa I do," he said, making a study of the cork with eyes and nose. "My wife lives in Fresno. I commute down to see her most weekends. We have a very nice house there, and she has a very nice job." This he said without rancor.

"I take it there's not much work for geologists in Fresno?"

"Not for this geologist." He poured the wine into two plastic tumblers, picked his up, swirled the ruby liquid, and stuck his nose into the vapors at the top of the glass. "Mmm. Davis Bynum. Nice little vineyard up along the Russian River. Not far from here. Do try a sip, my dear."

Sip, I did. Beer, I know, a little bit, but wine may as well be tart grape juice. "Mmmm," I murmured, pretending to have an oenologist's palate. It was good; good enough to strike me as darned *good* tart grape juice.

I set my glass down and studied my host. Here he was, a connoisseur and something of a gourmet, well dressed and cleanly groomed, a decent, warm human being living in a depressingly barren apartment far removed from a wife he clearly loved, just so he could call himself employed. That was dedication. "I bet she misses you."

Pain tensed his face. "And I her. But I suppose I won't be here much longer."

"Why?"

"Why? Oh, my, because the young Turks have yanked almost all the tanks. Something will have to give."

"The young Turks?" The alcohol seemed to be helping keep Pat Ryan's conversation on track, but I still had trouble following his verbal shorthand.

Pat carved into his steak. "You remind me of a woman named Janet Pinchon, who . . . used to work for HRC."

An odd combination of warmth and sadness swept over me. I found myself wanting to say, *But I am Janet. Don't you know me?* Realizing that the wine must truly be getting to me, I settled for asking, "How so?"

A bemused smile warmed Pat's face. "I don't know. You're put together the same way physically, I suppose; you could be . . . not exactly sisters, maybe, but certainly cousins. But there's more. Something in the intensity. Full of questions. Nothing was straightforward with Janet. Each answer just spawned another question." He laughed to himself. "I used to feel like a sheep around her. She was the sheepdog, snapping at my heels." With his fingers he pantomimed a dog's jaws. Snap, snap, snap. He bent back over his steak and carved.

Okay, if I was a sheepdog, I now had two conversational sheep to chase: the young Turks and their tanks, and Pat's conversations with Janet. I'd just have to herd one and then the other. "Who are the young Turks?"

"A figure of speech, my dear. The reformists. I use the term advisedly. H, R, and C. They used to work for Jones and Roux. Big firm. Didn't like the way they were treated there. Few people do, of course; Jones and Roux run a fully draconian shop, complete with torture specialists who pile on unpaid work on the one end, and bean counters with righteously tight sphincters who cut salaries on the other. So H, R, and C said, 'We can do better, be ethical and considerate, create a decent working environment, what ho.' A nice dream, eh? So they went out on their own during the tank-yank boom back in eighty-six, eighty-seven, thinking they'd outdo Jones and Roux in their own backyard, really show those bastards. They did pretty well for a while."

"What changed all that?"

"Well, for starts, my dear, if your favorite seasoning is spite, it's hard to keep the dish from spoiling."

I remembered the vanity and avarice in Fred Rauch's eyes and put my fork down for a while. "So they're bad businessmen?"

"Well, define 'bad business.' It's kind of redundant, isn't it?"

"Are we bitter?"

"Are we answering a question with another question? Besides, the success or failure of a business is based on external causes as much as internal talent. Coming from the oil business, no one should have to explain boom-and-bust economics to you."

"Supply and demand. So have most of the leaking tanks already been yanked?"

"Let's say most of the ones in HRC's bailiwick. There will always be tanks to yank and replace, as long as gas stations pump gas, but most stations are owned by big companies nowadays, and they hire a big firm to look after them, someone bigger than an HRC. The HRCs are fighting to the death over the last few ma-and-pa and ag tanks."

"Ma-and-pa groceries don't put in a new tank?" I thought of the hopeful words of Phil the grocery owner that morning.

"No. When Ma and Pa have their tank pulled, it hurts them so badly financially that they usually don't want to risk putting in another. But as importantly for the HRCs, the regulatory climate has turned bust."

"Please explain. First fill me in on the boom."

Pat smiled. "*Just* like Janet. The boom. In the mid-eighties, the government regulatory agencies—the Water Board and County Health, the nice folks who saunter out to watch you work—said that tanks no longer in use and tanks that were leaking had to be pulled and examined for 'unauthorized releases to the soil and groundwater.' My dear, even the tiniest amount of contamination would set off further investigation. Benzene contamination in the parts per billion. That's like a thimbleful in a swimming pool. How can you have a tank in the ground for fifteen or twenty years, filling it, say, once a month, and not spill that much? Impossible. Good-bye fifty, a hundred, two hundred thousand dollars."

"I was wondering about that. Neither of the tanks I saw come out today had obvious holes in them, but there was so much fuel in the soil around them that I had to stand upwind."

Pat smiled sadly. "Sure. I spoke with a fellow who used to deliver gasoline in a tank truck. I asked him how he knew how much gas to put in the tank. He said no problem, he'd just open the overflow valve and pump until he saw fuel flowing through it." He made an arc with a forkful of salad. "And sometimes he'd get to talking with someone . . ."

"And the bust? Lady Lucy of County Health said the mess would have to be cleaned up. Isn't that more work for HRC?"

"Well, regulations change. After sticking it to tank owners for eight years, they're adopting a much less stringent code, only requiring cleanup when drinking-water supplies are threatened. And Lucy and her pals in the state legislature have clamped down on the consultants.

The HRCs used to be able to charge liberally for their services, maybe even put together a big enough budget to find out how far the contamination has traveled and maybe how best to clean it up. The RPs—"

"RPs?"

"Responsible Parties; people with the mess—paid and paid. By and by, Mom and Pop with their leaking tank screamed rape to the legislature, and rightly so."

"What about 'mess up, clean up'?" I asked, mimicking Lucy's officious tone.

Pat rolled his head back and stared at the plain white Sheetrock ceiling of his plain white apartment. "Ma and Pa generally didn't know what they were getting into when they bought that grocery in the late seventies. They thought they were investing their life savings in a comfortable little community service. 'Hey, how nice; it's even got a gas pump! Extra income, and we save the neighbors a trip to town.' "

"So what did the legislature do about it?"

"The legislature passed a law. SB2004."

"Right, the cleanup fund. Lucy mentioned that. How does that change things for the HRCs?"

"SB2004 has a few rules. You only get Fund money if you get three estimates, proving that the firm you hired will do the job as cheaply as possible."

"So the competition is now fierce."

"Exceedingly so, and Mom and Pop are also getting sophisticated and learning how to stall the job. They used to think they had to get the work done right now or something horrible would happen to them. Now they know their property's probably a write-off anyway, so why not just ignore it and go on with life? The HRCs aren't getting much work at all."

"Why's the property a write-off?"

Pat downed the last of his wine and refilled his glass. "Because the banks got smart and all but quit lending money on properties that have those filthy little tanks in them. Imagine you're a lender who's taken a property as collateral for a loan, and you find out your collateral is contaminated and your landowner has skipped because he was mortgaged up to the eye sockets in the first place and hasn't two cents to put toward the cleanup. Now the regulators are coming after you to clean it up. It's going to cost, say, three hundred thousand. Suddenly your property worth a hundred and a quarter doesn't look very good to the bank."

I sat back in my chair, hands in my lap. This story was all too familiar: the economic shock waves that crash through a society as it finds out about the little flies that come in the ointment of technological advance. I wasn't sure I was going to like working in the environmental services industry, even for a week.

Pat advanced the wine bottle toward my glass. "Sorry. I didn't mean to burden this happy occasion with my defeatist zeitgeist. Have another drop or two?"

"You were telling me about a woman named Janet."

"You don't want to hear about all that. This is a fine steak I've served you, and I intend that you should digest it in peace."

"Why did she leave HRC?"

Pat sighed heavily. "Oh, I don't know. She didn't play nicely with the boys. No, that's too simple. She didn't really tell me. My dear, I plied her with a lot better vintage than this, trying to find out. She was not a person who liked answering questions."

"She mostly *asked* them?"

"Just so."

"What kind of questions?"

"The same sort you ask. How do things work. Who's pulling the strings. What do things really cost. Who's really responsible. How to live with the consequences of our actions. A veritable sponge for ideas and information. I called her the rabbi: she was intent on getting at the truth."

"What kind of work did she do?" I asked, hoping to at least find out what a Phase One was.

"She drilled wells. She sampled wells. But the boys around the shop competed rather harshly for those jobs, and Janet often lost out and did environmental assessments."

"Why?"

"Sexism."

"No, I mean why were some jobs more prized than others?" No one had to explain to a survivor of the oil patch what sexism did to the levelness of the great playing field we call the workplace.

"Oh. Well, the drilling jobs pay better. Bigger margin. Lower liability. The boys aren't dumb, they take the jobs that will make them look the best at the bottom line. As luck would have it, Janet happened to like doing the assessment work."

I stared at him expectantly.

Pat shook his head at me, smiling, and made the snap, snap, snap gesture again. "*Just* like Janet. And the answer lies within the question: she liked to ask questions. A natural detective."

"And what did she detect?" I asked, proud of my alter ego.

"Well, like I said, the banks don't like to make loans on contaminated properties anymore. That hesitancy has spun off a whole other line of investigations, namely reviewing past property usage to see if they're clean. Have the past owners used hazardous materials on the property, that sort of thing."

"A Phase One review?"

"That's what it's sometimes called."

"How's that done?"

"The client comes to us saying he needs a property reviewed so he could get a bank loan, and Janet would go out looking for potential contamination. Janet was in her element. She'd really dig in there, go right after the quick of the matter. She had all sorts of sources: old codgers who liked to talk, old phone books, fire insurance maps that show where the tanks were buried back in the twenties. She became something of a sleuth. She was good. Almost *too* good."

"Especially if she cared about the truth more than her job?"

"Especially."

13

When we were done eating, Pat recorked the remainder of the wine, then suggested what he termed a postprandial perambulation. "I have to walk off some of that wine," he explained. "I have more work to do tonight."

"On a Friday night? That's sinful."

"I agree."

We put on our jackets and began to stroll among the apartments and out onto the avenue. "Big workload?" I inquired.

Pat's face and shoulders sagged. "Oh, just a report. A compliance document called a Work Plan. I'm afraid it's due Monday."

That meant office work over the weekend, and another chance for me to get into HRC's offices. "Will Cynthia be running some overtime to help you get the report done?" I asked, hoping the answer would be no. I wanted as few witnesses as possible for what I had in mind.

Pat's jaws tightened. "No, she will not. This one is on me."

I wondered what was going on in Pat Ryan's professional life. Something about it was not stacking up quite right, which worried me. He was a nice guy—no, an extremely nice guy, the sort I like to befriend—but somehow not perfectly equipped for the rough and tumble of the office place. I resolved to drop by HRC the next day to see if he was there and might let me in, but I would make it worth his

while: presuming my advance money had arrived from Murbles, I
would bring Pat a nice picnic lunch.

❖

THERE WAS NO Federal Express package from Curt Murbles waiting
for me at my motel.

I checked with the woman in the office, who was sitting behind the
counter with a girl about four years old, brushing her rich coal-black
hair. I loitered for a while, watching the sensual slide of the brush
through the child's hair, wondering how it felt to love a child so, and
at the same time, what it would be like to have a mother who would
lavish such care on me.

❖

PAT RYAN DID not appear at HRC's offices Saturday morning.
"Dropping by" became a stakeout, which, after another night of poor
rest at the motel, became a fitful snooze while the overcast burned off
and the truck slowly heated up. I phoned the Sonoma County Sheriff's Office in search of Deputy Sheriff Dexter, but he was off duty and
not expected in until late afternoon. I was advised to try after six. I
couldn't think of any other lines of inquiry to follow, and after hitting
Murbles for a week's pay in advance, I didn't feel right just taking the
morning off.

At eleven I wandered into the deli, where Reena was refilling the
ketchup bottles. She smiled, asked what she could get for me. I scanned
the menu on the wall, searching for something fantastically cheap with
a lot of calories, my hands thrust deep into my pockets. I was, of
course, dreaming.

"Have some coffee," Reena said. "Here, is on the house. I need to
make a fresh pot anyway."

With gratitude, I took the proffered mug and loaded it down with
half-and-half.

"You looking for Mr. Ryan?" Reena inquired.

"Yeah, how'd you know?"

Reena smiled sadly. "Lots of people wait for him," she sighed, and went back to her chores.

◇

BY NOON, MY stomach was beginning to gnaw and rumble with hunger. At one o'clock it propelled me back to the motel in the tender hope that Murbles had marked the FedEx for a Saturday delivery. Failing all else, I figured I could heat up some water in the little coffeepot in my room and fill my stomach with that. Murbles was no longer a man's name, it was a sound my stomach made.

Murbles had, in fact, come through—sort of. There was a FedEx letter waiting for me, but the check inside was not drawn to the full amount I'd stated. Instead, he had sent half of that, with an offhanded note of explanation scrawled on "From the Desk of Curt Murbles" notepaper:

On consideration, the enclosed check will compensate you for services you will have rendered by the time this reaches you, rather than anticipatory wages.   —C.M.

To add insult to injury, the check was drawn on an account somewhere in Virginia, impossible to cash in California on a Saturday. I decided there was a special seat in hell for the Curt Murbleses of the world. It was a hard seat with a straight back, and it was real, real close to the fire.

◇

I ENDORSED MURBLES' check over to my credit card account, called the 800 number on the back of the card to get an address, and shoved it in an envelope supplied by the Wagon Trail Motel with a note indicating the urgency with which I needed it credited to my account, then drove it to the express office north of town that took shipments on Saturdays. Luckily, their system was down, so my credit card was not refused in the act of paying itself off. "Yes," the clerk assured me, "your shipment will be in Simi Valley Monday morning."

Monday noon I will again be able to feed you, I told my stomach, as I drove back toward town, *so please hang on, I'm doing what I can.*

My stomach allowed as how it couldn't wait.

Saturdays are big shopping days in neighborhood supermarkets. I drove around until I found a Lucky's store, parked the truck, picked out a shopping cart to push around so I'd look like a serious shopper, threw in a couple of boxes of Froot Loops and a package of tortillas to complete the effect, and trolled the aisles for freebies. Sure enough, I found a nice middle-aged woman who was rabidly anxious to have me sample some Polish sausage from her table near the meat counter. Heavens, I just *had* to taste three different chunks before I was sure I didn't want to buy that brand for my houseful of growing children and that husband of mine who was always saying, "Gosh, honey, why don't we have kielbasa tonight?" It was a great day: over by the dairy counter, an elderly man with a winning smile pushed Gouda cheese on me, and score of scores, there was a woman in the junk-food aisle dealing taco chips with a new bean dip. Hey, all three food groups: fat, salt, and fat.

Back at HRC, I found Pat's car parked neatly by the front door. I parked the blue truck out of sight to cover my subterfuge should Adam or Mr. Rauch drive by, and circled back to HRC. The door was locked, but Pat's face brightened when he trotted down the hallway in response to my pounding. "What ho!" he cried, as he pushed the door open. "To what do I owe the pleasure?"

"Oh, I was just passing by," I answered. "Okay, so I thought I'd come see if I could help you with your report."

"I'm not sure—"

"Come on, you fed me a fine meal last evening; the least I can do is be neighborly. Show me what I can do. It'll help me learn my way around HRC," I added, nearly gagging on the irony of my own words.

Pat's mouth opened and closed like a carp's for a moment before he seemed able to form his mouth around the English language again: "Nay, kind lady, I'm doing drudge work right now. I was just getting ready to process some words on yon computer. I can't ask you to be my secretary."

"Yes you can. I accept. I'm computer-friendly. Try me," I insisted, pushing past him and hurrying down the hall toward the one lighted office. I plunked myself into his chair, adjusted it to my height, and pulled his neat pile of lined notebook pages toward me. "Is this what you need typed?"

"Well . . ."

I turned on the computer. It *grr*ed and *beep*ed at me as it began to check its memory and boot itself up. Screens full of gibberish flew past, including one that showed me the machine was attaching itself to a local area network. I mentally licked my chops: the computer was on a LAN; what luck! With a little creative hacking, I could search all of the company's files from this one machine. The computer *beep*ed me again and the screen prompted me to type in a password. I turned to Pat expectantly, flashing him my best smile.

Pat rocked back and forth heel to toe, heel to toe, his hands in his pockets. Presently one of those lovely Pat Ryan smiles bloomed across his lips, and he said, " 'Grace.' It's my wife's name. But really, dear Emily, if you do that for me, it means I have to write the next part, which requires further thought. Thought means upper cognitive function, something on which I've run a bit low."

"Coffee usually helps me with that problem," I said, typing GRACE into the machine. It whirred and grunted and welcomed me into the secret land of HRC Environmental, Inc.

For a moment I felt exhilarated. But as I navigated through the menu of the shell program, my spirits sank. Getting past Pat had been a game, and I had played it well. Too well. I had taken advantage of a nice man to get into his company's stronghold, and by doing so I could get him into a great deal of trouble.

Self-chastened, I booted up the resident word processing program and began to type. I would at least do what I'd said I would, as if that might in some small way redeem me.

Pat leaned forward and wrote something at the top of the first page of his manuscript. "When you get to it, save the file to this file name. You may as well learn the filing system here. Everybody does his own primary typing, and everything goes in this format—see? The file name is the job number, and the extension is a kind of code for the type of document and where it is in the series. LT1 is letter one, SR2 would be summary report two."

"So this is WP for Work Plan?"

Pat grimaced. "WP2. The first version was rejected. When I'm done with the document, I'll E-mail it to Cynthia, and she'll archive it to a read-only file on her local drive." He laughed, a mirthless grunt. "Usually she does the final formatting and printing of the document, but if God is in Her heaven, this one will done before Cynthia comes in on Monday."

"Got it," I said, and began to type.

It took Pat nearly twenty minutes of fidgeting and pacing before he finally got down to writing again, and even then he was clearly having trouble. Actually, that much was clear from what I had been typing. His handwriting was small and neat, but what he had to say was a mess. Apparently he had as much trouble keeping to the point with his writing as he did with ordinary conversation.

After another fifteen minutes, Pat stood up and put his pen down with a sigh. "I'm going across to the deli and get a little pick-me-up. Can I get you anything?"

"No, thanks." I straightened up, ready for a chance to get at what I'd really come for. *Just go, Pat. Go now. Take your time. . . .*

"Sure," he said, staring disconsolately at the floor. After another few minutes of dithering, he left. And I went to work. And almost immediately hit a wall. The LAN was set up with the rudiments of security-consciousness, limiting Pat's password access to little more than his own work and final outgoing letters and reports that Cynthia had archived into read-only memory. I scanned through those, running a search command for Janet's signature line, but found relatively little. Either she hadn't written much, or she hadn't been credited for what she had written. My distaste for HRC Environmental increased.

There were a few short reports entitled *Quarterly Report of Groundwater Sampling,* with Janet's name on them. Each one was co-signed by Rauch. They appeared to be little more than a presentation of analytical data, but I printed one out and jotted down all of the addresses. I found and printed out two reports that dated back a ways entitled *Environmental Assessment,* also signed by Rauch. I wondered how Janet liked working with him. I suspected I knew.

I got back into the shell program and took a tour of all the programs Pat had access to. I found a spreadsheet, which was interesting because there were two canned user files attached to it, one for running job-cost estimates and one for figuring his time sheet.

When I booted the time sheet up, it automatically called up a current client list, coded by account number. My mouth watered a touch as I wondered how to decode that list into names and addresses, and oh, how I wanted to get at Janet's time sheet. I called up one completed time sheet at random and printed it. I was appalled at how much Pat had worked. Seventy hours in one week. He might as well have been a lawyer. There was a line at the bottom that calculated how much of that time was billable. Forty-two percent. Pat had worked that long and not even booked a forty-hour week. I had a sinking feeling that that record wouldn't be considered very high by an employer who looked on his employees as commodities.

I struck a vein in my computer mining when I found the client address records. Fat cats, alphabetical by cat. This I gleefully printed out for perusal in the privacy of my motel room.

From the client list I bounced into an interesting little scheduling program. It could move either forward or backward in time, beep you a warning of impending meetings, let you reserve equipment such as company trucks or well pumps, and send requests to co-workers for attendance at meetings or job sites. I got to fiddling with it, trying to find out if it could look backward and query what Janet had been doing during her last days on the job. This resulted in a very frustrating loop of commands which I couldn't find my way out of.

About there I heard the front door opening and Pat's muffled footfalls on the carpet. Adrenaline shot through me as I grabbed the reports and client list, frantic to hide it before Pat could see what I had done. I tried to stuff the pages under my jacket, but they immediately began to slide. As Pat's footfalls drew close to the doorway, I yanked open a drawer of his desk and tossed the pages in on top of some files. Slammed the drawer shut. Cursed under my breath at the sound that made. Berated myself for my stupidity. Freaked at the realization of how sloppy I'd gotten from hunger and lack of sleep.

"I brought you a Danish, my dear," Pat crooned, intent on extracting the gooey marvel from a very rustly bag. Perhaps he hadn't heard the drawer slam over his bag rustling. "Junk food of the gods," he said, proffering the goodie with courtly gestures and flourishes.

My nostrils picked up the scent of lemon Danish, my favorite rendition of the refined sugar/white flour/saturated fat class of gut bomb. Saliva gushed into my mouth. The flames of my gastronomic furnace leapt in anticipation of this fuel. I received it humbly into my hands, I bit, I chewed, I swallowed, I sighed.

The problem with eating refined shit like that when I'm that hungry is that I'm instantly even more ravenous. With my last ounce of self-control, I refrained from licking the inside of the bag. And found Pat staring at the computer screen. Frowning. I had left it set on the scheduling program. *Shit.*

"What's this?" he asked.

"I don't know," I squeaked. "I hit a couple oi keys by accident, and wound up in this. How do I get out?"

Pat smiled. "You hit the hot keys. An easy mistake." He leaned forward and hit Alt and the W. The screen immediately flashed back to the word processing program. But then Pat straightened up, his eyes hooded with suspicion. "The only thing is, I don't remember booting up the scheduler. So how could you have just switched into it like that?"

A sickly grin spread across my face. I said nothing.

Lowering himself into a chair, Pat stroked his jowls as he made a careful study of my eyes. "My dear Miss Hansen," he drawled, "I think it's time you told me more about yourself."

14

UNDERSTAND THIS ABOUT ME: I AM A TERRIBLE LIAR. I DON'T like to lie. What little thrill I get from even the smallest obfuscation is quickly crushed by a world of guilt. Moreover, I try to avoid lying if for no other reason than because I have trouble remembering anything other than the truth. Forgetful liars can get themselves in a great deal of trouble when they slip up and forget which lies they've told whom, and at that moment, I was so far from known territory that I couldn't remember what I'd told Pat before, or—and this was worse—what was true about me.

So I panicked.

I just sat there, staring back at Pat. Swallowing nervously. From inside my guilty little head, all that saliva rushing down my throat sounded as loud as a storm sewer.

"You were saying," Pat prompted. His eyelids had drooped to half-mast. He was *pissed*.

"I'm a friend of Janet's," I blurted. "No, that's not exactly right, either." And here I got confused, because wasn't I the best friend Janet had left in the world? Certainly her family hadn't kept very good track of her, and her roommate seemed to have written her off. "Well, I am her friend, but—well, I'm trying to find out who killed her. So yeah, I'm infiltrating your company. I was trying to find out what she was doing toward the end. Would you like me to leave?"

Pat's eyes closed the rest of the way. He let out a big lungful of air and caved slowly into himself, like an inflatable Patrick doll with a leak. "Oh, so that's all. God, I was afraid the boys had sicked you on me."

"What?"

Pat set his jaw in frustration. "Oh, you don't want to hear about it. It's my problem. Doesn't need to be yours."

"I don't understand."

Pat drew circles with his index finger on the desktop. "Let's just say I'm under a little pressure here to perform. Beyond that, I really think you'd be best advised to stay out of it. Consorting with the Company Loser can be considered impolitic."

I couldn't believe it. I'd just confessed something close to breaking and entering, and all he could focus on was whether I was on *his* case in particular. Whatever was happening to him had to be *bad*. "Can I help?" I asked lamely.

Pat drew another circle on the desktop and then folded his hands. "Sure, help *yourself*. Don't be a hero. H, R, and C don't like heroes."

"But—"

"No buts."

"I could keep on typing."

Pat gave me a wry smile. "Your kind of help, I don't need."

"Would you mind keeping it to yourself what I'm doing here?"

"Emily, my dear, I have enough trouble; I don't want to get involved." His shoulders sagged. "Well, that's not altogether true."

"Why?"

"Janet was a friend. Believe me, I'd love to take you on a big tour of this place, for what good it might do you, but the fact is, I haven't the courage. I'm not proud of that. Furthermore, I don't have the keys it would take, computer or otherwise. Besides, the bastards shredded all her notes and work files, even what she had on the computer."

"Why?"

"Paranoid bunch of bastards. Standard procedure when someone leaves."

"Her father didn't know why she left HRC. Do you?"

Pat leaned back in his chair and rubbed his eyes. "I have no idea.

Except it seemed they had some sort of falling out. Hell, they marched her to the door when she left."

I had meant, *Why did Janet decide to leave?* not *Why was she canned?* Then I wondered, *Why didn't I think before to ask Pat why Janet left HRC?* The answer clearly was, *Because I'd thought she'd left of her own accord. Why had I thought that?* I reached to the back of my memory bank, to that first conversation with the Senator. . . . Yes, he had clearly stated that Janet resigned from HRC, not that she'd been fired, or that he was uncertain which way she'd left HRC's employment. Had he been saving the family face? Or had Sheriff's Department detectives told him that? And if that was the case, then who told *them* that? "You mean she was fired?"

"I guess you could say that."

"But not exactly?"

"I expect the feelings were mutual."

"What did she tell you about it? If you were friends, didn't she confide in you? Something? Anything?"

Pat shifted uncomfortably in his chair, then shifted again, his large body wrestling for comfort in a smaller person's world. He leaned forward with his elbows on his knees and stared at the floor. "She wasn't happy here. Well, who is? But understand, Janet was a person who didn't say much about herself. Didn't offer confidences, and didn't reply to personal questions. I told you before: she mostly *asked* questions."

"Like what?"

Pat was no longer listening. He had buried his face in his hands. "I let her down."

"How?" I persisted, as gently as I could.

After a pause, Pat said, "I could see that she was into a row with the boys."

"How could you help, if they were on your case, too?"

"I mean I was sitting right here when they marched her out of here. She walked right past this door, back straight, shoulders square. God, she looked straight at me, said, 'Next time I'll take a subtler hint.'"

"What do you suppose she meant by that?"

Pat shook his head, grinding the tips of his fingers into the angle where his brows met his nose. "She just looked at me, said that, and kept right on walking out that door. Kind of 'Do your worst, I am on the side of the righteous.' I've seen men on the battlefield run straight into enemy fire with that look on their face."

"But what could you have done?"

"I could have called her. Or gone to see her. And then she was dead."

As delicately as I could, I took Pat back and forth through what he'd seen, and what had been happening at HRC before and after, try-ing different angles of questioning in the hope of jarring loose some minuscule clue that would give me another thread to follow. His mind was a shambles, a bomb site to his emotions; he didn't know what Janet had been working on, wasn't sure even from her questions what she had been thinking, and had no idea what could have made Rauch mad enough to goose-walk her out of the building. I apologized for any risk I'd put him to, apologized also for adding to his depression when he had so much work to do, and took my leave. It seemed the only decent thing to do.

Pat saw me to the door. "Where are you staying?" he asked. "If I don't make my deadline, maybe we can get drunk together."

"The Wagon Trail Motel. On Santa Rosa Avenue, bordering scenic Highway 101, where the dainty semis rock the weary traveler to sleep."

Pat nodded and shuffled back into the building, his shoulders bowed under the weight of the work that lay before him.

I thought about him as I drove back to the motel, wondering what lay ahead for him. Would he be the next victim Rauch marched down that hallway? I felt wretched at the thought that I might have hastened that moment.

The printout pages from Pat's computer lay on the seat next to me. Pat had said nothing as he watched me pull them out of his desk drawer. Maybe he didn't care anymore what anyone did to his employer, or maybe he had been too far saturated in despair to realize what I was doing.

Back at the motel, I pulled up by the door to my room and took the pages inside, whipping up a cup of coffee sludge to lighten the reading.

I've never liked reading technical papers. So before starting to read, I made a list of people I had to locate and talk to: Deputy Dexter, Suzanne Cousins, and the marvelous omnipresent Duke. Dexter would be easy to find. Suzanne might require a stakeout. Duke; hmm. It was time to turn the tables on him. I'd seen him on Highway 116 just before it rained; did that mean he lived nearby, or that he didn't mind getting wet? I could check his whereabouts with a few bicycle shop owners. Toward that end, I copied a list of shops and their addresses out of the telephone book and put the list in my pocket.

That accomplished, there was nothing left to do but read.

The environmental assessment reports were terribly boring. Dry recitations of what potentially hazardous materials were where on a property, why, when, and put there by whom. Yawn. I set them aside and pulled out the client list, leaned back against the pillows on the bed. Sipped the sludge. Yawned. Confirmed client Wilbur Karsh, Misty Creek Winery. Sipped. Yawned again, thought about taking a short nap. Thought uncharitable thoughts about Curt Murbles. Considered driving out to the ocean to watch the sun set. Kept reading. Halfway down page five, I saw a name that made me gag on my coffee: Valentine Reeves, of Reeves Construction.

Perhaps the Karsh family could convince the Sheriff's detectives that it was mere coincidence that put their dead geologist in a ditch in front of their home, but the additional presence in the same place of Valentine Reeves, a second client, made coincidence look a lot more like design. I thought of the figures I'd seen laid out in Reeves' notebook in Mrs. Karsh's kitchen, and suddenly the diagram seemed less cryptic. Surely that division of $40,000 meant that Reeves and Mrs. Karsh

were in business together. Hadn't "RConst" been set up to shunt part
of its portion to a "DK," and hadn't Reeves called Mrs. Karsh Dierdre? But what about the notations to "Bank" and "Trust"? Okay, to
do business they might need a startup loan, but that didn't explain the
"Trust" entry.

I sat up and swung my legs over the edge of the bed, grabbed the
telephone off the bedside table, and tugged the telephone directory out
of its drawer. Flipped through the yellow pages. Reeves Construction,
address on Petaluma Avenue, Sebastopol. I dialed his office number,
hoping that he might just be there on a Saturday, and got a polite
woman's voice. "I'm sorry, Mr. Reeves has stepped out for a few minutes."

"But he'll be back?"

"I think so. May I say who's called?"

"No, thanks," I answered, already standing up and straightening my
shirt. "I'll just drive on over and wait for him."

I PICKED UP Highway 12 off of 101 and hurried across the flatlands
toward the low hills to the west. As I left the Santa Rosa city limits, I
once again enjoyed a feeling of release as the road broke free of tract
housing and strip malls, giving way to pasturelands. Egrets hunted laconically in the tall grasses, suggesting that the gathering rainy season
was spawning vernal pools, and a turkey vulture glided overhead. As
Highway 12 ran parallel to Occidental Road, it dipped gradually to a
bridge that crossed over the Laguna de Santa Rosa. I looked for and
found a similar causeway leading up to the bridge, but here the Laguna
was choked with cottonwoods and gnarled oak trees, obscuring my
view of the floodplain. Abruptly past the Laguna, I found myself in
downtown Sebastopol, inching through a little late afternoon shopping
traffic. On my left lay a development of new commercial buildings built
on engineered berms to keep them above winter's floodwaters; on my
right, a refurbished railroad station turned upscale shopper haven. Two
automobile dealerships and a delicatessen later, I arrived at the traffic

light that graced the main intersection in town. As I waited for the light
to change, I perused my detailed map again, making sure which way
to turn.

Reeves Construction had its offices in a tastefully refurbished Queen
Anne–style house. I pulled the blue pickup to the curb and hurried up
the walk.

And nearly body-slammed straight into Valentine Reeves, who had
returned and was just leaving again. His thick, wavy white hair was even
more vivid by daylight, almost decadent in its lavishness. It curled just
over the collar of another blue shirt, this one a richly overdyed indigo
chambray, the sort of work shirt worn by people who don't actually
do any work. He wore tan work boots, and the kind of Levi's that come
predistressed, the knee and butt already worn pale. I revised my opinion about just how much, if ever, this man might work with his hands.

A look of patient indulgence occupied Reeves' handsome face. He
was a big man, used to other people giving way to him, and I was blocking his path. A heartbeat later, his lips spread into a flat smile. I presume he displayed his perfect teeth to me so that I could admire them,
because the cool glint in his eyes said he wasn't glad to see me. "Emily
Hansen, isn't it?"

"Yes."

"How nice to see you. You'll excuse me——"

"This won't take a minute," I insisted. "Perhaps Mrs. Karsh told you
why I was visiting here the other evening. I'm trying to talk to people who might have known Janet Pinchon. I'm thinking you did."

Reeves studied me like I was some unusual bug that had landed on
the path in front of him. Impatiently he said, "I believe I met her once.
She seemed a very earnest young woman. Does that help?"

"How did you know her?" I was deciding that I didn't like Valentine Reeves. Didn't dislike him, actually, just found him a bit . . . too
pretty, too glad to know himself.

The flesh around Reeves' eyes tensed. He took several breaths, the
little wheels under all that lovely hair squeaking on their axles. "I'd love
to help you, but I'm afraid I really am in a hurry. Where can I reach

you, Miss Hansen? I understand your mission, and it's a good one," he said condescendingly, pulling a small notebook and a mechanical pencil out of his pocket to emphasize his request of my phone number.

"I can come again," I said hurriedly. "When's good?"

Reeves' eyelids lowered ever so slightly. "Just give me your phone number."

I took a deep breath. Not only am I bad at lying, I'm hopeless as a poker player. I don't bluff well, particularly when someone is calling me on it. So I dug into my pocket and pulled out the card for the Wagon Trail Motel and with considerable misgivings read him the number.

Reeves rewarded me with his very sleekest smile. The kind of smile a mouse must see on a snake just before it strikes. My stomach tightened. Reeves watched me for a while, evaluating my reaction. Satisfied, he put one hand on my shoulder, patted it cozily, maneuvered me out of his way, and strolled comfortably out to the curb, where he climbed into his truck and drove away.

I forced myself to breathe. My mind scrambled like a lost ant, hurrying to reevaluate the man to whom I had just so unsuccessfully spoken, trying to understand why I had so thoroughly underestimated him. I had gazed upon his self-satisfied exterior and presumed him too busy with his own reflection to notice Janet, let alone wish her ill. But here he was, a man connected to her murder, and I had walked right up to him and gotten in his face like I'd thought he was a pump with a well-oiled handle. Well, he had instead pumped me, finding out just where to find me.

I heard a voice inside my head. It was screaming, *Why can't you remember to watch your back?*

15

I TRIED TO TELL MYSELF I WASN'T FRIGHTENED, THAT I WAS just a little overtired and anxious. Anxious that I didn't know what I was doing. Anxious that people knew where to find me. Anxious that if the blows fell, I wouldn't even see them coming.

I sat in the truck for a while, staring at my hands. It was four-thirty. I had another hour and a half before it was time to go to the Sheriff's Department to look for Deputy Dexter, an exercise I found only a little less frightening than facing off with Valentine Reeves.

I drove north to the town square, parked the truck, got out, sat down on a bench, and tried to collect myself. I figured no one would pick me off right there in public.

Sebastopol looked like a small-town America kind of place peopled by a lot of superannuated hippies who had settled down to raise kids late in life. The downtown area was a few blocks of spruced-up hundred-year-old shops interspersed with cupcake Queen Anne houses. The town square where I sat had a gazebo with a metal silhouette of a great blue heron stalking across its slate roof, a fond reference to the wildlife of the nearby Laguna de Santa Rosa.

My stomach was hard as a brick; the only breaths I could draw were shallow ones. I was losing my edge, and not only that, I was losing my grip on myself. Who was I? I was a geologist, going undercover as a . . . geologist. I was Em Hansen being Janet being Em; no, I was a scientist, yes, a trained, skilled person, using this training and these skills.

If police procedure wasn't working, the scientific method would. Tonight, in the safety—no, keep it straight, the privacy—of my motel room, I'd go over my notes, line out my hypotheses, quit running on intuition alone. I would make a list of suspects, and remember to consider anyone even tangentially connected with the case. Especially big men, with big hands. Like Valentine Reeves, and Pat Ryan, and—

No, that's ridiculous, I told myself. *Pat Ryan couldn't hurt a fly.*

Except he was in the service. They teach people to kill in the service.

Don't be ridiculous!

I pressed the heels of my hands into my eye sockets. Clearly I was losing my mind, going paranoid.

Work, damn it! I pulled the list of bicycle shops out of my pocket. There were candidates right there in Sebastopol, and hadn't I last seen the Duke just a few miles north of there? Hoisting myself resolutely to my feet, I shambled up to the corner and crossed Main Street, looking for a likely informant. A pack of high-school-aged kids were lounging about the sidewalk on a bench in front of a cookie shop. Most were dressed in oversized denims, dark T-shirts, voluminous winter coats that sat crooked, and heavy black shoes. Stringy hair appeared to be in. Some were smoking cigarettes, trying to look degenerate. One ripening fruit of a girl was bouncing her body against a male of equivalent age, who was in turn trying to appear uninterested, but in fact looked scared. He was trying to hold himself steady against the girl's attentions by bracing himself against a mountain bike. "Excuse me," I said, "but do you know a skinny bicyclist named Duke?"

The boy goggled at me in horror. "No. Should I?"

"Okay, then," I said, pulling the list out of my pocket, "can you tell me where to find a place called the Bicycle Factory?"

The boy's eyes widened further. The girl stopped bumping him, fixed me with a virulent stare, and began to fiddle with a small diamond stud that was pierced through her nubile nose.

I gave her a back-off-I'm-older-than-you glare and spoke again to the boy. "The Bicycle Factory?"

He bunched up his shoulders and frowned like the whole world had gone crazy and he had the misery of being the only one left sane. "Jeez, it's across the street, lady. You just came from there."

Trying not to look as stupid as I felt, I recrossed the street and passed into a turn-of-the-century brick building, where I located a salesperson and repeated my question.

"Duke? No Dukes here," he drawled.

"Oh. You know a Janet Pinchon?"

"No, should I?"

I eased jangled nerves a while in a bookstore called Copperfield's, then hit the sidewalk again and walked until I came to the post office, a smallish Greek Revival job. There was a phone booth under a winter-naked Japanese magnolia tree in front of the building, so I took another shot at reaching Suzanne Cousins. Again a machine answered, and again I left my name and phone number, imploring her to phone me back. I wondered if she was actually there and just using the answering machine to screen her calls.

Of course, the telephone kept my precious coins.

Getting back into the little blue truck, I searched out the other two bicycle shops in Sebastopol, found that one had closed and the other sold mostly kids' knobby-tire specials. I drove next to Santa Rosa, which boasted a longer list of shops, and managed to find two of them before closing time. One person knew Janet—as a customer only, good taste, lots of cash—but no one knew a skinny spandex freak named Duke. This saleswoman suggested I try a repairman named Arnie, who worked at a place called the Pedal Pusher. *Arnie* was a cool dude, like totally balls-to-the-wall. *Arnie* knew everyone. *Arnie* "left skin" on half the rocks and bushes up the single-track mountain-bike trails up in Annadel State Park. *Arnie* clearly made the saleswoman's pulse beat faster.

It was now six, time to look for Deputy Dexter. I decided to wait until six-thirty before presenting myself at the Sheriff's Department, let the man get settled in. Okay, so I was stalling. I find it kind of difficult to walk into a police station and sound coolheaded regardless of the circumstances. And I was now hungry enough that my head was beginning to feel more light than cool.

So I drove around downtown Santa Rosa awhile, dreaming that I had the nerve to walk into one of the restaurants I was passing and order a nice, big dinner, then present my burned-out credit card in payment. That way, I reasoned, I would be forced to enter the Sheriff's Department, but at least my stomach would be full.

A little red idiot light on the dash began to blink. Perfect; I was now not only starving, I was running out of gas. So what was I supposed to use to refill the tank, Murbles' check?

No, sucker, you mailed that away, and your credit card won't be any good until Monday afternoon at the earliest.

Oh, cool your jets, I have a gas credit card!

I realize it's a sick habit to argue with myself in the second person, but sometimes it supplies me with critically important information.

I pulled over at a copy center that was coming up on the right, hurried in, and asked the narrow-necked student type behind the counter where the nearest Chevron station was, which query clouded his face with overwhelming strain as he tried to think. Turning to a big woman behind him who was slapping pages rhythmically through a copy machine the size of the *Queen Mary,* he whined, "Chevron station, Milly?"

Without looking up, Milly said, "Left on E Street to College Avenue. Left again. It's just beyond your 101 overpass."

Milly was right. And after filling the tank, I discovered something wonderful: Chevron stations can also be minimarts. My blood sugar level was saved.

I ran my eyes hungrily over the tightly stocked shelves in the glass kiosk where the cashier sat, fairly licking my chops in anticipation. Humming greedily to myself, I grabbed three burritos out of the cooler and a big bag of tortilla chips off a wire rack, then added a tub of bean dip to keep with the Mexican theme. I chose smokehouse almonds for the roughage, a Slim Jim for the B vitamins, and a quart of juice-flavored fizzy water to wash it all down. And for dessert? A couple packages of Reese's Peanut Butter Cups. Thinking ahead toward breakfast, I pulled two pints of orange juice and an egg salad sandwich out of another glass-fronted cooler, added a pint of milk in the name of dietary diversity, and grabbed several packages of beef jerky for future need. I was all but chortling in my glee. Munching cheerfully on one of the Peanut Butter Cups—why not begin with dessert?—I got back in the truck and aimed it north toward the Sheriff's Department.

THE SONOMA COUNTY Sheriff's Department is located right off Highway 101 in a large compound of county buildings. Just follow the signs for the "Adult Detention Center" (and no, that big stone building with the tiny little windows is not a high school study hall, it's the county jail), and you'll find the Sheriff's offices sandwiched in between the jail and the courtrooms. I parked the truck off Ventura Avenue and tried to enter from the north, but realized I was at the sally port where the bad guys arrive in ankle irons. Circling around to the south side, I found my way into the public waiting room past the courtrooms, where an information desk fronted a catacombs of low-ceilinged, fluorescently lit bull pens. I asked for Deputy Dexter and was told to wait.

As I waited, I perused the photo portraits of Sonoma County Sheriffs Past and Present that hung as a decorative frieze around the tops of the walls of the room. They dated back to the mid-1800s. I was just making a scientific study of how many of the preponderance of Sheriffs from the first half of the twentieth century had chosen to have their portraits taken wearing hats when Sheriff's Deputy Dexter emerged.

"Bull pen" was an accurate term for the place this fellah belonged. He was big and muscular, a devotee of a gym somewhere, with a broad chest glistening with official hardware. His reddish-brown hair was trimmed in a butch cut short enough that the speckles of gray hardly showed above his ruddy, freckled face. His hands were the size of catcher's mitts. "I help you?" he asked in a sodden growl, taking me in from the top of my uncombed hair to the soles of my red roper boots.

"Deputy Dexter? I'm Em Hansen, a friend of Janet Pinchon's, the, ah, woman who was killed here in Sonoma County recently. I understand you were the officer who took care of things when she was found. I'm in town to pick up her things, and I was just, well . . . I'm trying to understand the circumstances of her death."

Dexter turned to the woman behind the information desk, rumbled, "See if you can find Detective Muller, please. Send him around to conference room B." To me he said, "Step this way, please," and led me back past the counter to a tiny little room—about six feet by eight—that held only a small table and two chairs. The room had no windows and no decorations on the walls. Conference room B, hah; I knew an interrogation room when I saw one. I ran my eyes around the room, searching for the video and audio pickups for the taping system that would be hidden behind the walls.

Dexter gestured to one chair and sat down on the other, lounging back with the ankle of one leg crossed over the knee of the other, the better to display his thick, muscular thighs.

Moments ticked by. I had time to realize that he hadn't bought my story, or at least not at face value. I sat down and tried to remember to breathe.

I made a deeper study of Deputy Dexter. His eyes were bloodshot, the lids puffy. He wore his radio mike festooned through his right epaulet, and the holster of his Sam Browne belt on the left. *Great,* I thought distractedly, *a lefty named right.*

I began to squirm in my chair.

Dexter pulled a nasal aspirator out of a breast pocket and gave himself a good snort on each side, all the time staring straight at me.

I cleared my throat. "I was saying—"

"Mrs. Karsh phoned me about you." He let the statement drop like a turd from a tall horse.

Well, that kind of made me angry. I was there to do a job, just like him, and we didn't have to get nasty about it. I felt that distinct heated sensation I always feel when I'm up against some damned kind of cowshit-chucking intimidation specialist who isn't going to give me an even break. I forced myself to take a very deep breath, and said, "Allergies?"

That froze him in midsniff. His hands stopped in midair, halfway to his pocket to put the nasal aspirator back.

"My cousin Lester had allergies," I blathered. "Man, did he suffer. You ever think of moving somewhere dry? I'm from Wyoming, and it's real dry there. I bet you'd like it there."

Dexter's head tipped slowly to one side, eyes widening with amazement or alarm, I wasn't sure which.

"Lots of fishing, hunting, hiking," I prattled on, kind of getting into it. "I ride horses myself. I get out there on horseback in that dry air and I always feel better. Athletic guy like you would like it. You should try it."

"Huh." Dexter's forehead was beginning to rumple with the strain of listening.

"So hey, I just want to ask a few questions. I'll bet Janet's dad's been all over you guys like a cheap suit. That can't have been fun. That's why the family's asked me to step in, kind of low key. You understand. All this has been a real shock for them."

Dexter put the tips of his broad fingers gingerly to the bridge of his thick nose.

On a roll, I said, "So I understand you were the one called out to the site where Janet's, uh"—here I paused and averted my eyes, laying on a little anguish for effect—"body was, ah, found. I've seen the pictures that amateur took. That looked like a lot of evidence. We're just trying to find out why this hasn't led you to a suspect yet."

Dexter began to probe an ear with one of his kielbasa fingers, perhaps to figure out where the babbling noise he was hearing was coming from. He was saved from my next salvo as a second man bustled into the room.

This one was the same vintage as Dexter, but hadn't worked as hard to keep gravity from having its way with his soft tissue. He had become quite oval: oval face, oval gut, oval feet in soft oval shoes. Bright blue eyes. Plain clothes. He smiled. I braced myself, because he had one of those very unassuming faces that can really take you for a ride if you think you've gauged the guy at first glance. "Hi, I'm Detective Muller. And you're?"

"Em Hansen."

"*M* for?"

"Em. Emily."

Dexter coughed. "Says she's a friend of the Pinchon family. Wants to talk about it."

Muller gave me one of those bright smiles that tell you absolutely nothing about his mood.

I leaned back and made a lousy attempt at looking relaxed.

Muller arranged his face in a sympathetic mask and said, "Miss Hansen, is it? There's nothing more I can tell you that we haven't told Janet's mother. It's highly regrettable, but we don't have a suspect. We've pursued all the angles, and we're going back over them all, got plenty of men on it. But so far it seems like a random killing, and they're the hardest to solve. Do you have any ideas for us?"

Muller's line did what it was probably designed to do: I felt the urge to tell him everything I knew just to comfort the poor man. But I managed to restrain myself and say only, "What did Janet's boss say?"

"You mean her former employer?" asked Muller.

"Yeah. Doesn't it seem odd that she died two days after leaving that employment?"

"Yes, Miss Hansen, we checked that out. They seemed as perplexed about it as you and I."

"But—did you ask her co-workers?"

"I assure you we are very thorough."

I was stunned. Either they hadn't asked Pat, or Pat had been afraid to tell the truth. Or had Pat fed me a line? I changed gears. "Can I get a list of what you took from Janet's room?"

Muller cocked his head like a bird examining an unusual seed. "No. Why?"

"Because—" I broke off. I'd been about to say, *Because I'm conducting a murder investigation here,* but Muller was not exactly welcoming me as a colleague. "What did Murbles tell you about me?"

"Who?"

"Curt Murbles."

"Who is Curt Murbles?"

"He's—" I closed my mouth. Detective Muller had said he had spoken to Janet's *mother*. Did that mean he had not been visited by the Senator and Murbles? If not, why not?

Muller was asking, "Where can you be reached?"

"I'm staying at a motel. It would be hard to reach me there."

Muller cheerfully pulled out a notepad and pen, prepared to write, his opaque little eyes trained on me.

I sighed. "The Wagon Trail, on Santa Rosa Avenue."

On his way out of the room, Muller said, "Thanks for coming in. Dex, you see her out?"

"Sure." Deputy Dexter shifted his weight, preparing to stand.

Desperation loosened my tongue. "What about Mrs. Karsh's son?" I said. "He looks like he has a head of steam up. And his hands are big enough."

A flare of raw irritation shot through Dexter's swollen eyes. His jaw tightened. "You mean Matthew?" he replied, his voice going oddly soft and silky. It reminded me of the tone Mrs. Karsh had used as she addressed her son from the porch outside her kitchen.

"Yes."

"Matthew is *disabled*. You are not the first to draw the *wrong* conclusion from his appearance."

"You mean, as in mentally challenged?" I said sarcastically. That seething heap of flesh had been mentally competent enough to unleash a pair of guard dogs at me.

"*Yes,* as in mentally challenged," Dexter said, his eyes narrowing. "Mrs. K has looked after him all these years, giving up more than you could imagine, just to keep him out of harm's way, away from people like you who don't understand. His father wanted to send him to a home, but no, she wouldn't send him. That's what a fine lady *she* is."

Dexter and I had locked eyes. I was afraid to look away, but just as frightened to keep staring. He leaned back in his chair and began to rock slightly, laying his thick fingers on the table and tapping it softly with the rhythm.

Muller's voice sounded from the doorway behind me. "Why do you wonder about Matthew Karsh's hands, Emily?"

I jumped up and whirled around. "I saw the photographs. Big, nasty finger marks on Janet's neck, grabbing her from behind like a coward. It looked awful." My throat tightened. I could practically feel Matt Karsh's disgusting apelike fingers closing around my neck. The sensation was so startling that I jerked backward, watching Muller watch me.

"Photographs? Which photographs?"

I froze, mouth open. Had Murbles gotten to that photographer ahead of the police? That was fast work! "Ah, that amateur photographer who was hanging around the ditch that morning."

Muller said, "Is there something more you need to tell us, Emily?"

"No! I mean, no, I don't have anything else. But Murbles does. Better yet, talk to the Senator." I was about to add, *He hired me. Ask him. He's not coming clean with you, and I'm beginning to think he knows more than he's telling you,* but I wasn't sure what I meant by that, not yet, and running off at the mouth with Sheriff's detectives is never a good idea. Instead, I just grumbled something like, "Thanks for your time."

"The Senator?" Muller echoed.

"Forget it," I whispered, and found my own way to the door.

16

Back in my room, I punched Murbles' number into the phone. It rang twice, then Murbles' irritating voice came on the line.

"This is Em Hansen. A, you didn't send the right amount; B, what the hell are you doing, hanging me out to dry with the Sheriff's detective?"

"Oh, it's *you*. Call me back at a reasonable hour. On Monday."

"No, this is a reasonable hour. *I'm* working, why aren't *you*?"

There was silence on the other end of the line. At least he hadn't hung up.

"Listen, *Mr.* Murbles. I am working for the same man you are, trying to find out who killed this man's daughter. Are you going to support me in this, or do I have to go around you?"

Murbles snorted.

"Well?"

"*Miss* Hansen, why don't you just do your job?" He laughed again, louder this time.

I didn't like this. He was having a joke, and it was clearly on me. "Isn't there something else you need to tell me about my job, Mr. Murbles?"

"Oh, no. You're doing just *fine.*" His sarcasm was thick enough to cut with a knife.

"All right, if you want to play it this way, then listen to this: you owe me for plane fare, food, lodging, and et cetera, and by the time you can FedEx a check to me, another four days' work. I'll expect those three thousand dollars by Monday eleven A.M., and it had better be a cashier's check this time."

"And where will I acquire a cashier's check at this time of night, and how will I express it on a *Sunday,* Miss Hansen?" he purred, really enjoying himself.

"Listen, Murbles, if you want to play rough, I'll call you up each night this time with a full accounting, and you can run to the bank daily. Will that make you happy?"

The line went dead.

THE BURRITO AND taco chip munchfest wasn't half as pleasant as I'd hoped. Not after my visit with Dexter and Muller. In fact, halfway through the second burrito I began to feel a little nauseated, so I took the remainder of the food out to the truck for overnight refrigeration. It wasn't very cold out, well above freezing, but much cooler than my room, which had conspired to overheat.

I leaned against the truck for a while, feeling the cool air against my face, letting it settle my stomach. I watched traffic groan by on Highway 101, wondering how much too far I'd gone with Deputy Dexter. Even though I seemed to have hit some kind of nerve, it had been reckless to dig into him about Matthew Karsh. What was my problem? Hadn't Muller said they'd been thorough? That would mean they'd interviewed everyone within sight of the ditch, and all their neighbors. Surely if there had been something to find at Mrs. Karsh's, they would have found it, wouldn't they? Or was Dexter hiding something?

I was normally content to leave police work to the Sheriff's Department, no matter how irritated I might be with them: they had the training, the personnel, and hopefully the budget to run materials through laboratories, run the routine interviews and detailed checking of leads, not I. But were they really doing those jobs?

And if so, then what was my job?

The dampness of the night air began to cleanse my mind of upset and confusion.

My job was to get inside. To follow those avenues that would only occur to someone with Janet's—and my—background and training. My job was to think like Janet, to slip the rest of the way into her boots and figure out where she had been those last days, and what she'd been doing.

I squared my shoulders and headed back into my room to get to work.

◈

A GEOLOGIST IS first and last a scientist. In simplest terms, a scientist is someone who works up a list of possible answers to a question, and then figures out which one is correct. This system used to scrutinize and test possible answers is called the scientific method.

Possible answers are called working hypotheses. By testing several working hypotheses at once, the scientist avoids spending too much time chasing the wrong one and further avoids getting entranced by a wrong answer that happens to fit most criteria of looking right. By eliminating hypotheses through scientific testing, I would eventually develop a formal theory that could be tested with a special test: in this case, a murder trial. All very neat and logical. Unemotional. Keep me out of trouble.

So first I needed hypotheses.

That meant I needed to figure out what the question was. Okay, on the face of it, the question was, *Who killed Janet Pinchon?* but each hypothesis that might answer this question needed to address subquestions, such as, *Who needed her dead? Who had the opportunity to kill her?* and so forth.

The only hard, clear evidence I had was that Janet Pinchon was dead, found in a ditch on Sanborn Road with her bicycle and wearing a bicycling outfit, which, of course, suggested that she had been out bicycling. I didn't know the official cause or time of death or the place she was killed, and was not privy to information such as fingerprints and blood samples.

In the photographs, Janet's bicycling costume was in disarray. This could mean one of several things, that she was a slob (I knew better), that she had been handled sexually by some necrophile who had happened upon her dead body (far-fetched but possible), that she had been sexually assaulted by her killer (most likely), or that her killer had taken the trouble to make it look like the killing was sexually motivated (hold on to that thought).

Circumstantial evidence was another matter. The circumstances were that Janet was a geologist who had recently been fired from her job installing and sampling wells and doing environmental assessments, that she was single, apparently a loner, and a bicycle freak.

From there it wasn't tough to come up with several working hypotheses that would explain how Janet came to be dead. I got a pad of paper and a mechanical pencil out of Janet's boxes and wrote down my hypotheses:

1. Accidentally killed by hit-and-run driver, body later shifted in position and abused.
2. Killed so she couldn't bear witness to being sexually assaulted, body dumped at separate site to mask evidence.
3. Murdered for other reason, body dumped at separate site to cover evidence.

Possibilities one and two are the police's problem because they had nothing to do with Janet's occupation, I reasoned, cheerfully delegating them the work. *But number three has possibilities for me.*

The possible motivations for killing a geologist could form a long list, all of which seemed to fit in one very obvious category: What the Geologist Knew.

Well, I didn't yet know what Janet knew. *And maybe someone just thought she knew something. . . .*

My neck started to ache in a place I had once landed when a horse changed course and I didn't. I closed my eyes and massaged it. I was getting hopelessly snarled.

Brushing aside the pages of notes, I clicked on the TV and flopped onto my belly on the bed. After ads for mouthwash, luxury automobiles, a brokerage firm, frozen dessert, and a fitness salon, a sitcom blessed the screen with inane laugh track and hypercute family hanging out in a middle-American living room. Little sister was sassing big brother.

For some reason, this made me feel worse. I rolled onto my back and stared at the sparkles in the cottage-cheese ceiling of my motel room, wondering what it was about that little sister that made my skin crawl.

I closed my eyes, opening my mind to another tool indispensible to a geologist: intuition.

17

Late in the evening the wind came up. I lay on my bed in the dark listening. It whined like an immense, irritated aunt, complaining, chattering at the window frame, searching out small objects to rattle in its angst, its timbre rising and falling as the sky filled and emptied its ghostly lungs.

At midnight I took a break from trying to sleep. I put my jacket and jeans on over my T-shirt and stepped outside. The stars had been swallowed by a heavy, dank overcast.

I inhaled deeply, smelling the air for moisture. By Wyoming standards, those clouds were boxcar-loads of moisture waiting for the tiniest shimmy to rip loose the flood. The muscles of my arms twitched restlessly. Back home I would have been helping Dad move equipment into the barn and check on the animals. I fought off a pang of loneliness. I could still do those chores, but never again with my father. Those days were gone. My mother owned the ranch now. I supposed her name had always been on the deed, along with his, but she hadn't lifted a finger in decades. What would become of the place?

I waited awhile, hoping to catch the first drops of rain on my face, but all I felt was a fine wetness. Here in California, weather seemed to lean in gradually, with no consideration for drama. No sudden onset with raindrops the size of sparrows to send you running for cover. Even the wind was muted by Wyoming standards, a nattering old woman

with cold hands next to the blue howler that would have blown hay
bales sideways and uprooted fence posts back home.

Yet the air had refreshed me some, in spite of all that worried me.
I went back inside, and for a while, I slept.

❖

THE NEXT MORNING was Sunday. At first light, I doused myself in
a shower that hit me in the elbow, dressed in a warm sweater and clean
jeans, opened the curtains, turned on the TV set to keep me company,
and dined on the orange juice and sandwich I'd bought at the Chevron
station.

The first real drops of rain broke free of the overcast at seven. They
seemed speculative and uncertain, tentatively sampling the atmosphere
to decide if they really wanted to fall through it. Convinced that this
chickenshit rain wasn't going to amount to much, I loaded myself into
the little blue pickup for another pilgrimage to The Ditch. It was too
early to visit bicycle shops, and maybe I'd catch Mrs. Karsh on her way
to church, or even Jaime Martinez.

As I drove across the Santa Rosa Plain, I wondered what it had
looked like before European settlement changed it. I supposed the
craggy oaks that studded the pastures and lined the roadway like arthritic
sentinels were native, but wouldn't they have originally formed a con-
tinuous wood? And grasses might have grown between them, although
I doubted this particular species; the revamping of species populations
in American grasslands with the advent of cattle grazing was an all-too-
standard story. Here and there I saw trees I knew to be exotics: euca-
lypts, Lombardy poplars. And the holstein cows were not native, and
neither were the sheep I passed.

The rain blurred my view of the landscape, but when I flipped on
the wipers, they only smeared the windshield. The wash button
brought no sluice of fluid. I turned off the blades, quitting while I was
behind. This rain was landing on clay soil, God's own raincoat, quick
to saturate with the rain. If ever a hard rain were to fall, it would run

off faster than it soaked in, and if those man-eating ditches didn't carry the water away fast enough, the place would surely flood. Pair up them animals and call for Noah.

About a quarter mile from my last turn, I brought my attention back to the center of the road just in time to swerve and avoid hitting an old man and woman who were marching along the edge of the ditch. He swung a cane, and she, a plastic trash-can liner. I took this all in with the flash of intense concentration that comes with the jolt of adrenaline. I squeezed the steering wheel until my knuckles turned white, forcing myself to concentrate on the here and now.

I got out of the truck. As I waited for the couple to catch up with me, I looked up at the sodden gray sky and smiled appeasingly. It chose that moment to open up and pelt my face like spit.

I jumped back into the truck. Drops greased the windshield. *Ratta-tatta-tat,* down it came, cold and icy, sucking the heat out of the air.

The older couple closed in from the east, their heads bowed and shoulders now hunched up under their ears, but their pace didn't quicken. The woman was large and cushiony, the roundness of her face exaggerated by the pointed hood of her robin's-egg-blue jacket, all pulled up tightly by the drawstring. Her mate jerked along with his teeth clenched, his eyes hooded by the brim of an old cloth fishing hat. As they passed, I rolled down the window of the truck. "Can I give you a lift?" I called.

The man hoisted a stiff arm in greeting. "No, thanks, we're dressed for it," he barked.

At that moment the woman lowered her bulk toward the ground, snatched a beer can out of the ditch, and flicked it into her plastic bag.

A woman who combed the ditch for debris? The perfect observer! "Are you sure?" I urged. "Seems right cold out."

"No, missy," the man insisted, waving a hand dismissively. "First good rain of the year. Blow itself out in a minute anyway. A celebration to walk in it."

"You live around here?" I begged.

"Got to keep moving, or the old bones stiffen up."

They hitched on by. The woman never looked up from her obsession with the contents of the ditch.

I pulled the keys, locked the truck, and hurried after them, quickly catching up to their elderly gait. "Do this every day?" I asked, as raindrops splattered me in the eyes.

"Purt' near," said the man, raising a leery eyebrow at me.

"Get many cans?"

"Why you care?"

"I'm new here," I suggested. "Sorry. Just trying to get to know folks."

The man stopped and looked around, gesturing at the surrounding landscape. "Here?" he demanded.

"Ah, no, I mean new to Santa Rosa." I smiled, admitting my foolishness.

The man laughed, not a very nice laugh. "Obviously." He peered at me suspiciously.

I let my face fall. It was not hard to look bedraggled; the rain was beginning to plaster my hair to my forehead. "Okay, I'm a friend of Janet Pinchon's, the woman who died out here two weeks ago, I—"

"That bicycle girl?" he cried, with alarm.

The woman tugged at his arm to try to get him moving. "Leave it, Fabio."

The man stood still, staring at me. "I knew her. All those questions. Always questions."

"Fabio!" his wife barked, swatting him with the bag. "The devil's business! You're raving!"

He shook his head. "Terrible thing: woman dead in a ditch."

"Fabio! Not our business!"

I struggled to hold the man's attention. "Do you walk up that road past where she was found?"

"Every day," he replied, eyes growing larger as he warmed to the topic. "Start at six, home by seven-thirty. We live just here." He pointed to a driveway a hundred yards or more away. "Walk up Occidental here to Sanborn, up Sanborn to Hall Road, say our hello to Mrs. Johnston."

"Fabio! Sucker for a woman," the woman nattered. She was running out of steam. I had won.

"Mrs. Johnston's getting old," Fabio continued, warming to his narrative. "Kind of cheers her up, having a visitor."

"I'm sure," I soothed, trying not to stiffen as the rain began to soak through the seams of Janet's down parka. "Then where do you go on your walk?"

"Oh, back here along Occidental until it gets to be seven, then back home."

"And you didn't see her body in the ditch? Were you walking on the other side of the road?"

His eyes went vague. "It wasn't there."

"You're sure you walked past the place where she was found?"

"I'm not senile! It was not there when we walked *up* Sanborn Road. It *was* there when we walked *home.*" His eyes filled with suspicion again. "Why you so interested?"

"Fabio . . ." His wife's bag began swinging with increasing menace, describing a larger and larger arc, colliding with the raindrops. They coalesced and skidded down the plastic, drawing paths as long as tears.

So Janet's body had not been in the ditch when Jaime came to work; it was dumped only moments before Mrs. Karsh phoned 911. "Did you tell this to the police?" I urged.

The plastic bag slammed into the old man's side. "Now you done it, Fabio! You always got to get involved!"

"*Basta rompere i miei colcoglioni!*" he bleated. "Holy Mother, woman! You and your secrets! This girl's a *friend* of hers!" He spat, a well-practiced gesture aimed at the space between his feet and hers. "I think *this* of your secrets!" Having settled this argument to his satisfaction, he turned to me and intoned, "We don't talk to no police," underlined it with a firm slash of his hand, left to right, murmured, "Excuse me," turned, grabbed his wife's arm, and continued down the road, chewing at her in Italian.

I stopped. There was no point in following. The rain seemed to be stopping, too, so I returned to the truck and leaned on it, trying to conjure my next move. Either Jaime himself had dumped Janet's body and come back to report the job done, or someone else had just left it there, barely missing being seen. A mysterious X. Which I didn't buy.

I got back into the truck and continued on to Sanborn Road. There were no cars parked by Mrs. Karsh's weathered house, and no battered yellow truck.

I proceeded down the road a bit and parked on the left. Taking binoculars in hand, I got out of the truck and looked out across the floodplain of the Laguna de Santa Rosa, assuming my bird-watcher pose. The Laguna was a narrow, sleepy stream that wandered dreamily through a belt of willows and oaks. The trees that formed the riparian belt were dotted with songbirds, and the nearby grasses sprouted the white heads of cattle egrets.

I stepped up to the barbed wire fence that paralleled the road, popped the top and middle strands a bit farther apart, bent forward from my right hip, and swung myself through. I've climbed through fences that way so many times in my life that I barely broke stride. From the fence I wandered down to the stream, pulling a strand of grass to chew. The grass was greener there, and much richer. Cattle grazed laconically along the stream bank, and some lay peacefully chewing their cuds in the rain-dampened grass. A great blue heron fished in the shallow waters. A flock of blackbirds rose and fell through the air with the careening whims of their leader, then abruptly coalesced along the power lines that followed the road. I raised the binoculars to my eyes and focused on the wires. Yellow eyes; Brewer's blackbirds. Beautiful, glossy black feathers. I watched the egrets for a while, then a great blue heron that stood motionless in the slowly flowing waters.

I shook my head, thinking sadly of the article in the Sebastopol *Times & News:* somewhere along the Laguna, developers hoped to build new housing. Right here in the wetlands, nature's great filter, which catches the polluted runoff from the land and cleans it through ion-rich clays before releasing the waters to the oceans. But while farmers prefer wetlands for their flat, moist soils, developers lust after them as inexpensive land on which to build town homes and factories, shopping malls and business parks. Before the human race got so good at multiplying its numbers, the damage to the balance of nature wasn't critical. But now human populations increase geometrically, and with them, their effluent load, full of brand-new man-made toxins. They are increasing faster than we can invent the filters to catch them, at the same time that we are destroying the wetland filters nature built, draining them and paving them, rationalizing that we can do without this one, or that we won't miss a few or even most.

I thought of Janet, riding her bicycle out along the Laguna, admiring what Mother Nature had done right. Had she seen a threat to what she held dear?

West of the Laguna, the ground rose steeply into the wooded hills studded with orchards, vineyards, and the occasional farmhouse. I trained the binoculars on them. The drier ground above was full of sheep and a few goats. A small, square farmhouse stood in the middle of that range, near a large, aging barn. A band of children were chasing the goats, one medium-sized boy joyously wielding a stick.

I swung the binoculars back to the farmhouse. A short, dark man was climbing into a familiar-looking battered yellow pickup. Yes, it was the man who had fetched Matthew Karsh back from the gatepost the first time I visited the neighborhood. Jaime, the hired hand. Was this where he lived? And these his children?

I hurried back to my truck, climbed into the seat, and pulled the detailed map I'd copied at the library out of the door of the blue truck and took a good squint. The road Jaime was driving down was called Ferris Road. Why was that name familiar?

I dug through my notes, found the photocopies I'd made of the Sebastopol *Times & News*. Sure enough, there it was, on the weekly "County Sheriff's Log" for the date Janet's body had been found:

**Miwok Mills: Jaime Potrero Martinez, 43, 10225 Ferris Rd.,
was arrested for public drunkenness. He was released the
next day on a citation to appear in court.**

I had no idea what connection this incident might have to the death
of Janet Pinchon, but I didn't believe in coincidences when murder
was involved. Had Jaime Martinez dumped Janet's body and then
spent the day at the bar in Miwok Mills drowning his fear and guilt?
Or had he killed Janet himself? No, he was a petite man, his hands too
small to have left those marks.

I was just trying to decide whether it would be safe to pay a call on
Jaime Potrero Martinez at his home when I heard a vehicle approaching. I glanced up into the rearview mirror. It was a battered yellow
truck, pulling up behind me.

Jaime Potrero Martinez had come to me.

18

I STAYED IN MY TRUCK, FIGURING THAT IF JAIME WAS GOING to try something hostile, I was safer sitting at the controls of twenty-five hundred pounds of steel than challenging him on foot. He stayed where he was. He was short enough that all I could see over the dashboard of his truck was the upper half of his dark, ruddy face topped by a green and white cap that advertised pizza. Even with such a limited view of him, I had no trouble identifying him as the man I had seen bullying Matthew Karsh into that same yellow truck; those hard, coal-black eyes and black, angry brows were unmistakable.

Through those eyes he'd seen me from across the Laguna and had hurried over here to confront me. Why? His eyes burned with the same fierceness I'd seen him use on Matthew Karsh, but now they held something else, too; I could see the whites nearly all the way around the pupils. That looked to me like fear, but not ordinary fear; he seemed less afraid *of* me than of something *about* me.

I waited. He stayed in his truck. What was frightening him? Was he one more person who mistook me for Janet? Did he believe in ghosts?

Hell, it was broad daylight, or as bright as it was going to get, and this was a public place; how dangerous could it be to get out of my truck and talk to him? If he steered his truck toward me, I reasoned, I could always vault the fence.

So I climbed out and walked back to his driver's-side window. Not too quickly. Hands in pockets, kind of casual. Still chewing on that stalk of grass. As I moved closer, his eyes narrowed, and he seemed less frightened and more enraged, so I stopped about ten feet away. *"Buenos días,"* I said. "I help you?"

He nodded his head, one quick, sharp motion, driven by force of habit and ingrained manners, but frowned, his eyes still bugging. *"Buenos,"* he replied. "You trespassing." He stared defiantly at the ground, nostrils flaring.

Oh, how I do hate to be told to bugger off. Such gracelessness, such utter lack of hospitality, really truly gets under my skin. I moved closer. "This is a public roadway, *verdad?"*

"Before!" he insisted, pointing over the fence at the pasture. "I seen you from my house."

"Ah. When I was watching the birds. Lovely, aren't they?"

Jaime clenched the steering wheel. "This is *private* land. You keep *off."*

Just what the hell did I think I was doing taunting him? What *was* getting into me? I reminded myself I should not take this man lightly, reminded myself also that I was afraid of Matthew Karsh, and that Matthew Karsh was afraid of this man. I used this thought like a nail, jabbing myself with it to make myself pay attention, not be foolish. "You're Jaime Martinez," I said, as evenly as I could. "I've been wanting to talk to you."

Jaime's jaw muscles bunched.

"I understand you were the man who found Janet Pinchon's body. She was a friend of mine, and—"

Jaime rolled up his window fast, his mouth working furiously in a streak of Spanish curses, ground the battered yellow truck into reverse, and punched the gas.

"Hey!" I slammed the window with the heel of my hand, ripping the flesh on a bit of bent trim as the truck accelerated away from me.

The yellow truck backed wildly for twenty yards, careened into a gate access, crashed into first, and charged away.

I stood squeezing my hand, trying to stop the bleeding.

Down along the Laguna de Santa Rosa, the cows still chewed their cuds, the egrets and the heron kept on hunting, and once again, it began to rain.

19

CHEVRON STATIONS DON'T SELL FIRST AID KITS ALONG WITH the junk food. I returned to the Wagon Trail Motel and prevailed upon the manager to bandage me up. She arched one handsome black eyebrow as she expertly bound my wound with homemade butterfly bandages and gauze. Her doe-eyed daughter watched with amazement and her infant son slept peacefully in his bassinet, oblivious to my foolishness. Now the girl tugged at her mother's elbow. The woman whispered something to her in Spanish. The child looked at me with alarm and withdrew halfway inside the inner door.

"Your Elyria Kretzmer phoned while you were out," the manager announced, as she cranked an extra wrap of adhesive tape around my wrist. She gave it a tug, to let me know what she thought of women who go around cutting their hands, and while she was at it, she gave a good stare at my lacerated knee.

"Ouch. Thanks."

"She wants you to call her."

"Yeah, I'll get to it."

The eyebrow arched again. "She said she was worried about you. Now I am, too."

"I just caught it on a fence," I lied. Embarrassment is the one thing that can make a truly talented liar out of me. "Thanks for your help. I'll go to my room now and be good."

"She left her number."

"I have it," I snapped, as I hurried out the door.

I did go to my room. I went there and paced for a good ten minutes, cradling my aching hand. Every fifth or sixth time I turned, I would glance at myself in the mirror, trying to figure out what a Mexican campesino had seen in me that would both enrage and spook him. So I looked like a dead woman; was that a sin? I had been thinking of Jaime as a lackey, a hired hand, but what I had just learned of him suggested that his involvement went far beyond that. Had Janet once stood along that stream bank and stared?

I looked around the room, staring into Janet's boxes for an answer. "What scared him, Janet?" I whispered. "Did he threaten you, too? What's so important about a few acres of bottomland that he has to run me off?"

The boxes didn't answer.

My hand began to throb. Finally I sat down to write my thoughts out on paper, so they'd quit fluttering around I stared at the pad for a while, then gingerly picked up my pencil. I couldn't put any weight on the heel of my hand, but I managed to write legibly. I made myself a list of questions:

Did detective question P. Ryan?

Who and where is Duke?

What isn't Suzanne Cousins telling me?

Who profits by that division of $40,000 in Valentine Reeves' notebook?

Why was Janet fired?

Where was Murbles at the time of the murder?

Then I took up the telephone and phoned Pat Ryan, finding him at his desk at HRC.

"Ryan," he answered, in a dull moan. I could hear his fingers tapping at the keys of the computer. Click-click. Click. He sniffed, clearing congestion from his voice. Had he been up all night?

"It's Em. I had another question, if you can stand it."

"Sure." He sounded like he was speaking, if not from the grave, then at least from its lip.

"Did the Sheriff's Department ever question you or anyone else at HRC about Janet, like right after she died?"

"I wouldn't know. I wasn't here." Click, click, click.

"You weren't?"

"No, I was on a job out of town."

"But you were there when she was fired. What day of the week was that?"

"It was a Monday. An odd day to fire someone, don't you think?"

"Odd? Why?"

"Oh, you know; they usually fire people on a Friday."

"Who does? Why?"

"They always do it that way, every place I've worked. That way, the other boys and girls have the weekend to cool off. Limits the gossip and breast-beating."

"I see. So you were on a job out of town?"

"No, well, you see, it wasn't really a job. That Hollingsworth."

"That Hollingsworth, what?"

"It was a glorified errand. Adam Horowitz could have done it. I tell you, these guys—"

"Wait, slow down. When did Hollingsworth send you out of town?"

"Oh, half an hour after Janet left."

"And you were gone how long?"

"Well, it was supposed to be two days, but when I called in, he had another errand, and that one put me near Fresno, so he said why didn't I just take some comp time and see my wife for a week?"

"Didn't that seem odd to you?"

"Well, frankly, yes, because I knew this Work Plan I'm doing was pending. It's on a short fuse, tight deadline. Any day we were supposed to get the comments on the first draft, and I was supposed to respond to them. But I didn't complain; I've logged an extra ten to thirty hours a week for these guys since the day I started working here two years ago, and I haven't been able to take more than a few days off."

No wonder Pat Ryan looked like the walking dead. "So you just got back this last week?"

"Right."

"Did they tell you about Janet's murder when you called in?"

"No. Or the Turks didn't, but Jaki did."

"Who's Jaki?"

"Jaki was the secretary before Cynthia. She phoned me down in Fresno to tell me. Real heads-up kind of babe."

"Well, that opens another question. Why and when did Jaki leave?"

"She said she didn't like working here anymore. She left the week Janet was, ah . . . was killed. Cynthia is a temp. They probably ought to be interviewing for someone else, but I don't suppose they have to pay a lot for Cynthia, so they'll probably string her along awhile. Or until she makes a big enough mistake they decide to execute her," he said bitterly.

"Can you give me a home phone number for this Jaki?"

Pat told me to hold on for a moment. Then gave me a number in Rohnert Park, a town he said was south of Santa Rosa. I wrote it down on the pad of paper, adding Jaki to my list of questions. "Jaki's a nice kid," he said. "Be gentle."

"I will. One more question: who's Valentine Reeves, and what's he got to hide?"

"Got me."

"You don't know him?"

"No, sorry. Should I?"

"He's an HRC client. He runs a construction company."

"That would have been Janet's territory."

"Why?"

"Because it's construction people who get environmental assessments done. They need a clean assessment, remember, in order to buy land to build on, or to get a construction loan."

I pondered that for a moment. Then inspiration struck. "Can you dig a site address out of the computer where a job was done for Reeves?"

"Spell the name." I did. I heard Pat clicking away at his computer. "Here it is. Or wait, we've done several for him. Yes, he's a big customer, it looks like. Let me read them to you."

I scribbled as fast as I could, given the pain in my hand, but I might as well have saved myself writing down the first three. Number four was getting to be a familiar address: 10225 Ferris Road. The home of Jaime Potrero Martinez.

✧

JAKI WAS IN and willing to talk to me. When I pulled up in front of her cracker-box little town home, she was sitting out front on a concrete step, pulling a weed from the minuscule flower bed next to it. She was petite and had short, dark hair cut in a butchy ruff that was longer down the back of the neck than on top of her head. She had on purple lipstick and wore big purple trousers and a black vest encrusted with antique buttons. Her eyes were dark and limpid, yet lively, like a cocker spaniel on uppers. Politely not commenting on my bandaged hand as she sized me up, she shook my left hand with hers and motioned for me to step inside her abode, which featured a tall, spindly fir tree decked out with popcorn strands, lights in the shapes of hot chiles, and slick photographs of male bodybuilders that had been cut out from a calendar and hung up with ribbons through holes punched in the middle of their self-admiring heads. Jaki stretched her purple lips with pride as I admired her efforts at Christmas decor and said, "Pat Ryan just called, said you were okay to talk to, but to watch my back. What's up? And what happened to your hand?"

Candor seemed the best policy with anyone who wore purple lipstick. "I caught it on a truck door. And I'm trying to learn what I can about Janet Pinchon's murder. I've gone undercover, taking her job at HRC. I'm crosswise with Rauch, Adam Horowitz, at least one client, and the Sonoma County Sheriff's Department. But I was hoping you could help."

Jaki grinned. "My kind of woman. I liked Janet. Who gets along with Rauch anyway? And Adam Horowitz—well, pissing him off just means you're breathing. Yeah, if you can leave me out of your fight with the Sheriff, I'll help. If I can." She showed me to a futon couch and curled up at one end of it, pulling a box of fat-free cookies out from under a cushion and leaving it communally open on the coffee table.

I sat down and greedily snatched a cookie. A long-haired cat with fish breath briskly claimed my lap. I munched. The cat purred.

"That's Brutess. She has good taste in humanoids," Jaki informed me. "So speak: how can I help you bust Janet's murderer?"

"First, why did you leave HRC? Did that have anything to do with Janet?"

"No, the Janet thing just tore it. I got a better job. That's code for 'I couldn't stand the sons of bitches a minute longer.' "

"Can you expand on that?"

"For hours."

"Okay, can you think of anything that would pertain to Janet's relationship with the company?"

"Well, she was a pretty honest babe. Into doing good and all that. I'm sure it rubbed her the wrong way to work for those slimeballs. But beyond that, she was kind of quiet, you know?"

"That's what everyone keeps telling me. Okay, were you there the day she left the company?"

"Yeah, but it was lunchtime. I was gone. Let's see . . . come to think of it, I'll bet no one but Rauch and Hollingsworth were there when it happened. When I came back from lunch Hollingsworth tells me she's gone and I'm supposed to pull her time sheet off her computer so he could advise payroll to make out her last check."

"Did she keep her time sheet that current?" I knew Janet was tidy, but that was anal-retentive.

"Yeah. We were supposed to update them the end of every day directly into the computer. Hollingsworth and Rauch would go over them and E-mail them over to the company that did payroll."

"No paper copies?"

"Nope. We'd E-mail them to H and R directly from our individual computers."

"But doesn't that make it a little easy for someone like H or R to kite the numbers?"

"Yup." Jaki popped her eyes and smiled in a "happy clown" face and nodded. "You're getting it, ain't ya?"

"This is part of why you left?"

"You got it."

"I copied one of Pat Ryan's sheets off his computer."

"So have I."

Jaki took me to her home computer and got it running. As she booted her programs, she said, "This is for your information only. I kept this backup tape from the payroll company's system just in case anyone at HRC got rough with me." She glanced at the date and fiddled with some keys. "There." She pointed at the screen. "I'll pick a week at random. On the payroll, Pat shows sixty-two billable hours. You can see here on the time sheet Pat actually filled out that he reported less than thirty. Of course, Pat's on salary, which means he gets paid for a standard week regardless of all the overtime he logs."

"Wow."

"No shit, Sherlock."

"Did they kite Janet's hours?"

"What do you think?"

"You have a record of that, too?"

Jaki moved back to the futon couch. "Sure, I used to copy everyone's time sheets off the computer every Friday. Aside from losing them clients if the chumps ever found out, it's against federal law to defraud people through the mails, and the clients are billed guess how."

Like Pat had said, Jaki was a heads-up kind of babe.

"Did Janet know about this?"

"Well, we all suspected it. . . ."

"But you did not confirm her suspicions."

Jaki's eyes dimmed for the first time. "Janet and I didn't talk that much about things."

Which meant, I supposed, that Jaki had wanted to keep her job until she was ready to leave it. "Okay, let's go back to the day you came back from lunch and Janet was a newly ex-employee. Did Hollingsworth seem angry?"

"Naw, but butter wouldn't melt, you know? Now, Rauch, he had a head of steam up. He told me to crack into her computer so he could delete all her files. Then he had me clean her desk out and bring everything into his office that didn't look like a paper clip or a rubber band. I heard him running the shredder after that."

"So you had everybody's computer passwords?"

"Yeah." She raised a skinny arm and made a muscle. "Power!"

"Did you tell the Sheriff's detective about all this?"

Jaki's rather pale skin turned paler against the purple lipstick. "Well . . ."

"You held some of it back?" I didn't mean it to sound accusatory, but it did.

"Look, all that was nothing unusual. Really. Rauch is always going off half-cocked at people, and with what he's up to, he's so damned paranoid he shreds his own toilet paper when he's done with it, you know? I mean, it was weird that Janet was killed and all, but I didn't think it had anything to do with HRC. Did it?"

It was time to be a little less gentle. "Maybe. Why didn't you tell the Sheriff's detective? The real reason."

Jaki cringed. "I got a record."

"Dope?"

"Yeah. It was a long time ago, but I really got to watch it. I figure anyone coming from money, like Janet, they can figure out who killed her without *my* help, what little *I* know. See? They hired you, didn't they?"

"So why talk to me, if you won't talk to the Sheriff?"

"I break into a rash when I'm around cops! You ever had a cavity search? Well, and Pat told me you were okay, and . . . okay, it's been a while, right? I figured they'd get it cracked right away, but they haven't. So someone's still out there creeping around, maybe gonna nail someone else, for all I know." Jaki sat up straight. Her eyes took on a gleeful, almost avid light. "And maybe it is Rauch or Hollingsworth, what then? Am I supposed to let *that* go? Uh-uh. See, I can talk to you, and maybe you'll tell the cops you just found the information lying in the street." She slumped back and looked at me out of the corner of her eye. "But you won't tell them about me. Right?"

I sighed. "Agreed. If I need the stuff about the time sheets, we'll figure something out."

Jaki relaxed back against the arm of the futon couch. The fickle cat stood up and stretched, ambled over to Jaki's lap, tested it for tenderness, and flopped down again. Jaki scrubbed her fingers into the ruff around its neck and murmured, "We's gonna chase bad guys together, Brutess. Ain't we? Huh?" To me she said, "So: what else?"

"You know a client named Valentine Reeves?"

"Val? Sure, known him all my life. Pretty good guy."

I cocked an eyebrow in surprise. "You like him?"

Jaki shrugged. "Why not? What's there not to like?"

"Well . . ."

"You mean because he's a bloodsucking capitalist pig land developer?"

"Something like that."

"Yeah, he makes a buck, but he's pretty socially responsible about it. Mostly he's into building housing for low-income people."

"But still, it's how he makes his living."

"I didn't say he was doing it for his health."

"What kind of job was HRC doing at the Martinez place for Reeves Construction? An assessment?"

Jaki looked blank. "What's the address?"

"It's 10225 Ferris Road. Just east of Miwok Mills."

"Oooh. Yeah, Jaime lives there, but he doesn't own it. That's the old Ferris place."

"Ferris? Like the road?"

"Yeah, I haven't lived here in Rodent Park Town House City all my life; I grew up in Miwok Mills. Oh, yeah, old man Ferris owned a guzillion acres along the Laguna. An apple-packing plant, too. It's a winery now."

God bless the prurient mind and long memory of the small-town gossip. "Misty Creek Winery?"

"Yeah."

"That fits, I suppose. Martinez works for Mrs. Karsh. Janet's body was found in the ditch along her property."

"That was where she was found? I didn't know that. Well, the whole family was weird. Was it in the paper? I'm sure the detectives didn't say anything about that."

"Why weird?" I asked, pulling my legs up under me and getting comfortable. "Tell me about Matthew."

Jaki grinned, getting into this new line of gossip. "Oh, yeah. Matty's pretty wacko, isn't he? He went to school with my oldest brother."

"He went to school?"

"Sure, for a while, anyway. He may be crazy, but he isn't stupid."

"Has he always been like that?"

"Well, sort of. In a small town like the Mills, everyone has a theory about a guy like Matt. Lots of people think it was because he got slammed too hard on the playground once, way, *way* back. He wasn't more than five or six. This other kid kind of conked Matty's head against some concrete at the bottom of the slide. Matty's never been the same. Then again, he never was real great before."

"Explain. Before, after."

Jaki shrugged her shoulders. "Well, I didn't know him before—I wasn't born yet—but my older sister said he was always quiet, always stuck to his mommy like glue. Kind of broody. Got scared by things other kids didn't get scared of. I always wondered if they didn't just blame things on the accident so they wouldn't have to admit that he was just plain weird. But they say that after the accident his temper got a whole lot worse, and he was in school then, too, and even though he was smart in some ways, he couldn't keep up. They kept him back in school once or twice, and he got to where he was bigger and bigger than the kids around him, and somewhere in high school he just quit showing up."

"Was he violent?"

Jaki thought. "It was weird: The kids would taunt him and throw apples at him because he was so big, but he'd just freeze, go all blank-eyed. Then afterward he'd get real frustrated and bellow at his sister, even take a swing at her. He's a sad case."

"Sad? You don't find him frightening?"

Jaki frowned. "Well . . . no. Of course, I haven't seen him in years and years, but all I remember is this big, pathetic kid."

"I see," I said, although I didn't. "He has a sister?"

"Yeah, somewhere. She took off with this older man in the middle of high school. It was a real scandal."

I thought, *I'd have run off, too,* at the same time feeling guilty for harboring such resentment against a damaged, demented child. Matthew Karsh was a conundrum to me, someone I instinctively feared yet begrudgingly felt sorry for. Part of me certainly wanted to prove him a killer, especially after that scene in the apple-pressing house. I tried to clear my mind of my own prejudices. He was frightening to look at, and certainly capable of some pretty scary mischief, but was he a killer? Maybe his bluster was just a front he put up to cover his own fears. Yet I found myself saying, "I had an older brother once, and he was pretty rough on me."

Jaki's bright little eyes focused sharply on me. She didn't say anything.

Embarrassed at letting my personal stuff work its way into the conversation, I asked, "How old would Matthew be?"

"He'd be forty, I guess; same age as *my* brother. Yeah, that's about right."

"And his sister, was she older or younger?"

"Younger, by two years. Her name was Sonja." Jaki reached for a cookie. "People always say how sad it was, like she was real charming and smart, so why did she have to leave and Matty stay; that kind of stuff. Then I've heard the old birds say she was a little hussy, like she had her daddy wrapped around her little finger and all the other men and boys swooning, but you know how people talk."

"Ah. Mr. Karsh. What happened to him?"

"What do you mean?"

"Well, it doesn't look like he lives in that house."

"Oh, no, he hasn't lived there for who knows how long. He's got a cookie. He lives with her."

I pondered this bit of information. If Mrs. Karsh had been left for another woman, and worse yet, had been left caring for a brain-damaged, tempestuous son, perhaps that explained her apathy toward her surroundings. The woman must be bitterly depressed. "So they're divorced?"

"No, like I said, he lives with his cookie. That's my mother's term for mistress. That means Mr. K is still married to Mrs. K, otherwise you'd call his cookie his significant other."

"Why?"

"That's just what they call it."

"No, I mean why didn't they get divorced?"

Jaki shrugged her shoulders. "I dunno. Catholic? But it's all still one big weird happy family. He runs the family business."

"So Mrs. K doesn't work?"

"No, she stays home, always has. She's kind of a dinosaur, like she remembers when she was a girl and her family had money. At least, that's what my mom says. She only comes out to do the marketing, on Friday afternoons. I know that because I used to check at the Lucky in Sebastopol before I went to secretarial school."

Friday afternoons. Yes, that fit, and I knew just who baby-sat for Matthew while she was shopping.

Jaki chattered on. "Once a month she goes to the ladies' auxiliary meeting over at the grange hall in Miwok Mills. My ma sees her there. She calls her the grandee."

"Why's that?"

"Never gives anyone the time of day."

"She seemed pretty nice when I dropped in on her. Gave me tea and cookies."

"Wild. You're probably the only visitor she had this year, unless she talks to the meter reader. Oh, and once a year she cooks sauce for the fire department's Christmas Spaghetti Feed. That's tonight. You going?"

"It's an idea," I murmured, not wanting to admit my own fall from financial liquidity. And I had bigger things on my mind than spaghetti feeds. Seemingly miscellaneous pieces of the puzzle were falling together: Dierdre Karsh proudly frozen in a loveless marriage, grieving a runaway daughter, living on a decaying farmstead with a deranged or perhaps just damaged son, while her estranged husband sought his comfort with another woman. Perhaps he gave her only enough money to live on; not enough to paint the kitchen or buy fresh curtains.

But what was the connection with Valentine Reeves? Wait, Jaime Martinez worked for Mrs. Karsh, and Reeves was getting an environmental assessment done on the place where Jaime lived. "Was it an environmental assessment that was being done on the old Ferris place? You know, where this guy Jaime Martinez lives?"

Jaki furrowed her brow. "I don't know. I'm sure I finalized the contract and all that, but God, there were so many of those. The addresses stick with me better than the work, because that's how I thought about them. Well, it probably was an environmental assessment, because that's mostly what we did for Reeves Construction."

I fell silent, trying to think of anything else I could ask Jaki. That was always the problem in this kind of an investigation: trying to figure out what the questions were so I could get the right answers. On a whim, I asked, "Do you know of a bicycle guy named Duke?"

"No. Should I?"

I shook my head. "I'm just trying to connect the dots. How about Janet's roommate, Suzanne Cousins?"

"Suzanne. Sure."

"You do?"

Jaki slapped her knee, scaring the cat. "Grew up together. You think this county's a big town, don't you? Well, uh-uh. It only grew this big in the last ten, fifteen years. And let me tell you, sister, if you grew up in Miwok Mills, you knew *everybody.*"

"Well then, was it you that connected Janet with Suzanne? Suzanne said she didn't really know Janet."

Jaki looked at me like I'd just sprouted feathers. "Huh? Naw, they lived together at least two years, and I don't know how you can do that without getting to know someone pretty darned well. And no, I didn't introduce them; they knew each other through that women's drumming circle that meets out in the Mills. Shit, yeah: Janet and Suzanne were *tight.*"

As I drove back up Highway 101 toward Santa Rosa, I vowed that I would never, ever again believe a word any of these people told me. I would assume they were all lying until I could prove otherwise. Except maybe Pat Ryan and Jaki. Or were they simply the best bullshitters of the lot? I was going to find Suzanne Cousins, and she was going to talk to me, drum and all. She could tap it out in Morse code on a tom-tom, for all I cared; I needed information, and I needed it now.

Suzanne's car was parked in front of her place, and I thought I saw a brief movement near a window as I was approaching the door, but on knocking, I got no reply. I peered in every window, staring past prisms and candles clear to the back wall of each room, but no Suzanne. I did spot a book left open on the couch and a still-steaming cup of tea on the table by the candles and whale vertebra. Either she had just gone out the back door for a brisk walk to the convenience store, or the sly she-dog was in there somewhere, lurking out of view.

I wrote my name and phone number and "Please call me, it's important if we're going to know who killed Janet" on a piece of notebook paper, jammed it in the doorframe, and left. Hardly knew Janet indeed.

Still fuming, I descended on the next few bicycle shops on my list, finishing up at the Pedal Pusher on Cleveland Avenue. The place was packed; everyone was buying bicycles for their kids for Christmas, and it took quite a while before I could find someone who could talk to me. As I waited, I stared into glass cases at lovingly displayed bits of bicycle paraphernalia, gimcracks and gewgaws that fit on handlebars or clamped to this or that tube to make the bike work better or look prettier or whatever. I tried on several ultralightweight helmets, and hoisted a couple of thousand-dollar bicycles to see what that kind of money could buy.

By and by, a very tall, athletically slender man wearing a tight black jersey and bicycling shorts strolled up to me. His eyes were shiny black and intelligent. His socks and athletic shoes were black, too, and his skin was dark as coffee. A fabulous headful of dreadlocks hung almost to his shoulders. He exuded a healthful, soul-deep beauty, an athletic angel done in shades of shadow. In a low, warm voice he asked if he could help me.

"I hope so. Are you Arnie?"

"The same."

"A woman at another bike shop said you know everyone in the business. She also said you left skin on rocks and trees," I added, taking in his taut, linear musculature, "but you look pretty complete to me."

Arnie nodded demurely. "A figure of speech. The lady's suggesting that I ride with a certain *je ne sais quoi*. So. Are you looking for someone?" His eyes glinted with restrained curiosity.

"Well, a guy named Duke, who looks nothing like you."

Arnie thought, shook his head. "Can't help you."

"Well, I'm also trying to learn what I can about a woman named Janet Pinchon, who loved bicycles. She owned a rather expensive one."

"A Merlin."

"Yes. You knew her?"

He nodded gravely. "And the bike."

"Duke said he helped build it."

Arnie rolled his eyes in sudden recognition. "A rather slender young man with, shall we say, afflicted skin?"

I sighed. "Arnie, if I had any money in my pockets, I'd offer you an early lunch, but I'm broke. I really need to talk to you. I haven't been able to find anyone who'll admit to knowing much at all about Janet, and it's very important that I do."

Arnie's eyes closed for a moment, as if in prayer. Then he turned toward the back of the shop, motioning for me to follow. He led me past the repair counter, past several bicycles pinioned in repair racks, and back into a storage room. There he reached up to the wall and took down an eight-by-ten color photograph in a cheap frame. It was a picture of five people in gaudy spandex standing with their bicycles held jauntily between their legs, all grinning in the glory of brilliant sunshine. Arnie was second from left. Janet was far right. It was a tender thing to see her alive and smiling.

Arnie spoke. "The fellow you called Duke took the picture. He's a funny kid, likes to make up nicknames for himself. He had a crush on Janet, liked to hang around and talk about her while I built the bike." He smiled. "So I guess you could say he helped."

I was still staring into Janet's smile, kind of falling slowly into the image. I heard Arnie say, "You look like her, you know that?"

"So I've been told."

"Then you didn't know her?"

"No." I was tired of lying. And I was caught in a tide of sadness, irrationally grieving a woman I'd never known. She looked so young and hopeful, so fragile, so earnest; a person I would have enjoyed knowing. Perhaps I was grieving the loss of the opportunity to meet her, to explore friendship.

Or perhaps I was grieving Janet because it was a simpler, easier grief to feel than the loss of my father.

Arnie said, "She was a really nice kid."

"A kid? Wasn't she twenty-five or so?"

"Hmm. Years isn't everything. Sometimes it takes a person a lot of years to give up certain dreams from childhood."

I looked up at Arnie, certain now why he knew everyone and

everyone knew him. He was paying attention, for one thing; people would gravitate toward him like sheep crowding into the lee of a hill. "What dreams couldn't she give up?"

"She thought that doing right is the point of living."

"Isn't it?"

Arnie's eyes reflected my sadness. "Not the whole point. And that's my point. And now she's dead."

"What killed her, Arnie?"

"You mean who."

"Okay, who?"

It was Arnie's turn to sigh. "I don't know, not directly. We used to ride together on an evening out along the Laguna. She loved wetlands more than anything, even bicycles, loved the way the birds dipped in the water and—well, just the quiet, I guess. She'd kid me that I needed her so I wouldn't get hit, because I dress so darkly, no reflective clothing. Then the last weeks before she was killed, she was really preoccupied. We rode out on a Sunday, and she wanted to go out toward the Laguna. She kept looking for a road up on the hills where she could overlook this place on Ferris Road, wanted to leave the bikes and head through the trees to a look-off, but she never found one."

"What was she looking for? Or at?"

"She said she couldn't tell me, that it was for her work. I remember her pointing out a bird of prey—it was one of those black-shouldered kites, beautiful birds—it just hovered over the ground, wings flapping like this." Arnie raised long-fingered hands and fluttered them by his shoulders. "Janet said that bird could see everything."

I smiled. In the fat years before I'd been laid off from Blackfeet Oil, I had begun to take flying lessons. My instructor had suggested the Piper Tomahawk, a low-winged trainer, but I had preferred the Cessna 152, with wings set above the fuselage where they wouldn't interrupt my view of the ground. I loved the freedom of flying, but most of all, I loved the view of the ground, with all its shapes and lines and patterns. How well I could understand Janet's desire to hover above the land she wanted to study. "Did you ride together the Sunday before she died?" I asked.

Arnie shook his head, closed his eyes in pain. "No, I was out of town that weekend for a race. She left a message on my machine at home, to see if I wanted to ride with her that Monday, but I couldn't. I was working late, making up some of the time I'd taken off." Arnie opened his eyes and looked deeply into mine. He didn't have to tell me what he was thinking: if he'd been with her, she might have lived.

"Arnie, Janet was fired. For all we know, she left on that ride early in the afternoon, while you would have been at work, regardless of overtime."

Arnie looked straight into my eyes. Words weren't proof against what he was feeling.

I changed the subject. "What about Duke?"

"Timothy Swege."

"I beg your pardon?"

"He doesn't think 'Timmy' is macho enough. He's tried Thor and Ivan, too, but somehow couldn't get them to stick, either."

"Oh. Did they ever ride together?"

Arnie shrugged his shoulders and smiled. "I guess she'd ride with him if he got darned lucky. The roads are public places, after all."

"So she found him obnoxious."

"I didn't say that."

"Where can I find him?"

"He lives with his grandmother out in Miwok Mills. Kind of drifts around sticking his nose into things. I haven't seen him lately."

"Can you give me his address?"

Arnie looked into my eyes once more, just double-checking that I was a decent person, then scribbled the address out on a business card from the shop. After that, he walked me out to the parking lot. The heavy gray overcast had thinned, and I could even see a patch of blue sky. As we headed up to the little blue truck, Arnie jerked to a stop as if he'd been tugged from behind.

"What?" I spun around, startled by his motion.

His eyes had gone very large, the whites showing all the way around those dark irises. He was staring at the truck.

Suddenly wary, I backed away from him, pulled out the keys, and unlocked the door.

Arnie's eyes grew very narrow. In a voice pitched low in anger, he hissed, "What are you doing with Janet's truck?"

20

I YANKED THE DOOR OPEN, RIPPED INTO THE GLOVE COMPART-
ment, dug furiously through a pile of papers for the registration. Sure
enough, the little blue truck was registered to Janet Pinchon, 3006 Via
Robles. "Damn him!" I bellowed. "Damn him, damn him, damn him!
That son of a bitch had me figured right along!"

I felt cold from the top of my head to the soles of my feet. The im-
plications of Senator Pinchon's act were not clear, but it looked bad,
very bad. And why hadn't I looked at the registration? Because I'd been
thinking of it as a rental car, that's why, and I never bothered to look
at the registrations on rentals. That son of a bitch, that oozing, pestilent scab of vanity. To set me loose driving his dead daughter's truck
around her town without telling me was deceitful at best, and endan-
gering at worst.

And now I had a very tall, very fit, very angry man in bicycling spandex gripping my shoulder. It was clear that at that moment this man
thought I had killed his friend, or knew who had. "How did you know
this was Janet's truck?" I pleaded.

Arnie pointed angrily at the back, to a bumper sticker that read *Save
Mono Lake*. "That, and the bicycle rack."

"The what?"

Arnie bent inside the pickup bed and pointed at a metal bar with
wing nuts that was bolted inside. "That bar. You pop the front wheel

and lock the forks onto the bar." It felt like his coal-black eyes were drilling holes in my skull.

To hell with the Senator's privacy; the man had endangered me. "Arnie, I have to tell you something I'm supposed to keep my mouth shut about. I'm here because Janet's father hired me. He *said* he wanted me to find out who killed her. God, what an idiot I was!"

Arnie released his grip on my shoulder. "Janet hated her father."

"I begin to think the feeling was mutual. But wait, did she *tell* you she hated him?"

Arnie knit his brow. "Not straight out. Just little things she'd say. Like, 'I'll show Father what has value,' in an angry voice."

That was an odd statement. "And what does have value?"

"I'm not sure."

"What was the context?"

Arnie gripped the tailgate of the truck in frustration. "When we looked out over the Laguna, for instance. And she was reading the paper one time, and she slapped it and said, 'I bet Dad's behind this.' "

"What was the article about?"

"It was in one of the leftist papers that are printed around here. It was an exposé of some plan to build housing along the Laguna."

"What would that have to do with her father?"

"I don't know."

"A housing development would be mandated under county government, not federal. You know he's a United States Senator?"

"Yes. It's funny about that: Janet loved the truth more than anything, but that was one thing she'd lie about. When people asked her if she was any relation, she always said no."

"Then how'd you know?"

"One time, when she was in a really down mood, she told me about it. Said it was embarrassing. Said she wanted to make it on her own merits, and didn't want to answer for his."

"Did she tell you anything else?"

Arnie shook his head miserably. "No."

I stared uncomfortably at the ground. "Were you—ah, special friends?"

"No. Not that I didn't wish. Janet was lovely, clear down to her soul. Intense. Kept to herself, except for riding and work. She wasn't one to say much about herself."

I touched Arnie's shoulder softly. "If it's any comfort to you, it sounds like she opened up to you a lot more than to anyone else."

❖

THERE WAS A break in the rain, and I felt a strong need for wide-open spaces. I drove west on Highway 12 toward Sebastopol to the middle of the Santa Rosa Plain and parked the truck, got out and walked along a paved bicycle path that followed the highway along open, level ground. I needed to get away from the truck while I decided what to do about it, get away to a place where I could see people coming if they were interested in making me a target.

Who had seen me in that truck? Mrs. Karsh and Matthew, Valentine Reeves, Duke. Arnie. Jamie Martinez; maybe that was why he had looked so spooked, and the same went for the rest of them. Had Suzanne Cousins seen it? Yes, but she knew I represented the family, so it might not have seemed odd to her. Why hadn't she said anything? The people at HRC had seen it—or maybe they hadn't: I'd never parked it right under their windows. Pat Ryan would have seen it in his rearview mirror as I followed him to dinner, and I'd left it in plain sight in the parking lot when I helped him type his report, but heaven knew Pat was preoccupied, and he might just not have noticed. Jaki? Yes, but I'd come clean with her. And it wasn't an unusual make or model, or color; not everyone would notice.

Cars and trucks whizzed by along Highway 12. To the south, the land rolled away in gentle meadows punctuated by spreading oaks that sheltered birds in their branches. I found a bench beside the path and sat in thought, staring upward through the gnarled branches and twigs of an oak tree. The grasses in the meadow were beginning to show a lush green in answer to the rains, and the hills uncoiled beyond the

distant oaks like an undulating blue ribbon. The sky breathed dampness in wintery white, but here and there a pale shell-pink tint rode
the heavens like an ethereal light. Such splendor, yet so fragile against
the cruelty of human designs.

A beefy young buck on in-line skates careened past my bench, followed by two women shuffling along pushing baby joggers. I bowed
my head and concentrated on the ground so I wouldn't have to make
eye contact.

I thought about Valentine Reeves staring in the window of my—
Janet's—truck. He had certainly recognized the truck, and had bent
to confirm his recognition. From there he would have tipped off Mrs.
Karsh. She would have told him what I'd said, that I was a friend of
Janet's. Wouldn't it make sense that I might borrow her truck from
the family? But why had the family, which cared so little that it had
not yet bothered to pick up her possessions, bothered to collect her
truck? Just to leave it by the airport for me? No. There was still an important piece of this picture missing.

A bicyclist hit his brakes, and then accelerated again in order to miss
hitting my feet. I glared at his wheels but resolutely did not look up.
This wide-open space was not so wide-open as I had hoped.

I picked up one of the stiff, dry leaves that had fallen from one of
the oak trees that grew beside the bench and crumpled it along its veins,
noting how easily it snapped. I was beginning to think that Senator Pinchon and his vile sidekick Murbles had sent me here not as an investigator, but as a decoy. Leaving me the keys to his daughter's truck was
a setup, I was sure; I remembered that wry, almost contemptuous smile
that broke across his face when he had said, "A private vehicle will be
available."

And I had put the idea in his head. How that must have amused
him. Then there was the way Murbles treated me, fending off my attempts to speak with the Senator. Until this moment, I'd written this
off to Murbles playing some power game, jealously filtering access to
his powerful employer. Now I wondered if he wasn't following his
boss's instructions within a gnat's eyelash.

What did all this mean? Janet had told Arnie she was going to teach her father something about value, or about what to value, and now she was dead. Her teaching was so important that the Senator had not publicly acknowledged his own daughter's death.

For that matter, how had he managed to keep his connection to a murdered woman this quiet? And why hadn't the Good Senator played this occasion to the hilt, sobbing through the newspapers and on national TV, hauling in the sympathy votes hand over fist? *That would have held value for him,* I thought contemptuously. I could just see the headlines: Senator's Daughter Slain, Bereaved Father Demands Justice, Anticrime Bill to Follow.

And the Sheriff's Department—wait, they knew who Janet's father was, didn't they? Or did they? Muller had acted as if he didn't know who Curt Murbles was, or the Senator, for that matter. Was knowledge of Janet's parentage something that Muller was withholding in order to be able to spot people with special knowledge of the murder? I didn't like that idea, as that meant the Sheriff's Department would be watching me as a possible suspect. Damn. But what if Muller had not in fact met the Senator or Murbles? Surely the Senator had been to Santa Rosa since his daughter's death, because he had been able to draw a map directing me to the site where she had been found. Or Murbles had. . . .

So why was the Senator keeping quiet about his daughter's death? This question set off a flurry of doubts about the Senator's and Murbles' true interests in any information I might uncover. The kindest conclusion I could draw was that Janet's murder had somehow hurt the Senator right where he lived: on Capitol Hill. And how could I work for a man who might be implicated in his own daughter's death?

I couldn't, but it never occurred to me to quit.

I hoofed it back toward the truck, stopping some ways out from where it was parked to make certain I wasn't being watched. I tensed. There was a piece of yellow paper underneath the windshield wiper that hadn't been there when I parked it. And the binoculars were in the truck, not my pocket, where I could have used them to take a look at the paper before I approached the truck. I actually found myself hoping that it was a parking ticket, but the shape was wrong.

Suddenly I knew exactly what the paper was about, and who had left it. I closed the final distance to the truck at a run and snatched it off the windshield, cursing myself. *The Duke watches your every move,* it read, in loopy script.

Great, a ha-ha note from Timothy "Duke" Swege, the bicyclist who had passed me on the trail while I was so studiously staring at my feet. That little snake. He could have stopped, but no, how much more amusing to leave the private investigator with her head in the sand and instead pen a little billet-doux to chide her about how unobservant she is. My head began to pound.

It was high time I chased that knock-kneed spandex freak down and squeezed a little information out of him, but he might be miles away by now in any direction. No, I'd wait until the rain drove him home, because I now knew where that home was.

I climbed into the truck, still wound as tight as a watch spring. I considered phoning Washington and shouting at Murbles until I felt better, but if he and the Senator had indeed sent me in as a decoy, it wouldn't do to let them know that I knew. To hell with phoning in every day—I might be a decoy, but I wasn't a puppet! It was time the tables turned in this game of cat and mouse, time that the Senator started to provide information for me. Because I was too far into the investigation to stop. I would see it through to the end, one way or the other.

It *was* time I got Suzanne Cousins to talk, and I now knew how to force her to do so. I stabbed the truck key into the ignition, smiling grimly as the other keys on the chain swung against the dash: if this was Janet Pinchon's truck, then it followed that one of those keys would open the front door to Suzanne Cousins' duplex.

21

I STOOD ON THE STOOP OF THE DUPLEX GETTING SOAKED BY the rain, which had come back in force. I knocked on the door, hard. No answer. I lifted the ring of keys and got to work.

Key number one was a nice, hefty Schlage, the wrong make for the lock. *It probably opens the front door at HRC Environmental,* I thought wryly, tucking the notion away in case I needed to get back into that building.

Key number two was tiny, and had a small dolphin stamped into it. *This one opens HRC's monitoring wells,* I reasoned, remembering the Dolphin brand lock Adam Horowitz had muscled open at the Misty Creek Winery. *Good thing I'm not some renegade who likes pouring toxic chemicals into holes in the ground.*

Key number three, a simple old Kwikset, did the trick. I kicked the door wide, all my fury and frustration at being misused, ignored, and kept ignorant rending the last frayed threads of my manners.

Suzanne was sitting on her couch, sipping another cup of tea. "You forget something?" she asked dryly.

"No, but this time we're going to talk."

"And why is that?"

"Because I finally understand why you don't want to talk to me about Janet."

Suzanne arched one of her lovely eyebrows ever so slightly. "Oh?"

"You don't trust Janet's father."

She shrugged. "And?"

"We have that in common."

Suzanne thought about that a moment, then rose calmly from the couch and turned toward the kitchen. "Tea?"

I nodded my head and followed her deeper into her domain.

❖

STRONG HERB TEA on a disgruntled stomach is a strange experience. It wasn't anything out of a package; Suzanne brewed it from a handful of twigs and dried flowers and berries that she pulled from half a dozen glass jars. She wouldn't speak while she was preparing it, except to ask about my hand and to give me a towel to dry my hair. "Is it infected?" she asked casually, staring at the bandage.

"No. Just happened."

Suzanne opened one more jar and dropped something that looked like dried moss into the pot, then excused herself to the bathroom while it steeped. I considered following her, to make sure she didn't climb out a window, but instead waited in the kitchen, uncomfortably aware of this brew that smelled like damp things from the woods. When she returned and poured me a cup, I sniffed it suspiciously before I took my first sip. Which I found oddly refreshing. I sipped again. The decoction at one and the same time soothed and roused me, making me feel even more bold.

Suzanne examined me with those big smoky-gray eyes and sipped from the teacup she had been holding when I arrived. She held her cup with both hands, elbows on the table coyly drawn close to her breasts. Steam rose in pale curls around her eyelashes.

"Why did you tell me you didn't know Janet?" I demanded.

"Janet's gone."

"I know that, damn it, that's why I'm here."

"Don't you like to let people go when they're done being here?"

This was the limit. I'd heard about this California New Age poppycock, and here it was, herb tea and all. "Sure. And sometimes it takes a little more than a 'too bad' to lay the dead to rest."

Suzanne mapped my face with her eyes. "So you're taking her ghost for a last little ride."

I didn't like the way she said that, kind of half-mocking, half-serious. Her steady gaze was becoming increasingly unnerving. "Listen, Suzanne, Janet was a friend of yours, and a sister geologist to me. I'm trying to find out who killed her. Let's just stick to that, okay?"

"Okay. So. What have we found out?"

I shook my head. "No, that's not how this is going to go. I'm not reporting to you. I don't know you, and right now I barely even trust myself."

"That's reasonable," she purred.

"So you just answer a few simple questions and I'll get out of here."

"Lovely."

I began to feel the urge to look over my shoulder, like someone was watching me. "What was Janet working on at HRC just before she left?"

Suzanne smiled beatifically. "I don't know. Really."

"Come on!"

"Come on, yourself. You must have learned this about Janet by now; she was tight-lipped at the best of times, and she took matters of honor very seriously. Even company proprietary interests were part of her code of honor, no matter how dishonorable her employers."

"What do you know of the dishonor of her employers?"

Suzanne just smiled.

"Now you come on," I said. "You're not going to come this far and stop, are you?"

Suzanne put a hand to her breast in mock sincerity. "I? Stop? We are not on the same pathway, dearest. And we never were."

"Quit twisting my words! Listen, I don't get this. You lived with the woman for two years. I'm told that you were close, that you beat drums together or something. Now she's brutally murdered, and all you seem to have on your mind is getting her belongings out of the room so you can rent it to someone else. Excuse me if I'm missing something here, but that seems to lack a little in compassion."

Suzanne's gray eyes took on the deep, predatory gleam of the mountain lion, that single-minded look of the creature hunting meat. Either this woman was insane, or I had hit a nerve that ran deeper than the grave. But she said nothing.

As we continued to stare at each other, another voice broke the silence, making me jump: "You leave her be!"

I spun around in my chair. A short, ugly woman stood in the doorway. Drop earrings thrashed beneath closely cropped hair. Her belly sagged out farther than her breasts, suggesting that she exercised her tongue and her jaws more than any other part of her body. Her skin had the look of cold oatmeal, and her eyes reminded me of halved hard-boiled eggs set in tomato aspic. Her lips were drawn into a crazed pout, and her neck thrust forward far enough to draw her double chins taught. In a bleating, nasal voice, she declared: "Janet was doing the work of the Goddess. She has fought her good fight, and we are releasing her!"

I grasped my chair, ready to spring if necessary. Was this one apt to get physical?

Suzanne narrowed her eyes at the other woman in warning. "Liza, this is Em Hansen. How was your meditation?"

Liza's wild eyes flared. "Shitty. Like you said, there are too many unsettled vibrations in Janet's room."

I wasn't going to let Suzanne swerve the subject without a fight. "Liza, I'm trying to finish Janet's work. Can you tell me anything about what she was doing?"

"Janet loved the Goddess!"

Suzanne cut across her words. "Janet had a thing for wetlands, Liza; she didn't give a hoot for your religion."

Liza shot her neck forward at Suzanne. Heading off an argument that might distract them from what I wanted to talk about, I interjected, "Can you tell me about her wetlands work?"

Liza looked blank.

"Or anything she might have said about her employers?"

"*They* were for sale!"

"Can you give me a for instance?" I asked politely.

"The list is *endless.*" She swept a hand dramatically through the air between us, her pestilent eyes wild with drama.

I couldn't imagine Janet confiding in a person like Liza when she wouldn't confide in anyone else. "Did this 'for sale' stuff have anything to do with why Janet was fired?"

Liza bristled. "Yes, they crucified her because Janet wouldn't lie for the bastards!"

"About what? The job she was doing?"

Liza's bombast faltered. Clearly she was not privy to certain details, but she blustered along anyway: "Yeah."

"And what do you know about the job?" I asked, letting my tone suggest that I didn't quite believe her. I knew I wouldn't have to goad her very hard; wackos like that take everything personally.

Liza puffed her chest indignantly. "The thing was on a tight deadline."

"How do you know that?"

"Because she'd been working through the weekend to get it done, and couldn't help me with The Project. She had to have a draft of some report for Monday morning. All she'd tell me was that there was something in that draft that her boss would want out, but she was going to leave it *in.*"

"She told *you* that?"

Liza tilted her chin up in defiance. "She told Trudy."

And you wormed it out of Trudy, whoever she is. "So he fired her? For that? Why didn't he take whatever it was out and remove her signature line?"

Liza and Suzanne looked at me like I was speaking Greek.

"I've looked at one of her older reports. It's constructed like a letter with a long documentary text. The state requires registration on such documents. Janet wasn't registered, but Rauch is. So it ends with sincerely yours and her signature, her title, then Rauch's under that. So I wonder why he didn't just take her report and do what he pleased with it. You can do wonders with a computer," I concluded dryly, thereby answering one of my own questions. That was why I hadn't found her report on the computer. My mind skipped ahead, wobbling slightly in the effort, as I considered breaking back into the computer system at HRC to retrieve that file. But then, all I would find in that report would be what Rauch had left in, not what he had taken out. "Did Janet bring home a draft of that report?"

Suzanne waved a hand casually. "If she did, the Sheriff's detectives would have taken it when they went through her room."

My head was beginning to feel a little thick. "Do you have an inventory of what they took?"

"No. They gave that to her mother."

"Her mother?"

She shrugged. "Isn't that who gave you Janet's truck?"

It was hard to keep the shock from showing on my face. "No, it was left for me at the airport. How can I reach Janet's mother?"

"The lady didn't leave a number."

Liza blasted in on the conversation again. "Janet hated her parents. *Hated* them."

To Suzanne I said, "Why didn't her mother take the rest of Janet's possessions with her?"

"She didn't even come in. She just rang the buzzer and demanded the keys."

"Then why did she take the truck? Didn't that mean she left another vehicle here?"

"No."

The room began to seem a little far away, Suzanne's voice more distant. "Speak," I insisted, struggling to stay focused.

Suzanne arched an eyebrow. "Someone dropped her off. I gave her the keys. She left."

"Some man? Who, Janet's father?"

"I'm sure I wouldn't know him if I saw him."

"A vain old fart with wavy hair?"

"No."

"Then who? Come on, Suzanne," I whined, "what aren't you telling me?"

Liza bellowed: "Hey! You back off my friend!"

Suzanne turned toward Liza, a well-oiled gun turret shifting its aim, and fixed a glare on her. Liza evaporated from the doorway. Turning back to me, Suzanne said, "Nothing. It was the day after they found Janet. Janet's mother came by only to get the truck after identifying her body. The Sheriff's deputy had found the next-of-kin information when they searched Janet's things and called her. That much I know. You want speculation? I rather think she didn't want to ride back home with the man who was driving the car she arrived in."

"Did she tell you his name?"

"Burble; something like that."

I was beginning to feel tired, even lethargic. "Murbles," I said doggedly. Murbles with the long fingers, who seemed bent on filtering his boss's communication with his hired detective. Murbles, slipping in and out of the county like a mist . . .

"Yes."

So the inestimable Curt Murbles had driven Janet's mother to Santa Rosa to identify Janet's body, and had pissed her off so thoroughly that the woman wouldn't ride a mile farther with him. That argued well for her character. "Where does Janet's mother live?" I asked, beginning to wonder how much time she spent with her famous husband.

"San Francisco?"

I set Suzanne's strange brew down. "Do you know the Karshes?" I asked, trying to be thorough. My head felt like wool. I wanted to leave.

Suzanne set her cup down abruptly. "Stay away from Mrs. Karsh," she said, her face hard. To herself more than to me, she muttered, "I told Janet that, but would she listen to me? No."

At last Suzanne was showing some passion. "Mrs. Karsh seems like a nice person," I taunted.

"Then you met the tip of the iceberg."

"What aren't you saying now?"

She stared out the window, as if at something far away.

I was getting tired of Suzanne Cousins. I was tired of her attitude, tired of her selective interest in reality, and very tired of her tea. "What did you put in this brew?" I demanded.

"A little chamomile. You seemed tense."

"And what else?"

Suzanne grinned, her eyes narrowing like a cat who's getting rubbed just right. "Oh, this and that."

"A little eye of newt to chase away the ghosts?" Something was wrong. My tongue was too loose. I needed to get out of there. I stood up.

Suzanne stood up, too. "I think it would take a little more than herbs to help you with your problem, dear." She advanced on me, smiling like the cat who is about to catch the canary.

I backed toward the door. "I'll stick with plain water, if you don't mind."

"Fine, whatever works for you."

"You think of anything else important, you just give me a call, okay?"

"Sure," she purred, and slammed the door behind me.

22

IT TOOK ME TWO HOURS PARKED NEAR A NICE, SAFE SUPER-market to sleep off that tea. When I awoke, I stumbled out of the truck to the phone booth under the supermarket portico and called information hoping to talk to Janet's mother if her father couldn't be bothered, but found no listing for a George Harwood Pinchon in San Francisco. In case Suzanne's guess had been wrong, I also tried Sacramento, the state capital, but had no luck there, either.

I steered the truck down a side street in Miwok Mills, to the home of Timothy "Duke" Swege, where I found Duke's granny, but no Duke. She came out on the front porch of her petite brand-spanking-new town house and chirpingly announced that "Timmy" was out riding his bicycle. Granny Swege was a shrewd little tub of a woman, with tiny eyes like hard little beetles. The tight, tidy waves in her apricot-colored hair gave her a misleading cuteness. "What happened to your hand?" she inquired.

"My hand?" I lifted it and stared at the bandage as if it had only just materialized. "Oh, just a little scrape."

"Hah."

"Timmy be back soon?"

"He promised to be back by five so he could clean up and take me to the Christmas Spaghetti Feed." She looked at her watch. It was three forty-five.

"Oh, the Spaghetti Feed at the firehouse," I said. "I hear that's quite an affair."

Granny cocked her head sideways, a gesture that brought to mind a mountain chickadee that had once watched me from a nearby perch as I sat eating my lunch in Yellowstone. Suzanne's tea was still having its way with me: as I stood there on that tidy little front porch in California, the memory of the chickadee set off a cascade of associations, one of which was inevitably Frank, and it was some moments before I began to make sense of the words that were coming out of Granny Swege's mouth. ". . . all my life, that's seventy-two years, and the Feed has been going on only since the Coulter boy took over as fire chief, which was, let's see, back in sixty-eight, so that's . . ."

I did the math for her. "Almost thirty years."

"Exactly. Of course, they just use the money to buy beer, but I figure our boys can have a drink now and then if they want to."

Bless her heart, Granny Swege was a self-starting gossip! I fell quickly into the small-town cadence. "I reckon."

"Of course, that Ted Coulter was a smart boy. Too bad he had that mishap with the tractor."

"Yes . . ."

"Left three kids, and his wife pregnant with a fourth. Tchh." Tragic shaking of head.

I shook my head, too. "The best and the brightest."

"Tchh."

"Like the Karsh boy," I lured.

Granny's eyes brightened. "Oh, and he was a bit odd to begin with, don't you know."

"Really! What was he like?"

"Oh, always an uncoordinated child. His mother sheltered him, so he never quite developed, you see." Knowing shake of head.

"And so when that other kid hit him on the slide at the playground . . ."

Hand to mouth, ritually aghast at the memory. "A terrible thing.

198 ◇   *Sarah Andrews*

Even starting out peculiar, he could have become someone, coming from his family, but now you never see him."

"Never comes to town?" I asked hopefully.

"Like he's buried out there on that ranch."

"It must have been awful for the child who hit him."

"Oh, Dexie was in torment, he was so sorry. Everybody blamed him, poor child, but *I* didn't. I told him, 'Tom Dexter, he probably saw you coming and just didn't move hisself out of your way. He never was quite normal, sticking to his ma like that.' "

"Dexter, you say?"

"Yes, you know, the one that joined the Sheriff's Department. Like I say, he felt responsible, always did. Wanted to pay his debt to humanity." Granny pursed her dry old lips, shook her head again, and added, as an aside, one knowing woman to another, "Kind of a Jesus Christ complex."

I almost dropped my teeth. "Nice guy, though, that Tom Dexter. Big guy, still fit for his age," I said, double-checking.

Granny fixed those lively little eyes on me. "Noticed, did ya?"

Moving right along, now . . . "Ah, sure. But I suppose the whole Karsh family suffered, having a brain-damaged son."

"Oooh, yes. Hmm-hmm." Knowing nods aplenty.

"And then the daughter . . ."

"Sonja, yes. Wasn't she a spirited girl, though. Bright as a button. It was the personality, not the looks, that always drew attention."

"Something like me?" I joked.

Granny Swege laid her head back and took a squint at me. "Yes, I'd say so: kind of average, but game for a hard day's work or a good gallop."

Swallowing my pride, I said, "Rode, did she?"

"Uh-hmm. A real horsey girl. The apple of her daddy's eye. *And* her granddaddy."

"But she ran off?"

"Thankless child."

I lowered my own lids, knowingly, nodding ever so slightly. "But no one's ever heard from her."

"Makes ya wonder, doesn't it? Course, they say she went off into the drug culture down in the city, but that's what they said about every kid that slipped the traces back in the seventies."

"Seventy- . . ."

"Three. Easy to remember. It was the summer we all lined up to buy gas, and Sonja had a job at the burger stand next door to the filling station. In the time you'd wait for a pump, she'd take your order, grill one up, serve it to you, and take away the trash. Always was an enterprising girl."

This didn't sound like a drug addict to me. No, I'd file her under F for Future CEOs of America. "So she disappeared, and . . ."

"Mm-hmm, girl disappears, Ma's cuckoo over the boy, and Pa drowns his sorrows with Miz Redhead."

"His secretary."

"Like they thought nobody'd ever notice."

"About when did Mr. K move in with her?"

Lips pursed in concentration. "Oh, he quit going home at night right after the girl went missing. When he started his dalliance is another matter. I'd say *years* earlier."

So far this jibed well with what Jaki had told me. "Do you know Suzanne Cousins?"

"Little Suzy?" she said wryly. "You mean Martha Cousins' girl."

"Ah, sure. Did she know Sonja?"

"Close as two sardines in a can."

My mouth sagged open. Of course, Suzanne must have known Sonja. She was the right age, and she had grown up in the right town. "How did Suzanne feel when Sonja went missing?"

"I wouldn't know. Strange girl. All those drums and such."

"Suzanne go over to the Karshes' much?"

Granny looked at me like I was a fool. *"No* one goes over to the Karshes' much."

"What about Val Reeves? Isn't he paying court?"

"Val Reeves? Dierdre Karsh? What have you been smoking? Val Reeves sticks by his wife like glue. He's a good churchly kind of fellow, always trying to make things better for everyone. Why's everyone got to bad-mouth him, just because he's a developer? Getting on him for trying to give us good homes and good water. It's jealousy, I tell you, bald-faced, lily-livered jealousy. They got a problem with him making a decent living? He could build for the country club crowd, but no, he builds low-income projects, so the old folks like me on fixed incomes can have a place to live. Pah!"

I made a quick appraisal of Granny's town house. The siding was of composition board with battens nailed every eighteen inches or so to keep it from buckling with the weather.

Following my gaze, Granny said, "Yes, your Mr. Reeves built this place, and a good job he did, too. He could have cut corners, but he didn't. Stick that in your pipe and smoke it, smarty!"

"I quite agree," I said quickly, trying to mollify her.

"You're one of them county folks working against the community water project, ain't ya? I shoulda known!"

"The what?"

"Damn gummint tryin' ta tell us how to live! Get off my porch! You're letting the cold air in! You think heat is free? I'm on a fixed income, damn it. Get off with you!"

As I wandered back to the little blue truck, my mind buzzed with a theme that spells trouble to any westerner who's ever tried to live off the land: Granny Swege had mentioned Val Reeves and water in the same breath.

◆

DOWN IN THE center of Miwok Mills, the rain was again stopping and cars and trucks were beginning to gather near the fire station. I parked the little blue notice-me truck a hundred feet or more down a side street in a vain attempt to disassociate myself from it and wandered back toward the fire station and its coming Spaghetti Feed. The Feed was my one chance to corner Mrs. Karsh in a public place—a place where, hopefully, Matthew Karsh would not be found.

I was just admiring a bumper sticker on a Chevy four-by-four that read FIREMEN ARE ALWAYS IN HEAT when one of the roll-up doors on the fire station opened and a big red pumper loomed out into the street. Jim Erikson was at the wheel. He parked the pumper at an angle, blocking traffic, hopped out, sloped back into the fire station, and repeated the process with the emergency vehicle that was parked in the second bay. And the fire engine from the third. It had a large rowboat mounted upside down on top. "Preparing for the next great flood?" I asked as I strolled up, real casual like.

Jim Erikson blushed right up to the roots of his sandy hair. He shoved his strong fingers into his jeans pockets. "Sure. Have to be ready." He smiled uncertainly, twisting his long, lithe body around in an effort to look shorter. Then he noticed the bandage on my hand. Taking hold of my wrist to get a look at the dressing, he asked, "What happened?"

I jerked my hand away. "Oh, nothing," I answered, confused and embarrassed by the tenderness of his touch.

The breeze shifted, and the intense aroma of spaghetti sauce assaulted my nostrils, reminding me that all I'd had for lunch was beef jerky and Suzanne's draft of witch's brew. "Smells like a flood of spaghetti to me," I crooned, glad to have something else to talk about.

Jim continued to smile but stared at his feet. "Ah, yeah. We're just getting ready for tonight's big Feed. It's our annual fund-raiser."

"Can I help?"

"Help?" he echoed.

"It's a volunteer force, isn't it? I could help set up chairs or something."

Jim scratched his head and smiled. "Follow me."

We marched into the fire station through bay number three, stopping to lower the roll-up door. Inside, a passel of young bucks wearing flame-red long-sleeved T-shirts with "Miwok Mills Volunteer Fire Department Keep Back 300 Feet" stenciled across the back were bashing about, setting up folding tables and chairs for the event. Loud rock music from an oldies station boomed from the back of the room. The young bucks rocked and howled with the beat, slapping out time on the backs of the chairs as they popped them open in lines down the sides of the tables. Canned Heat gave way to Pink Floyd's *The Wall*, with appreciative bopping and heavy grunts at the "hey!"s.

"Looks like they got them all but set up," Jim said.

"Oh, there's Mrs. Karsh," I chirped. "I could help her at the stove."

"Sure," Jim said doubtfully. He led me inward through the fracas to the kitchen area, which was a big portable steel range with a couple of thirty-gallon pots simmering on it, behind which stood Mrs. Karsh. Her eyes were focused on the contents of the pot to the right, which she stirred as if nothing beyond it existed.

Jim Erikson said, "Hi, ah, Mrs. Karsh, this is Em Hansen."

Mrs. Karsh looked up and jerked her head back as if dodging a fly. Collecting herself, she arranged her face into a blank mask, her eyes pointed straight toward me, but focused several feet short of my face.

Jim concluded, "Em would like to help."

"Help?" said Mrs. Karsh, as if she'd never heard the word before.

"Yeah, I could slice bread or whatever else you need done."

"Ah, thanks, Jim, but things are pretty much under control."

"Em wants to sing for her supper."

Mrs. Karsh's face expression shifted to a submissive demi-smile. "Oh . . . well, okay, Jim. Tell her she can take the bread over to that table and cut it. The bread's in those boxes, and the knife is on that table," she said, pointing to one that was safely twenty feet from her. "And the cutting board . . ." She left off stirring, searching for the board. I found it in another box and got to work, somewhat clumsily bracing the handle of the knife too high in my hand to avoid pressing against the gauze bandage on my palm.

If I thought I was going to get Mrs. Karsh to talk to me, I was wrong. She kept her back to me, her attention trained firmly on the sauce pots, and her gaze turned tightly inward. All attempts at conversation were deflected with vague hmms, um–hums, and excuse-mes. By and by I gave up and turned my attention to the rest of the room.

A community event is like a patient's pulse, affording a quick reading of the patient's state of health. Or lack thereof.

The fact that Miwok Mills could support a volunteer fire department was a point on the healthy side of the ledger. The firemen seemed to have good enough morale, sopped as they were in the usual esteem-building good time men have when they engage in organized heroism: puffed-out chests, raised chins, raucous singing. Once, a call came in for the rescue vehicle, and with ungainly athleticism, the men hurled themselves at the switch that interrupted the siren before the roar could shatter everyone's eardrums, then drew straws over who was going to drive the truck to answer the call. As the hour grew later, wives appeared with kids in tow. Lots of little kids in a community also argue health, as it suggests an adequate local source of employment for their parents, who are too young to draw from Social Security. The kids ran around among the chairs and tried on their dads' hats and turnout coats. At five o'clock we all sat down and ate a quick plate of spaghetti (which the younger kids threw at each other, much to their mothers' dismay), and after cleaning up, we opened the doors to the public.

I faded to the back of the room and surreptitiously wolfed down a second plate of Mrs. Karsh's excellent spaghetti sauce dished up on overcooked pasta and positioned myself to eavesdrop on conversations held by people waiting in line. I needn't have worried that they'd hush up around me; the diners were far too busy glad-handing and gossiping with one another to take notice of one stray female in red boots.

Jaki came through the line early on in a phalanx of nearly identical-looking siblings (she was cool, didn't even wink), and Jamie Martinez queued up with his brood. There were nods all around, but I quickly got the impression that, small town or no, not everyone in this place knew each other. Mixed in with the ancients and the Jakis and others who had clearly lived in the neighborhood since God was a small child were a population of younger couples whose big-city version of casual attire stood out a lot more than my boots did. These citizens found themselves drawn into conversations with the old guard that ran something like this:

Old coot (in polyster slacks and Fire Department jacket): "You're the Smiths, aren't you. You bought the old Jones place."

Young coot (in predistressed denims and one hundred percent cotton sweater in this year's fashion color, flashing expensive orthodontia in an overly earnest yet somehow impersonal smile): "Yes, and we just love it here in Miwok Mills. I tell you, getting out of L.A. was the smartest thing we ever did."

"I hear you're opening up a café hereabouts, fixing up one of the older buildings."

Young coot, putting hands on wife's shoulders: "Yes, my wife is the little entrepreneur in the family. Going to serve biscotti and lattes, live the good life here in the country. I telecommute to my job in the city myself."

Old coot, removing sweat-stained cap to scratch head: "How things change. I grew up right here in the Mills, farmed all my life. Retired now. My boy's trying to keep the orchard going, but prices aren't much these days, and the cost of farm equipment and chemicals being what they are . . ."

Young coot: "Quit using that poison and go organic! My wife's café's going to be all organic. Will you excuse us? I see our friends the Thompsons. . . ."

In between half-heard mutterings about the community water project, I heard riffles and snippets of other political chat, such as development versus keeping to the land, industry versus the carriage trade, community face-lifting versus keep it homely and maybe the slick assholes will leave. Talk seemed split between several camps, including the *Who Are These Young Upstarts?* mutterers, the *Keep Miwok Mills Messy* curmudgeons, and the *La Dolce California Move Over I Got Mine* interlopers. I heard one tradesman with rough hands and a *Go Niners* ball cap admit shamefully to a burgeoning addiction to decaf cappuccinos. His compatriot looked both ways and asked if he'd tried the ones at a bakery in Sebastopol where, "the foam's extra good and they let you shake your own chocolate powder."

I hung close behind Mrs. Karsh. It seemed to make her pretty nervous to have me standing there, so I moved up even closer. Sure enough, her spine grew stiffer. I wondered just what she was thinking.

I got part of my answer at about six, when I saw a familiar mane of rich, wavy white hair looming above the throng. Valentine Reeves was in line, moving toward us, walking next to a man so impeccably groomed and smiley that I figured he had to be a politician. I watched Mrs. Karsh, waiting for her to notice Reeves. Yes, the instant she saw him, she glanced furtively my way and back at him. Reeves was definitely part of the equation, but to what did these numbers add up?

When Reeves was ten feet away, a young man with rough hands shouldered his way into line next to him. "Say, Val, anything more on the new project? I could really use some work this winter."

Valentine Reeves flashed his splendid teeth and clapped the man on the shoulder. "As soon as I hear, I'll be in touch, Herb. I can always use a hard worker like you."

"Yeah, well, Jim Erikson had me on his crew the last time, you'll remember, but he and I are—"

"Don't worry about a thing, Herb." He clapped the man's shoulder again and moved closer to us.

Mrs. Karsh nodded hello to Reeves and his well-dressed companion. "Val. Harold."

I stepped forward and stuck out my hand. "Nice to see you again, Mr. Reeves." I turned to his companion and grinned like a Junior Leaguer at a barbecue. "Hi, I'm Em Hansen, I'm new here," I said winningly.

Reeves looked doubtful, but the man grinned back and enclosed my hand in his before Reeves could open his mouth. "Harold Grimes," he said sweetly. "County Supervisor for this district. Welcome to our community."

A shrill voice stabbed into the conversation: "Harold Grimes, you're bringing me *dowwwwwwn!*" I glanced around to see the raw-faced Liza, the bug-eyed woman who had experienced a "shitty" meditation in Janet's room, lunging through the crowd. "Over my dead body you'll poison our children's water! You still think you can squash our project, don't you? And, Val Reeves, what are you doing talking to this man? These government bloodsuckers are all—"

Another woman grabbed her arm and pulled her back. She was big and muscular, but still had to tug hard. Liza roared, "Let me go, Trudy!" but lost her balance and started to pedal backward with the bigger woman's motion. I was just calculating how to get around the table and talk to them when Trudy zipped Liza out the door and they were gone.

Harold Grimes turned to give an elderly lady a flirtatious squeeze, his attention already miles beyond me. Valentine Reeves pulled himself up tall and continued his conversation with his would-be employee as if he had been interrupted only to swat a fly. "Don't worry about a thing, Herb. Jim's a good man. I'm sure he'll draw his help from local talent. You have a good Christmas, and say hi to your wife for me."

So Jim Erikson was in construction? Yes, he'd said he was an electrician who worked for himself. That's why he'd been available to take the call the morning Janet's body was reported. I glanced over toward where Jim stood recharging the coffee urn.

Reeves finished his conversation with Herb the laborer and took a very long look at me. He inhaled slowly, expanding his broad chest and laying his leonine head back in an elaborate neck stretch that showed me all the most impressive angles of his face. He was not smiling.

Mrs. Karsh grabbed a cloth to wipe up an imaginary spill. "Emily's helping," she said, sliding into that same rich, unctuous tone she had used when she had spoken to her damaged son from her kitchen steps. My breath caught in my throat. I had to remind myself that I was not on her back porch, that there were hundreds of people looking on, that I was safe. Reeves spread his lips in a smile that showed me every last intimidatingly perfect white tooth but did not warm his cool blue eyes.

"How very nice of you, Emily. Our community needs *all* the support it can get."

I stared defiantly back into the lion's eyes. "I hear you have lots of projects here in town," I said. "How nice. I'll bet this place will become a regular magnet for the *bicycle* crowd."

Reeves' eyes narrowed, intensifying the threat latent in his chilling smile. "Just what kind of mischief are you up to, my dear?" he purred.

"I'm just interested in understanding what you have going on here," I said quietly, serving bread to the people who were beginning to move around the obstruction Reeves was forming. "I want to know what's out by the Laguna that has young women dying. And I won't stop until I find out."

Mrs. Karsh's eyes widened. "I don't know what you mean," she whispered.

Reeves' gaze lingered on me like the smoke that hangs in the air after the explosion of a cannon. When he was content that I had gotten his unspoken message, he moved down the serving line toward the tables, set down his plate, and motioned sharply to Jim Erikson, who hastened over to see what he wanted. I could not hear what they were saying, but Jim glanced over toward me and blushed.

Mrs. Karsh appeared at my elbow. Very urgently she whispered, "We're running low on bread. Get some more, please!"

"Where?"

"There's another box out in the trunk of my car. Here, take my keys." She fished them out of her apron. "Go through that back door and turn right. It's the blue Dodge at the foot of the parking lot, near the willows by the creek."

I didn't think the bread supply was that low, but I headed out through the door into the chill darkness beyond, still trying to assess what I had just witnessed between Liza and the County Supervisor, and just exactly what Valentine Reeves' unspoken message to me had been. My feet crunched on the wet gravel as I wove my way back among the cars toward her ancient Dodge. I fingered the keys, flipping past the square one to the round one that would unlock the trunk. Bending, I slipped it into the lock.

Matthew Karsh rushed out of the dense shadows beneath the trees, moving his bulk toward me at frightening speed.

I jumped backward, jerking the key free of the lock. Dropped it on the ground. Slipped on the gravel, fell backward—

Matthew kept coming, hands rising, thick fingers tense with intent.

"Hey!" I shouted as I crashed backward into another car. I regained my footing and dodged backward through the pack of cars, but the pocket of Janet's jacket caught on a side mirror, throwing me off balance. I slipped again, banged against the door of the car. "Your mother sent me for the bread! Calm *down!*" I screamed, desperately shielding myself with the only weapon I could muster: the illogic of family obligations.

Matthew stopped ten feet from me, hands clenching, his eyes dark pockets of hatred. Then he began to move toward me again.

I grabbed the place where the jacket was caught and ripped. Still I was not free.

From behind me, a bit of gravel whizzed past my ear, plinking Matthew Karsh squarely in the face. He brayed in rage, grabbing at his eyes. The jacket pocket ripped free. I jogged backward several steps, stumbled up against another car.

I heard whistling, then, "Hey there, Sherlock, how's life been treating you?" The voice was familiar: Timothy "Duke" Swege, in the flesh.

At the skinny little man's approach, the enormous Matthew turned and lunged back into the trees. Duke swaggered up like he was joining me at the bar, all reek of aftershave and broad-toothed bonhomie, ready to make a hit. His thin blond hair was slicked back, a gold chain glinted from the base of his chicken neck, and the heavy cuffs of his jacket were turned up to expose his bony wrists where they rose from the pockets of his jeans.

"Thanks," I panted.

" 'Twas nothing, fair lady," he soothed, taking my bandaged hand and kissing it. With his opposite hand, he produced another fair-sized chunk of gravel and added, "I always got something hard to offer someone as lovely as you. You just gotta call me a little earlier next time, so you can save your lather for me."

I leaned on the car, adrenaline crashing through my veins, uncertain whether to thank him or slap him across his pustule-ridden face. I settled for muttering, "Got a flashlight, Galahad? I dropped some car keys here."

The Duke turned. "Hey, Grandma! Got a flashlight?"

"What, dear?" I heard, from beyond the cars toward the street.

"Don't call her in here!" I urged. "That monster's still out there somewhere in those bushes!"

Duke laughed. "Matthew? Don't worry about him. He's a big coward."

I stared at him. "That coward was coming straight at me!"

"Oh, really?" he taunted. "Well, he took off fast enough, didn't he? You just can't let them know you're scared, darlin'."

This was the limit. After getting scared witless, being lectured by a banty rooster about how to strut was beyond what I could stand, even if the rooster in question had just saved my skin. I lunged toward him, grabbing at the front of his jacket, but as I did so, I kicked the keys and heard them ring against the gravel. I sighed, my anger collapsing under its own weight. "Want to help?" I said, opening the trunk of the car and dropping the load of bread summarily into Timothy Duke Swege's scrawny arms. "Into the hall. Double step!" I slammed the trunk. Hard.

"Hey, don't get so jumpy." He looked me up and down, his eyes lingering on my none-too-awesome bosom. "You're taking life way too seriously, Sherlock. You know what you need? You need a man around you, that's—"

"Oh, dry up!"

Duke turned his narrow shoulder toward me and shrugged it. "Okay, darlin', but just remember, things get too tough for you in Sherlock land, you just give old Duke a call."

◆

INSIDE THE HALL, I marched straight to Dierdre Karsh and pushed the keys into her hands, making a point of brusque physical contact. She took the pressure impersonally, as if hit by a sudden gust of wind. I stared into her pale gray eyes, ready for whatever bullshit excuse she might hand me.

A tiny light kindled in her eyes. She used that tone. "Is there something wrong, dear?" she inquired.

"Your son just tried to assault me. Again," I seethed, wondering why I couldn't say it more directly: *You set me up.*

"I'm sure you're mistaken," she soothed, offering me a lovely little smile, a prim thing that suggested a curl of her dry lips could make the last five minutes mean nothing.

So innocent was the look that I almost bought it. "No. I am not mistaken," I assured her.

Her eyes went dead. They did not shift, did not stray from their focus on mine, but one moment she was seeing me, and the next instant her eyes were vacant. Blip. Door locked. Occupant gone away.

I heard a voice behind me, too close for comfort: "Is something the matter, Dierdre?"

I turned. Valentine Reeves stood inches away. He peered down into the well of my eyes, arrogantly taking his time, searching for the exact nerve on which he would apply his pressure. When he spoke again, he smiled as if we were having a lovely conversation, but kept his voice too low to be heard beyond my ears: "You're a stranger here. I've checked you out. You'd best consider leaving now, because this is a *very* tight community."

The gloves were off.

I STAYED IN the firehouse until the Feed was over, waiting until the firemen were close enough to cleaned up that I could ask Jim Erikson to walk me to my truck. But before I asked, he said, "Want to maybe go out for a beer?"

"Me?"

Jim glanced around like, *Can't you be a little quieter about this,* and said, "Yeah. You know, like a beer."

"Well, okay."

As I waited for him to get his jacket, I began to wonder just what he and Valentine Reeves had been saying to each other. A beer, huh? Just whose idea was this tête-à-tête, really?

As Jim and the others shuffled out the door, I let myself be carried along in the flow. As the flow ebbed away, Jim turned to me and smiled shyly. "My vehicle's right over here," he said, as he put a hand out and touched the small of my back, guiding me toward his truck.

I stepped away from the warmth of his hand, wary from my earlier foolishness. "No, that's okay," I said firmly. "I have my own truck right here. I'll follow you; that way I can just continue on from there, and you won't have to bring me back."

"Okay," Jim said. I couldn't read his face. It was in shadow. We got in our respective vehicles and turned west on Occidental Road, which twisted and turned for several miles before spilling us out in a little town stuck in a cleft between wooded hills. The shop fronts were early-twentieth-century clapboard specials done up with trendy signs advertising restaurants and knickknack emporiums. Jim led me into the bar in the Union Hotel, a nice old joint with wooden tables and chairs, and ordered a couple of long-necks. He hadn't spoken as we walked in from the parking lot, just kept his hands in his pockets and his head down, and now that we were seated, he didn't seem have a whole lot more to say.

My heart sank. If indeed this man had ever found me attractive, the combination of Reeves' private words with him and my standoffishness had quashed it. Sure, I had good reason to be cautious around Jim, after what I'd been through and with where I was heading, but as I sat there watching him look everywhere in the room but at me I realized that I did indeed like him, even though he wasn't Frank Barnes. Unfortunately, in that lonely moment, sitting with a man I didn't know in a half-empty bar in a town I'd never seen before, I needed Frank sitting beside me.

I made an attempt at conversation. "You're an electrician?"

"Yeah." He waved at a friend who passed through from the street to the restaurant beyond.

So much for conversation starters. With a heavy spirit, I gave up trying to be sociable and put my mind back on my work. "So Reeves builds lots of projects around the area?"

"Yeah."

"Low-income stuff?"

"Yeah."

"That seems fairly enlightened."

"Oh, he's helped out a lot around here, building housing for old folks and poor folks, so they can be part of the community they work in or grew up in, and he's been buying up old places and renovating them, so the area keeps the old flavor."

"You sound doubtful."

Jim stared uncomfortably at the tabletop. "Oh, I guess some people think he's doing it *to* us instead of *for* us."

I asked some more questions, but Jim didn't seem to want to say any more about Valentine Reeves. The silence began to drag. Our beers came. We nibbled chips. He waved at another friend. I felt even lonelier and more out of place and even more frustrated, and wanted to leave. The combination of loneliness, fatigue, and my burgeoning paranoia began to send my mind to places it didn't belong. I began to imagine things. Such as that he was working directly for Reeves. Reeves had set the entire community against me. Therefore, Jim had brought me here so that Reeves' henchmen could wire a bomb to the undercarriage of my truck.

"I kept overhearing people talking about a water project," I said, trying to distract myself. "What's that all about?"

Jim took a pull on his beer and stared at me. "The Mills has its own local water district, a set of wells with water treatment, supplies about half the community."

"And that's a problem?"

"Well, everyone had their own wells before, and most still use them to water their gardens. The problem was more quality than quantity. They say the water stank and tasted like, well, you know."

"So what's the problem now?"

"Well, there's this group that doesn't like having the county manage it for them."

I recalled the fanaticism in Liza's eyes, and the combativeness of her words. "Why?"

For the first time since we'd sat down, Jim smiled, a crimp at one corner of his mouth. "I'm not in the district. Thank God." He looked away across the room.

The conversation lagged again. I couldn't think clearly about the investigation, let alone any questions that Jim might be able to answer for me. I began to count the minutes before it would seem polite to leave.

A weird sense of agitation started to gnaw at me. Suddenly it began to feel *important* to leave, and to leave *soon*. I began flashing on Janet's boxes back in my motel room. The sense of urgency grew, a need to get back to the motel and protect those boxes.

"Is something the matter?" Jim asked, his spine straightening as he went into EMT mode.

My ears began to ring. "No. Yes. I'm sorry, but I got to go. I—uh, don't feel well. Yes, I really think I ought to leave now. Sorry."

Jim reached across the table and touched my forehead with the back of his hand. "Has this happened before?"

The agitation had my mind racing, and my skin felt oversensitized. The last thing I wanted at that instant was someone touching me. "No. I have to get back to where I'm staying. Now."

Now Jim had hold of my wrist, feeling for my pulse. "You look pale, and you're perspiring. Your pulse is fast. Here, put your head down on your knees," he said, getting to his feet and pulling my chair out from the table so I'd have room. His hands moved over my neck and shoulders with authority, urging me to lower my head. "Had anything unusual to eat lately? Drunk water from a pond or anything?"

I fought his attempts to lower my head. "No, never." But as I thought that thought, Suzanne's weird tea came to mind. Was this some aftershock from whatever toxins had been in that draft? At that instant I could almost taste it again, all woody and astringent on my tongue, now badly entwined with the garlic and beer. "I'll be okay, really; I just want to get going. Please." I stood up abruptly.

Jim gripped my arm. "I'll carry you."

"No, damn it, I can walk. I just want to go!" I hurried out of the bar and lurched back to my truck. My hands shook as I pressed the keys into the door lock.

Jim hovered by my side, the authoritative fireman quickly crumpling into an uncertain boy. "Let me come with you, just to make sure you're safe."

"No need," I insisted, opening the door of the truck into his face.

"How can I reach you? I'm—worried about you."

"I'll give you a call."

"Promise?" He thrust his hands deep into his pockets, and raised his shoulders up to his ears like he was cold.

"Sure. I'll leave a message at the firehouse," I said, my mouth spitting out any words I thought might get him to let me go.

"Okay," he said doubtfully, but I cut him off, slamming the truck door as I drove quickly away.

23

I FOUND THE DOOR TO MY ROOM AJAR.

I stepped to one side of the door and pushed it farther open with my toe, but even as it swung open those few inches, I knew the maid hadn't just left it unlocked while leaving. The lock had been struck with a heavy object, and a light was on in my room. It looked like a tornado had touched down. Janet Pinchon's personal effects were strewn madly across the floor.

I'm not a complete idiot. I didn't go right in, I ran to the lobby and told the manager what had happened.

Her eyes grew wide. "Someone is in your room?" she spat, indignant at the thought.

"The place has been ransacked. Call the police," I said, turning to see if anyone was coming around the side of the building. I heard her say, "I'm right behind you. I'm dialing now." Still watching the walkway, I waited until I heard her speak the essentials into the phone and then the clacking sound of the phone landing back in the cradle, and started to run back to my room. Kicked the door open. Saw no one. Ran in and roared with anger: each box had been dumped; each book, each item of clothing, whipped into chaos. The bedclothes had been ripped back as if by one mighty hand. There were red letters on my sheets, scrawled in big ugly strokes from one of Janet's marking pens. The letters formed just one word: WHORE.

I heard a sound behind me. I dully remember thinking it was the manager coming in.

Thick, rough fingers closed around my throat and squeezed. I tried to scream. I pried at the fingers, trying to free myself, trying to twist around and get a look at the person who was pressing the life from my neck, but my head was held firmly in place and all I could do was flail at the heavy form that stood rooted behind me. My fists hit soft, cushiony flesh that covered a body as thick as a stump.

The hands began to force my face down toward the sheets. Before my face reached the bed, the room grew gray and splotchy, then very quiet.

I saw nothing but tiny stars in a dark heaven.

24

THE DARKNESS WAS MADE OF COAL-BLACK VELVET. THERE WAS a loud ringing in the middle of the darkness, and far away and below me there was a planet that called to me, but I didn't want to go there, I wanted to stay out here in the darkness. The darkness was comforting and lovely, and the planet such a cold and lonely place.

Then I found that there were words in my head, snaking around my brain like shining ribbons, registering more as sight than as sound. They said, "Oh, I see it's happening to you now. But you can live, so why don't you?"

I twisted in the darkness, searching for the source of the words, but instead began falling toward that planet. I called out, my words flying like bits of color, "Who? Who are you? Let me see you!" When the reply came it was muffled, the colors fading out: "I'm Janet. I live out here now."

Then the velvet darkness extinguished, degrading into just an absence of light and a dull throbbing. As the world swept up under me, smacking me with the law of gravity, I felt the soft pressure of bedclothes against the front of my body, and knew that I was lying across my bed. My legs canted painfully off the edge of my bed, their weight resting on the tips of my boots, which seemed to be filling with the pressure of settling fluids and agonized flesh. I couldn't find the strength to open my eyes. I tried to cry out, but could manage only a tiny *aaah*.

I heard a clearing of bad sinuses and a familiar voice. "She's coming to. Is the ambulance here yet?" Why was Deputy Dexter here, and who was he talking about? Who needed an ambulance?

A numbness at my throat gave way to the beginnings of pain, and I understood at last what had happened. I had been strangled. And an old riding injury in my coccyx began to throb. I managed to slide a hand over toward one hip to make sure that my jeans were still in place, and said a prayer of thanks that I had been spared at least the humiliation of showing my bare buttocks to Deputy Dexter.

"Here it comes," said a second voice, distraught, feminine. The manager. "Ah, she's alive then? *Gracias a Dios!*" I felt her cool hand against mine. I tried to thank her, but my voice still hung in ribbons back there in the velvet darkness.

"Did you see who did this?" Dexter asked her.

"No. When I came, she was already like this, the door open. No one else was here. I called the ambulance from that phone by the bed and covered her to keep her warm. I couldn't tell if she was still breathing. Can I put the blanket back on her now?"

Dexter let out a long, tired breath. "She's lucky. The perp must have heard you coming and had to run for it before he could finish her. Yeah, you can go ahead and cover her up."

I heard the siren grow louder and louder, impossibly loud, then shut off. The sound of a vehicle pulling up outside the door. Footsteps.

I felt the manager's warm breath close to mine. "Help is here. You be okay, hear?"

"What's the name?" Dexter asked the manager.

"Mine?" she replied.

"No, hers. She looks familiar."

"Her name is Emily Hansen. Wyoming license. She's been here about five days."

There was a pause, then Dexter's voice again. "Hansen? Oh, her."

More people hurried into the room, feet trampling Janet's beautiful books into a sorry mat of frayed pages. "Watch it," Dexter barked. "This is a crime scene. Leave me a little evidence, why don't you?"

"What do we have here?"

"Strangulation. She's breathing."

Sure hands touched me here and there, feeling for pulse and respiration. A firm voice told me to take it easy and rest, that I was going to be okay, not to worry. Someone pressed a protective collar into position around my neck. I grabbed at it, tried to tear it away from my throat, tried to push myself up from the bed. Big hands flew all around me, restraining me. I tried to speak, to beg them to take the collar off, but my tongue seemed to fill the entire cavity of my mouth. Then they rolled me over. The room spun and I wanted to vomit. I opened my eyes.

The first person I saw was the manager, her eyes soft and deep with concern. My vision swam. I wanted to put my head against her bosom and wail.

Metal clicked against metal as the medics adjusted the gurney to the height of the bed, and a moment later, I was shifted onto it, my head cradled in a brace to keep me from turning it.

"Okay, Ms. Hansen, what happened in here?" Dexter demanded.

"Hands—" I began, but a rip of pain in my throat stopped me.

"Did anyone else see anything?" Dexter asked, turning back to the manager.

I started to say, *Janet did,* but knew that wouldn't do. Then I began to worry. Had I really *seen* Janet? No, I had heard her, or no, seen her words. Like beautiful ribbons. And now she was gone. Or was she? Was I hanging on to her, like Suzanne said? Hanging on to those ribbons of speech streaming out across an infinite void. Why not? They were beautiful, they were—

"No," the manager replied. "It's been very quiet, no one in the nearby rooms. I'm the only one here tonight, except my daughter and the baby. The baby called to me just as I was coming. I feel awful. If I hadn't gone to him, I might have seen—"

"And been assaulted yourself. Any strange vehicles parked around here? Anyone hanging around?"

"No, but a person could come from any direction. Except I guess the freeway."

"Anyone come to the desk and ask for a key? Any phone calls for her, asking the room number?"

"No. Just her aunt called this evening."

Frida? Frida had called? That meant Elyria had called her, and . . . My head began to pound with pain.

A medic spoke. "We're ready to move her. You can question her at the ER later on."

Dexter bent down toward me. "Do you have any idea who did this?"

I tried to speak, but still could not, my nightmarish fear of not being able to cry out visiting me as I woke. I began to shake. I closed my eyes and pressed back tears.

Dexter stood up and turned away. "Take her away."

25

Deputy Dexter never came to the hospital. An officer who identified herself as a member of the Domestic Violence Sexual Assault Unit arrived at the hospital with the ambulance and stayed with me, asking questions as the doctor and nurses examined me and took pictures of the bruises on my neck and at the base of my spine. She was just going over the problem of where I was going to stay that night—the detectives were still combing my room for evidence, she said, and another room at the same motel was no more secure—when this problem resolved itself. I saw a familiar face: Aunt Frida, poking her head around the doorframe of the examining room.

Frida's intelligent eyes shone with both pleasure and pain at seeing me. As usual, her short hair stuck out in inelegant, unkempt tufts, but it was grayer than the last I'd seen her. When had that been? She hadn't been at Father's funeral. I struggled to remember why. Or had I ever known? So much had been left unspoken on that most painful of occasions.

Having caught my eye, she stepped the rest of the way into the room. She seemed stooped, and her aging eyes were framed with worry. She had moved away from Wyoming when? Five years earlier. Had it been that long since I'd seen her? She shook her head at me. "Is that Emmy Hansen I see here, the little whippersnapper who tried to ride my worst stallion when she was only four?"

"Hi, Frida," I sighed. I immediately began to relax enough to feel jittery.

"Well, you little marmot, what the hell you gone and gotten yourself into this time?" She crossed the room and touched my cheek with a cool, rough hand. "Hah. So you're a private de-tective now. Don't you know you could have got yourself killed doing that? Stick to breaking horses, Emmy; they let you down kinder."

I tried to smile. "Who let you in here?" I rasped. My throat felt like I'd been gargling broken glass. "I mean, how'd you know to come?"

"Oh . . . this woman calls herself Elyria Kretzmer phones up and says, 'Secure the livestock, Em Hansen's in California.' "

"I'm not sure that's exactly how she'd put it."

"Words to that effect. Anyways, I tried to call you earlier, do my Christian duty and get you out to the ranch to dinner. Well, but you weren't there, were you? No, you were out playing Lone Ranger. I had quite a little chat with your motel lady. She allowed as how you already ripped a knee and near to lost your hand somehow, and how it looks like you been living on tap water and the glue off of old cans. I told her that warn't no surprise; you're half coyote and half goat, and more stubborn than either parent. And dumber." Her expression sobered. "*She's* smart; she called back soon's this happened. Well, hospitals make me sick. Let's get you out to the ranch and get you rested up."

About then, I would have cuddled under her jacket like a newborn lamb in a spring blizzard. The need was so strong it scared me. "I can't go yet," I blustered. "Deputy Dexter hasn't taken my statement yet."

Frida screwed up her face. "You under arrest or something?"

I scowled back. "No, I'm the assault*ee,* not the assaulter."

"What's wrong with that lady cop who was in here with you just a moment ago? She ain't doin' her job?"

"Well, yeah, *she* asked a bunch of questions, but I'm not letting Deputy Dawg brush me off."

"You want a date with him or something?"

"Goddamn it, Frida, this ain't funny!" I snapped, briefly sucked into the family aw-shucks speech patterns. Then, pulling myself up on my dignity, I said, "Whoever did this killed a woman just like me, and I'm not going to let him get away with it!"

Frida's eyes turned to flint. "I know that, missy. Don't you think I been all over the Sheriff's Department like a cheap suit already? I got a phone in my truck, and we had quite a little talk while I was driving in here. I told them come morning to put on their saddles, as we'd be riding them 'til they's broke. Nobody, but nobody messes with my flesh and blood without *payin'* for it. But right now, missy, you're going to get a square meal and some sleep!"

DETECTIVE MULLER GREETED us the next morning with the same breezy, uninformative manner he'd used two days before to brush me off. He showed me into the same tiny room, inviting Frida to stay outside. Frida insisted on coming in. She stood behind me rather than sitting, and fixed Muller with her nastiest stare. Muller appeared unmoved.

I chose the direct approach. "It was Matthew Karsh," I asserted. "Or Valentine Reeves." I didn't mention Pat Ryan. I couldn't stand to even think that idea, and the last thing Pat needed was the cops down his collar. "Or even Curt Murbles."

"Who?"

"Janet's father's personal assistant. But it was Matthew Karsh." Why was I saying that? Through the night I had tried again and again to dispel his image from my mind, his hateful eyes, his grasping fingers, but I could not. On the way to the Sheriff's Department that morning with Frida I had promised myself that I would deliver my evidence and— and yes, demand action, but try to maintain an open mind, try to remain in some small way a scientist, ready to consider all possibilities. But now I had let my emotions get the better of me. I could see in Muller's eyes that he thought less of me for it, and would discount whatever I had to say.

Muller raised his eyebrows politely. "And how do you know that, Ms. Hansen?"

I jerked open my collar in reply. "I measured his glove size." Between my teeth, I added, "Strangulation from behind and attempted rape. Same M.O. as Janet Pinchon. And when I swung my arms behind me, I hit . . . someone sloppy." That was true, I had. Murbles was a slender man, and Reeves seemed fit. Had my assailant just been wearing a heavy jacket? But there was more, a sense of why I knew not who it was, exactly, but what he had been like. I just couldn't put my finger on what that sense was telling me.

Muller stepped forward and took a look at my neck, examining my throat with the same interest a stone cutter would show the crown jewels. "Hmm, hmm. Yes, those are nasty bruises. My problem is, though, that it says here in your statement that you did not actually see your assailant. So how do you know who it was? Did he speak to you?"

"The son of a bitch tried to kill me!" I snapped.

Muller nodded. "I'm so pleased that you survived."

"And rape me, Goddamn it!"

Muller looked at the report in his clipboard. "Yes, a nasty bruise, but there's no mention here of semen. . . ."

I heard a rushing in my ears, and my body began to shake. I felt Frida's strong hands descend upon my shoulders. I closed my eyes. "I'm not naive. I know damned well that a great many rapes are not performed with penises."

Muller continued to speak as if we were a couple of government employees discussing a recipe for Christmas cookies. "I understand that, but you see, we need physical evidence to connect us to a particular rapist."

I took a long, deep breath and continued. "You know what case I've been working on."

"Case?" Muller's already peppy frame straightened up even further.

"Oh, for Christ's sake. Janet's Pinchon's father hired me to look into her murder."

"You're a P.I.?"

"I am a geologist."

"You're saying a—Mr. Pinchon, would it be?—hired a geologist to investigate his daughter's death?"

"I am looking at things from the perspective of the deceased."

Detective Muller sat down on the edge of the table and draped his hands over one knee. "And what have you discovered?"

"Where's the camera?" I demanded. I was tired of the runaround. It was time to show him that I knew a few things, that he should respect me.

"The what?"

"And the audio pickup. Come on, Detective, I know the drill. Who's listening in? I'm not the criminal in this investigation, I'm one of the good citizens who's *trying* to help." It was a stupid display, and probably only went further to convince the detective that I shouldn't be trusted.

Frida stepped around beside me and stretched herself up as tall and as intimidating as her five-foot-three-inch frame could muster.

Muller tipped his head, giving me his Botticelli angel impression. "Ms. Hansen, you may rest assured that the crime against your person is being taken very seriously, and investigated thoroughly."

Frida butted in: "Didn't you even check this Karsh fellah out?"

Muller blinked at Frida, turned back to me, smiled a Mona Lisa smile. "Ms. Hansen, we want to make sure that, while obeying the law is every citizen's concern, enforcing it is the work of our department and the courts. I think you ought to know, just so you're not tempted to get confused, that we visited Matthew Karsh last evening, and were told by his mother that he was with her all evening, ever since riding straight home from the Spaghetti Feed with her—which he did because he does not drive a car. He was, in fact, there with her when our deputy arrived at their house directly after securing the scene of last night's crime and turning it over to the detectives."

I pressed doggedly onward, furious that I couldn't clear my mind of my emotions and lay out my thoughts and evidence logically, cooly, compellingly. Some detail kept eluding me. I wasn't getting through.

"How long after he—after I was hit? Jaime Martinez could have driven him. Was he agitated or sweating? Can he *prove* he was there the whole time? And what about Reeves? Where did he go after the Feed?"

Detective Muller gazed blandly into my eyes. "Let me be even more direct. I understand that you're upset, Ms. Hansen, but for all we know, that murder and your assault are not even connected. Now, don't you think it better to leave this investigation to us?"

FRIDA HELPED ME down the shallow steps in front of the courthouse like I was an invalid. About then I felt like one. "Let's go back out to the ranch," she said soothingly, "maybe take a ride. Life always looks better between the ears of a horse."

"But I *know* things."

"I believe you."

"But, Frida—"

"But, Em, these Sheriff guys is slick as wet soap."

"They treated me like *I* was the criminal."

"Now, that's not altogether true. They got a job to do, just like you, and you kind of tried to tell them what their job was. And they're right, it's best you leave any contact with suspects to them. So why don't you just get off the skyline for a while? A woman could get shot out here in the open."

I barely heard Frida's words. I felt dirty, stupid, and scared. My legs were shaking too hard to carry me onwards. I sat down on the bottom step. Why had I gone into that motel room when it had so clearly been violated? Had I lost the capacity to care about myself?

Pieces of the puzzle spilled about in my mind, spinning, looking for connections. Valentine Reeves and his construction projects. Senator Pinchon hiding in the weeds, trying to cover some political bombshell. Rauch and Hollingsworth stealing from their clients and firing their most dedicated employees. Jaime Martinez prowling like a fox around the Laguna. Missing sisters. Aging catatonic fathers, attack dogs, and

redheaded secretaries with attitudes. Just how were they all tied together, and what secret secured the knot?

I felt Frida tugging at my arm. "Come on, I'll let you chop a cord
of wood and then muck out the stables. You'll be fine."

As I rose again to my feet, I glanced around, taking in the array of
two-story government buildings around me. "This the County Administration Center, right?" I asked.

"Yeah. Why?"

An idea was forming in my overheated brain. "Then the Assessor's
Office is near hear. I'm going there."

IF YOU EVER WANT TO KNOW WHO OWNS WHAT AND SINCE when, take yourself to the County Assessor's and Recorder's Offices. They're usually right across the hall from each other, and they keep the records of all births, deaths, marriages, and deeds. Sonoma County's records were in good shape, all nicely reduced to microfiche and microfilm and carefully stored in pleasantly decorated public offices. I asked a few questions at the counter, getting my bearings on the local filing system, and then took Frida over to one of the microfiche readers to get started. Within an hour, we were beginning to see what the rub was with Family Karsh.

For a dollar a page, I purchased photocopies of parcel maps that showed the area on both sides of the Laguna near Sanford and Ferris roads. Matching up the parcel numbers with the ownership records (numerical listing), we quickly found out that the Dierdre F. Karsh Trust, Wilbur Karsh, trustee—and not Mr. and Mrs. Wilbur Karsh—was the listed owner of not just the twenty-acre tract of land on which Mrs. Karsh's house stood, but also of myriad other parcels nearby.

The Dierdre Karsh Trust. Was this the third piece of the monetary pie that Valentine Reeves had been dividing? And if so, if Dierdre Karsh had such enormous trust holdings, why would she need a piece of Reeves' pie forked back to her under the table, as it were, out of sight of both the lenders at the bank and the trustees?

Turning to the alphabetical listings, we looked up all other current holdings deeded to the Dierdre F. Karsh Trust, and found hundreds of acres of choice agricultural land and one five-acre parcel zoned commercial/industrial. This last parcel was registered as Misty Creek Winery.

Moving over to the Recorder's Office, we searched back into prior ownership of each parcel, digging for the source of the Dierdre F. Karsh Trust. It was rough going; my eyes burned from staring into the microfilm screen, and my throat began to throb, but bit by bit we uncovered a fascinating picture. A man named Rheingold J. Ferris had bought all of the holdings between 1915 and 1970, and then deeded them all at once to the Deirdre F. Karsh Trust in his last will and testament. It seemed that he had been her father.

His will was on record. Handwritten, no less. It made such good reading that I carried the microfilm to the desk and requested a photocopy.

I, Rheingold J. Ferris, being of sound mind and body, bequeath the sum and total of my worldly estate with the exception of that forty-acre parcel on Ferris Road which is my home to my sole heir, Dierdre Ferris Karsh, to be administered in trust. Upon her death, I decree that the trust shall pass to her children, Matthew James Karsh and Sonja Ferris Karsh.

I appoint Wilbur Henry Karsh, husband to Dierdre Ferris Karsh, as trustee of the Dierdre F. Karsh Trust, and assign him the office of executor of the estate, for all portions excepting that forty-acre parcel of land on Ferris Road which is my home. It shall be the task of Wilbur Henry Karsh to maintain the rest of my estate in its totality, neither selling real assets nor drawing moneys from it, excepting that he shall be given a yearly salary equal to one-half of the net income from the operation of the industrial facility of which enterprise he is currently manager. Wilbur and Dierdre Karsh may continue to inhabit the house on Sanborn Road which is a part of my estate and will be part of the trust.

That forty-acre parcel of land and improvements thereon on Ferris Road which are my home shall be held in separate trust for my granddaughter, Sonja Ferris Karsh, to be deeded to her on her twenty-first birthday. Until her twenty-first birthday, said property shall be under the trusteeship of my daughter, Dierdre Ferris Karsh, to be maintained for Sonja Ferris Karsh. If Sonja Karsh does not survive until her twenty-first birthday, the property shall be deeded instead to the German Emigrants' Pension Fund, to be disposed of as they see fit.

All other income and assets derived from the operation of the estate shall be invested and managed by the firm of Jordey and Hawke, Santa Rosa, who will administer both trusts toward the future well-being and maintenance of my grandchildren and their children, and their children's children. During the lives of Deirdre Ferris Karsh and Wilbur Henry Karsh, moneys may be drawn from the estate only to support the educational attainments of my grandchildren.

Upon the death of Wilbur Henry Karsh, the trusteeship of the estate, and the half income as above stated, shall be assigned to a qualified person to be identified at the appropriate time by Wilbur Henry Karsh.

Upon the death of Dierdre Ferris Karsh, the estate shall pass in trust to my afflicted grandson, Matthew James Karsh, and to my

granddaughter, Sonja Ferris Karsh, in even parts. The estate shall
be managed in trust by Wilbur Henry Karsh, by his assigned suc-
cessor, and so in perpetuity.

I chased back over to the Assessor's Office and looked up the ownership of the land on which Jaime lived, the old Ferris place, a name
Jaki had mentioned and that I now had reason to recognize. Sure
enough, that was the forty-acre parcel being held as the Sonja F. Karsh
Trust, Dierdre F. Karsh, trustee.

I was appalled. Never in my born days had I seen a plan so bent on
maintaining control of the lives of one's descendants, even from beyond the grave. He was treating his daughter like a mental invalid. The
vision of a stiff and rage-filled old man filled my mind, disdainful eyes
bulging and gnarled hands bent in fists. I wondered in what form this
specter haunted Dierdre Karsh.

FRIDA WAS TUGGING on my shoulder. "Enough. I'm taking you
home and back to bed."

I spun around, dropping the photocopied pages of Rheingold Ferris' will. "No! I'm just beginning to get somewhere!"

Frida drew me firmly out the door and onto the cement portico in
front of the building. "Em Hansen, I'm going to tell it to you straight:
I think you're coming unhinged. You're talking to yourself. Not generally a habit of yours, is it? Look, your hands are shaking. And just a
moment ago, you looked like you'd seen a ghost. That ain't healthy.
Now, come on, before I have to hog-tie you and drag you out that
door."

I pushed the pages toward her. "No, Frida, look: this will is the key
to everything."

Frida read it. "And?"

"This Ferris guy was a control freak. Don't you see? That's why

Dierdre Karsh is the way she is. And why her disgusting son is the way he is, and why it all happened."

"You mean the old man treated her like an incompetent, so she's raised her son to be one, too?"

Not exactly what I'd been thinking, but it would do. "Sort of."

Frida gave me a long, gauging look. "Em, nothing's ever as simple as all that."

I glared at her. She was right; when stated that simply, all the poisonous subtlety was lost. Frida had never met Mrs. Karsh, or Matthew. She hadn't heard that sweet, almost seductive tone Mrs. Karsh used around him, hadn't seen his eyes ignite with free-floating hatred when he heard it. But come to think of it, why had I seen these things if a whole community of people had not? "Okay, then, let me explain," I began, hoping I could. "Everyone in town sees Matthew Karsh as a pathetic mess. They all seem to think he's still about six years old; I've seen two guys who are downright petite make him cower. But in fact, he's all grown-up. He attacked me two times I'm sure of, and I feel in my bones that that was him last night in the motel."

Frida looked sadly at the bruises on my neck. "Define grown-up. Define attack. No, sorry, it doesn't fit: if he's so busy cowering, how's come he can strangle people? You just said you seen two little guys he was scared shitless of."

"Frida, he's a bully, and that term I can define. A bully is a coward who's found someone he's not afraid of. Those little guys were men. I'm a woman."

"That's not brain-damaged, that's crazy."

"I won't argue that."

"Emily, you saw what you saw at that dinner and the winery and at that house, but this business at the motel is another matter. It's a long way from trying to scare someone to trying to kill them, and Muller's right, your motel is a long way from where that woman got killed. And make up your mind: is this Matthew guy brain-damaged or crazy?"

"Why do I have to choose? I've seen him with his family; his be-havior is blatantly hostile, yet they treat him like he's just an oversized child. It's like a bad dream. Ma kind of goes into a trance and talks to him all sweetie-like, almost goading him along, and Dad just trots along behind him hoping he hasn't done any damage. A more despondent, self-pitying old wimp I haven't met lately. And that's being nice. Look at it another way: Dad has everything to gain by going along with the status quo, staying in charge of that trust, not rocking the boat. The only person who's the least bit direct about things is the redheaded mis-tress who doesn't want her deal to go down. You should have *seen* how she stared me down."

Frida sighed heavily. "It's not that I disbelieve you, Em. Somebody certainly attacked you, and I'm not letting that drop as long as Sheriff is an elected office. But they've just told us they didn't find no evi-dence, and I don't believe in conspiracies of silence. Why, if this guy Matthew is that big a monster, is not one *resident* of this county, who knows him a lot better than you, crying foul?"

Frida was right, my case was full of holes. My mind wobbled with uncertainty, considering her side of the argument, quickly bogging down in reasonableness. That's the trouble with being a geologist. Our minds are constructed to spot the errors in our own thinking, and the more certain we become about anything, the more easily we worry that we've missed something crucial.

I thought of Janet, out there alone along the Laguna, trying to doc-ument the truth about whatever it was she had been looking for. I could almost see her riding up and back, watching, searching, now stopping to take a closer look. She would have double-checked each datum, confronted each allegation of the use of toxic materials on that prop-erty by interviewing the people who had used it. Her very honesty would have drawn her that extra inch closer to harm's way. . . .

Yes, Frida was right, I had not a shred of evidence that Matthew, or for that matter, anyone else I had identified, had attacked me or killed Janet, but somebody had. I kept arguing, if only to delude myself, that

I was doing something to track that person down and put him away. Doing nothing was just too painful. "The people who know Matthew Karsh never *see* him anymore. Or if they do see him, they see the Matthew who freezes when a skinny boy throws a piece of gravel at him."

Frida touched my shoulder gently. "Maybe that's all he is, Em. Just a big cripple who likes to scare little girls. And if Ma seems a little loco, maybe it's because she's been cooped up with that kid all them years. Or maybe Granddad knew what he was doing, Em. Maybe she's *non compos mentis.*"

"No, Frida, that's not my take. A little peculiar maybe, but she's also *shrewd.* She suffers in silence, but she gets her licks in: drops the boy off at the winery when she goes to her ladies' meetings so Pa can spend the afternoon chasing him around through the warehouses."

Frida blew a hank of hair off her forehead. "They call that 'passive-aggressive.' "

"Fine, passive-aggressive."

Frida shook her head, dropped her tone to emphasize that all kidding was over. "Em, you got yourself throttled and now you want to lynch someone. That's normal, but it ain't healthy to brew all this up from what little you know about these folks. And you still haven't shown me why any of these people would want to kill your geologist lady."

I sighed. "My geologist lady walked right into the middle of that family and didn't come out again alive. I feel it in my bones. They're just not normal folk. Look what Mrs. Karsh's father did to her: he installed her in a depressing old house, left her inheritance in trust where she can't control a dime of its income, set up her philandering husband—who he probably chose for her—to administer it, and then, just to really rub it in, he made her trustee of her girlhood home, which his granddaughter will get free and clear as soon as she's of age. Do the math: that granddaughter was only thirteen when Granddad died; Mrs. K had eight years to gaze at that lovely place across the Laguna, knowing she's got to take real good care of it for everyone's little cupcake. Come on, how would that make you feel?"

Frida snorted. "Jealous as hell."

IN THE END, Frida won out and took me home. I was beginning to give in to a fatigue so deep I was stumbling, and besides, I couldn't think just then of much else I could accomplish, at the county offices or anywhere.

It had begun to rain. We slopped southward down Highway 101 first to the Wagon Trail Motel to pick up a few of my things, and to arrange to keep the room a few days longer. Packing up just now felt way too difficult, and I was content to leave the little blue truck right where it was. Frida insisted that I borrow one of her vehicles in future. She knew better than to think I had let go of the investigation.

The manager shook her head when she saw me, taking in the bruises on my neck with proper horror, whispered a prayer, and said there were a few messages for me. Frida grabbed them. "You'll have plenty of time to worry about these at the ranch," she said.

Before we got there, I was asleep, my neck gone stiff as my head bounced against the cool window glass.

FRIDA'S RANCH LAY along a hillside high above the Russian River, the main drainage into the Pacific Ocean into which all other waterways of the Santa Rosa Plain fed. On a topographical map Frida had on the wall of her living room, I could see that the Laguna flowed north into Mark West Creek, and Mark West into the Russian River at Wohler Bridge, a short trestle that joined its banks along a narrow part of its floodplain. Into the Laguna flowed the Piner and Santa Rosa Creeks, two channelized rivers that carried the runoff from the City of Santa Rosa westward across the Santa Rosa Plain. In aggregate, the winding blue lines that marked these drainages looked like the fingers of an open hand reaching in from the ocean. From a glance at the topographic contours, it looked like the floodplain of the Russian River was narrow enough that it would act like a tourniquet, backing draining floodwaters upriver to the Santa Rosa Plain. I studied the relatively flat topography around the Laguna. I had no doubt it could live up to its Spanish name.

Frida sent me out to my quarters, one of the guest rooms that had been carved out of the loft space above the office in the central barn. "You take a nice, long nap," she told me. "This rain ought to let up before long, and I have several three-year-olds who need exercising. But you rest first. The way you look now, you couldn't handle a hundred-year-old mule with the mange."

I fell into a deep sleep until late in the afternoon. When I woke up, I ventured into the house, laid out my change of clothes, and drew myself a bath. I undressed my injured body, trying not to see myself in the mirror, but something made me pause before immersing myself in water. It was an old, confused feeling I had not consciously felt in a long time, a mixture of guilt, anxiety, and sadness. It reminded me of being very little and painfully alone. Something had been let loose in the hours since those awful fingers had closed around my throat. Soap and fresh clothing helped dispel the feeling somewhat, but I still felt dirty, as if the marks on my body carried shame.

Frida banged into the house a few minutes later and shucked off her oilskins. "Still raining. I don't know about this climate. It don't rain all summer and fall, and then wham, you get the year's deluge in three or four months, and it's all this piss-poor rain. No snow never."

"How much precip altogether?"

"Oh, twenty-four inches, maybe. Some years only twelve. Other years, forty. It all depends."

I looked out the windows toward the line of trees that marked the river. It formed only a vague smudge of darkness in the gray mist of falling droplets. "I'll bet that thing floods if you get that much."

Frida nodded. "Yes, damned thing jumps its banks and all hell breaks loose. I met a fellow downriver by Guerneville, said it was his job during floods to poke the couches under the bridge with a stick so they don't cause a jam."

Our conversation lapsed.

Frida's was a modest ranch by Wyoming standards, not much more than a hundred acres, and with just a two-bedroom house, but the stables and barns were spacious and in good repair. The porch on the south side of the house was nestled in among white-blooming camellias, and commanded a view of the river, the low-lying vineyards, and rolling hills leading down onto the Santa Rosa Plain. Most important, the horseflesh at Frida's ranch was superb. She always did know how to breed a winner. Once again, I wondered why she'd left Wyoming. She'd left a full life's worth of friends and acquaintances behind, and even though the grass was better here and she'd obviously been able to improve her breeding stock of horses, I'd always heard that land prices were sky-high in California, and it couldn't have been easy to change her base of business. "Frida, why did you move out here? Did it have something to do with your husband dying?"

Frida didn't answer right away. She poured herself a glass of water at the sink in the kitchen and took a swig. After a while she said, in a low voice, "Yeah, something like that."

It wasn't like me to ask direct questions of my kin, but I was home-sick and my throat ached and if anyone in my family could help me find a new direction in life, Frida could. "You need help with this place? You got, what, thirty head out there; must be a lot of work mucking out all those stables."

Frida didn't turn her head, but I felt her attention on me as she tipped her glass once more to her lips. "Yup. I got help."

"Well, I—"

"I got a couple boys come in, and anyways, I got a partner'll be back by the end of the week."

I had stepped over the line. "Sorry."

"Don't apologize."

"It's just that—"

Frida's hands formed fists on the drain board. "Emmy, we all lose our fathers some time or another. I lost mine, and I didn't like it all that much." She pitched the rest of the water into the sink, set down the glass, and headed back out to the horses. I didn't see her again until eight.

27

THE NEXT DAY WAS TUESDAY. IN THE MORNING I PUT A CALL through to HRC Environmental and got Cynthia, who treated me to a loud snap of her gum as she said good morning.

"This is Em Hansen," I said, holding the earpiece a bit farther from my head. "I was sorry to have to just leave a message like that yesterday on the answering machine, but it was kind of an emergency, and—"

"What message?"

"That I couldn't make it to work yesterday. And today, for that matter." I wasn't certain if I was ever going back to HRC, but I wanted to maintain the option, just in case there was some other smidgen of information I thought I could extort from that closemouthed pack of thunderclouds.

"I didn't get no message. We thought you'd just left town or something. Mr. Rauch was real mad, and Adam, he—"

"But I left a message!"

"Jeez, I'm sorry. You know, I'm new here, and I wondered why there weren't no messages there from a whole two days of weekend. Maybe I hit the buttons wrong or something."

"Yeah, you did," I growled. "Well, can you put me through to Rauch? I suppose I've got to explain myself now. I'm, ah . . . ill."

"He ain't here."

"Well, hell; can I talk with Pat?"

"Pat Ryan?"

"You got any others around there?" I mentally slapped my own wrist. Mouthing off at people never helped in situations like this.

"Um, he ain't here either."

"When will he be back?"

"Um, he won't."

"What?"

"He quit."

"Quit? You mean he was fired."

"I'm not supposed to talk about it."

"You got a home number for him?"

"No, I'm not allowed."

So the bastards had canned him. I ran off and grabbed the phone book in search of a number for Patrick John Ryan. There was no listing in the book or with information, which meant I'd just have to go to his apartment to catch him before he left town. I felt an echo of his guilt, kicking myself just as he had kicked himself for not being in touch with Janet toward the end.

Just then, Frida came in from the barns. "Morning," she said, nodding cheerfully. "You look better."

"I'm feeling fine, actually. I'd like to help you feed the horses, or whatever you need done."

"Got it covered. Why don't you just rest awhile longer? I got the hired hands here, and my boy Abe'll be out in a few days for Christmas, so I've got plenty of help. You haven't seen your cousin in years, have you?"

Christmas. It was coming, and too soon. I had to get this investigation wrapped up before the holidays locked the whole town up like a vault. "Well, then, where are those phone-message slips you pocketed at the motel?"

Frida shook her head and pulled them out of her jacket pocket. There were three, all crumpled up. The first was from Elyria, from Sunday evening, saying call please, giving her home number in Denver. The second was from Pat Ryan, from Monday morning, saying good-bye and have a good life, and giving a local number. The third, also from Monday morning, was from Curt Murbles, ordering me to phone Washington ASAP. Frida brushed a hank of gray hair off her forehead and mumbled, "I called that Elyria person back for you, so she wouldn't worry any."

I shot her a look and grabbed the phone. Elyria could wait, then, but Pat Ryan might already be on his way to Fresno. I dialed the number and got no answer in seven rings. "Shit, the poor man probably needed someone to get drunk with. He just got fired," I gloomed.

"Now, don't get pissy with me, young lady; you ain't no candidate for a ritual drunk in your condition."

I glared at her. "A good drunk might be just what I need."

Frida glared back. "And be just like your mama."

I opened my mouth to speak, but closed it again. She couldn't have gotten her point across better if she'd slapped me.

And she didn't know that things had changed. That two weeks after my father died, my mother had checked herself into a clinic and dried out, and had gone to AA and stuck with it, and had written me a God-damned letter of amends. I buried my face in my hands and moaned, "Ma's sober now, Frida."

Frida shot up straight from where she'd been leaning on the counter. "Good on her! I always knew she had a little starch in there some-where!"

That was the limit. I wasn't ready to hear my mother spoken of as a woman with starch, not after all her years of drinking, not after putting her to bed passed out night after night and sneaking around in the mornings so I wouldn't wake her into one of her rages, and help-ing Dad do her chores and— "I'm going to town," I said coldly. With frigid civility I added, "May I borrow that truck, please?"

Frida laughed derisively. "What, did you want her to stay drunk for-ever?"

I wheeled on her. "Don't you understand? My father worked that ranch alone, day after punishing, blistering day! And where was she? Drunk in the house! He might still be alive if she'd—"

"No, Em, it's time *you* understood. Just who do you think went into town and bought her all that booze? Not her! It's eight miles into town from that godforsaken ranch, and you know damned well she quit driving near to fifteen years ago. So who bought her that booze, Emmy? Who? It was your father, Em! Your father bought her every Goddamned drop!"

I stared at my feet so Frida wouldn't see me cry. My voice came out in a whine: "I want to go to town. May I have the keys, *please?*"

Frida made a sound like a dry spit. "Have it your way."

◈

FRIDA MAY HAVE a temper, but she's a very practical woman. When it came to selecting a vehicle for me to drive, she chose a brand-new Ford F-250 pickup. Why? "Because it's plain vanilla and it'll climb a sheer cliff. If a V-eight was good enough for Al Capone, it's good enough for you."

I smiled grimly, having so recently learned what it was like to drive around in a moving target. Frida's truck was plain vanilla, all right: all white, and it was so new that it had no easily identifiable marks, not even a nick on it, and she had not yet had the ranch insignia painted on the door. As she handed me the keys, she showed me how to use the cellular telephone, which she kept hidden in the glove compartment. "You plug this here cord into the cigarette lighter, punch these buttons, then talk into it like it was a real phone or something. And use the damned thing, will you? You get your ass in another crack, you dial 911 first and me second, y'hear?"

I may be ignorant, but I learn fast: the first thing I did was go through the glove compartment and check the registration of the truck. All was copacetic. Registered to Horizons Ranch, Incorporated. Having established the legitimacy of my carriage, I stood back for a moment and admired the thing. It was high, wide, and handsome, with plenty of clearance, big knobby tires, pristine white paint, and lots of chrome. It was a dream truck, all rigged out with wide side mirrors and a big hitch for hauling a horse trailer to the shows, so Frida and her partner could make the best possible impression and get top dollar for their stud and training. I cinched myself in behind the wheel, turned the key, let the smooth resonance of the powerful 7.5-cubic-liter engine ripple through my body, and put her in gear with a smile on my face and a song in my heart.

◇

PAT WASN'T HOME. I considered climbing onto his balcony to peek in and see if his things were still there, but decided I was more likely to get arrested as a Peeping Tom than learn anything through that exercise. Instead, I scribbled a note saying I was looking for him and here's my new number, and jammed it into the crack between the door and the jamb right above the lock.

I drove next to the County Health Department, LUST Division, in search of Lucy. When I presented myself at the long governmental counter at this agency, I had to first *ahem* the attention of an overworked secretary who seemed intent on getting a memorandum typed. After signaling three times that she'd be right with me, she hurried off to refresh her coffee, took a sip, and then joined me, panting as if she'd just run the mile in under four minutes.

I cleared my throat and tried to smile. "I'd like to see Lucy, please."

When the secretary spotted the bruises on my neck, her jaw descended in rapturous horror as one hand rose to touch the same places on her own body, and curled her upper lip, like I'd smeared some unmentionable substance across my skin.

Tugging my collar up to cover the marks, I repeated, "Lucy, please?"

"Lucy McClintock?" she said, to my throat.

Gritting my teeth, I replied, "You got two?"

Still fixated on my throat, she picked up the receiver of a phone on the counter and dialed. What shame did she think I was carrying? I was the attacked, not the attacker. And yet a part of me felt that shame, like a cow too dumb to avoid being cut out of the herd by a wolf.

In a few moments, Lucy emerged from an inner room. When she saw me, she didn't smile. "Em Hansen, isn't it?" she asked crisply. From the tone of her voice, I gathered that she didn't look on me as quite the object of social stimulus as Earl the Earth Mover Phipps. I was in the "consultant" category, dog's bodies to be directed with martial precision into impoverishing one mom-and-pop grocery store owner after another.

"Yes. Thank you for seeing me, Lucy." I tried to smile again, but all I managed to do was stiffen my lips.

Lucy led the way through a rabbit warren of tiny office cubicles to the one she called home and pointed to a chair. Plopping her own girlish curves into the chair behind the desk, she said, "Go ahead and talk, I've got to finish my time sheet."

"You charge the client, too?"

"Oh, yes. They complain, but let 'em. Mess up, clean up." She picked up a paper form in a clipboard and scrawled some entries on it. I noticed that one of these was the mom-and-pop grocery where we had met. How long ago had that been? Had it really been only five days?

Lucy casually assessed this project five hours, although I was certain she had been on site no more than forty-five minutes.

"You charging for your lunch and driving time?"

"Of course. And the time it took to pull my notebook together, and file my forms when I got back, and the time it takes to fill out this form. I have the best charge record in the place."

"I'll bet you do."

Dropping the form in her Out basket, she said, "So HRC canned Pat, and now they're sending you into battle. Does that really seem wise, sending someone as inexperienced as you?" She leaned back in her chair, slung one leg over the other, and lowered her eyelids at my red boots, the better to emphasize how unconcerned she was with my emotional comfort.

"Replace Pat? I'm not on duty," I said, fighting off an urge to slap her. "As a matter of fact, I haven't been in at HRC this week. What's going on?"

Lucy shrugged her shoulders carelessly. "Pat Ryan blew another deadline. Weather-All's looking for blood."

"Who's Weather-All?"

Lucy knit her eyebrows at me in irritation. "The client."

I stared at her blandly. "I'm new here. Kindly enlighten me."

Lucy flicked a bit of lint off her pant leg. "Just a messy little site out by the Russian River. Old lumber-processing center. Leaking tanks all over the place. Soil and groundwater both totally contaminated with gas, diesel, waste oil, solvents, all sorts of slop they used to soak wood in. The groundwater's so shallow that product comes clear to the surface when it rains. You can see it running off in lovely rainbow sheens right into the river. Real idiots: We found this when we went up to inspect the site before approving their application to put in a well farm. We slapped a Cleanup and Abatement Order on them so fast their heads swam, and there's no way they're going to pump potable water out of there in our lifetimes."

"What's a well farm?"

Lucy looked bored, more interested in her own heroics than "the client's" business. "Oh, they wanted to make a municipal water system, pump a bunch of water out of the riverbank gravels and pipe it to Occidental. Developers." She said this last word with the same tone some people save for the word "leeches."

"Why do they need that?" I asked, remembering the glimpses of the quaint little town I had followed Jim Erikson to Sunday, just before . . .

My mind slipped out of gear, avoiding thinking about the way that evening had ended. I came back into focus as Lucy was saying, ". . . has lousy aquifers, won't make water like the aquifer around Sebastopol and Miwok Mills. And they need to show the county they have water to get a permit to build."

"So Weather-All wants to develop Occidental?"

"There's always someone up there who's bought a big parcel thinking they can make a buck on it. They never quit. They circled like

246 ◇ Sarah Andrews

vultures waiting for the kill when we condemned Camp Meeker's failing septic tanks."

"Camp Meeker?"

"That's a little place right outside Occidental. They figure great, let's
get a municipal sewer system to Camp Meeker and then hey, Occidental's only a hop, skip, and a jump away."

"Why does it make a difference to them whether they're on a sewer
or septic systems?"

"Because their ground fails the perc tests for septic systems for the
same reason the wells won't make water. Your ground has to perc or
we won't okay the leach fields. You can have a huge parcel of land—
say, ten acres—but if it won't perc, we won't permit more than two
bedrooms on the whole parcel. No water, no sewer, no development."

Was this what the horrifying Liza had been so het up about that she'd
tied to take on the County Supervisor at the Spaghetti Feed? "Doesn't
Miwok Mills have some kind of water project?" I asked.

Lucy stretched, starting to get bored. "Oh, yeah, bunch of local cra-
zies want to take their water district back from the county, run it themselves."

"Why?"

"They think we're dumping poison in it."

"Are you?"

"No."

The conversation seemed to be turning about an elusive central
point. I fought to keep it on track. "So Pat Ryan was writing a Work
Plan for emergency cleanup?"

"Yeah. The Water Board served the Cleanup and Abatement Order
a month and a half ago, and all we've had from the consultant—"

"HRC."

"—Pat Ryan, lead investigator, is a totally unacceptable Work
Plan."

Lucy's arrogance and condescension had gone way beyond grating on my nerves; it had nearly cut through them. I couldn't keep a certain tone of derisiveness out of my voice as I said, "You said the State Water Board served the Cleanup and Abatement Order. So why was the Work Plan sent to *you?*"

"County Health has to review it, too. We have to help keep the consultants honest."

"So what was wrong with it?"

"What was wrong with it? It looked like it was thrown together in five minutes by a drunk. We threw it out a month ago and told him to do it right, due yesterday. Now, late again, hand-delivered this morning by your Adam Horowitz, we get this," she said, rapping a document to the right of her time sheet with her knuckles. I took a squint. Sure enough, Work Plan Draft 2, HRC Environmental Consultants, Pat Ryan officiating as sacrificial lamb. "More rambling trash; it'll never work. I *told* Weather-All you were too small a firm to handle a job this big."

All I could think of to say to this was, "Pat's a nice guy."

Lucy canted her head forward and looked at me through her eyelashes. "He's a loser, honey."

I dug my fingernails into my palms. How dared this woman flaunt her power like this? And how dared she speak of a kind, decent man like Pat Ryan as if he were a hapless drifter? "What will the client do now?"

Lucy shrugged her shoulders. "Nothing. Hiring you was probably a ruse to look like they're taking action. Like they really mean to clean it up."

"What do you mean? Aren't there fines levied against them?"

Lucy opened a drawer in her desk, took out a half-eaten candy bar, and unceremoniously chomped into it. "Weather-All's just a front, a corporation. The boys who set it up will string this out as long as they can, which is quite a while. They've already managed to get the case assigned to a student intern over at the Water Board who's pretty green and easy to maneuver. When they've gotten their assets moved, they'll file for bankruptcy and take their dirty business somewhere else."

I had to hand it to Lucy. Under all that pompous self-importance she had a brain. "Who are the boys behind Weather-All's front?"

"We don't know. They're pretty secretive. My guess? It's drug money getting laundered. Or a bunch of fat cats from Washington running a scam and hiding behind a dummy corporation while they're in office. There are all sorts of funny guys out there along the river."

Needless to say, the moment Lucy said, "Washington," a red light went off in my head. Could the Good Senator be involved? "Doesn't the Cleanup Order name the officers of the corporation?"

Lucy yawned and bit into her candy bar again. "Yes, but they're front men. Losers."

My mind sped forward, making connections. "Is Valentine Reeves one of them?"

Lucy thought a moment. "No." Stuffing the last bit of candy into her mouth, she stood up. "Listen, I got to go. I got an appointment to get my hair cut."

I looked up at her, jolted into the realization that for Lucy, all these foul doings were just an eight-to-five job. She would leave now and go to the beauty salon, spruce herself up for the holidays, and forget all about Weather-All and dozens of other festering sites of contamination until tomorrow, while the dirty boys moved their assets and the Pat Ryans moved home to Fresno. "Just one more thing: I came to ask about a property by the Laguna de Santa Rosa. For an environmental assessment."

Lucy shrugged her shoulders again. "Fire away."

I gave the address of Janet's last job, the old Ferris Place, Jaime Martinez's roost.

Lucy shook her head. "That's not a site."

"Meaning?"

She pulled a sheaf of papers out of her file drawer and passed it to me. "These are all the properties we have files on, or active investigations—all the sites in our jurisdiction with known or suspected releases of toxic materials to soil and groundwater. It's cross-referenced by address and site name. There's nothing on Ferris Road. Is that what you came to ask me? You could have looked at the copy on the front desk."

With that I had heard one too many snide remarks from Lucy Mc-Clintock. I would not slap her, as I so dearly wished to do, but later, in the privacy of my room, I promised myself that I would disassemble her to her last curling eyelash, picking through all her obvious flaws for the one down deep that was truly offending me.

"Are we done here?" she asked impatiently.

"No. If I wanted to find a missing tank, how would I look for it?"

Lucy's eyes brightened. "A tank? What kind of a tank?"

"An underground tank, of course. Say I thought there might be a tank that someone had on their property that they didn't want found. How would I go about finding it?"

"Well, we've already done that. When our governing laws were promulgated and the regulations drawn up that opened this shop, the first thing we did was make a list of all known or suspected tanks. Lots of people hadn't registered their tanks, but we sent around a questionnaire, and you'd be surprised who came right out and bragged about them. We have lots of lists," she concluded smugly. "Just what are you after?"

"I want to know if there might be an unregistered, unreported tank on that site on Ferris Road."

"Could be. Lots of agricultural properties have outlaw tanks. The ag lobby fought like crazy to stay outside the regulations. That's why they're at the bottom of the SB2004 priority list. Even if that property's zoned residential but used agriculturally, use prevails in its classification. Now, do you have a suspected tank to report, or are you done here?"

I looked up. "So you found no tanks at that address?"

"I already said. If you want to subpoena the delivery records of all the bulk plant operators in the area, and believe me, they have their ways of losing old records, or if you want to find a farmer who'll squeal on another about his outlaw tank, then you can probably find all kinds of tanks out there that no one's copping to. Diesel, gasoline, heating oil, waste oil . . ."

"Thanks," I said. "If I—*when* I find it, I'll come straight to you. Then what happens?"

That question earned me one more shrug. "Then we send them a letter telling them to register it and show it's fit to hold what's it's built for, or pull it. You know the rest."

This would have to do. As far as the Karsh family went, it was the only pry-bar I had.

28

I found a listing for Swege in Miwok Mills. Granny answered on the sixth ring, not moving as fast as she used to, no doubt. "What do *you* want?" she shouted into the phone, when I told her who I was.

"I'm looking for Timmy," I said sweetly.

"Timmy? Oh, he's down at that bike shop, spending money." I heard a click, then a dial tone. So much for chatting with Granny.

I found the Duke sitting on the work bench next to Arnie's bike stand eating the latest thing in sports candy. "If it ain't Sherlock Holmes," he crooned with his mouth full. "How's tricks?"

Arnie looked up from the wheel he was balancing and smiled. "Hey there," he said. "What can I do for you?"

"Loan me Watson awhile."

Arnie's smile broadened. "Sure."

On my second pass past his apartment, I found Pat Ryan carrying a cardboard box of kitchen supplies out to his car. His face was blank, unreadable. It seemed to be melting in the rain.

I got out of the truck, closing Timmy Swege in so that he couldn't overhear our conversation. "I heard," I told Pat. "At least you get to go home for Christmas."

Pat stopped, water dripping from the tip of his nose. He stared at the pavement and said nothing.

"You're not?"

Pat forced a smile. "Going to Mother's. She's a good cook."

"Um, what about Fresno?"

"Fresno has tired of supporting a husband who cannot stay employed. Who's your sidekick?"

We both looked toward the truck. Duke arched an eyebrow, presuming, I suppose, that we were admiring him. "God's gift to hyenas," I answered. "Say, when did Rauch give you the assignment to rewrite that Work Plan?"

"Friday morning. Why?"

I thought about telling him he'd been set up so that the client could look like they were trying when they weren't, but decided that on some level, he must already know. Instead, I offered to distract him. "No reason. Have time for a little vigilante work before you run off?"

The corners of Pat's mouth curled into a dreamy smile. "Just let me get a bottle of antifreeze," he answered, flicking the rain off his hair, gently so as not to mess it up. "A man could catch a chill in weather like this."

TWENTY MINUTES LATER, I stood in the drifting rain myself, talking to Pat through the open truck window as I tried to focus the binoculars on the old Ferris place. I could hear the neck of his wine bottle clink against his stem glass as he refilled it. "I think Janet found a tank out there," I said.

"Which would kill the construction loan," Pat answered merrily. The cabernet sauvignon he had chosen had warmed him quickly, and his spirits seemed to be rising. Timothy Swege was enjoying the experience, too, crammed in between the big man and the far door of the cab with a glass of his own.

"So she put the tank evidence in the first draft of her report, and Rauch got mad and fired her. Why?"

"Well . . . he might have thought her evidence shaky, but knowing Rauch, he cared not for facts. More likely he stood to lose the client if she sank the loan. And we all know how far the lad will go to please a client."

"Do you think he cares that much about this client? I thought you said there wasn't much money in environmental assessments."

"No dollar is too small for our Freddie Rauch."

Timmy took a long slurp from his glass. "Got any more of this, man?"

"So where's this lovely tank of yours?" Pat asked, daintily crooking a pinkie as he raised his glass once more to his lips. "By the house, where the children are chasing the wee doggie with sticks? Or mayhaps by the barn, where three old cars sit stripped of their wheels on cinder blocks, blithely dripping crankcase oil into the ground."

Timmy said, "Good eyes, Ryan."

"I was a sharpshooter in the service."

I lowered the binoculars for a moment and tried to envision Pat Ryan set to plinking men in black pajamas just because his eyes were unusually good. Maybe that was why he seemed to have a little bit of trouble dressing up nicely every day and trying to act just like the rest of us. "Think this place might flood soon?" I asked, unconsciously changing the subject to matters of the weather.

"Could be. It floods most years, and the ground's saturated now."

Timmy said, "Yeah, the ants have come inside for the winter. They found a jar of honey I left out on the counter. The lid was on, but just a wee bit of the golden sticky had dripped down the side," he said, starting to mimic Pat's language. "The wall from the dishwasher over to the sink was black with the little blighters. Granny 'bout roasted my nuts."

"So how high does this thing rise?" I asked.

Duke pointed out the window toward the span and causeways where Occidental Road crossed the Laguna. "See that bridge? Two years ago you couldn't even see the railings. Just the top of the stop sign down at the other end."

"Give me Wyoming any day," I muttered, resting the binoculars on the roof of the truck to steady them. "Duke, you ever ride out here with Janet?"

He shrugged. That meant the answer was no. "She said the Laguna was like this sacred place, and we ought to like leave it in peace."

"I did hear she liked wetlands."

Pat said, "She did a special project on the ecological value of riparian corridors while she was at Sonoma State. I think this was her study area."

I said, "I can see how she might fall in love with it."

"I met her environmental studies professor once," Pat continued. "He came to take her to lunch. He seemed genuinely fond of her, in a fatherly sort of way."

Janet had been in need of good paternal influence, and she loved nature. Put these ingredients together in the form of a good teacher, and you had the best kind of devotion. "Duke," I asked, "did she ever pick your brains about the Miwok Mills Water District?"

"Oh yeah, all the time. Wanted to know who was for it and against it, that kind of stuff."

"What exactly *is* going on?"

"There's a bunch of freaks call themselves the Citizens against Poison petitioning to take the water district away from the county, run it themselves."

"Why?"

"Something about teeth."

Pat said, "The rallying cry is their claim that the county wants to fluoridate the water. You know the old saw. 'Twill poison us all, our children, or old and infirm. Just think of the poor souls on the end of the line, they'll get a concentrated dose!"

"Yeah, that stuff," said Timmy, pulling down another gulp.

"That's nonsense," I said. "If they don't want it, they don't want it, but fluorine's dissolved in the water, not suspended; its concentration doesn't increase at the end of the line."

Pat chuckled. "You understand basic chemistry, and I understand basic chemistry, but our average paranoid citizen was passing notes that day in school."

"You say that's the rallying cry. What's the real reason they want to privatize the district?"

Duke had the answer for that one. "Granny says they're a bunch of ungodly abortionists who moved here to blow dope, and now they want to control the water hookups to keep anyone else from moving in."

Pat said, "The old *I've got mine, now the rest of you get lost* prejudice. But if they take over the district, they still have to administer chlorine to kill the bugs in the water."

"And that's a problem?"

"Sure. If they put the chlorine in too soon, they form a whole host of trihalomethanes."

Timmy belched. "What?"

"Chloroform. Bromoform. Dichlorobromomethane. Dibromochloromethane. A nasty little stew. You wouldn't want to drink that, laddie."

"Just so," said Timmy the Duke. "Gimme more of that wine, bro. I got some stew to wash out of my system."

Pat took a swig. "Myself, I may not warm to engineers as a class, particularly not the unadventuresome sort that go to work for county governments, but at least they know better than to plug my drinking water full of bromoform."

I said, "So tell me, Duke, who *is* behind the water district uprising?"

Timmy shrugged again. This time, I presumed, because he didn't know the answer.

Pat intervened. "We shall divine the answer. Where does this cabal of sorcerers meet?"

"Bob Weatherall's office there in the Mills."

"Who's that?" Pat asked.

"Just this guy."

"He own a lumber company out by the river?" I asked.

"Sort of. 'Weatherall's Weathers-All.' Real lame. It got taken over years ago by some guys from out of town."

"He own land locally?" Pat asked.

Duke shrugged. "Plenty. Why?"

To me, Pat said, "That's who's behind it, then."

I stared into the cab at Pat. "How'd you think to ask where they meet?"

Pat chuckled merrily. "This water district stuff came down many times when I was working for the Water Board. The righteous citizens intent on good deeds, justice, and self-regulation storm the Bastille of government. But who's back there whipping the fanatics into a lather? Why, someone with bucks to hire the lawyer and a vested interest to go with it, just biding their time 'til the hotheads win the day and then piss their neighbors off by mismanaging the project. Then huzzah, the next time they get together to elect themselves some managers, the developers start looking pretty good to them, and *wham,* they vote in all sorts of expansion. Nay, 'twas easy to divine, fair Emily; when you see the sheep line up, just look behind them to see who's driving the flock."

◇

THE WIND PICKED up, binding my dampened hair against my face. I squinted into the misting rain, willing my eyes to see what Janet had seen. I wished I could rise up and hover like a bird.

Hovering. Like Janet's black-shouldered kite. Yes, a bird could see everything, peer right down onto the patterns of the land, right into everyone's backyard and bad housekeeping. It was part of what had drawn me to take flying lessons during the fat years before Blackfeet Oil had gone under. How I wished I had gotten that license, and could rent a small airplane right now and hover just like that lucky bird. I could get a camera and document what I saw, and—

Suddenly I knew what Janet had done, knew how she had gained her bird's-eye view of that property. Like any geologist worth her salt, she had used air photographs, those marvelous hawk's-eye views straight down into the messy backyard of every citizen. "Pat! Who has air photographs of this area?"

"Current or historical?"

"Both."

"County Assessor's Office."

I jumped back into the truck.

I dropped Duke off at the bicycle shop and made a beeline to the Wagon Trail Motel. There I dug through the mess and picked up Janet's stereo viewer, a sort of binocular magnifying glass that would permit me to look at pairs of air photographs and see them in all the glory of three dimensions. Before I left the room, I dialed Jaki's number at her new job and told her where I was going, who was with me, and what kind of shape he was in. The man needed help, and I had too much going on to provide it for him.

As I pulled away from the parking lot, the motel manager hurried out of the office, waving another telephone message for me. Again it was Murbles, commanding me to call. I stuffed it in my pocket next to the last one. He would just have to wait.

I proceeded north on Highway 101 with caution, pulling off at the Yolanda Avenue ramp and back on again to see if anyone had picked up my tail from the motel. We were alone.

Back at the Assessor's Office, Pat and I set up shop at that long government counter and perused a map that showed the flight lines and photograph numbers for the aerial surveys of Sonoma County, one each for 1961, 1971, 1980, and 1990. When we had the two photographs closest to the Ferris property identified for each year, Pat picked up a magnifying glass and started with the oldest, while I set up the stereo viewer and began with the most recent, figuring I should start with what the place looked like now and work backwards in time.

And immediately ran into a problem. The 1990 photographs were flown at very high altitude, affording poor resolution. I couldn't make out anything smaller than a barn or a large tree. The photograph served only to orient me in a general way.

Next I looked at the aerial photographs taken ten years earlier, in 1980. Here my luck was better. I could see the tops of the three cars up on cinder blocks beside the barn, or three others just like them, along with several other automotive derelicts. The driveway leading back to the barn showed patterns of heavy wear leading around the barn in a sloppy circuit, as if the barn were the center of a loop in a motocross event.

The pictures from 1971 were better yet. The disused cars were not there, but trucks and other farm implements were, and I could see the vehicular tracks, as in the 1980 pictures. I showed them to Pat.

"Yes . . ." he purred. "That barn had heavy traffic all around it. And what's that little blip? A pump? Put it under the stereo viewer. If it sticks up pretty sharply, but not so high as the barn, I'll bet it's a pump. Makes sense if it was an apple orchard. The hired hands might have brought the tractors there to fill them up. It's a good thing this year is good, because these ones from sixty-one are unreadable. Too contrasty."

I checked my mental notes. In 1971 old man Ferris would already be dead, but Sonja had not yet disappeared. Who was using the place? Was Jaime there? "Okay, Pat, after looking at air photographs, what would Janet have done next?"

"Question people," Pat said quietly. "A blip and heavy traffic patterns are only clues. She would need a firsthand account from someone who had seen the tank in use."

"Who would she ask?"

"The owners, first off."

I clenched my teeth. The owners, I would not be asking. "Who else?"

"An old orchard worker, if you can find one, or someone who delivered the fuel." Pat fixed the woman behind the counter with a good old blarney smile. "We just love air photographs," he cooed. "You know where we can find any more of them?"

The woman preened. "Go over to the County Water Agency. They have even older pictures you can look at there. And ask for Bartolo Colotti. He used to pick apples all over that area."

◈

JAKI WAS RIGHT on schedule, waiting for us at the curb outside the building at eleven forty-five. "Darling Jaki," Pat caroled, spreading his arms wide. "What luck to see your shining face before me."

Jaki grinned and opened the door to her car. "Step in, fair knight, your AA chariot awaits. C'mon, double step, we don't wanna miss the opening statements."

Pat hung his head and smiled, mumbled, "Just a little slip I'm having, is all."

Jaki enclosed the big man in her slender arms. "I know. Life sucks. Let's go." She pushed him into the seat and buckled him in, then came around to her side of the car, where I stood.

"He seemed so clear," I said. "And he didn't drink that much the first time I saw him do it. When my ma was drunk, she'd get more and more cloudy and then pass out."

Jaki smiled cheerfully. "Drunks vary like crazy. This one kids himself he can have wine because it's Jack Daniel's that he drinks to get seriously drunk on. And yeah, a little wine kind of calms him down and he gets clearer for a while, but when he's all the way gone, he cries. Be glad you missed that."

I went back around to Pat's side of the car, scribbled Aunt Frida's phone number and "stay in touch" on a piece of paper, curled and stuffed the paper into the top of the bottle so it wouldn't ruin his nice pressed shirt if it spilled, and kissed him good-bye.

29

I WAS ON A ROLL. IF THE SHERIFF'S DEPARTMENT COULDN'T
unearth the truth with all its power to dig into the privacy of everyone's lives, then I would show them what could be done with publicly available information.

Before driving out to the Water Agency on West College Avenue,
I figured I'd hit the County Planning Department. It was time to find
out a little more about Valentine Reeves' plans for the old Ferris place.

In that particular governmental agency, there is no long counter. Instead, one takes a number and waits. That's a bad sign. A person could
collect cobwebs. I took a seat, figuring to wait ten, maybe fifteen minutes.

After five minutes, the irrepressible Liza stomped in from the street
and barked to the receptionist, "Tell Martinez I'm here." Then she
plopped her barrel-shaped body into a chair, folded her arms angrily
across her breasts, and arranged her face in a scowl that could curdle
milk.

A moment later, her big friend Trudy came in, panting. "Liza, I
asked you to wait for me," she said. "You were supposed to wait while
I parked the car."

Liza pouted.

I said, "Liza, isn't it? And Trudy? Em Hansen. Liza, you and I met
at Suzanne Cousins', and I saw you at the Spaghetti Feed. You were
having words with the County Supervisor."

Liza eyed me askance, dredging through her memory banks for my face. Then her storm-cloud eyes cleared for a moment, and she said, "Yeah. Suzanne's."

Trudy settled herself in a chair, hitching her slacks to make room for her crotch as she sat down. She observed me calmly, but was clearly on the alert.

"Maybe you can help me with something," I said, in a neighborly tone. "Janet and Suzanne were friends, weren't they?"

Liza hunched her ample shoulders up under her ears, knocking her earrings askew. "Sure. Why?"

"Because I'm trying to find out what happened to Janet, and I can't understand why Suzanne's so blasé about her death."

Liza glared at me. "Janet was a warrior. We do not weep when a warrior dies in battle."

Trudy sank her face into her hands.

"What battle?" I prompted.

"We protect the Great Mother!"

"Oh. Are you guys a church or something?"

"We are the Covenant of the Great Mother. Well, Janet wasn't, but she was a good kid."

"Oh. What does the Covenant do to protect the Great Mother?"

Liza's eyes bulged. She had the look of someone who has awakened suddenly in the middle of a hurricane, and wonders pettishly why she wasn't aware of its arrival. "We protect Her daughters! We stop the filthy son-of-a-bitch government from deviling Her body!"

"Is that what you're doing here?"

Liza jumped up like lightning had struck her in the butt. "Grimes!" She began pacing erratically, swinging her fists viciously and muttering under her breath.

I wondered what in hell Liza had eaten for breakfast, so I'd know to avoid it myself. "You don't like the County Supervisor, I take it."

Liza advanced on me. She loomed over me, arms tight against her sides as if someone were pinning them back to restrain her from a fight, and as she spoke, a fine spray of saliva left her lips. "Fluorine coursing through our bodies and right down the drains into the Body of our Mother!"

"What's the matter with you?" I gasped, wiping at my face.

Trudy jumped up and pulled Liza away from me, but Liza's oatmeal-paste skin had turned an ugly purple. "I've worked *hard* on this project for *three years!* You're just like all the rest! You want to stay *ignorant!*"

Out of the corner of my eye, I saw a short, swarthy man in polyester pants who had just one black eyebrow extending across his forehead. He had beetle-black eyes and looked so much like Jaime Martinez that I had to look twice to make sure it wasn't him. He had wandered out of his office to attend the next visitor on his list, but when he saw that it was Liza, he began to back up quickly. Ready to get Liza off me, I pointed at him, blurted, "Liza, is that your planner?"

The man froze, eyes locked in fury. What had Liza said his name was? Martinez? This man could be a cousin of Jaime's, if not his brother.

Liza spun on her heel and closed on him. "About time!" she scolded. "Back there drinking coffee, weren't you? Who do you think is paying your salary?" She started toward him, Trudy still trailing from one shoulder like a pennant. The planner waved a limp hand, guiding them toward an office.

I jumped up. "Trudy, wait," I cried. "How can I reach you?"

Liza wheeled on me, her eyes narrowing to venomous slits. "You work for the paper? Or perhaps you're CIA! Hah!"

The planner rolled his eyes.

Trudy released Liza's shoulder. "You go ahead," she said. "I'll be there in half a minute." This last she said as much to assure Martinez as to calm Liza. When Liza and the planner had disappeared behind a room divider, Trudy came back to me, her body tense with indecision. "If you really want to help, come for Janet's drumming," she said.

"Her what?"

"Drumming. Wednesday evening, seven o'clock. The solstice. At

Suzanne's." She shrugged her big, meaty shoulders. "You seem to really need one, and your energy will provide the negative ground for the event."

❖

WHILE I CONTINUED to wait for a planner myself, I got to looking through a copy of the County Plan. It showed everything from zoning to hundred-year flood levels.

The patterns of rivers and floodplains on the hundred-year flood map fascinated me. A floodplain is just that, the plain bordering a river that floods. The channel down which a river flows is formed as the water scours away at the banks. This process of erosion proceeds laterally as well as downward, usually forming a much wider valley than the width of the river channel itself. Then, when the vagaries of climate—the patterns of rainfall, heating, and cooling—overload a river with water, it swells and spills out over its banks, inundating this surrounding lowland.

The hundred-year flood level is that line of equal elevation to which the supposed biggest flood expected within a hundred-year interval might rise. Planners love this line. It's a line above which it's considered okay to build, because gosh, you're above the highest line a river will rise to in a hundred years, and who lives even that long, right? Wrong. These predictions are based on limited data; and, every once in a while, perhaps every three hundred or a thousand years, even if global warming wasn't changing our climates anyway, that region could see an even more unusual climatic event, and the river could rise even higher, and how do you know where you are in *that* cycle? So building near a floodplain is like everything else in life: just a crapshoot.

The old Ferris place sat right along the edge of the floodplain of the Laguna de Santa Rosa, right near those fertile, water-rich soils farmers have always loved. Farmers are philosophical; they'd rather risk the occasional flooding of their crops and grazing lands than farm dry, stony, hillside soils. The forty acres of the Ferris place had plenty of each. As the topographic overlay on one of the maps showed me, the house and barns sat at the point where the hills and lowlands met, about two feet above the hundred-year flood line.

I traced Santa Rosa and Piner Creeks, which emptied their waters directly into the Laguna right near the old Ferris place. The Army Corps of Engineers had straightened them and ramped their banks into an engineering-approved angle designed to deliver water downhill faster so that during heavy rains the upper end of the drainage—in this case the City of Santa Rosa—wouldn't flood. But everything downstream from these creeks would. Faster. Deeper. And carrying more sand, gravel, brush, old tires, couches, and runaway Buicks. So if the Laguna, Mark West Creek, and the Russian River ever backed up at the same time some thousand-year freakish amount of water charged down the channelized creeks, the Laguna could flood to a higher level.

Maps are such fun.

At last, a slender young man with a vanilla-pudding face and polyester slacks called my number. "How can I help you?" he inquired blandly.

"I'd like to know more about the zoning of this property," I said, pushing the County Plan his way and tapping old man Ferris' parcel. "It says urban residential, but everything around it is zoned rural residential or agricultural. Am I reading it correctly?"

"Yes you are. That's a special zoning for mixed usage. See, it's almost contiguous with Miwok Mills"—he tapped his finger at the crossroads—"which is zoned urban." He squinted at the parcel. "But this parcel you're interested in must have been grandfathered in, because the way the plan's set up now, we wouldn't have allowed that."

Grandfathered. How appropriate. "What kind of building is being proposed for this parcel?" I asked.

The vanilla-pudding man shuffled away from the counter for several minutes. When he returned, he held a roll of blueprints and plot plans, outlining existing structures and those to be added. Slowly rolling the rubber bands to the end of the bundle, he opened it up and spread it out on the counter. "Looks like town houses," he sighed. "Rentals."

A raft of town houses all along Janet's sacred stream. I uncurled the rest of the plans so I could see the logo printed on the corner of the top blueprint. *Reeves Construction,* it read, and I thought, *Looks like our boy Valentine figured out a loophole in Grandfather's will.*

❖

THE SONOMA COUNTY Water Agency was a monument to that place where governmental spending and architectural vanity sometimes meet. Two-story atrium. Volumes of space with no one in it. Blond wood and extralong counters.

Bartolo Colotti was a robust man of Italian descent, scant on height but not on breadth of shoulders. He was at that forty-something age when his eyebrows were just starting to sprout rogue bristles a twisted inch long, and his hairline was starting to slip backward like he was losing his hat. "What can I help you with?" he asked.

As I explained my quarry, I was picking at the bandage on the heel of my right hand. The adhesive tape had begun to itch.

"Just north of Occidental Road, west of the Laguna?" Barto asked.

"Yes. There's a property on Ferris Road that interests me. I understand you used to work in the orchards up around there."

Barto pulled bundles of twenty-seven-inch square blowups of aerial photographs out of his vertical files. "There was a special survey flown in the fifties. Part of the planning for channelizing the creeks." He laid everything open on a large light table and bent over them. "The old Ferris place," he mused. His smile tempered a little. "Are you one of those environmental people?"

"No. Or not exactly. Why?"

Barto seemed about to say something, but then changed tack. "Oh, there was another woman came around looking at these same photographs a while back."

"About my size?"

"Yeah, kind of looked like you. Or your younger cousin."

"Did she ask you about tanks, too?"

"Sure. That's what you're all doing, right? Looking for tanks?"

I nodded. "Anything you can tell me about the old Ferris place would help. That other woman was—couldn't finish the job."

Barto regarded me for a moment, seemed to make a decision about me. "My dad worked for old man Ferris some, and my brothers and I used to go along during the harvest. Dad drove a truck, hauled the big crates of apples over to the packing plant. Picked a lot of apples on that ranch myself, but not until after the old man died."

"So you grew up here."

"Sebastopol born and bred."

I took a look at the laugh lines around his eyes and the gray hairs in his sideburns, trying to guess his exact age. "Then maybe you knew Matt and Sonja Karsh in school."

"Of course. Sonja was my year at Analy High."

I smiled at the tone of his voice. "You liked her."

"Sure," Barto said, turning shyly away from me as a blush bloomed on his swarthy face. "She had spunk. Real smart, too."

"I hear her dad favored her, too."

"Oh, yeah. He'd ride her around with him while he made the rounds to check the harvest, always showing off how smart and charming she was, always hoisting her onto his shoulders so's she could pick the best apple on the tree. Talk about the apple of his eye."

The image was a rich one, opening doors to memories of my own father, of riding on his shoulders so I could see beyond the sagebrush, of accompanying him to town to buy wire and staples for the fence. I understood the Sonjas of the world. Especially the Sonjas who had older brothers who were a shade too rough with them. "How about her grandfather?" I asked. "He liked her too?"

Barto laughed. "Yeah, that surprised everyone. He didn't generally have much use for the female persuasion. Dad used to cuss about that. He said Ferris asked him to 'put his woman to work' in the packing plant, but Dad would have none of it. Said Ferris treated his dogs better than those women. Heck, one woman got a sleeve caught in the paring machine one time. It ripped her arm right off. She nearly bled to death, but the old man seemed more concerned that work was interrupted. The men at least he'd address by name, like they were human."

"What became of his wife?"

"I don't know. Died young. He didn't want another, Dad said."

"And his daughter, Mrs. Karsh?"

"He all but ignored her. It's funny, every other female in the county, I know by her first name, but she is always Mrs. Karsh."

This bit of gossip clicked neatly into place, fitting smoothly with everything else I'd heard. "I read his will." I pointed to the old Ferris place on the 1971 aerial photograph. "He left his home, the whole parcel, in trust to Sonja."

Barto raised his eyebrows. "You don't say? Well, there you go, she just had a charm about her, you know? And she had a mind for business, showed it really young. If anything would melt that iceberg's heart, that would."

"He left the rest of his estate in trust for Mrs. Karsh, with her husband as trustee."

"Well, we always presumed . . . But no, I didn't know that about the trust."

"I'll bet people wonder why Dierdre Karsh lives so poorly, if she inherited so much land."

Barto's deep olive complexion grew rosy with another blush. "What do you mean? Property's not money, not if you can't sell it. It's hard to make money at farming and apple processing. It's not like it's a guaranteed living. You hear about government subsidies, but not everybody gets in on that game. Far from it. I hear Will had everything but his socks mortgaged to pay for replanting so much of the orchards to grapes and switching the apple plant over to a winery, and then the phylloxera came and—"

"The what?"

"It's a plague of mites. Kills the vines, right down at the roots. No, it's tough sometimes making a living in agriculture."

I saw my informant veering into the dignity of communal sadness and away from the joy of gossiping. "This barn here," I urged, pointing to the photograph. "Was this where the tractors and trucks fueled up?"

Barto squinted. "Yeah, right there. The pump's gone now, but that's where the tank was."

My heart leapt into my throat. I could practically feel Janet looking over my shoulder, getting as excited as I was, saying, *Yes, there it is. . . .* "Is the tank still there?"

"I'd be surprised if it wasn't. It costs to dig those things out. Even if you have your own backhoe, it's a couple days' work."

"How big was it?"

"Thousand-gallon gasoline. He had one at the apple plant—that's where my dad gassed up—but he put this one by his house, too. He was real proud of that, said he got the stuff real cheap from the old bulk plant on Abbott Street. Kept his drivers from spending time going into town to fuel up, the tight-fisted old so-and-so. They say the Grand Canyon was just a gopher hole 'til Ferris saw someone drop a nickel down it."

I laughed. "So you remember a gasoline pump right there by the barn."

"Yeah, right there. Yeah, I remember the location especially, because the summer Sonja ran off, I'd gotten my license and could drive one of the stake-beds during the Gravenstein harvest instead of just picking—they're the first apple in, usually they come ripe mid-August. Anyway, that was the summer we had the gas shortages, with everybody lining up at the pump, and Will Karsh swapped that tank out. There was a big hole in the ground for a while before they got the new one in, because everyone else wanted a tank that summer, too, and the supplier had to reorder. Big hole, with a pile of gravel. You had to swerve to miss it. And it stank." Barto wrinkled his nose.

"Stank of gasoline?"

"Yeah, the old tank looked like Swiss cheese. The water table's shallow there—just a few feet—so the old tank had been sitting in water and it rusted through and water was getting in. Dad said no one had used it since the old man had died, but then that gas shortage hit and they started using it again. Pumped as much water as gas. Dad said he had to pump it into a barrel and let it sit for a while, then he'd siphon the gas off the top and filter it through an old sock. My dad told Will he didn't need to go to all that trouble and put in a new tank, like the drivers could stagger their times at the pump at the plant, but you see, Will had bought Sonja this little red sports car for her sixteenth birthday, and—"

"And she needed a place to fill it up."

"Apple of his eye."

"I'll bet Matthew was jealous."

Barto shook his head and smiled at the memory. "Oh, boy, was he! He couldn't drive, you see."

"Couldn't pass the test?"

"No, he'd get all tense and mixed up and fail it every time. His behavior was getting pretty strange by then, anyway. He'd dropped out of school, and they kept him pretty close to home. Boy, he'd get into the machinery, though!"

"Like forklifts?" I asked, remembering the sound of machines echoing through the warehouses at the winery.

"He was a terror. Knocked over cases like it didn't matter. And that backhoe. He loved the backhoe, wanted to dig the old tank out so bad he had a fit. They had to sick Jaime Martinez on him. Jaime could always control him. You should have seen that little guy order Matt around!"

I grinned, thinking, *And men think women are gossips.* "Jaime worked for them back then?"

Barto thought. "He started about then, I'd say. He was a picker at first, but he seemed to like it there. Found ways to make himself pretty indispensable."

I could only imagine how useful he could make himself if he could control Matthew Karsh. "So they put in a new tank."

Thoroughly engrossed in his story, Barto continued. "Yeah, and like I say, Matt just had to get at that backhoe. The morning the men came to put in the new tank, Matt was already on that backhoe, shoveling the pea gravel into the hole—you know, the ballast for underneath the new tank—and Jaime was right there barking at him, telling him what to do. Lousy job Matt did."

I imagined Matthew Karsh in the backhoe, pounding at the controls with his enormous, clumsy hands, working furiously to be the big man, shooting nasty looks all around. How awful it must have been to be his little sister. "Why did Sonja run off? Really."

Barto's smile faded. "Well . . ."

"Please, it would help me understand a lot."

Barto rubbed at the back of his neck. "Well, that was a bad summer for her. You'd think it was a good one, because she'd just turned sixteen and had a job and that new car. To think we all envied her. It sounded real racy; you know, living by yourself . . . a red sports car . . ."

"But you knew things were rough for her."

"Well, her dad had moved out, and her ma was being pretty difficult, and—"

"I thought he left after she did."

"Yeah, well, I think it was a gradual thing. Will and Natalie—his secretary—had been friends for a long time, and who knows what happened when."

"And Mrs. Karsh was getting suspicious and getting on him about it?"

"Well, now, Mrs. Karsh would never say anything like that where any of us common folk could hear it. No, you know how people are, they can't fight about what's really going on. They get on each other about something smaller like it was the end of the world. And it was all over town that Will was treating Sonja better than his wife, so Mrs. Karsh would make *comments* about that car, really taking bites out of Sonja, making suggestions about what kind of female drives a red car, that sort of thing. I guess Will kind of threw in the towel and quit trying to keep up appearances. And then when Sonja was gone, I guess he really didn't see any reason even to visit."

"And what was it like for Sonja with him staying away more and more?"

Barto said simply, "Matt treated her worse and worse."

"You mean getting physical?" A memory of my own brother popped into my mind, of his face contorted with hatred as he pinned me to the floor of the barn and threatened to drip spit into my eyes. I grabbed the edge of the counter, took a breath. The line that divided Janet's life from my own had long since blurred, and now I was beginning to melt into Sonja's.

"I never *saw* anything."

"But you suspected."

Barto's face stiffened. "Oh, looking back, I can see all kinds of things, but you figure kids are always getting hurt. But not adults, and let me tell you, that summer Sonja was a woman." He shook his head at the bitter endings adolescence can bring. "One morning I came to work, and Sonja had this big bruise on her cheek." He touched his own face, tenderly, like it hurt. "But then when she left for her job a few minutes later, she'd covered it all up with makeup."

"Did Matthew otherwise get in fights a lot?" I asked, leading the witness. To hell with the scientific method, multiple working hypotheses, and all the rest. This was war.

"Not with anyone else. Everyone knew to leave off of him because he was already injured. I remember the apple fights we'd have. All the pickers' kids would get in on the act. Dexie, Suzanne . . . It's fun, you split up in teams and throw the windfalls at each other. You only use the rotten ones, or your dad yells at you for stealing bacon off the table. Beyond that there was only one rule: don't hit Matthew, or he'll go crying to Mama and the game's over. He was a real coward, you see."

"But Matthew wasn't afraid of Sonja?"

Barto shook his head, his eyes deep in the mists of remembering.

"Didn't anyone try to stop him?"

"Mr. Karsh broke up the fights when he was there, made them sit apart for a while. But Sonja got blamed. Boy, what you can see in hindsight you wish you'd seen at the time."

"Who blamed her?"

"Her mom. 'Sonja, leave Matt alone.' That kind of stuff."

"And her dad?"

"He bragged about her, how smart she was, how she could really look after herself. Like that made everything else all right. Ol' Will was telling himself it was a fair fight."

"And then he gave her that car."

"Yeah."

"And Matt couldn't stand it."

"That bruise was as big as a saucer."

"And then she was gone."

Barto sighed. "Yeah, then she was gone."

"What became of the car?"

"It sat in the barn for a year or two, and then I guess they sold it."

"Why didn't she take it with her?"

Barto turned and looked at me, surprised. "I never thought of that." He shrugged his shoulders. "Maybe she didn't want to be reminded of all the fighting."

"So the house was empty again, and Mrs. K rented it to Jaime. Because he doesn't own it. It's being held in trust for Sonja."

"No, it's part of his pay. Lots of farm people around here have a Mexican family living on their property, but usually it's in a trailer."

"So Jaime made out."

"He does well. Aside from staying there free, he makes wages working on the vineyards and orchards, and makes a little extra fixing his friends' cars."

That explained why the junk cars were there, and why Jaime might feel a little proprietary in guarding the place. "What does he do with the crankcase oil when he's done with it?"

Barto laughed dryly. "Who knows what he does? It's not exactly an up-front business. I daresay he doesn't charge sales tax or report his earnings to the Governor. And Jaime grew up the other side of the border; his idea of housekeeping isn't exactly like ours. It's pretty funny watching the liberal slicks who move in from the city. They're all, 'We don't want to impact their culture' with the campesinos, protecting their right to camp out in the blackberry brambles and get drunk in the middle of the road and all, then about two years later they start to get sick of picking beer cans out of their fancy landscaping."

"So how do the liberal slicks react to low-income housing projects? You know that Valentine Reeves is planning to put fifty units up that hillside where the apple trees now are."

Barto's tone grew icy. "Those city folks are the problem. When I grew up here, housing was affordable. Now we got them moving in, paying big-city prices for property, running the cost of housing way up, but hey, our wages are staying the same. That's my kids who are going to have to live packed into those new cracker boxes."

"So Reeves is on the level."

Barto set his jaw in exasperation. "Reeves is just making a living. Everyone jumps on him because they'd rather look at apple trees than houses. But hell, we've got a population explosion going on, don't we? I hear that even if nobody new moved into this county, the population would still double in the next ten years because we're so good at having kids. Me, I stopped with two, just so I could afford to feed and educate them. That hurt. I like big families."

I shook my head in sympathy. Back home in Wyoming, I was watching the quality of my own life slip away as hobby ranchers drove the price of land up and the value of the beef crop down. When I inherited my parents' ranch, *if* my mother didn't lose it to taxes before then, I'd inherit it with the U.S. government as a fifty-five percent death-duty partner. And there had never been enough land to parcel around to each rancher's child; I was only hopeful because my brother's fate had made me the only heir. "Going back to Sonja: There was a lot of talk about her messing around with an older man. Did you ever see him?"

"At the house? No."

"Anywhere else?"

"No."

"Then how does everyone know there was an older man?"

"Well, it's just what was said."

"When did they say it, before she went away or after?"

Barto thought for a moment. "After."

"Where did she go?"

Barto smiled into space. "I always wondered if she went to Hawaii. She'd talk about it like it was a fairy tale and not the fiftieth state."

"But you don't know."

Barto's face fell into wistful repose. "No."

A heavy sadness was beginning to settle on my bones, but I had just one more question. "The other woman who asked you about this underground tank; did she also ask you about Sonja?"

"No. Why?"

"No reason. Just wondering if she knew to stay away from Matthew while she was working out there, is all."

Barto thought a moment before saying anything more. "I can't see why that should be a problem. I mean, I haven't heard of any trouble with him in years. He almost never leaves the house, and that's half a mile away from the Ferris place. And he was just a kid back then, or a teenager, anyway. Everybody grows up eventually, doesn't he?" he said, looking into my eyes for reassurance.

30

I MADE ONE FINAL STOP BEFORE ASSAULTING THE SHERIFF'S DE-
partment with my data: the Sebastopol Public Library. I asked where
the Analy High School yearbooks were shelved. In the 1973 Analy
High School *Azalea* I found ample pictures of Sonja Karsh, popular girl
that she was, including group shots for the Tiger Pep Band, the A Cap-
pella choir, the Independent Study Program, and something called the
Girl's League Cabinet. There wasn't a single girl's athletic team back
then, but there was a nice half-page shot of Sonja about to shoot a basket in gym class. Her smile was infectious, a glowing flash of young
womanhood in a plain but intelligent face. I flipped to the pages for
the senior class, but of course, Matthew wasn't there. I did find him
one book earlier. Where he should have been a junior, he was a fresh-
man, his awkward bulk looming over his classmates like a thunderhead.
He was already fully grown, though his flesh had not yet spread. He
looked lost, his eyes focused on inner space.

At the Sheriff's Department, I asked to see Detective Muller, recit-
ing inside my head a litany against losing my cool. I told myself that
he was a detective doing his job just like me, and that I shouldn't expect him to treat me as a colleague or even a human being, that I should
only hope that his ears were working and his brain was in gear. But to
my surprise, when he appeared at the counter to receive me, he surprised me by saying, "I'm glad to see you. How are things going?"

"Fine. You lead the way."

When Muller had shown me once more into the little room with the tiny table and two chairs, I sat down and laid it out to him. "You got your tapes running? Good. I'll name names and produce documents if you need them, but here's what I've got. Item one, Mrs. Karsh's father treated her poorly and left her inheritance in trust. Her husband's the trustee, and he's living with another woman and doesn't give Mrs. Karsh enough to live on. But our Mrs. Karsh is of the old school, and thinks ladies don't display their anger.

"Item two, the one bit of property she has any control of is the old Ferris place. She's supposed to hold it in trust for her daughter, who is God knows where. The law firm that's supposed to manage the trust has quaintly looked the other way for over twenty years now, neither finding Sonja and deeding it to her, nor declaring her dead and deeding it off to some old folks' fund. Bet they make a bundle overlooking that little detail, but Mrs. Karsh doesn't look like she sees a cent. So she's bartered herself a handyman by letting him and his tribe live in the house. This man, Jaime Martinez, is running an illegal fix-it shop out of the barn. He's probably throwing the waste oil and engine-cleaning solvents into an abandoned gas tank by the—" I stopped abruptly as Deputy Dexter sidled in and propped his muscly bulk against the wall. He folded his arms across his chest, making his biceps bulge menacingly.

I sat up straighter and continued, staring straight at Deputy Dexter. "Item three, everyone treats Matthew Karsh like he's a weakling, but he's a full-grown man and he's got a mean streak he doesn't mind applying to selected people of the female persuasion. For example—"

Dexter's eyes shrank into dark slits, eclipsed by the hardening flesh of his face.

I narrowed my own eyes in reply. "I have it on good authority he tossed his sister around most of the time she was growing up. Her father looked the other way, rationalizing that Sonja's normal brain gave her the advantage, but that only goes for mental processes; the boy outweighed her by a hundred pounds. She got Dad's attention, so Ma looked the other way while Matty beat her up. Then she ran off and never even dropped a card, and the whole thing's just written off like a chapter in a bad book." I leaned pointedly toward Dexter, added, "Everyone feels so guilty about poor little Matthew Karsh with his dented-can brain that they've gone blind to what's going on here. Still. Now. Today."

Dexter clenched his teeth and hissed, "And just what is going on here, Miss Hansen?"

"Mama likes to sic her boy on people who make her angry." I yanked back my collar, exposing the lurid bruises. "I think there's a pattern here, don't you?"

Dexter's face looked like it might explode.

Detective Muller broke in. "Why would Mrs. Karsh find you threatening, Miss Hansen?"

"That's item four: Sonja's inheritance, the old Ferris place. There it sits, one of the last large chunks of land in the west county area that is zoned to be developed as more than a single-family unit. It's probably worth a mint, but Ma Karsh can't sell it. But aha, along comes Valentine Reeves, who's figured out a loophole in the will: Can't sell it? Then let's build high-density *rental* housing on it, just give the trust lawyers a little slice of the action to keep them quiet. *Voilà*, Mrs. K can finally afford to paint her kitchen. Which brings us back to Janet Pinchon, who was performing the environmental assessment required for Reeves' construction loan application. Janet found out about Jaime's tank, which after twenty-some-odd years in the ground we may presume leaks like a sieve, right into the groundwater and into the Laguna, just like the tank it was put in to replace. Disclosure of that little detail would kill the loan because the banks won't lend on a property burdened by the overwhelming costs of cleanup." And my mind ran on, seeing the futility of Janet's death. Reeves had found another backer who would supply private money, and all he had to do was just pump that contaminated groundwater to Occidental.

I glanced at Muller. I clearly had his attention. He looked as cheerful as a kid on Christmas morning.

"So?" Dexter sneered, drawing my attention back to himself.

"You've made Reeves look bad, but he was Janet's client, not the Karshes."

"But Mrs. Karsh needed that development even more than Reeves. He could build anywhere, but for her it had to be there. And Janet took her job and her profession seriously. She would have interviewed Mrs. Karsh to corroborate her information about the tank. She would have made herself an absolute pest."

Deputy Dexter shot me a look. I guess he figured it took one to know one.

Muller asked, "Is the assessment public information?"

"No, it's proprietary."

"Then couldn't they just throw the thing away if they don't like what it says?"

"Yes, but Janet wanted that construction project killed." I paused, uncertain whether this was the moment to talk about Senator Pinchon and his unnatural desire to keep his connection to his daughter quiet.

"And?" Muller prompted.

"And Janet handed in a rough draft of that assessment to her boss. The boss immediately fired her, marched her right out the door, shredded all her notes, and scrubbed her computer files, leaving no record of her draft of the report. Kind of gets your attention, doesn't it?"

"Why would he want to do that?"

"He can be bought."

"Lovely. But a shredded document is not a motive for murder."

"It isn't, but the threat posed by Janet's knowledge was, especially now that she no longer worked for HRC. I'll bet she got on her bicycle and rode right out there to let Dierdre Karsh know that if that tank wasn't out of the ground pronto, she'd report it herself, proprietary knowledge be damned. Her mistake was in going out there alone." I waited for Muller to speak.

He didn't.

"Well? Aren't you even going to say anything?"

Muller smiled pleasantly. "You say you can document your sources, showing that Janet knew about this tank. That's nice. But do you have any *proof* that she went beyond that and threatened the Karshes?"

"Proof? Just what do you guys need, a road map?"

Detective Muller spoke calmly. "I am sorry, Ms. Hansen; your story is very interesting, but your evidence is circumstantial. We would need more than circumstantial evidence to make an arrest. And we have none."

"None? What about the chaos in my motel room? Whoever attacked me tore that room to shreds. Surely you've measured his tracks and processed the prints by now."

"I'm sorry, but you are wrong. Worn carpeting like that does not preserve footprints, nor does rainy pavement. And while your motel room, like all motel rooms, was a veritable library of fingerprints, we found nothing we could use."

"Nothing?"

"We found *your* prints."

Dexter spoke, one corner of his mouth curling with pleasure. "People think we can get prints off *shit.*"

Muller's gaze flicked from me to him. "You will excuse us, Deputy," he said quietly. When he was gone, Muller turned back to me, spoke soothingly. "Please, Ms. Hansen, I wish you would go on out to your aunt's ranch and get some rest. We'll be in touch with you. And rest assured we are doing everything we can."

I felt deflated. I rose to go, but stopped. "How did you know where I'm staying?"

"We ran a make on your aunt's plates. I had a cruiser spin by last night to make sure you were safe."

"Oh."

As he walked me out through the lobby, past those blank governmental counters and the photographs of Sheriffs present and past, Muller murmured: "Oh, and to answer your questions, the lens to the video camera is hidden in the corner, and the microphone is behind the light switch. Have a good afternoon."

31

PROOF. IT'S A DIFFICULT THING TO COME BY SOMETIMES.

I went back out to Frida's. She was gone somewhere, so I set myself up in her kitchen with the phone book and made some calls. I called Lucy McClintock at the Sonoma County Environmental Health Department and reported the outlaw tank at the old Ferris place. She was avariciously ecstatic to know of its existence, assured me she'd put it on one of her lists, and was certain something would be done about it by the end of January. Christmas holidays, you know: everyone would be out of the office for weeks.

With this cheering bit of news, I tried to call Pat Ryan but got no answer. Curt Murbles, I had no intention of phoning.

Needing something to do to justify my existence, I went through the tack room and oiled the leathers and polished every bit of brass I could find. They hadn't really needed it. Neither did the animals seem to need attention; all were freshly combed and watered, but I curried a nice-looking mare anyway, and cleaned the sawdust from her hooves with a pick. As evening drew near, I saddled her up and set out on a ride, but was soon turned back as the skies ripped open and emptied huge, sodden drops of heaven down my collar. So much for the Christmas season in California. Cold and miserable, I returned to Frida's, took a hot bath, ate a cold dinner of leftovers and beer, and went to bed. I won't say that I slept.

◆

THE NEXT DAY was the winter solstice. I never saw the sun; it was clouded over the entire day, even when it wasn't oozing rain. The air was mild, so I spent the day exercising horses in the ring in the hope that putting my body to work would free my brain to discover a solution to my troubles.

By dusk I was still a woman with no proof or strategy to find it, and the tension was about to drive me wild. Normally riding puts me in a deep state of relaxation, but on this one occasion the rhythmic motion of horse and rider was one more thing that wasn't happening fast enough.

I had one more appointment. It was one I had not been certain I wanted to keep, but I was antsy for something to do, and fate sometimes conspires to move a restless soul to the place it needs to be. I took a shower, put on clean jeans and a turtleneck shirt I'd borrowed from Frida, fired up that beautiful truck, and headed out in search of Suzanne Cousins and her drumming circle, Goddess help me.

The night was damp and cool, and the windshield kept fogging as I struggled to master the controls of the ventilation system. Giving up, I cracked my window a ways.

When I got to the duplex, I found that I was the last to arrive. I hurried inside, forgetting to close the truck window. Suzanne didn't look very glad to see me when she opened the door to her candlelit living room, but Trudy intervened and pulled me into air thick with heat and incense, placed me on a cushion on the floor jammed in with a dozen or more unsmiling women, and put a stick in my hand and a skin drum in front of me. I had just enough time to glance around among the dimly lit faces to see if I could recognize a few others.

My survey was cut short when a big woman with lank hair that hung to her waist raised her right hand, closed her eyes, and screamed. Or at least, that's what I thought she was doing, but it seemed this was something expected of her, because I was the only one who jumped.

Her scream ran on and on, swelling and vibrating against the plaster walls. The others chimed in, howling like a pack of coyotes, shrieking like banshees, until I feared the plaster might crack.

Banf! She slammed her hand against the eighteen-inch drum she held propped against her ample chest. *Banf! Banf!* She struck it again, and again. The rest of the women echoed the beat. *Thud! Thud! Thud! Thud!* The small room rang with the beat, thundered with the beat, churned with the beat. The reek of incense filled my hair, curled downward through my nostrils, saturated my lungs. *Thud! Thud! Thud! Thud!*

As the sound swelled into monotonous pulsing, I grew irritable and decided to leave, rationalizing defensively that these women were too weird to tell me anything dependable, and besides, no one was going to talk to me about Janet while they were all getting ripped on drumbeats. But where my mind was unwilling, my soul found something in the company of these women comforting. How long had it been since I'd been with a group of women who were just being women together? I couldn't remember if I ever had. They didn't seem to have any particular expectation of me, which was kind of nice. For however long they wanted to play their tom-toms, I figured what the hell, I could be part of the gang. It was better than trading scowls with Frida.

Beat. I closed my eyes. In time, I became fascinated by it. It seemed simple at first, but by and by I realized that it had changed, shifting from a straight four-four time into patterns that swelled and ebbed with my breathing. Or perhaps I was breathing with the beat; I wasn't sure. I watched the beat as one dropping pebbles into a well, watching the ripples spread through the dark liquid so deep below. Some time had passed when I noticed that I had begun to beat my drum, too, and that its warm resonance had found its way beyond my brain and into my heart. I followed it into a dream place where I could feel stronger and more whole. I wanted to cry over its warmth, and found, to my pleasure and relief, that I could. Hot tears rolled down my cheeks, washing away a hurt that had no name.

The rhythm shifted, and my dream with it, and I was alone in the prairies of Wyoming under skies pregnant with rain. I was fleeing an enemy, running up the ramparts into the mountains, fast as the wind, leaping from one prominence to another like a bighorn sheep. All around and ahead of me the skies were opening. Great warm drops began to fall. The waters built up and engulfed me, carrying me away past the mountains to a place I found familiar. Father stood on the front porch waving, and I knew then that the waters were my tears.

Then the door opened, and Mother came out. She was young and strong and beautiful, and she was also crying. She was holding a small child, a boy, and he was dead. I wanted to die.

Leaping up from the floor, I began to scream. I screamed and screamed, and no one tried to stop me. They were all still drumming, their eyes closed, all except Suzanne Cousins. I found her eyes on me in the candlelight, watching me like a cat.

I couldn't breathe. I wanted out of there. Stumbling over women and their drums, I found the door, opened it, and slammed it behind me.

Outside, it was dark as pitch. Heavy clouds blanketed the sky, soaking up the heavens and all street light. Sucking in great lungfuls of the cold night air to still my tears, I found my way to Frida's truck, climbed in, and began to drive. I headed westward, taking the swiftest route past the last of the tract housing and into the farmlands, searching for the calm of open spaces.

Beyond the city limits, the roads dwindled, and I soon found myself on Occidental Road heading toward the Laguna. I thought of turning around, but rushed onward, drawn now by a perverse urge to be near the swelling waters of my dream.

A fog lay thick against the ground as I descended toward the Laguna lowlands. It became thicker yet and thickest as the great truck rolled over the causeway and across the bridge. I had a sudden urge to floor the accelerator, fearing that Matthew Karsh might find me there, or that my tears might sweep up behind me, carry me off the bridge, and drown me, but I crept nervously along through the cloying mists, finding my way along the line that marked the edge of the road. As I cleared the far end of the bridge and causeway, the grade began to rise and the line swung away abruptly to the right, opening out to Ferris Road. Unable to control myself any longer, I pressed down on the accelerator. The truck surged forward into a clear pocket within the fog.

And I saw someone—no, two people: kids!—in the road ahead of me. I skidded to a stop, hit the emergency flashers, lowered the window to yell at them.

The kids were cuffing each other around, a boy and a girl, brother and sister, dark hair and cheekbones struck from the same mold. The girl was greatly outmatched by her much larger brother, but she fought doggedly, returning blow for blow. In the heat of their battle, they did not appear to see me.

Intense feeling gripped my chest. I struggled to breathe, trying to pinpoint the nature of this overwhelming emotion. Was it fear? No, it was heavier than that: it was rage weighed down with guilt. I felt tiny, smaller than the little girl. My overheated mind struggled to understand, deciding first that I was feeling a ghostly echo of Matt and Sonja fighting thirty years ago. Then my heart said, *No, it's me. And my brother.*

The thought made no sense. I shook myself, furious that the drum's liquor still roamed my brain. I lowered the window, leaned out, and thumped my hand against the door panel, begging the kids to get out of the road. *"Por favor, niños! Por favor!"* Still they ignored me.

The fog shifted, now hiding them, now bringing them sharply into view, like the changing images of a dream. I thought of swinging to the left to pass them, but feared I might be hit head-on by an oncoming vehicle, or that worse, the next car going my way would run them over. I pressed the horn. They did not respond. Would I have to get out of the truck and physically remove them from the road?

No. A man was emerging from the mouth of Ferris Road.

Jaime Potrero Martinez. He strutted purposefully toward the kids, grabbed them by the scruffs of their necks, and started to bellow at them in Spanish. Then he struck each of them. Hard.

Incensed, I pounded the horn. Jaime dropped both kids and stormed toward the truck, shouting and waving his fists. As he reached the door panel, I slapped the lock down and pressed the button to raise the window. It closed too slowly. Jaime slammed at the window, catching the top edge of the glass before it met the gasket and shattering it.

My fear vanished like snow, melting in the heat of my anger. "You stupid son of a bitch!" I bellowed. "Now you can pay for this!"

Jaime's eyes finally focused on me, popped wide in recognition. *"Bruja del diablo!"* he shrieked, his voice straining between rage and terror. He turned and ran into the fog.

I gunned after him down Ferris Road, my aunt's window crumbling in against my shoulder. "Hey!" I shouted. "Hey! You! You're breaking the law, *chingaso!* Hey, I know about you! You want to pay for this window, or you want me to turn you in?"

Jaime glanced back at me as he ran, his eyes bulging with terror. Suddenly he leapt off the road into the trees, vanishing from sight.

I began to tremble, my rage collapsing into fear. What had I just done? Was I tired of living?

Glancing quickly into the rearview mirror to make certain that Jaime's children were not behind me, I slapped the truck into reverse and backed out onto Occidental Road. The children were gone, sprung into the same rabbit hole their father had used.

I punched the truck back into forward gear and floored it, asking all seven and a half liters of that truck's engine to give me everything they had.

32

Frida was not happy with me. "You used to be a more cautious girl," she muttered, as she picked at the remnants of the window on her brand-new truck. "Or at least you knew when to quit. Boy howdy, my partner ain't a-gonna like this."

All I could do was apologize. I'd pulled the truck into the barn to hide it, but morning follows night, and Frida had come early to make a call from her office, spotting the mess before I could get it downtown to a glass place and fix it up. "I can have it fixed by this afternoon," I grumbled. "When's your partner coming back?" Oh, how my face burned. The one person on earth I hated to have think so little of me just now was Frida.

"By noon. You get gone now, and just stay gone until you've redeemed yourself, you hear?"

"I hear."

Her aging spine unstiffened then. "Your cousin Abe will be here by suppertime. That's six o'clock, young lady. You make sure you're on time." .

I promised.

With Christmas so close at hand, the glass shops were shorthanded, but I found a place that would have it by four-thirty. I whiled the time away loading a little Christmas shopping onto my newly resurrected credit card: a nice fleece sweater for Frida, and a book of cowboy poetry for Cousin Abe. That left me wondering what to get for Frida's partner, who I'd begun to presume lived at the house with her. There were clues to this all over the place, like the interior decor, for instance—the fact that there was any. Frida wouldn't have bothered.

As I squirmed through the Christmas rush at Coddingtown Mall, I got to ruminating on who or what this partner might be. Had Frida taken a new lover, or was he just a friend? He had to be one or the other, or she wouldn't share lodgings with him. Had I seen any clues about this guy, any photographs or framed memorabilia with his name affixed? No, but I hadn't gone into the bedrooms yet. He'd be there when I returned, so my speculation would be over. *Well,* I told myself, *I'll just get him a horse book of some sort, and if he doesn't like it, he can exchange it.*

I got to dawdling, putting off facing Frida's contempt for me. I cut things as close as I dared, not going to pick the truck up from the repair shop until five. When I had finished paying the bill, the man handed me the keys and a sealed manila envelope. "This was on the floor," he said. "We dug it out as we were cleaning up the broken glass."

I turned the envelope over, examining it as I walked out to where the truck had been parked in the lot. I had assumed it belonged to Aunt Frida or went with the truck, but no, there in handwritten letters it said, "For Em Hansen. EYES ONLY." Raindrops began to fall, pelting the envelope and making the ink run, so I hurried with it into the truck.

Inside the envelope was one thin sheet of paper and a second envelope. The note on the paper said:

To Em Hansen:

Suzanne said you were trying to work out who killed Janet. Well, I don't know if what's in this envelope will tell you anything about that, but I'm sure I don't know what to do with it, and you seem an honest sort.

Janet gave it to me for safekeeping about a month ago. She

said she found it while she was doing some sort of survey, going through boxes where fungicides were stored out in the barn at the old Ferris place. She figured Jaime Martinez's wife Magdalena must have put it out there, as it was in there with some other junk mail and things that must have been lying around when she and Jaime moved in. Janet didn't feel it was right to leave it there.

This is a letter from Suzanne to Sonja Karsh, who you may know ran away back when we all were in high school. I read it. Maybe that wasn't right, but I had to know what to do with it. When Sonja left it really hurt Suzanne, and now I know why.

The note was simply signed *Trudy*. She must have gone out sometime during the drumming and slipped it through the open window of the white truck.

I opened the inner envelope. The letter was dated September 1973, the month after Sonja disappeared. The paper had yellowed, and the glue on the envelope had turned to dust. It read:

My Dearest Sonja,

You've been gone six weeks now so I hope you've found that place you were looking for all right. I remember when you said sometimes a person just has to let go and leave and I shouldn't miss you if you ever just had to go but I've waited up night after night hoping you'd call me at least and say that you're all right but I guess you think I'm the worst. I can only hope the post office forwards this letter to you.

Sonja I'm SORRY SORRY SORRY. Matt cornered me. How can you think I'd do anything like that on purpose? I didn't want to do it you have to believe me, he just backed me into the barn where your car was and said he wouldn't hurt me if I'd let him kiss me. It was gross his breath is like farting you have to believe me I hated it. Then I tried to get away and he pushed me into the car and pulled up my dress and that was when you came in. That was all, really you have to believe me. I shouldn't have run away. I came back the next morning before work to tell you what happened but you were gone.

You're my best friend and I need you. You were the only one I dared tell when my brother did it to me and you understood then so why can't you understand now? Even if you don't come back I'll wear my friendship ring forever and hope you wear yours. Please come back Sonja I'm sorry.

Your best friend,

Suzanne

The paper was brittle in my hands, even with the dampness that hung in the air. I smoothed it, folded it carefully. Then I slipped it back into the envelope in which it had waited for all those years, as grief and longing decayed into bitterness.

I had seen no rings on Suzanne's fingers.

I WAS LATE for dinner.

I decided to take an aggressive tack on things, burst in on the meal in progress with buckets of Christmas cheer, and hope the excitement thereof and the joy of two cousins seeing each other for the first time in who knew how long would bridge the chasm of Frida's irritation with me. So in I came, hurrying through the kitchen smiling and whooping, ready to gather Abe up in a good hug.

I stopped short, all sound gone from my lungs.

Frida's partner was home, all right, full in the process of trying to smooth my oh yes, *very* irritated aunt. Yes, soothing: holding Frida closely in big muscly arms, squeezing her, calming her with words, tenderly kissing her—

I had never seen two women kiss before. Not on the lips.

Abe saw the look of shock on my face, put his head down on the table, and groaned.

Frida quit moving, like she was in a different dimension from the rest of us, one in which time moved so slowly it appeared to have no dimension at all.

I just stood there, fool that I was, staring, thinking: *Oh,* that *kind of partner.*

Abe finally lifted his head and sighed like he'd just woken up from a long sleep.

Frida's partner broke the silence. "Abe, honey, aren't you gonna introduce me?"

Abe smiled faintly. "Kitty, this is Em. Em, Kitty."

"Well, isn't this nice?" said Kitty, in a loud, throaty growl. Hers was a voice that came from the gut and spoke of Marlboro cigarettes, years and years of them. She was over fifty, her big-bosomed, well-muscled body spread with the menopause, putting the rivets on her jeans to the test. Her steel-gray hair fell in a cascade of curls past her shoulders, framing a wide, lively face that did not lack for beauty.

I'm no homophobe, or at least I hadn't thought myself one until that moment, but it is a shock of titanic proportions to have an aunt you've known all your life—or at least thought you've known, all married up to your uncle and shucking out cousins like peas from a pod—suddenly turn up gay. Or lesbian, or whatever the hell they like to be called.

Kitty shook her head. "You look pretty dumb, standing there with your mouth open like that. Why'n't you apologize to your aunt for being late and scaring the piss out of her and sit down, for crap's sake, so we all can eat? I'm starved, for one, and this shit smells great."

I muttered an apology and we ate and we all got through it somehow. I wish to hell I could tell you I showed enough mettle to straighten up and apologize for the insult my lapse into silence leveled at my aunt, but I didn't. My courage runs thin near matters emotional.

It wasn't until I was walking out to the barn afterward with Abe that I found my voice at all. "I feel real dumb," was all I could say.

Abe was shuffling along with his shoulders up, but otherwise ig-noring the rain. He's a lanky guy, none too graceful, but nice-looking in a hayseed kind of way. He said, "It was a shock for me, too, the first time."

I was glad it was dark out, so he couldn't see the embarrassment that was heating my face. "But you're okay about it now?"

Abe shrugged.

"Abe, is this why she didn't go to my dad's funeral?" I asked, glad to focus on my father's intolerance rather than my own. "I mean, he didn't hold by alternative lifestyles and such, and—"

"Yup." Forcefully changing the subject, he said, "This letter came for you." He pulled a much-traveled envelope out of his pocket and handed it to me as he wrestled open the door to the staircase that led up to the spare bedrooms above the office.

"Thanks. But really, Abe, don't you find it, well . . ."

Abe stopped and stared into space, the rain falling through the glow around the overhead spotlight and soaking into his bad haircut. "Oh, Em, she's just who she always was. It ain't like she's turned into some-one else."

"But—"

"No buts about it. The more things stay the same, the more things never were what you thought they were in the first place."

33

SLEEP WOULD NOT COME.

Abe's words had hit their mark, setting off a cascade of anxieties. If things were not what they had always appeared, then what were they?

Opening the letter didn't help. It proved to be from Frank, forwarded through good old efficient Elyria:

Dear Em,

Guess you know I got married. She's not much like you, doesn't have your fury or sense of adventure, but she's a fine and good woman and loves me well.

After all these years a bachelor, I gone and got hitched the hard way. Well, tonight the most wonderful thing, I held my newborn son in my arms. I saw him born too, all wet and squalling, and I wanted to thank you. If you hadn't forced my heart open, I never would have let her in, and he'd never have been born. Thank you Emmy, from the bottom of my heart. Thank you again and again.

Frank

The letter dropped from my fingers.

As it spiraled to the floor, the world seemed to spin with it. Frank, who had been my lover, was now a father and husband. My own father was dead, my aunt was gay, and my mother was sober. I wasn't sure which was the hardest to confront. My mind kept buzzing, churning around and around those things that nag you in the night, like, *Was Frank my only chance at happiness? How could Dad go and leave me? How can my mother fail to ruin that ranch? Did I hurt my aunt's feelings?* and finally, *Why the hell didn't she just tell me she was gay? I could have handled it, truly. I just need time to adjust.*

Time to adjust, that's what I'd been needing, but Elyria had felt she knew better. She'd pushed and pushed, and now here I was more frustrated and demoralized than ever, up to my scalp in pain and bruises, huddling in the dark, scared out of my mind that somehow, somewhere, the monster who had attacked me in the motel was going to finish what he'd started. How could I explain to Elyria, whom everybody loved, what it was like to be hated, to feel those raging fingers close around my throat? No, I told myself angrily, the only one who might truly understand this agony was Janet Pinchon, who lay rotting in an early grave.

Janet. I had chased her ghost into the same trap that had swallowed her, and in the process, I had lost her. Gone was my sense of closeness to her, my pleasure in avenging her loss. Elyria wouldn't understand about this, either.

I pressed the heels of my hands into my eye sockets, writhing with anger at Elyria, missing her, wanting to call her, afraid to call her, dreading the loss of companionship that was to come. I wanted to plead with her not to marry Joe, or not just yet, so I could go on living in her spare bedroom just a little while longer, until the weight of all this pain and loss could leave in its own time.

One thought chased another for hours, until my fear of Matthew Karsh and his mother and whoever else out there might have done what was done to me and to Janet, and my rage at not being believed or helped by the Sheriff's deputies, and Frida's little surprise, and all the rest that had happened in recent months became one with my rage and loss over everything else in life. At five A.M., when my eyes snapped open for the hundredth time over some inconsequential noise—the stomp of a horse in its stall, or the clatter of the rain overfilling a leaf-choked gutter and finding a new channel over aging tin—I shrugged Janet's torn down parka over the flannel pajamas Frida had lent me and made my way down into her office in the dark. By the dim green light on the telephone keypad, I tapped in Elyria's number and the number of my telephone credit card. It would be six A.M. in Denver, a barely acceptable hour to awaken her, but it was time to talk; no, it was *past* time, and if I'd been up all night, well then, Elyria could survive without her last hour's sleep. And maybe she'd understand, and . . .

A male voice answered on the second ring, heavy with sleep. "Hello?"

"Joe. I'm sorry to wake you. I'll call back later," I said miserably, and hung up. Thirty seconds later, the phone jangled, echoed loudly by the outdoor ringer that would summon Frida if she were in the paddocks with a horse. I grabbed the phone off the hook and said hello, but heard only a dial tone. The infernal instrument was ringing for the second time before I realized that the call was coming in on the private rather than the office line, and that I had to push the flashing button to get it. By the time I did this and said hello again, Frida had picked up the extension in the house. She croaked into the line, her voice amplified by the short connection. "That you, Em?" Frida shouted. "What the hell you doing, calling me up at this hour?" Frida never was one to welcome intrusions to her sleep.

"It's for me, Frida," I asserted. "Go back to sleep."

"What's going on?" she insisted, now fully awake and riled.

"*Please* go back to sleep. This call's for me."

"Shit!" Frida barked, and hung up.

"Em?" said a softer voice on the line.

"Yes, Elyria."

"What's going on?"

"I don't know."

"Then who called just—"

"It was me. I didn't know you had Joe there with you. I'm sorry to have wakened him. And you."

"Well, you did, but I'm glad you finally called, damn you. And don't worry about Joe, he has a breakfast meeting. The alarm would have wakened him any moment. He's in the shower now. So what is this I hear about someone breaking into your motel room? That's terrible!"

"Yes, in a word, it was."

"Were you injured?"

Injured? Was that the word? "Well, some. They took me to the hospital, but let me go a couple hours later."

"Who was this creature? Did the police catch him?"

"No, they didn't. The problem was, I didn't see him. But I know who it was," I added hastily.

"Oh? How?" Elyria has an organized mind. It likes to file things under Yes or No, but not under Maybe.

"Well, it's a long story, but you see, his mother's trying to sell off his sister's inheritance, and I pushed a nerve, and he—"

"Wait, you're not making sense," she said, sleep still fogging her mind. "Start over."

"I think it's related to the case I'm working on."

"How do you know that?"

I said testily, "To be honest, I don't."

"Oh." There was a pause on the other end of the line, then: "So . . . will you . . . be out there much longer?" This wasn't like Elyria, to brush aside something so obviously important to me for whatever was on *her* mind. Or it wasn't like the old, pre-Joe Elyria. And she sounded overly encouraging, like she'd really prefer I stayed as long as I could.

"Don't worry. Frida's asked me to stay for Christmas. My cousin Abe showed up, and Frida's . . . ah, partner's back from some trip somewhere. It's a regular party."

"You don't sound so sure."

"Well, Frida's kind of . . . I think I put her off somehow. I used to think I knew her." At least maybe we could talk about this.

Elyria came back with something soothing and big-sisterly, that sort of "chin up" kind of chatter. Then she changed the subject again and talked about her work for a while, and when I started to sound more pulled together, she ever-so-casually mentioned, "Joe and I are going to his parents' for Christmas."

"Where's that?"

"New York."

"And you're going when." I wasn't asking her a question. We were speaking on the twenty-third of December.

"Tomorrow."

I couldn't keep the harsh, disappointed edge out of my voice. "So this is the big trip: he's taking you home to meet his parents. On the big family holiday, no less. That means he's proposed, and you've accepted. And this must have happened a while ago, didn't it, because it's pretty damned tough getting plane reservations into New York on Christmas Eve. So when were you planning on telling me?"

There was a long silence, and when she spoke again, there was a chill in her voice. "Em, you have at last found your calling. You are a fine geologist, but you are an inquisitor without peer."

Now it was my turn to stay silent. Into that empty phone wire I exuded all my pain and disappointment, all my terror of being alone and lost and forgotten, all my fear that in the time it takes to turn one's back I could be replaced, bumped out of Elyria's heart—or anyone else's—by someone more charming and whole. I waited, wishing the voice on the other end of the line would tell me it was all a joke, that it was over now. The soft green light on the telephone's keypad lit only a small sphere of the space in which I sat, and at that moment it seemed that was all that was left of existence for me, just one eerie green glow in a cold, empty office. My mind played a little trick then, abstracting me from the finality of that cold ending, by telling me that Elyria no longer existed, that I was holding an empty phone connected to nowhere. I was thinking about hanging the telephone up when I heard her voice, all tiny because I'd let the instrument fall away from my ear: "Em, listen to me," she scolded. "I can't be more for you than I am. What I am is your friend, not your umbilicus to the rest of reality. If you can pull yourself together, things will be fine for you and for us, but if you want to keep hanging off your emotional cliff by a thread like this, I'd make a sad waste of my efforts if I tried to save you. You've got to save yourself. Em?"

"Mm-hmm."

"Call me when you're feeling better? Please."

When I didn't say anything more, she hung up.

Outside, the rain poured down incessantly in the predawn darkness. I sat there awhile longer, staring numbly into that green glow as the phone emitted first a dial tone, and then an odd little voice that said, "If you want to make a call, please hang up and dial again," and then that nasty beeping noise, and then eventually silence.

34

THERE'S AN ODD FREEDOM IN HITTING BOTTOM. IT COMES with a not unreasoning conjecture that everything will be up from here. Little did I know that I had further down to go.

That came when I phoned Murbles. "This is Em Hansen," I informed him, bracing myself for the inevitable joust. "What do you want?"

"Ah, Miss Hansen," he began, his voice oddly warm. "*Good* of you to call. My message is simple. You have not reported to us anything of value. The Senator and I have decided that the line you are pursuing is nonproductive; or worse, your rash techniques are contrary to his privacy. As this smacks of *incompetence,* we feel we are best served to terminate your employment."

For a moment I was stunned, unable to reply. Then I got mad. Seething, spitting mad, one of those reckless mads that comes from having nothing more to lose. I gripped the telephone receiver so hard my knuckles turned white and sparks seemed to fly out of them. "Cut the shit, Murbles," I hissed. "Just where do you get the idea that—"

"You were *supposed* to report to *us.* Instead, you are out annoying the *police.*"

"You've been talking to Muller?" I asked, confused by the thought that Muller might have been in touch with them all along.

Murbles' voice carried a smirk. "Hardly."

"But—"

"Now, good-*bye*, Ms. Hansen. And don't think it isn't a pleasure to be done with you."

The line went dead.

I sat in stunned silence, trying to absorb what had just happened to me.

But then my mind started moving again, careening through this newest bit of information like a roller coaster out of control. *Of course, what was I thinking of? A slime like Murbles wouldn't be direct about how he got his information, he would bend rules and cut corners. So he had an informant in the Sheriff's Department. That figures; such custodians of the law as Murbles and his boss care little for its letter, and prefer to crush its spirit. Murbles sure covered a lot of ground the day he brought Janet's mother to identify her body, recruiting that contact and hunting down the man who took those photographs. And what did he say? I have not reported anything of value? Does that mean they were uninterested in all that stuff I laid out to Muller and Dexter, that they don't really care who murdered Janet? Or does he know damned well who killed her?*

I picked up the phone and dialed again. When Murbles answered this time, I said, "Murbles, you put your man on the line or I'm going straight to the media."

There was a moment of silence. "And just what could you tell them that was of interest, Miss Hansen?"

"You left footprints all over this county, Mr. Murbles."

Another silence. A second instrument picked up. I heard the Senator's voice. "All right, Miss Hansen, you have my attention. Now, what exactly are you going to do with it?"

I took a deep breath and let it fly. "Okay, this is it: I've got things pretty well in hand here, but the Sheriff's Department wants a bit more proof. I'm not certain just yet how I'm going to find that proof, but I'm going to find it, and you are going to pay me for every minute of the time it takes me. The reason you're going to pay me is because your daughter was murdered, see, and that's important. It's not escaped me that finding her murderer is not the real reason you sent me here, but it's the reason you gave me, and we therefore have a verbal contract that I intend to fulfill. Now, if you'd like to let me in on the big gag, the real reason you sent me here, tell me what mysterious chuck-hole in your political roadway I'm supposed to fall into so you can spot the joker that's really bugging you, well, this is your big chance, because the next time you hear from me, it'll be to call in my final bill."

Senator Pinchon's voice burst loudly over the line: "You don't really think you can—"

"I damn well can. You sent me out here to retrace Janet's steps. You wanted to know if she'd found your little chuckhole, and if she had, to make sure she hadn't told anyone about it. You people should be ashamed of yourselves." With that antiquarian bit of vitriol, I hung up, went upstairs, and fell soundly asleep until ten.

35

THERE IS COMFORT IN COMPLETING WHAT ONE HAS STARTED, just as those who have found the end member of despair and plan to kill themselves seem calmed as they clean their houses to set the stage. It was in this spirit that, on awakening, I came to peace with the notion that, no matter what it took, I would complete the task I had come to California to perform. There seemed, after all, little difference between Janet's questions and my own, and sometimes, when life begins to look like death, we discover that finding the answers to our questions has become the reason for living.

Cousin Abe helped me pack Janet's belongings into her little truck and lash a tarp over the load to keep off the now incessant rain. On my previous visit to that room at the Wagon Trail Motel, I had checked to make certain that nothing had been taken the night of the assault, and it had appeared that nothing had. But this time, as I sorted carefully through books and papers in order to repack them, I saw what I had missed: the eight-by-ten photographs of Janet's body in the ditch were gone.

I squared things with the manager of the Wagon Trail Motel. I paid her for the room, encouraging her to charge extra for damages, which I would pass on to the Senator, then made arrangements for her to receive messages for me, along with any further payment envelopes that would hopefully be forthcoming from Murbles. She was pleased to do it. "He was such a *cabrón,*" she purred, giving the word extra charm with her melodious accent. "If he calls again, I will tell him, 'Ms. Hansen is away from her room just now.' I will keep him ignorant."

Abe drove the F-250 and I drove Janet's truck back to the ranch, taking care again to make certain I wasn't followed. I drove Janet's truck right into the barn, where it could stay until I could figure out what to do with it. Clearly her family didn't care.

Next, I drove to the downtown Santa Rosa Library and paid a call on my blissed-out reference librarian, asking first for biographical information on the renowned Senator for California, George Harwood Pinchon. She directed me to good old *Who's Who* for a start.

George Harwood Pinchon, educated here, worked there, married 1) Lillian Abigail Torkelson, 2) Jennifer LaRue Mason. Married *twice*? I scribbled down the dates, and calculated Janet's birth year from her age. Janet was the spawn of marriage number one. Hmm. I dug through the bank of city telephone directories the library housed and found a Lillian Torkelson in San Francisco. It was an uncommon name, and if it was indeed her, she must have retrieved her maiden name upon divorce. And if she felt that way about things, I reasoned, some of Janet's dislike of Daddy might have been learned from Mama.

To the pay phone by the door. She answered on the third ring, sounding tired. "Ms. Torkelson?" I inquired.

"Ye-es, who's this?" The voice was low and heavy with Long Island vowels, and clotted with cigarette damage.

"My name is Em Hansen. Um, excuse me, but are you Janet Pinchon's mother?"

She replied with a guarded yes.

"Well, ma'am, this is a long, complicated story, so please stay on the line," I said, then explained what I was doing and why.

"That self-serving shit," she spat, when I added, strategically at the end, that I'd been hired by her ex-husband. I could hear a match strike, and an intake of breath through a cigarette.

"Tell me about that self-serving shit, Ms. Torkelson. Are you in touch with him?"

"The only time I've spoken with him in the past twenty years other than to ask where my check is was to tell him that Janet was dead."

"Was he upset?"

"Him? He said a few soppy things, you know how those pols are. Then he had the gall to say I'd called at a bad time. I'll bet he'd have hung up if I hadn't mentioned that Janet was found murdered by the Laguna, smack in the middle of Sonoma County!"

I tried to sound suitably disgusted as I asked, "What did he say *then?*"

"He asked what she'd been doing there." Ms. Torkelson sounded impatient. Apparently she didn't like saying anything that suggested that her former husband was big enough to take even this much interest in his daughter.

"And?"

"I said she was living there."

"And?"

"He asked what she'd been doing for a living."

"Exactly what did you tell him? I'm sorry to pursue this, but it could be important."

I heard a long intake of cigarette smoke from the other end of the line. "I told him."

"Told him who she worked for, or on what project?"

"The latter. He asked who her clients were."

"And you knew."

"Yes."

"Janet *told* you what she was working on?"

"Well, yes," she said defensively. "Her *work* was proprietary, of course, but she'd just been home for a visit, and when I asked who her client was, she . . . told me."

Pried it out of her, no doubt. "Then you knew she was working on an assessment for Valentine Reeves."

Ms. Torkelson's reply cut like a saw through wood: "*Beautiful* Val."

"You know him?"

"Val Reeves? Sure. Sonoma County was in George's first constituency."

"Politics," I said, again evidencing disgust.

"That's *all* he ever cared about. When I told him Janet had been out fighting the good environmental fight in his backyard, *that's* when that bastard started sounding upset! *God,* but I wanted to kill him!" The line filled with a thick smoker's cough.

"And he didn't come out to help you?" I drawled, certain I was pouring fuel onto her fire.

"*Him?* No, he hasn't bothered to see Janet since the divorce! Why spoil his perfect record? He sent that egregious assistant of his—what's his name, Mumbles?—to drive me to Santa Rosa, said *he* would help me, thank you very much, though I *told* him I could handle it my*self.*"

"So you didn't like Murbles."

"What a low form of life *that* one is, running around doing his filthy *spin* control. Showed *no* respect, *none.* I found my *own* way home, let me tell *you!*"

"And let me guess; he called back ten days later and asked to borrow Janet's truck."

A pause. "Well, what did I care? It was just sitting there on the street collecting parking tickets."

I skipped over the fact that I now had the truck and what was left of Janet's possessions; I didn't want to distract her with her own shortcomings. "Next question: does Senator Pinchon have any financial connection with a group of investors incorporated as Weather-All?"

When she was done coughing herself hoarse, Ms. Torkelson said: "Bob Weatherall, that sniveling old sot! Always had some big plan or another to develop some blackberry-encrusted piece of swamp or start some half-assed business. Well, he finally bet it all on a scam to build lawn furniture and it went belly-up and all the big sharks just swam in and gobbled him up, saying they were saving old Bob from bankruptcy. Hah! They bought his soul bag and baggage, and they've been using his name for any kind of deal they've wanted to pull off ever since."

"And your ex-husband is one of the boys hiding under his skirts."

From the other end of the line I heard a low, nasty chuckle. And glass clinking against glass, followed by a soft gurgling, a sound I'd know anywhere: Ms. Torkelson was pouring herself a late morning drink.

"Let me guess again," I continued. "His connection is something embarrassing to do with campaign funding, or perhaps an investment his constituency would not admire. Money laundering, perhaps."

"Right you are. It started twenty-five years ago when George was just a state assemblyman looking for a fast ride upstairs. That son of a bitch took my father's money and invested it with that den of thieves, and Dad never saw a cent back. A failed investment, George called it. Hah! I saw that money go in as investment and come out tenfold as campaign contributions, then disappear into the price of taking the tart he's married to now on the campaign trail with him. I married a common con-artist thief, just like his *associates* at Weather-All, and by God, I *divorced* him. My father's dead now and I know I'll never see a cent of that money for his estate, but if you've found something that can embarrass that weasel today, I'd just love to hear it."

"Do you follow his voting record?"

"With zest." Peals of derisive laughter. "He has the gall to call himself the Environmental Senator. My Janet knew the environment! She said companies like Weather-All shouldn't build on such environmentally sensitive lands. I told her the skunks will always try to build on the cheapest land they can find."

Guessing was getting easy for me, too easy. Ma Torkelson had raised her daughter to serve her well, long on grudge and short on caution, and with an extra twist: growing up with an alcoholic can foster a compulsion to make order out of chaos. It took one to know one; how hard I'd struggled to keep my own family's secrets secret. Pressing onward, I asked, "How does his claim jibe with his votes on environmental matters?"

"Votes? Hah! He makes all the right speeches, but he's right in there with that 'Pave the Wetlands' gang. You think they do things out in the open? Hell no, they do all their deals behind closed doors."

"So if Weather-All and friends needed to build along, say, the Laguna de Santa Rosa to get a source of water and a sewer tap into western Sonoma County to develop marginal lands, he'd help them."

The laughter on the other end of the line spiked into a giddy frenzy.

"Ms. Torkelson, this isn't really that funny. I think Janet was killed trying to find out about this connection."

The laughter stopped.

"Ms. Torkelson?"

When her voice came back on the line it sounded drained of all life. "My God, I never thought—"

The line went dead.

I thought of calling back, but knew what I could expect: either sobbing, fruitless grief, or scorching verbal abuse. Instead, I called the next number on my mental list, the offices of Reeves Construction, Sebastopol. When a woman answered, I shifted my voice up a half octave and chirped, "May I speak with Mr. Reeves? It's personal," and then, when I heard his voice, I warbled, "Hello, this is Wendy over at Weather-All. Can you help me? I'm new here, and I remember there were special instructions, but they're all gone right now to a meeting, and I have this check for you, and—"

"Under no circumstances do you make that check out to me or to Reeves Construction! You make it to the Ferris project escrow account and deposit it directly to the bank. It's bad enough I have to take your filthy money to get this project going, but I draw the line at selling my soul for it! This accounting is going to be aboveboard for anyone to audit, do you hear?"

Yes, I heard. *These* books were to be aboveboard, but his special kickback to Mrs. Karsh was not. But then, that's the way it is with the self-righteous: they have a way of deciding for themselves what is righteous and what is not.

I dialed him back. This time, when his secretary answered, I used my normal voice and said, "This is Em Hansen. I need to speak with Mr. Reeves."

I was put on hold, and some moments passed before he came on the line. "Ms. Hansen," he said. Very noncommittal.

"Mr. Reeves, I know you to be an honorable man. I just need you to confirm one thing: Janet Pinchon told you about that tank at the old Ferris Place, didn't she?"

The other end of the line was silent.

"I'll take that as a yes," I continued. "I'm guessing it was just after Rauch fired her, and just before she was killed."

As Reeves' silence continued, I said thank you and good-bye and hung up.

The next call was a bit more difficult to make, as it involved tracking down an old classmate on the East Coast: Marcie Jacobson, the woman who had recommended my services through her father to Senator Pinchon. My grandmother had a number for her mother, who was able to give me Marcie's work number in Virginia. "Jacobson," she barked, as she picked up the phone.

"Hansen," I barked in reply. "Yes, me; your old schoolmate. I understand you've been giving out my name for a certain kind of work."

There was a pause. "Oh, Em . . . yes, my dad asked about you recently. You know, I'd mentioned what you did there in Denver, and . . ."

I'll bet. I'll bet that grisly bit of gossip kept your tongue wagging all the way through the gin and tonics one evening. "What exactly did you tell him about me?"

Her tone became more guarded. "Oh, you know . . . that you were good at finding things out . . . that kind of thing. . . ."

"I think you were a bit more direct."

Amused snort. "Like *you're* being?"

"Just tell me which quality interested him the most," I said, goosing her arrogance toward greater candor.

Snort, snort. "Oh, let's see . . . I think it was a comment I made about where your talents lie."

"And where might that be?"

"I said you drew trouble like a lightning rod." Self-satisfied giggles.

I had counted well past five before I had calmed down enough to continue. Then, in a low, even voice, I said, "Marcie, you're correct, to a certain point. My life has had its difficulties. But the particular trouble I'm in now found me because you sent it. This I resent very, very deeply." When she didn't say anything more, I hung up.

◈

I SAT DOWN and wrote out in detail, and with references to each and every source except for Jaki, what I had learned about Janet Pinchon and what I believed to be the cause of her death, right down to the missing photographs and where I thought Detective Muller could find them. Matthew Karsh had killed Janet, I was sure of this now, but he hadn't acted in a vacuum: he was little more than an instrument of his mother's rage, which had seeded into madness so slowly that the whole family—no, the whole community—had as slowly come to accommodate it. A community that demoted Matthew's brutality to the acts of an overgrown child, and considered it private business when Sonja went missing. After all, it takes extra effort to mark the line between sanity and madness, more effort than many of us can spare as we struggle just to get through our days.

I found it difficult to write out my own miserable experiences. I was rightfully frightened, and angry and embarrassed to admit that my own weakness—my inability to face the changes life had brought me—had propelled me into harm's way. The difference between Janet's fate and my own had been luck: Matthew Karsh had removed his filthy paws from my throat a little sooner than from hers, and I had lived.

I included what I thought was going on between Senator Pinchon and Weather-All, and Valentine Reeves, Mrs. Karsh, her crooked lawyers, and HRC Environmental: a couple of nice little business arrangements, where certain laws, environmental regulations, and zoning ordinances were being bent just a little for the greater benefit of the investors. I wondered if, in their contempt for anything but their own greed and lust for power, they had simply disregarded some of the laws, because after all, a law that didn't suit them couldn't be much of a law, could it?

While Valentine Reeves had (in proposing his development of the old Ferris place) baited the trap that had sprung on Janet, he had neither killed her himself nor consciously suggested to Matthew and his mother that she be killed. I knew this because murder wouldn't fit with his self-image of enlightened despot, and as I thought of his impeccable clothing and perfectly combed hair, I knew he would never ransack a motel room or mutilate a bicycle. Vanity seldom gives itself over to such outbursts; they're messy, and hold little appeal for one so comfortably in love with himself.

I still reeled at the thought of a father who cared as little for his daughter's life as Senator Pinchon had, or for that matter, Will Karsh, and tried repeatedly to assure myself that *my* father would *never* have shown so little regard for *my* happiness. But little by little I was coming to face the fact that Frida was right: my father had driven me a mile farther down the road to hell with each drop of liquor he'd fetched for my mother.

At least I could rest my conscience that I wasn't working for a murderer. Janet's mother had assured me of that when she told me how little Senator Pinchon had known about his daughter's life. But while he hadn't ordered her killed, what she had stumbled into would indeed have embarrassed him, had she lived long enough to make it public. The sweet irony was that in employing me, he had guaranteed that his embarrassment would be delivered.

I MADE THREE copies of my handwritten document, thanked my friend for her help, and got directions to the nearest post office, where I bought four prestamped envelopes. One copy I mailed to Detective Muller, marked "Merry Christmas from Em Hansen." The second I sent to Elyria, with a brief note suggesting that she'd know what to do if I turned up dead. The third, I mailed to Senator Pinchon with a current bill for my expenses, including replacement of the window of the F-250. The original copy of my tome, I sent to the news editor at the Santa Rosa Press Democrat, figuring the PD would know what to do with a story like that.

36

CHRISTMAS CAME AND WENT. AS I HID OUT AT FRIDA'S AND waited for my letters to find their ponderous ways through the holiday mails, my temper grew short. I kept to myself, ruminating darkly off in my room or out on the porch by myself, rubbing at the fading marks on my throat and snapping at Frida and Kitty and Abe when they asked me innocent little questions, like, "How are you today?"

Within my growing hermitage, I gradually grew used to Frida's new life, and to her partner, who was after all pretty easy to like. I would have liked to talk things out with Frida, but the one time I tried to apologize for my breach of manners, she was curt with me: "Em, there's some things I don't like to discuss." So instead we took a longer, less fearsome route to our new state of normalcy.

I watched the papers for splashy exposés about Weather-All and Senator Pinchon, but nothing happened. Lucky McClintock got sick of hearing from me and quit returning my calls. Detective Muller, while continuing to receive my calls with polite good cheer, was no more forthcoming than Lucy.

As December and the year ground to a close, it continued to rain; thick gray clouds sliding seamlessly overhead, pelting us with wet. I suffered. It was like getting wiped with an endless gray sponge. Moisture fell from the sky in pulses, now a thin drizzle, now a downpour, now a needle-keen drifting wet; now, just for a moment, stopping. Frida said she'd never seen so many rainy days together, not in California and not nowhere. Abe sat glued to the Weather Channel on cable TV, watching the satellite images as one frontal system after another bowled rain and wind across the Pacific at us, and reported that it was all because of El Niño, the warm equatorial current that flows across the Pacific. He said El Niño had shifted north this year, pushing air thick with rain up the California coast.

"Yep, the old pineapple express, hauling rain to you straight from Hawaii," Kitty agreed. "The ground's saturated now; there'll be flooding soon. 'Bout time we set some sandbags beside the driveway, so the sheetwash won't gully it out. Pretty soon the tack'll be growing mildew, and we'll be treating the horses' hooves for thrush. What a hoot."

I was not as easily amused. I was restless and ill at ease, riddled with exhausting fantasies of getting even with Matthew Karsh. When I could hold still no longer, I swathed myself in oilskins and started exercising horses in the corral, making them lope around to get their hearts beating faster. Little by little I got used to working in the rain.

A few days before New Year's, I rode out from the corral in a steady rain astride a nice sorrel named Jack. New grass was sprouting up everywhere, turning the hills from a tired brown to a dazzling green. At first it was an exercise in cold, stiff misery, but the sensual rhythm of Jack's stride warmed my body and soothed the complaint my little monkey brain had been dishing out, and I kept on riding, forgetting how soft the years of office work had made me. And I caught the mother of all colds.

When Kitty pronounced my influenza a "healing crisis," I rolled over and gave up. "What's that, Kitty, a hint?" I snapped. "You ready for me to leave?"

"No, but whatever it is that's eating you is beginning to eat at me."

I threw down the cup of herb tea she'd just brought me, spilling it into the saucer. "What could that be, Kitty? Now, let me think. Could it be the assault? Or how about—"

"How about the way it reminds you of your family?"

"It *what?*" I bellowed, not wanting to admit that she was right.

"Your light's on at all hours, you're trying to get out of bed when you're running a fever, and there's a weird look in your eyes like you're seeing right through the wall at someone who's not here. Oh, maybe you'll be fine for a day or two, then you blow your stack over something trivial, like just now. I asked Frida, and she said that wasn't like you, that you were more the slow seething type, and as there's nothing here that should be riling you up like that, I figure you're being chased by your own shadow."

"You take your ten-cent psychoanalysis and shove it!" I hollered, knocking the tea onto the floor.

"I rest my case."

I opened my mouth to order her out of the room, but something in her eyes stopped me. Something more powerful than sympathy: I saw recognition. A chill went up my spine. Burying my head in my hands, I whispered, "What's happening to me, Kitty?"

Kitty sat on the edge of the bed and took my hands in both of hers. "Frida told me about your brother. I think something you've tried to forget is coming back to haunt you," she said.

"I was just a little kid. How could I remember?"

"In one way or another, we remember everything. Maybe it isn't a conscious memory, but we remember sounds and smells, and how things felt. We remember being touched."

I shook my head. "Come on, Kitty," I begged, "my father just died. I'm out of sorts."

"I'm sure that helped. Sure, your dad's gone now, so it's safe to look at what he wasn't. And perhaps his death helped break down those walls you built to protect yourself from the past. It's funny how this works: You need to be strong enough to remember things, yet at the same time something's got to weaken you enough so you can't keep it down. Like the trauma you had here in California."

"Matthew Karsh attacking me."

Kitty nodded. "Has anyone ever done that to you before?"

I opened my mouth to say no, but there was no point in lying to Kitty. And with that acknowledgment, fear flooded through me, soaking every muscle with a horrifyingly cold weight. I squeezed my eyes shut to push the feeling away. Felt myself choking for breath. Threw my hands to my throat, only to find none there but my own.

Opening my eyes again, I whimpered, "I keep wanting Daddy to come back and help me."

Kitty put a strong arm around my shoulders and hugged me to her breast. "There's not a woman alive who doesn't have just a tiny bit of that little girl in her. Hang in there, kid, you'll be amazed how much you can handle without your old man. As you begin to remember, you'll be afraid like whatever it was that scared you is just happening now, but as you acknowledge it, you lay it to rest. After that, it may still hurt, but it's out in the open where it can't run your life anymore."

THE MORNING OF New Year's Eve, the last business day of the old year, Kitty made an announcement to me and Frida: "Listen, you two, I like to leave things where they belong, like in the past. And I prefer an attitude of wellness around me. To prove my goodwill, I'm springing for mud baths for you both. There's no mood so black, and no snot so thick, that a mud bath in Calistoga can't lift it."

We knew better than to argue with Kitty.

Aunt Frida and I drove over the hills to Calistoga under gunmetal skies. Having elected to take Kitty up on her offer, we summarily left her behind. "I don't mind adjusting my attitude," Frida growled, as she wound the F-250 fiercely around the curves of Mark West Creek Road, "but I'm damned if I'm gonna let Little Kitty Wise-Ass gloat while I'm doing it."

Stifling a cough, I tipped my head back and looked at her out of the corner of one eye in appraisal.

"Yeah," she continued, "you can take the old hag out of Wyoming, but you can't take Wyoming out of the old hag. Sometimes, Em, I think Ms. Kitty's grown mildew between the ears living in this here loony bin all her life." When I began to laugh, Frida added, "Aw, hell, it'd happen to anyone."

Calistoga lay in a narrow valley between craggy hills, eroded remnants of a gang of volcanoes that had been born and died a few million years ago. They were steep and dark, coated with oaks and madrones. Volcanic heat still smoldered at their roots, heating a collection of springs and geysers into steam. One such geyser puffed and belched away at Indian Springs Resort.

We cruised through Calistoga, giving all the hip vacationers our best slack-jawed Wyoming hick smiles, passing shops full of chichi coffees, tourist gimcracks, and resort wear, before turning in at Indian Springs.

Kitty had signed us up for the works: mud, mineral bath, steam, showers, and a massage each. Frida had argued with her, saying that there was no way in hell she was going to get buried before her time, and I'd allowed as how I wasn't sitting up to the neck in no water. We had settled on a compromise: mud for me and the mineral bath for Frida. When we presented ourselves at the desk, an attendant led us down a hallway and into a white room fitted with lockers and low benches, where she handed us big white flannel sheets. "Please remove all your clothes and wrap these around yourselves," she whispered. "There's filtered water here for you to drink. I'll be back for you in a few minutes."

Okay, strip naked; I can do that. It was a pleasant room, all light and serene, and I was still half-stuporous from my flu. So Frida and I politely turned our backs on each other and got into our togas, then stood there making faces like we thought this was pretty silly.

There was a bowl of quartered oranges for us to munch on, and as we waited for the attendant to return, we got to seeing who could squirt orange juice the farthest. The flannel sheet was soft and comforting against my flu-ravaged body, and I found myself smiling in spite of my best intentions to remain ornery.

Soon the attendant returned and took Frida away. I poured myself a cup of water and took a seat on one of the benches. The water tasted of cucumbers. I liked it.

The attendant returned for me. "Your mud bath is ready, Miss Hansen," she said, beckoning me farther into the soothing recesses of the spa. We walked down another white hallway and into a room that had four low cement troughs full of black mud made from volcanic ash. A tiny woman with thick black hair pulled back into a heavy braid was working at the second trough, bending to spread fresh ash and scalding it with water hosed in straight off the geyser. She was dressed all in black, the sleeves of her dark turtleneck shirt pushed up her narrow arms to her elbows. She stirred the mud with a short-handled rake, using long, smooth gestures that spoke of reverence and a deep familiarity with her task. The rhythm was mesmerizing. The attendant guided me into a shower, murmuring that the woman with the braid would help me into my mud bath when I was ready.

The hot water drummed against my aches. I dawdled awhile, watching the woman rake the ash. When I stepped out of the shower, she came to me and looked up into my eyes with a sweet, welcoming tenderness. Her own eyes were dark as basalt, and her face was lined with age, yet peaceful and open as a child's.

That was enough for me; I would have been happy just to stare into her eyes awhile longer and go home figuring Kitty's money had been well spent, but she gently pulled my arm. I followed. At the trough, she spoke with her hands and a few words of Spanish-accented English, indicating how to settle on the edge and then swing my legs into the bath. I lay back onto the soft, warm mud.

"You okay?" The woman smiled. "Is not too hot?"

I shook my head, the motion dampened by the softness beneath me.

Then she turned toward the wall and raised her hands in supplication, and I recognized a practice I hadn't seen since my travels into the distant villages of Mexico: a devout Indian, praying at the start of work.

I felt blessed, anointed by God. I looked down along the winter whiteness of my form, seeing it for that moment as She might, admiring the slight rounding of my breasts, the sharpness of my shins, my hip bones. . . .

The prayer ended. Turning back to me, the woman bent to her work, dredging up great double handfuls of the warm black mud and stacking it quickly over my legs, my arms, my body, and then ever so gently against my cheeks, ending with a careful smoothing of a lock of hair that had come to rest across my brow. Then she went away to leave me to the embrace of Mother Earth.

⬦

FOR A WHILE I gazed upward at a frosted skylight in the white ceiling, watching steam condense into great hungry drops and fall lazily to the mud. Then I closed my eyes and let the warmth be all.

Minutes melted like chocolate, running through my mind, breaking the congestion in my lungs, drawing it away into the mud. My nose itched, making me smile.

Mud, I thought. *All these years, I've thought it was the lowest thing on earth. How ignorant I was. Mud is wonderful! Maybe Kitty's right; I feel my body healing. Mud!* I fell into a rhapsody of mudness. I smiled at the memory of drumming and the visions it had brought, and felt, for the first time in many months, whole.

Mud. I sang a mental hymn to colloids great and humble, and got to playing with its peculiar qualities, jiggling it with my fingers, now quickly, now slowly. . . .

Ashes to ashes, mud to mud, ashes to mud. Oh, thixotropy, receive now your daughter. . . . I laughed, tickled at the thought of that scientific term in these surroundings. Thixotropy, that quality of mud that makes it firm until jiggled by the shock of earthquake or the movements of a bather's fingers, whence it turns to liquid. Thixotropy. Once a geologist, always a geologist. Put a sick geologist up to her nostrils in hot volcanic mud and what do you get? A superannuated child lost in the blissful play of discovery.

In my mud-induced stupor, I recalled those stories of San Francisco earthquakes, of the ground heaving as fill soils turned thixotropic, of buildings sinking, of water shooting up in fountains. The idea of the earth receiving some things and expelling others tickled my mind, freeing it to think in any direction it pleased.

And just like that, I knew where Sonja Karsh had gone.

37

AUNT FRIDA ARGUED WITH ME ALL THE WAY BACK TO HER ranch. "You can't really believe that, can you, Em? Matthew Karsh killed his own sister? What kind of a monster would do that?"

I wanted to scream. "Why can't anyone see this but me? What kind of a human being ever kills another human being but a monster?"

Frida didn't have an answer to either question. "But his own sister! If *I'd* had a daughter, my boys would have protected her, or if they'd harmed a hair on her head, I'd—but not—Jesus, Em! Under the tank? How do you know that? That's disgusting!"

I kicked the dashboard in fury. "Don't you get it? That's why they don't want the damned tank pulled. All this time I thought it was because Val Reeves wanted his damned construction loan, but he knew he could get that money from Weather-All right along. They'd probably been courting him since he filed his plans with the County. And that's why Senator Pinchon's antennae were up." The irony made my head spin: Janet had told Reeves about the tank to try to block construction, but all she'd managed to do was drive him into business with her father's patrons.

Frida rolled her eyes. "Em Hansen, sometimes you analyze things to death, and you quit makin' any sense. See here, this Karsh woman would have just said, 'Take the money from Weather-All and let's get on with it.' "

"But Reeves didn't tell Mrs. Karsh about that money until that night

I happened by. That's what all his notes were about. He'd given up on getting a bank loan, and he was pitching her the deal with Weather-All. Anyways, I'll bet Janet caught her unprepared, coming to her and telling her the bank would want that tank pulled. Mrs. Karsh couldn't afford to have Sonja found. She panicked and called in her monster."

"Sure, the whole damned family's kept their mouths shut for over twenty years. Uh-huh."

"Well, they wouldn't *all* have to know. Just—damn it, Frida, she *knew* her daughter's body was under that tank. Her darling boy killed her, and Jaime Martinez helped bury her. *That's* why they'd already put the gravel ballast in place that morning the tank was installed. It all fits!"

Frida swerved to miss a slow-moving truck. "You'll recall, Em, that we don't even know she's dead. All you know is she hasn't been seen in close to twenty-five years. She could be anywhere. She could be a stockbroker in New York or a whore in New Orleans for all you know."

"They never found her, and the police would have looked," I muttered. "Or at least until they got bored. And the lawyers. They would have hired a tracer to find the heir on her twenty-first birthday." I considered this. "Or maybe not. They sure didn't hurry up and finish probating that will."

Frida went on. "Maybe she's no longer going as Sonja Karsh. Maybe she got a new name as—hell, these things can be bought, Em."

"She was only sixteen when she left; you think in all those years she'd never show up once or even phone her best friend to say happy birthday?"

"Or maybe she died in a bus accident in Spain five years ago, or—"

"Damn it, you just don't want to think a boy could have offed his sister," I seethed, my voice beginning to shake. "You're just like everyone else!" Now my hands began to tremble, and that feeling of terror began to rise in a wave.

Frida sighed with exasperation. "Em, even if it's true, how are you going to prove it? You gonna dig up that tank yourself?"

I stared out at the blackening clouds. I had an idea how I could force the truth to rise.

◇

BACK AT THE ranch, I settled myself in the office with the telephone book. Mrs. Karsh was listed and answered on the third ring. "Happy New Year," I said. "This is Em Hansen. I know about the underground tank by your father's barn. Your man Martinez has been pouring oil and solvents into it for twenty years."

"I'm sure I don't know what you're talking about."

"I'm sure you do. And Janet told you to pull it, didn't she?"

Another pause. Nice ladies don't lie, they just don't answer.

I sighed theatrically. "Well, it's an environmental hazard, ma'am, and if you won't do anything about it voluntarily, I'll tell County Health you have an illegal tank and they'll force you to pull it. But I'm a nice person, and I'll give you twenty-four hours to report it yourself." The illogic of our interchange delighted me. I was certain it would make perfect sense to a woman who lived by her rules. "Well, good-bye."

Hanging up the phone, I gave them an hour's lead, then got into the F-250 and began to drive. It was almost dark.

When I reached the turnoff for Ferris Road, I parked the truck and started hoofing it through the trees.

The rain had briefly ceased. A dim, foggy twilight enfolded me as I dodged through the thicket of oaks and followed the road from a safe distance inward. Under the trees, it grew darker and darker. I looked at my watch. Almost five o'clock. The sound of a heavy engine coughed into life by the barn.

I hurried through the brush and trees, racing to get as close to the barn as I could without being seen. Making it to within fifty yards, I could just see the shape of a backhoe lifting its claw.

A backhoe, right on top of the tank site. And a flatbed truck, its stakes pulled from one side, waiting.

I slid in behind an oak, pressing myself up to its damp, mossy bark.

The claw dropped, gouging at the ground just next to the barn. Matthew Karsh sat at the controls of the backhoe. He worked hurriedly, ripping at the soil, scooping it up, and sloppily shifting the spoils. Jaime Martinez waited nearby, pacing and gesturing. He was shouting something at Matthew, something I could not hear over the grind of the engine.

Sprinting back to the truck, I climbed in and dialed the cellular phone. When a voice answered, "County Health," I asked for Lucy, saying it was an emergency.

She was there. "Lucy," I said, "I'm glad I caught you."

"Who is this? I'm just leaving."

"This is Em Hansen. Remember that waste-oil tank I found? The one on Ferris Road?"

"Yes, yes, keep your shirt on, I'm working on it. I checked with Fire Services. No one ever permitted a tank there, or permitted removal, for that matter."

"Well there's someone out there with a backhoe right now, trying to get the bugger out of the ground."

"How do you know?"

I told her where I was calling from. "He's digging like mad, and he's got a stake-bed truck all ready to haul the thing away in the dark."

"But they can't pull a tank without a permit to close, nor can they take it off the property without a transfer permit, not to mention proper precautions."

"Precisely."

Lucy laughed a cruel laugh. "Keep an eye on them. I'll be right there."

❖

LUCY'S A SMART woman. She showed up in a government vehicle with an escort of three big men, carrying officious-looking documents.

It had taken her about twenty-five minutes to get there, long enough that Matthew had all the earth removed from the top of the tank and Jaime had a strap around it ready to lift the thing out of the ground. Matthew was giving it its first hard pull with the bucket of the back-hoe when the County Health posse arrived, bathing them and their efforts in their headlights. Matthew took one quick glance and vanished. I was amazed at how fast he moved.

Lucy turned to Jaime. She informed him that he was to cease what he was doing and stay away from the now fully visible tank by order of state legal code number such-and-such. Jaime climbed up and shut down the backhoe and stormed off toward his house.

As he came past me, I couldn't help saying, *"Si solamente pagas por la ventana."* If you'd only paid for the window.

❖

WATER IS A powerful force.

The ground had long since become saturated, shunting the rainfall into sheetwash. Over the next days and weeks, as one storm after another continued to pound the coast of California, the rivers began to rise.

The waters backed up first along the Laguna, inching across the floodplain, rising drop by churning drop toward the causeway where Occidental Road crossed the once narrow stream. It was a lake now, at last living up to its Spanish name, and growing deeper. Then, as one storm brought six inches of rain in thirty-six hours, the Russian River swelled and leapt its banks, backing up Mark West Creek and flooding low-lying vineyards. The waters of Mark West Creek stalled backward up into the Laguna, now gorging on fast-moving runoff from the flood-control channels of Piner and Santa Rosa creeks. Passage over low-lying roads became impossible.

As the waters continued to rise, Sonoma County became the focus of reporting on cable TV. I watched in fascination as the cable brought images of bridges and roadways awash, of National Guard helicopters plucking stranded residents from homes half-submerged in roiling, turgid waters. One particularly wet reporter spoke into a sodden microphone, reporting that, "Along the Laguna de Santa Rosa, the flood level has now exceeded the one-hundred-year level."

It was time to move.

I phoned Detective Muller's office, but he wasn't there. I left a message asking him to meet me by the Laguna and fired up that nice, high-clearance Ford F-250 truck and drove through the slashing rain. It was a long drive through congested, storm-deflected traffic to get around the flooded roads and bridges. Instead of driving ten miles south, I had to wind eastward, then drive fifteen miles south on Highway 101 and ten west again along Highway 12 and onto Occidental Road, but that was not enough. Even before I reached the causeway and bridge, I met a sign that read, FLOODING, LOCAL TRAFFIC ONLY. I inched onward, perversely needing to take a look.

Rain fell in sheets, consuming the sky. The roadway was slick with runoff, and here and there awash as bank-full ditches spewed muddy water onto the pavement. As the ground fell toward the floodplain, I brought the truck to a stop. The bridge and causeway were gone, deep underwater, not even Duke's stop sign at the far end visible to mark their position. More frightening was the Laguna itself. It was a mile wide, and all along the far side it had swallowed the lower halves of trees, houses, and barns.

I turned around and made my way southward over farm roads, crossing over Highway 12—also cordoned off, flooded above the engineered berms and into the fancy new buildings that had stood so high over the banks. I continued southward, now fetching up behind lines of other travelers inching their trucks south along the Santa Rosa Plain in search of a crossing. Miles farther south, this road, too, dipped low and was itself awash, but I drove around the barricade and crossed gingerly, the door panels of the high-clearance truck licking water. At Highway 116 I turned back to the north to begin the run along the hills to Miwok Mills.

And stopped. Traffic, compressed from all other roads into Sebastopol and its outlying communities, was at a crawl. A highway patrolman stood by the intersection passing out information: Storm winds had dropped branches on power lines. All power was out to the north, including the traffic lights. The delay would be at least half an hour to go four miles.

I got out my county map and plotted another course through the orchard lands among the hills, dodged around Sebastopol to the west, and reemerged onto Highway 116 north of town. Two miles farther north, I came up to another barricade, this one stopping traffic that approached the Laguna eastbound on Occidental Road from Miwok Mills. Swerving around it, I headed down off the hills toward the distended flow.

I couldn't reach Ferris Road. It, too, was awash, but half a mile short of it I found Jaime Martinez's battered yellow pickup parked, the waters lapping at its tires. It was empty, but the motor was still warm.

Leaving the truck, I climbed overland through the woods above the roadway. It was dim and, with the dying of the light, getting darker. I continued on across slippery slopes until I could discern the barn and confirm what I expected: the tank had risen from its grave and was afloat now, a huge rusted drum of iron three-quarters visible, rolling sickly in the muddy water, held in place now only by its tether and a few small hills of soil left as spoil piles the night Jaime and Matthew had tried to pull it.

I turned back for help.

I found Jim Erikson huddled up by the coffee urn at the firehouse trying to get warm. He had a blanket around his shoulders and his long legs were braced, so that he leaned stiffly against the edge of the desk. His hair stood up in wet spikes and sodden loops, and his eyes were red around the rims. He looked so bad I almost didn't ask. Almost.

"Em," he whispered, eyes wide at the unexpected sight of me.

"Just tell me one thing: did you set me up?"

His brows knit in offended confusion. "Did I what?"

"Take me out for that beer so Matthew Karsh could get to my room ahead of me."

"What are you talking about?"

"Reeves. Did he tell you to take me out after the Spaghetti Feed?"

Jim's face clouded. "I may work for the man, but I'm not in the habit of taking personal orders from Val Reeves."

"Good. Then I need your help."

"Name it."

"There's a thousand-gallon gasoline tank lying uncovered down by the Laguna. The tenant's been throwing waste oil in it, and probably everything else anyone wants to get rid of. Solvents. Paint. It's probably part-full, maybe a nice explosive mixture of air and volatiles. Well, now the water's up high enough that the thing's floated up out of the ground, and it's about to head downriver."

Jim jumped up and threw off the blanket. "Why didn't you say so! Hell, that's all we need is a thousand-gallon bomb floating toward the bridges." He grabbed his turnouts on his way out the door. I had to run to keep up. "I'll take the pumper with the boat on it." Turning briefly back to me, he asked, "Where'd you say it was?"

"I'll show you. You're taking me with you."

"The hell I am!"

"Oh? Then you tell me where that tank is."

THE METAL BOAT churned slowly through the brown floodwaters, swept along in their slow but powerful flow toward the ocean. Jim sat at the controls of the tiny outboard motor, squinting into the driving rain. I sat in the bow in borrowed turnouts and a Mae West life preserver, pitting every ounce of my rage against my fear of the brown, swirling waters. "Over there," I shouted over the grind of the boat's motor, pointing through the gray curtains of rain. "There! By the barn!"

Jim turned the boat, putting the current to his advantage, pressing us toward the dark, rain-blurred shape that was the barn. We glided over cross-fences, slipping between the tops of iron posts that anchored barely submerged strands of barbed wire. Here and there, bits of grass and twigs and even logs caught on trees and bushes, streaming down-current toward the sea.

Even through the gloom, I could see that the barn was awash. The entire farmyard was underwater, and the railings on the back porch of the farmhouse stood up like a savage grin. Not even a candle burned in the house. Jaime had taken his family to safety.

I heard Jim's voice over the sound of the motor. "Aw hell, Em, it's under control. There's a sling on it from the bucket of that backhoe. Even this water won't carry that backhoe off."

"No, Jim, look!" I could see someone at the controls of the backhoe, a huge, dark shape in water to his knees. A second, smaller man stood with his back to us on a pile of gravel, hunching against the rain.

The engine of the backhoe burst into life, and in no time, the bucket began to swing. The tank followed, docile as a cow, then snagged on a pile of gravel spoils. The bucket swung the other way, and tugged. The tank bucked once, then leapt the brim of the excavation and floated downstream. There it hung, slowly rolling, a giant can of toxic death bobbing on life's stream.

"Hey, stop that thing!" Jim shouted, but he was not yet close enough to be heard over the roar of the backhoe. "Em! Turn on that spotlight in the bow!" I hit the switch and aimed, lighting up the black-browed man like a Christmas tree.

Jaime jerked, jumping around on the spoils pile, scowling, venom oiling his black, black eyes. "Get back from here!" he shouted, his voice rising in panic. "You not s'posed to be here!"

"What are you doing, man?" Jim hollered.

Jaime staggered off the spoils pile and into the water, then half swam and half ran through the slurry of water and muck, hurrying in through the gaping doorway of the barn. Another motor sounded and he reemerged, this time at the controls of a boat with an engine powerful enough to tow a skier. As he neared the backhoe, he screamed an invective stream of Spanish at Matthew, exhorting him to join him in the boat.

Our boat was a hundred yards from the hole now and sliding by downstream with the current. I swung the spotlight this way and that, picking out a route through the fencing and half-submerged farm equipment. Jim hesitated, uncertain of running aground in a flooded yard strewn with such obstacles. A disk harrow bore its knives above the waters here, and a wagon rested there, half-emergent. "I'm not sure about this, Em," he called. "I think I should get on the radio here and report this and get the hell out. Those guys are leaving, and that backhoe's heavy enough to anchor that tank."

"No, look." I swung the light. "The one on the backhoe isn't going to leave."

Matthew gunned the engine and swung the bucket again. Jaime called to him one more time, then opened the throttle on the speedboat, speeding away.

Matthew Karsh's enormous hands moved wildly among the controls of the backhoe, his precious backhoe. Now jerking the bucket wildly, once, twice, three times, he tried to flick loose the sling that held the tank. Then, raising the bucket as high as it would go, he grasped the brakes that turned the wheels, jammed them opposite directions, and kicked the accelerator hard.

The backhoe slipped, fell sideways, and slid into the waters of the Laguna de Santa Rosa. We saw Matthew heave up out of the waters like a broaching whale, sputter, gain his footing, and try to regain his seat, which now lay sideways. The motor was still running on the backhoe. He grabbed the controls and jerked. The bucket swung again, finally spilling the sling, and the tank began to drift. The engine died.

We were fifty feet from the backhoe now. I looked back at Jim. He hesitated, trying to decide between the man and the drifting tank. He went for the man. "We'll get as close as we can," he shouted to Matthew. "Get ready to board us!" I gripped the spotlight with white knuckles, trying to convince myself that Matthew would come along quietly because Jim was aboard.

At first Matthew stood frozen in the spotlight, watching our boat churn toward him with blank eyes. As boat and man met, Jim swung the boat and braced himself, grasping the center seat, then reached his free arm out to Matthew. As Jim's fingers closed around his wrist, Matthew's face twisted with fear and rage, and he flung his arms sideways, spinning the boat. As Jim struggled, Matthew pushed, throwing the unsuspecting fireman overboard.

I clambered across the boat to pull Jim back in, but Matthew continued to thrash, frantically grasping him behind the neck and banging his head against the motor casing. I heard a neat crack. Jim's eyes closed. Matthew shook him once and, satisfied that he was gone, released him to the waters.

I watched in horror as Jim's body floated away, face down, his long legs dragging on the gravels below, keeping his life vest from turning him onto his back.

I looked back at Matthew. His mossy teeth gleamed as he lurched toward me, grasped the gunwale of the boat, and pulled it hand over hand. The boat bumped against the fireman. The motion rolled Jim over, but still he slid away from us, mouth agape, no bubbles issuing from his airway. Matthew was five feet from me and closing. I grabbed an emergency oar, swung it. It struck Matthew's arm with a sodden thud and skidded away. With one filthy paw he ripped it from my hands.

I leapt into the water and flailed, unable to touch bottom against the buoyancy of my life vest, sick that my shorter legs found no footing. I spread my arms and swam, hampered by the bulk of the life vest. Releasing the boat, Matthew Karsh followed me, striding through the dark waters like a heron in search of prey.

Panic consumed me. I didn't want to die. I struggled westward toward the barn, where the waters would be shallower. One foot found bottom, slipped, struck again.

I felt a tug at the back of my vest, now a jerk, now hands closing around my neck, and he was pressing me under. My hands found the side of a gravel pile and I pushed upward, briefly freeing my mouth. I gasped, only to feel the tug again, and knew that he was dragging me through the waters with one hand, ripping at the straps of my vest with the other. They gave, one after another. He handled me surely, like a flopping doll, oblivious to my claws and kicks. I gasped, drank up sodden air, my nostrils stinging with inhaled water. He had my vest off now. I felt my belly dragging over the spoils pile as he pushed me into the pit, pushing me down, pushing me—

With all my remaining strength I dove, swimming hard for the bottom of the hole, for that place where the tank once rested.

Bottom. I clawed, digging at the gravel to pull my way along the bottom, praying that I could move just far enough away from him before broaching that I could slither loose and gain my footing. . . .

Time slowed like jelly, flowing around me. A strange notion enfolded me, saying, *You've been here before, you've done this before . . . you've*—

Gravel exploded around my hands in bursts. The skin on my fingers tore with the effort. Something hard lay in the gravel, something rounded and smooth, like a buried cobble. My fingers plowed through the gravel, grasping the smooth roundness, gaining just enough friction to pull my way forward. Then it was loose and in my fingers, a smooth thing with two holes. Still grasping it, I popped to the surface and gouged it into the gravel, pulling my way over to the far side of the pile. My feet found bottom and I ran, slogging, slowed like a nightmare in the dark waters.

I gained the barn, footholds better now, wading knee-deep through the water, heading toward the hill—

He struck me from behind, slipping, his blow not true.

I spun and struck him with the thing in my hand for all I was worth.

38

When the Sheriff's men found me, I was forty feet above the waters, clinging to a high branch of an old apple tree. Sonja Karsh's skull was still in my hands. I had heard them calling from their boats, pulling Jim from the water. When their searchlights found Matthew, they had followed the muddy hollows of my tracks through the trees. I heard them calling me, had seen their flashlights dodging like fairies through the branches, but I was so cold it didn't occur to me to answer.

Detective Muller climbed up and gently took this burden from me, plucking it with a plastic bag lest he spoil any evidence. Then he helped me out of the tree, speaking softly, saying, "There, there now," as if I were a naughty kitten that had escaped its mother. When we were on the ground, he pulled my rain jacket and sodden sweater off me and draped me with a blanket. Then he shone a flashlight on the skull. "It's half-full of gravel," he said, smiling. "I wondered why it was so heavy."

"The rest of her bones will be at the bottom of the excavation."

"Why, thank you. Now we have enough to get a warrant on this place, too."

"You mean you have one for the other farm?"

"Mrs. Karsh's home? My, my, you have such little faith in us. You think we were giving the Karsh family hands off? We searched it when Janet Pinchon's body was found, and paid them another call the day after you were assaulted. But patience is everything. The farther people wander down the path of mischief, the bolder and more erratic they get, and eventually step right out into the open." He turned the skull around delicately in his hands, regarding this remnant of lost promise with sadness and respect. "Now we have habeas corpus."

DIERDRE KARSH'S EYES grew bright and alert at the sight of myself and Detective Muller at her door. "Why, Em, what brings you out on a night like this?" she asked brightly. "And who's this with you?"

I smiled. "I'm sure you've met Detective Muller."

"Oh, I didn't recognize you, Detective. Come in. Can I get you some tea?"

Muller extended the search warrant. "No need for that, Mrs. Karsh. We're just here to cover a few points we missed during our last visit."

"Well, I can't imagine what that might be, but you're welcome, of course. . . ." She turned away, her spine stiff with repressed emotion.

Muller turned to me, nodded toward the tank house. "Over there?"

"Yes."

The Sheriff's deputies fanned out across the yard, hands at the ready. One stood proprietarily by Mrs. Karsh. Detective Muller and I approached the door, which was dark with rain and lack of light, all power in the district still out with the storm. The door was locked. Turning back to Mrs. Karsh, Muller said, "You'll unlock this, please."

Mrs. Karsh's eyes held that light I'd seen the first evening we had stood in her dooryard. When she spoke, her voice had begun to change, taking on that seductive, disarming quality I had come to know so well. "Oh, that? I'm not sure I still have a key."

"Odd," said the ever-cheerful Muller, playing his flashlight on the lock, "the handle turns smoothly, and when I rub off this smear of dirt, the brass is shiny where a key has so recently worked it again and again. Unlock it, please."

Raising her eyebrows to suggest she knew nothing about this, Dierdre Karsh marched across the yard to the door and withdrew a chain of keys from her apron pocket. She made a show of trying one key after another, then managed to look surprised when a very shiny one worked. Shaking her head in disbelief, like this was all very unexpected, she stepped aside.

Detective Muller opened the door. A narrow wooden staircase led upward around two sides of the narrow space, spiraling toward a trap door. Muller's flashlight danced through festoons of cobwebs and ages of dust everywhere but on the stairs. We climbed.

The hatch swung heavily, but caught against a support, forming a railing to grasp as we climbed the last few steps. Preceding me, Muller swung his light and groaned.

I was assaulted by the reek of urine and feces. I saw the missing photographs of Janet, this one stabbed to the wall with an ice pick and that one spoiled by something that looked sticky. I sat down on the top step and held my head in my hands.

"That's good, Em," Muller said, his voice grown husky with feeling. "You don't want to see any more. Jane," he called to a uniformed officer in the yard, "read Mrs. Karsh her rights!"

As I reached the bottom step, I heard Dierdre Karsh speaking to the officer, her voice oddly cheerful, like a booster at a pep rally trying to exhort a dreary bystander to join the occasion. "Why are you doing this? Don't you see, I never go in there. My son's a frail creature, he doesn't know what he's doing half the time. Must you put these manacles on my wrists? Really, why are you doing this? There's no need. . . ."

I took a good look into her eyes. She was alone with her fantasy.

SETTLING MY WEARY BONES AT FRIDA AND KITTY'S KITCHEN
table two hours later was a pleasure that would be hard to exceed. Frida
had the late edition of the *PD* open on the table for me to admire. Ban-
ner headlines read: "Pinchon Connection to Money-Laundering Ring
Seen," with the subheading "Laguna Development Blocked by Dead
Man's Will." The eleven-o'clock news on television was even sweeter:
Curt Murbles mobbed by reporters' microphones, his sniveling face
drawn up in defeat, spitting out his last press conference before the long
walk into unemployment and oblivion.

As my universe shifted ever so slightly toward the state of balance I
crave, I savored the moment, even allowed myself a bit of smugness.

Frida was stirring cocoa on the stove. "So what happened with
Matthew?"

"They're holding him on two counts of murder, two counts of attempted murder, and assault," I answered, cuddling down into the thick
terry cloth bathrobe Kitty had given me to wear. The thing hung clear
to the floor and covered my feet, which were wrinkled like raisins after
the hot bath Kitty had prescribed. "Jim Erikson's in the hospital with
a concussion, water in his lungs, and exposure, but they say he'll be
okay. A Sheriff's deputy nabbed Jaime as he was beaching Mr. Karsh's
powerboat and making for his truck. He's being held as accessory to
murder."

Frida poured us each a cup of cocoa and brought them to the

kitchen table. Kitty had set out sticks of cinnamon to stir them with, but Frida pushed these aside with a snort and shoved a bag of marshmallows at me instead. "So then what happened?" She put her feet up on a free chair and began to chew on a chocolate chip cookie.

"After the deputy was done reading Mrs. Karsh her rights?" I asked, staring into my steaming mug. "She turned and looked at me, and her eyes took on this weird light. She said, 'Sonja darling, you know I've missed you, don't you?' It was spooky: She took my hand and held it with both of hers to her chest, as if I should comfort her. And then she turned back to the Sheriff's deputy and said, 'Isn't it nice? Sonja's finally home.' "

The rest I couldn't explain. Still clinging to my hand, Mrs. Karsh had begun to smile like an angel. Charm shone from her face, rolling back the years, showing me the girl that had bought Will Karsh's soul.

I had said, "You can't sell this to us. We know damned well you know who I am, and we know why you're doing this, too."

Detective Muller gave her a lovely smile. "This is not your daughter, Mrs. Karsh, this is Em Hansen. You remember Em. You drove your son over to her motel room the other night."

"Me? Oh, surely you have me confused with—"

Muller said, "No, it was you," like he was only making light conversation. "We found someone by the liquor store who saw you in your car." Muller chanced a quick look at me, enlisting me in his deceit.

Dierdre Karsh smiled innocently. "Oh, *that* night! That was an *accident*. Little Matty got carried away, you see. He was only supposed to *scare* her!"

Muller had turned toward the uniformed officer and flicked his wrist, consigning one more person to the courts and the penal system. Her eyes had gone as dead as her son's, the world and all its troublesome young women locked out.

Remembering this in the safety of Frida's kitchen, I shook my head. "You know, when she took my hands like that, I looked over at Matthew. They had him locked in the backseat cage of a police cruiser like he was an animal. He wasn't even shivering, but his eyes had gone

empty, like two tunnels leading nowhere. And you know, for a moment I felt his pain."

Kitty touched my shoulder in sympathy. "You've a big heart, Em,
and twisted as Matthew is, he deserves your sympathy." She shook her
head. "I remember when my son was born. You have a baby and your
confidence is shattered, your world changed. Every irritation with
your mate widens into a wound. But here's this little one whose absolute innocence and dependence on you fills his eyes with adoration.
When he's hungry, he needs you. When he's cold or tired or hurting,
he needs you. You are his comfort, his heaven on earth, and before
too long, the temptation to chuck the father and build your world
around the son grows huge. Think of what you can do with a slave
like that, especially when they grow up big. But a decent woman, a
woman with any maturity, bites the bullet and leaves the poor thing
to his innocence."

I set down my mug of cocoa and addressed my aunt's lover: "Kitty,
I remembered something, just like you said. It was when he was trying to drown me."

Kitty nodded.

A motion caught my attention: Frida's head jerking as she squeezed
her eyes shut.

I began to tremble, and fought an almost overwhelming urge to lay
my head in Frida's lap like I was a little child. "You were there, weren't
you, Frida? Please tell me."

"They said you'd never remember," she whispered. "You were so
little." She wouldn't open her eyes. Perhaps it's easier to tell these things
with the shutters to your soul tightly closed.

Watching the remembered pain etch her face, I said, "I remember
going down again and again underwater, something—some*one* pushing me." I closed my eyes, too. A chain of memory uncoiled then, bits
and pieces flashing by at high speed, remembered thrashing in the water.
"Then Mother was angry, and I'm running. Then I'm hiding, and I
can hear her telling me it's not my fault." I opened my eyes, and was

reassured to find that Frida was there; still aging, wise Frida, not the younger Frida she would have been then. "What wasn't my fault, Frida?"

Tears squeezed out from Frida's tightly closed eyes. "My God, that was a terrible day. I thought your father'd die when he saw that boy dead, stone-dead, all the meanness gone from him. He looked like an angel." Frida opened her eyes now, and the tears slid freely down her cheeks. "Em, to lose your husband is a terrible thing, but God help you, you should ever lose a child. You think it was easy for your mother to lose her only son? Mad as she was at him for throttling you and pushing you under and holding you down like that in the irrigation ditch? He near to killed you—and would have, if you hadn't of dove and wiggled away from him like you did tonight. You always were the survivor. You bet your ma was angry, and if some of it seemed aimed at you . . . well, no one's perfect."

I had to run her last words through my mind several times before their meaning came clear, so lost was I in the memory of that day, nearly thirty years before, when my brother had gotten just a little too rough to show his little sister what jealousy and wrath he held for her, had pushed me down just one too many times to show his cousins how tough he was. "And the hiding?"

"We couldn't let the picnic finish, what with what he'd done. Swimming was over for that day. Your ma was terrified, and Abe and you was crying. Even my little Jed got to screaming, though he was just a year and couldn't of known what was happening. The whole day was ruined. When we got you all back to the house, your brother took one more swing at you and you lunged at him, and your mother had to break up the fight. She sent you to her bedroom. If only it had been a bigger house."

"Why?"

"Because then she would have sent him to another room, but there wasn't one, they hadn't built it yet. And he was still spitting like a wildcat, real spiteful, so she did the only thing she could think of. She opened the door and threw him out, told him to stay out there until he was ready to behave." Frida sighed and hung her head. "Em, that boy wasn't much for behaving, never was. He had to show us all."

This part of the story I knew, the cleaned-up, tell-the-neighbors part of our family's history. My brother had gone back out to the irrigation ditch by himself—God knows why, my dad had always said—and thought he'd take another swim. And he had drowned.

Somewhere along the way, as Frida's tears dried, and my trembling quieted to a fine tingling, I whispered, "I'd always thought it was because she drank."

"Why would drinking make him drown?"

"Like she was out cold and he went for a swim."

Frida shook her head. "No, Em, it was the other way around. Your ma used to take a good swig now and then—hell, all those girls from the East could put away a highball like it was ginger ale—but I never did see her drunk until your brother was in the ground."

I touched my cup where it rested on the table. The cocoa had gone cold. As I began to pull my hand away, Frida took it up in her dry, warm hands and said, "And now your daddy's gone, and she's had to face it all."

I shook my head, bewildered. "And all these years I thought it was because she loved him better."

40

So that's how it all ended. Matthew Karsh pleaded innocent of murder by reason of temporary insanity and stood trial, to the greater horror and entertainment of the county and half the country, and I wound up with an apology from Deputy Dexter, very nicely if somewhat stiffly delivered. At first Jaime supported Mrs. Karsh in her plea of ignorance, her main defense against charges of accessory to murder and conspiracy to commit murder, but when he learned she had tried to lay the whole thing on him—Sonja's death, and Janet's—he opened up and told Detective Muller everything: about arriving for work in the predawn mists both times to find her waiting with corpses, about Mrs. Karsh's careful instructions regarding disposal of the bodies, about his frail attempt to dress Janet's death up like an accident when he didn't have a handy grave to bury her in. He had a witness to this later crime, or partly so; his cousin Eduardo of the County Planning Department, who had insisted on taking those terrible pictures, damn his eyes, and then sold them to some *cabeza loca* from out of town! *Ay Dios!* He had gone home, washed down the truck, and set out for church to pray for the soul of the dead woman before going to the bar in Miwok Mills to get drunk. Ask his wife! He was with her the entire night before, just like always, and after the grisly disposal, she'd seen how scared he was with the ghost clinging to the truck like mist.

All of this made me ponder a few things. When I held Dierdre Karsh up to my own mother, I could see a difference: My mother had not condoned my brother's fury, nor fed it. She had simply come up against her limitations with a difficult child, had made her mistakes, and had paid for them bitterly. And no matter how I tried to change the past by rethinking the present, my father, with all his frail intentions, was gone, and nothing would bring him back. A piece of my past I'd been too young to understand had surfaced, just like that great tank floating up in the flooded night of the Laguna. In rising, this piece had changed from a nameless, life-shaping monster to a thing I could mourn, and I began to feel better. A scar had been lifted from my heart, leaving it to beat more softly in the knowledge that the past does not have to control the future.

In this vein, I asked a boon of Detective Muller. I asked if, when Sonja's remains were recovered, a ring had been found encircling one bone of the left-hand fingers. He acknowledged that there had been a ring, an inexpensive thing, the sort of ring that teenage girls give each other in celebration of their friendship. They had puzzled over it while the medical examiner probed the bones of the neck for strangulation fractures we knew he'd find, wondering if it might help identify the remains as they waited for Sonja's dental records to be located in a re-tired dentist's garage. I suggested that Muller take the ring to Suzanne Cousins for identification. I didn't go along; I figured my presence wasn't necessary on an errand such as that, but when I saw him next, Muller said it was the strangest thing: Suzanne had dug like a mad-woman through trunks and boxes in her closets until she found a tiny jewelry case, and there inside, in somewhat better shape, was the ring's perfect mate.

So what's next? After I visit Pat Ryan at the hospital where he's dry-ing out, I'm going to look up Arnie at the Pedal Pusher and take him the last bits of Janet's bicycle gear from her boxes, as a memento. To-gether we'll pick out something for crazy old Duke. Janet's Filson vest, I'll keep for myself, and we'll give her books to a school and take the rest to a homeless shelter. Maybe they can figure out what to do with her truck. And I've promised Jim Erikson, I'll drive out along the Russian River to Jenner with him as soon as he's able, so he can show me the Pacific Ocean.

And what else? There's the rest of January, then three more bitter months until the spring warms Wyoming, and my mother has a herd of cattle to keep alive. She knows how; she worked alongside my father for ten years before the drink took her, but I reckon she'll need a bit of help just the same. I won't say I trust her, exactly. There's been too much pain between us, and too many years of caring have been lost to forget the damage just like that, but at least I have a mother who's shown the willingness, however late in the day, to face her losses and start to grow again.

You see, I've decided to accept her apology for all the years she lacked the courage to love me. In deciding that, I've had to accept the painful fact that she's a real person, not a monster, and I've had to see that she owns that ranch, not I. But I will offer her my assistance; humbly, too, because I have to face my own losses, and admit a tender need for a place to be while I prepare for my next beginning.

Author's Note

I WENT TO WORK FOR A SMALL ENVIRONMENTAL SERVICES FIRM in Sonoma County in 1989, the day before the Loma Prieta earthquake. Working that job was a painful experience for me, not unlike taking a long walk in tight shoes, and it was destined not to last, but it did put me standing next to a ten-ton drill rig and service truck watching the mast shake and the fluids in the decontamination tanks leap sideways as the ground began to roll. I knew it was a big quake by its amplitude and wavelength, and I judged by the rubbery feeling of the shaking that the epicenter had to be some ways off, but I didn't know whether the shaking was coming from north or south. I remember turning to the geologist next to me—a young buck not a bit less irascible than my fictional Adam Horowitz—and saying, to state the obvious, "An earthquake!" The guy raked me with eyes hot with fury and resentment, as if to say, *I'll be the judge of that!*

In the ensuing weeks, the quake was all anyone talked about. I described my experiences of watching the drill rig rock and witnessing the cloud of smoke that coiled over San Francisco that night as the Marina District burned. My cousin Greg in Santa Cruz told of his escape from a liquor store as bottles sluiced off the shelves and doing "tai chi break dancing" in the parking lot outside, and a friend who was driving down the ramp from Highway 101 onto Fell Street in San Francisco likened the experience to "skiing down a mountain made of Jell-O." Most eloquent to my ears, though, was the experience of a painfully shy woman who had been riding the BART train through the tunnel under San Francisco Bay when the temblor hit. Something of a claustrophobe to begin with, she found herself under ground that

was underwater, halfway between Oakland and San Francisco, in the dark and in a dead train. In the company of strangers, she walked out. She had this to say: she felt that Mother Earth had betrayed her.

Now, it's a peculiarly human habit to anthropomorphize nature as we do, and more human yet to take the motions of inanimate objects personally, so I think I know what she meant. I find that California's geology follows a negative female archetype in its personality: She is capricious, moody, given to fires and floods and earthquakes, entirely too ready to rid herself of the humans who persist in building along her shores and valleys. She is the very image of the Hindu goddess Kali, as viewed through the lens of Western patriarchal cultures. The geology of the Rocky Mountain province, where I trained as a geologist, seems by contrast to follow a more masculine archetype: the craggy, unchanging old man reigning stiffly over the androgynous plains.

I find it interesting that Kali is viewed so differently by cultures older than ours. She is indeed considered ferocious, but not disenfranchised from her anger as are women in our society. Her anger rises naturally as she moves to crush that which threatens her children. She is not a demon but a slayer of demons, a balancer of the unbalanced, and, it is said, those who find the courage to embrace her will transcend their fear and discover the greatest bliss.

I find these things interesting because as a culture, we move to control nature, denying its overwhelming power and increasing our numbers at the cost of its nonrenewable resources (which ultimately include clean water, air, and soil), rather than humbly seeking harmony within it while we still have time.

I dream a dream for my generation, a mother's dream. I dream that we are learning to raise our sons and daughters with Kali's ferocious love, not stunting their growth with toxins born of our disappointments and impacted anger. Our daughters will grow up strong, directing their passions in mature ways, neither scorned for their anger nor shamed for their desires, ready and able to use these energies to birth an even better world in the generation to follow. And our sons will grow up knowing how to grow, delighted by the strength of their sis-

ters and their wives-to-be, responsible for all their acts and feelings, mature and wise and strong.

It is a fine dream. In it we find the humility to admit our shortcomings in the way we've been treating our Mother. On waking, we embrace our limits and her vastness, and learn to live in harmony with the natural laws of her love.